Praise for the

Th

"As in the two previous novels in the series, set in Oyster Bay on North Carolina's southeastern coast, Adams concocts a fine plot; this one finds its roots in World War II. But the real appeal is her sundry and congenial characters, beginning with Olivia herself. Adams's heroine has erected a steel curtain around her emotions, but *The Last Word* finds her emerging from her shell with confidence, a confidence matched by Adams in this unusual and appealing series." —*Richmond Times-Dispatch*

"I could actually feel the wind on my face, taste the salt of the ocean on my lips, and hear the waves crash upon the beach. *The Last Word* made me laugh, made me think, made me smile, and made me cry. *The Last Word*—in one word—AMAZING!" —*The Best Reviews*

"The plot is complex, the narrative drive is strong, and the book is populated with interesting and intelligent people . . . Oyster Bay is the kind of place I'd love to get lost for an afternoon or two." —*The Season for Romance*

A Deadly Cliché

"A very well-written mystery with interesting and surprising characters and a great setting. Readers will feel as if they are in Oyster Bay." —*The Mystery Reader*

"Adams spins a good yarn, but the main attraction of the series is Olivia and her pals, each a person the reader wants to meet again and again." —*Richmond Times-Dispatch*

"[A] terrific mystery that is multi-layered, well-thought-out, and well presented." —*Fresh Fiction*

continued . . .

A Killer Plot

**A BOOKS
BY THE BAY
MYSTERY**

Written in Stone

ELLERY ADAMS

BERKELEY PRIME CRIME, NEW YORK

THE BERKLEY PUBLISHING GROUP
Published by the Penguin Group
Penguin Group (USA) Inc.
375 Hudson Street, New York, New York 10014, USA

Penguin Group (Canada), 90 Eglinton Avenue East, Suite 700, Toronto, Ontario M4P 2Y3, Canada
(a division of Pearson Penguin Canada Inc.) • Penguin Books Ltd., 80 Strand, London WC2R 0RL,
England • Penguin Group Ireland, 25 St. Stephen's Green, Dublin 2, Ireland (a division of Penguin
Books Ltd.) • Penguin Group (Australia), 250 Camberwell Road, Camberwell, Victoria 3124, Australia
(a division of Pearson Australia Group Pty. Ltd.) • Penguin Books India Pvt. Ltd., 11 Community
Centre, Panchsheel Park, New Delhi—110 017, India • Penguin Group (NZ), 67 Apollo Drive,
Rosedale, Auckland 0632, New Zealand (a division of Pearson New Zealand Ltd.) • Penguin Books
(South Africa) (Pty.) Ltd., 24 Sturdee Avenue, Rosebank, Johannesburg 2196, South Africa

Penguin Books Ltd., Registered Offices: 80 Strand, London WC2R 0RL, England

This is a work of fiction. Names, characters, places, and incidents either are the product of the author's
imagination or are used fictitiously, and any resemblance to actual persons, living or dead, business
establishments, events, or locales is entirely coincidental. The publisher does not have any control over
and does not assume any responsibility for author or third-party websites or their content.

WRITTEN IN STONE

A Berkley Prime Crime Book / published by arrangement with the author

PUBLISHING HISTORY
Berkley Prime Crime mass-market edition / November 2012

Copyright © 2012 by Ellery Adams.
Excerpt from *Poisoned Prose* by Ellery Adams copyright © 2012 by Ellery Adams.
Cover illustration by Kimberly Schamber.
Cover design by Rita Frangie.
Interior text design by Tiffany Estreicher.

ISBN: 978-0-425-25173-7   50452688
3/13

BERKLEY® PRIME CRIME
Berkley Prime Crime Books are published by The Berkley Publishing Group,
a division of Penguin Group (USA) Inc.,
375 Hudson Street, New York, New York 10014.
BERKLEY® PRIME CRIME and the PRIME CRIME logo are trademarks of
Penguin Group (USA) Inc.

PRINTED IN THE UNITED STATES OF AMERICA

10 9 8 7 6 5 4 3 2 1

ALWAYS LEARNING   **PEARSON**

To these Mavens of Mystery:

Kaye Wilkinson Barley
Lesa Holstine
Doris Ann Norris
Molly Weston

Chapter 1

"There's a witch in Oyster Bay," Dixie, the roller-skating dwarf and diner proprietor, announced. She set a breakfast strata made of eggs, tomato, basil, and mozzarella on the table and slid a plate of bacon onto the floor.

Immediately, the black nose belonging to the standard poodle sleeping on the booth's vinyl cushion began to quiver. Flashing Dixie a brief smile of gratitude, Captain Haviland lowered his paws to the checkered tiles and began to eat his breakfast with the delicacy and restraint of an English aristocrat.

Olivia Limoges, oak-barrel heiress, restaurateur, and aspiring author, reached for the pepper shaker and gave her eggs a quick dusting. "A witch? Does she lure small children into her house with candy bars and then lock them inside cages until they're plump enough to eat?"

Dixie put a hand on her hip and scowled, her false eyelashes leaving thin stripes of electric blue mascara on the skin above her lids. "I'm not pullin' your leg. Folks have talked about her for years. The stories have gotten wilder and wilder because only a handful of people have actually been brave or stupid enough to pay her a visit."

Watching as Dixie topped off her coffee, Olivia cocked her head to the side and asked, "Where does this supposed witch live?"

"In the swamp," Dixie said distastefully. "Word is you can only reach her house by boat and she's not shy about greetin' unwelcome visitors with a few shotgun blasts."

Olivia, who owned a rifle and was an excellent shot thanks to regular visits to the shooting range, approved. "Perhaps she values her privacy. People always talk about those who don't abide by societal norms. I know plenty of locals who believe there's something wrong with me because Haviland is my constant companion. They disapprove of my refusal to attend every street fair, regatta, shop opening, and ribbon-cutting ceremony. When I don't buy a dozen boxes of stale Girl Scout cookies or chemically laced Boy Scout popcorn every time I leave the Stop 'n' Shop, the troop parents fold their arms and shake their heads at me." She paused to glance out the large picture window at the end of her booth. "Things were getting better, Dixie. I felt anchored here again, like a boat fastened to its moorings. For so long I was drifting and that finally stopped. But then Harris found that painting under his stairs and everything shifted again. I feel like my tether is frayed . . ."

Dixie heard the pain in her friend's voice. "None of that was your fault, 'Livia."

Olivia's dark blue eyes glinted. "Wasn't it? I'm not so sure about that." She gestured around the packed diner. "And people are right to doubt me again. How could they see me as anything but an outsider after I led the police to the door of a person they all loved? I was Gretel, leaving them a trail of bread crumbs."

"You're givin' yourself a bit too much credit, don't you think?" Dixie turned, placed the coffee carafe on the counter, and faced Olivia again. "Chief Rawlings arrived at the same conclusion before you did. You told me yourself he gave you a head start so you could warn Wheeler that all hell was about to break loose. For a cop, the chief sure is kindhearted. Don't you go messin' with his feelin's."

A flush of pink spread across Olivia's cheeks. She hurriedly cut into her strata with the edge of her fork and filled her mouth with a bite of warm eggs, fresh tomatoes, and melted cheese.

"I see what you're doin'," Dixie said, shaking her pointer finger. "Stuffin' your face so you don't have to tell me what's goin' on between you and Sawyer Rawlings. The whole town knows you're an item so don't bother denyin' it. One of the chief's neighbors saw you doin' the walk of shame. *She* said Haviland spent the night too. Must be serious."

Olivia bristled. "There wasn't the slightest trace of shame on my part but I'm not foolish enough to discuss intimate details with the biggest gossip in all of Oyster Bay. Meaning you." The barb was softened by a smile, which was quickly hidden behind the rim of Olivia's coffee cup. "Get back to the witch. That's a far more interesting topic."

"No, it is not, but I'll play along. Hold on." Dixie skated over to the *Cats* booth and slapped a check on the table. She spent a moment chitchatting with an elderly couple clad in matching lighthouse T-shirts and was undoubtedly explaining for the millionth time why she'd decorated the diner using Andrew Lloyd Weber paraphernalia.

Next, she pivoted and moved on to the *Phantom of the Opera* table. A jowly man in his late fifties dug around in the pocket of his madras shorts in search of his wallet. Ignoring Dixie's question as to whether he enjoyed his food, he tossed bills on top of the check with dismissive little flicks of his wrist. His breakfast partner, a skeletal blonde in her early thirties clad in a miniskirt and a white tank top stretched taut over a pair of cartoonishly large implants, jabbed at the porcelain phantom mask with a long, curving fingernail.

From where she sat enjoying her meal, Olivia watched Dixie straighten to her full height. After donning her skates and teasing her hair a vertical inch into the air, she was barely five feet tall, but what Dixie lacked in stature she made up for in fearlessness.

"Y'all have a nice day," she said tightly, her farewell clearly meant as a command.

The top-heavy blonde grabbed her take-out coffee cup and shimmied across the vinyl seat, granting the diners in the opposite booths a clear view of her leopard-print panties.

"Hurry up, babe." The man in madras shorts began to walk away without waiting for his companion. He popped a toothpick in his mouth with one hand and jiggled a set of keys with the other. Using his elbow to push open the door, he let it go without bothering to see if his lady friend was directly behind him. She wasn't. The door slammed in her face and she jumped back with a little shriek. Jutting her lower lip into a collagen-enhanced pout, she followed her man out of the diner.

"High-caliber clientele," Olivia teased Dixie after she'd cleared the couple's table.

. Dixie wasn't happy. "Cheap bastard. Doctors are the worst tippers."

"How do you know he's a physician?"

"The caduceus on his key ring." Dixie pointed out the window. "And the vanity plate on his I-am-not-well-hung-mobile."

Olivia had been too absorbed rereading the latest chapter of her novel to notice the atomic orange Corvette parked outside Grumpy's Diner. She peered at the showy convertible as the man settled into his seat and revved the engine. The vanity plate read, "NIPTUCK."

"Having seen the missus, perhaps the plate should say, 'I Inflate You,'" Olivia said. "You could use the number eight and the letter *u* to save space."

"Lady Watermelons is *not* the missus," Dixie corrected. "I saw a picture of the missus and the doc's three kids when he opened his wallet. Such a cliché. Why do they come here anyway? Why not go to Vegas or Cancun?"

Olivia shrugged. "He wants to show off his car. See?"

The object of their derision was donning sunglasses as the Corvette's soft top folded back. The doctor glanced around, making sure he'd captured the interest of a few passersby before turning on the radio. The plate glass window above Olivia's booth began to vibrate as the Corvette's speakers pounded out a thundering bass.

Dixie shook her head in disgust. "Pathetic." And then her eyes narrowed angrily. "She'd better not do what I think she's going to do."

Olivia looked at the blonde, who'd pulled back her arm and was preparing to throw her take-out cup into a trashcan on the sidewalk. At the same moment she hurled the cup, the doc put the sports car in drive and launched out of the parking spot. The cup missed the rim of the receptacle by several feet and bounced off a lamppost, splashing coffee onto a parked car, the newspaper box, and the bare legs of a teenage girl. The girl shouted, her face registering pain and surprise.

Dixie swore through gritted teeth as the orange Corvette raced out of view.

"Maybe the witch can put a curse on those two cretins," Olivia suggested, sharing Dixie's indignation over the couple's behavior. It was bad enough that they'd both blatantly littered, but to drive on after splattering a young woman's legs with hot coffee bordered on criminal conduct.

Collecting Haviland's empty plate, Dixie put a hand on the black curls of his head and sighed. "I wish all humans had your manners, Captain. But the spell thing isn't a bad idea either. We just need to hop a boat, cross the harbor, head up the creek borderin' the Croatan National Forest, and hike a trail for a mile or so."

"She's hardly Oyster Bay's witch, then," Olivia said.

"Closest thing we've got," Dixie retorted. "Anyway, what kind of mystique would she have if she lived in a beachfront condo? A shack in the swamp is way better for business."

This statement piqued Olivia's interest. "What kind of business?"

Delighted to have her friend on the hook, Dixie was just about to answer when Grumpy rang the order bell in the kitchen. The breakfast rush was nearly over, but the family of four in the *Evita* booth was casting expectant glances at Dixie. When she skated over with a tray laden with stacks of buttermilk pancakes, sizzling sausage patties, cinnamon-laced French toast, and an omelet the size of a beret, their eyes grew round with appreciation.

"That should hold 'em for five minutes," she said, coming to an abrupt stop at Olivia's booth, her silver tutu billowing as she applied the brakes. "Back to the witch. Her name is Munin and one of my cousins went to see her over the weekend." Dixie pulled a stray thread from her left tube sock and lowered her voice. "He and his woman want a baby real bad but it's just not happenin'. They've both been checked out and there's nothin' wrong, medically speakin'. Been goin' on five years since they started tryin'. Munin is kind of their last hope."

Olivia dabbed her lips with a paper napkin. "And can they expect a healthy set of triplets nine months from now?"

"I reckon not," Dixie replied. "See, Munin doesn't take cash or checks. You have to bring her somethin' that's real precious to you to get her help. If the witch doesn't think what you brought is special enough, she won't lift a finger for you."

"What does she do with the objects?"

Dixie shrugged. "Who knows?"

Impatient to return to her manuscript, Olivia offered to tell Laurel about Munin. "The big shot of the *Oyster Bay Gazette* staff might not cover the story herself, but maybe one of the Features writers would be interested."

With a scowl, Dixie picked up Olivia's empty plate. "I'm not tellin' you about the witch so that you can turn her into a Disneyland attraction. I'm only tellin' you about her because she sent a message back with my cousin."

"For you?"

"No." Dixie piled Olivia's silverware and crumpled napkin on top of the dirty plate. "For you."

Bomb dropped, Dixie skated off to the kitchen with her tray. She then tarried at the two remaining tables, filling water cups, delivering a fresh syrup jug, fetching extra napkins, and exchanging small talk.

Haviland stood up, yawned, and stretched, indicating he'd had enough of the diner for one day.

"Just a few more minutes, Captain," Olivia promised her dog. "Let me strangle the resident dwarf and then we'll be on our way."

As though sensing her friend's ire, Dixie lazily coasted back to the window booth. "Ah, so now you're chompin' at the bit to hear about our witch. Well, I won't keep you in suspense another second." She grinned wryly. "Munin asked my cousin if he knew you. He said everybody knows who you are, but only a couple of folks know you well. The jackass mentioned my name and told Munin that you and I were friends. So the message came to me."

Olivia felt a constriction in her gut. She sensed that once Dixie relayed the message, her life would be altered yet again. Perhaps not greatly, but she didn't welcome any more change.

In the last year alone, she'd opened a second restaurant, reunited with a father she'd believed dead only to watch him die, discovered the existence of a half brother, and fallen for Oyster Bay's chief of police. Olivia Limoges was a woman who liked to be in control of her own future, and as of late, she'd been unable to exert much influence over her fate.

She turned toward the window, observing locals and tourists going about their business, unburdened by the press of circumstance. "What does the witch want from me?"

Dixie's grin faded, replaced by a look of solemn concern. Because she was adept at concealing her feelings, it was easy to forget that Olivia had been put through the wringer over the past few months. Dixie spoke to her friend very gently. "Munin wants you to come to her. Says she's got somethin' of your mama's to show you. Apparently, she's been waitin' for the right time to send for you and now the time's come."

Olivia was unprepared for this. "That's ridiculous. Why would my mother, a librarian and do-gooder, have given something to a woman known as the local witch? And I use that term loosely."

"Maybe you shouldn't," Dixie warned. "If your mama handed over somethin' she treasured, then she was lookin' for help outside the normal realm. She obviously had a problem that couldn't be fixed by the folks she knew. The question is, did she get what she needed from Munin?"

The tightening sensation in Olivia's chest increased. It was difficult for her to picture her beautiful mother, the kind and gentle librarian, traipsing through a barely discernible track in the swamp in search of answers.

"I am *not* going to respond to this woman's summons," Olivia said. "It's probably a scam, though more creative than most, I admit."

The family of four ambled out the door, waving at Dixie before leaving. Her mouth formed a smile, but her ale brown eyes were troubled. "Munin said you wouldn't agree at first. That was part of the message. I was supposed to wait for you to refuse and then tell you the rest. I wonder how she knew . . ."

Her impatience morphing into full-blown annoyance, Olivia growled, "Oh, please! What's the magic word, then? What's going to convince me to hire a boat and douse myself in mosquito repellant so I can waste an entire day finding some crazy hag?"

Dixie gestured at the hollow in Olivia's throat. Resting there was a golden starfish pendant attached to a delicate gold chain. Olivia's mother had given it to her only child shortly before her tragic death. Since reclaiming the necklace from the dollhouse in her childhood room, Olivia wore it every day. She touched it during moments of uncertainty or distress. It was her talisman.

Knowing that she was pointing at a sacred object, Dixie swallowed hard and then continued. "Munin said she has your mama's starfish and if you want to know why, you'll have to come. And soon."

Olivia reached her hand out for Haviland and he obediently moved closer. Her fingers sank into his soft curls and her tilting world steadied itself. "This is a hell of a way to start my day," she grumbled, overpaid Dixie for breakfast, and strode out into the sunshine, one hand gripping her laptop case, the other curled protectively around the gold starfish on her neck.

After settling Haviland into the passenger seat of her Range Rover, Olivia headed for home. It was late in the day for a walk on the beach, and the August sun seared the pavement, coaxing shimmering waves of heat into the stagnant air, but she wanted to make contact with the water, to wade ankle deep for a few moments.

The downtown streets were clogged with vacationers

in rental cars. Low-end convertibles and minivans eased through the business district, drivers scouted out eateries and boutiques or searched for a prized parking space.

Though she was accustomed to summertime traffic and knew that the crowded town meant that both of her restaurants would be filled to capacity for the remainder of the season, Olivia felt a sudden pang of longing for winter.

Oyster Bay possessed a quiet beauty during the somnolent stretch from November to March. It never turned bitingly cold, but grew gray and blustery enough to chase the tourists away. The sparkling sea became flat and lusterless. Sluggish waves rolled onto chilly sand beyond the decks of vast, empty beach houses. Without the calls of Canada geese and the shrieks of gulls, there was a hush along the shore. A few sandpipers still waded into the shallows, trilling softly, and terns picked their way over perfectly formed scallop shells that would have been instantly placed in a child's plastic bucket had they drifted above the water line during a balmier season.

Olivia saw plenty of kids now. Holding hands with their parents, they skipped down the sidewalk, sun kissed and content. Some carried dripping ice cream cones big enough to spoil their lunches while others held rainbow pinwheels that spun obediently in the salt-laden breeze.

At one time, the vision of a multitude of children wouldn't have moved Olivia in the slightest, but now she smiled and her thoughts turned from the witch to her niece and nephew, Caitlyn and Anders.

"We should get them some new books," she said to Haviland.

The poodle, who'd been poking his head out the window in hopes of receiving a welcome rush of air, turned his cocoa brown eyes to Olivia and issued a derisive snort.

"I know we just bought a small pile, but one can never have too many books." She sighed as the Suburban in front of them idled through the entire the green light. "But we won't go to Through the Wardrobe today. Flynn's got that ridiculous puppet show scheduled this morning." A wicked gleam flashed in her eyes. "I should encourage Laurel to bring the twins to see it. I bet they'd attack the puppeteer. They're still completely enthralled with pirates, you know."

Haviland, who undoubtedly connected the word "twins" with two pairs of sticky hands that pulled his fur and grabbed his tail in a most undignified manner, uttered a low growl before sticking his head back out the window.

Olivia was just about to tease her dog some more when the light turned from red to green again. Before the Suburban could lumber forward, an orange Corvette rocketed down the left turn lane, passed the SUV in the middle of the intersection, and began to ride the bumper of a Mini Cooper.

"Bastard," Olivia grumbled, instantly recognizing the car and its driver.

The Suburban turned right at the next corner and Olivia was stuck behind the plastic surgeon. His music continued to drown out all other sounds, and Haviland whined in discomfort. Dr. NipTuck and his mistress drew both curious and disapproving stares from the pedestrians. Feigning disinterest, they slapped their palms against the car's tan leather in time to the bass-heavy music. The blonde lit a cigarette while the self-satisfied physician took sips from a mega-sized fountain drink and crept even closer to the Mini's tiny bumper.

Traffic inched down the street and the more Olivia observed the Corvette's occupants, the more irritated she became. When the Mini stopped instead of racing through the next yellow light, the doctor laid on his horn and made impatient gestures with his free hand. Blondie tapped cigarette ash onto the road and Olivia could see the flash of her complacent smile in the sports car's side mirror.

The anger that had come to life after Dixie had delivered the witch's message regained its hold over Olivia. As she watched the occupants of the orange Corvette, she fumed over the realization that some enigmatic old woman living in a virtually inhabitable swamp had successfully manipulated her. She could not stop thinking about Munin and her mother. What was their connection? And how had the witch known about the necklace?

Olivia had worn her starfish necklace every day of her girlhood until she'd abruptly hidden it inside her dollhouse.

"Why did I ever take it off?" she demanded aloud, furious that her sharp memory could not provide an answer. Although she distinctly recalled pulling away the tiny fireplace in the dollhouse's living room and stuffing her treasure into the small cavity she'd carved within, she couldn't remember what event had influenced her to hide it in the first place.

The noise from the Corvette prevented her from concentrating and she glared at the back of the tourists' heads, wishing she could bore holes into their skulls with a single, venomous look.

This fantasy turned to very real outrage when the doctor blatantly tossed his extra-large plastic take-out cup onto the road. It bounced against the asphalt, and the lid became dislodged. Ice cubes ricocheted in all directions and the bright red straw rolled to a stop in the middle of the double yellow line.

"Bastard!" Olivia repeated, her lips tightening. No one littered like that in her town. Fuming, she considered her options. She could report the infraction to the police, but doubted they'd respond. Because the revenue generated from tourism kept many Oyster Bay families afloat during the off-season, the authorities were reluctant to inconvenience visitors over minor infractions.

Haviland, who also had his gaze fixed on the orange car, bared his teeth.

"You're right, Captain. It's up to us. At the next light,

I will calmly get out and tell that jerkoff to pick up his trash. If he argues, you can flash him your most fearsome snarl."

Olivia's plans for a peaceful resolution were quickly ditched, however, the moment Blondie finished her cigarette.

The next few seconds moved in slow motion. Blondie pushed a final plume of smoke into the air and then pulled back her arm. Olivia saw the movement and was reminded of a television close-up of a quarterback preparing to throw a winning pass. Unlike a highly focused athlete, Blondie hadn't aimed for a spot in the distance where she wanted her missile to fall. In fact, as she released the cigarette butt, still glowing orange at one end, she turned to speak to the doctor.

Olivia watched in horror as the lit stub careened toward the sidewalk. The object in its path was a stroller whose occupant was a chubby-cheeked toddler dressed in a pink sundress. Her fist was closed around a mermaid doll and her bare legs swung out before her as though she were running in place.

Before Olivia could call out a warning, the cigarette struck the child's right arm, just above the wrist, before dropping to the sidewalk. The child opened her eyes wide in shock and then her face crumpled, her mouth forming a huge O as she howled in pain.

All Olivia could see was Anders as a newborn, fighting for survival in a hospital NICU. The sight of her tiny nephew hooked to tubes and wires as if he were a human marionette replaced the little girl's round, healthy body. Over the music, Olivia heard only a child's cries and was transported back to that time of fear and dread, to those long hours when she didn't know whether her brother's son would survive.

Reliving those moments of helplessness, Olivia's grip on the steering wheel turned white-knuckled. While the little girl's parents knelt by her side to examine the angry red mark on her arm, Olivia pushed her foot against her accelerator petal until it hit the floor.

The Range Rover leapt forward. Three thousand pounds of metal plowed into the fiberglass body of the orange Corvette and a sickening *crack* resounded above the hip-hop music.

Olivia applied the brakes and cast a quick glance at Haviland. His custom-made canine seat belt had done its job, and though he was unsettled, he was also unhurt.

Putting the Range Rover into park, Olivia leaned forward to gain a clear view of the damage. The back of the Corvette looked like a crumpled soda can. The taillights were splintered and a large chunk of fiberglass had been violently detached from the frame. It sat like an amputated limb behind the left rear tire.

The plastic surgeon's license plate was mangled beyond recognition and the car's speakers abruptly stopped broadcasting any sound.

Olivia examined the wreckage and smiled. "Thanks for visiting Oyster Bay. We hope you enjoyed your stay."

Chapter 2

The smaller the mind the greater the conceit.

—AESOP

Olivia maneuvered the Range Rover to the side, put on her hazard lights, and phoned the police. She reported the location of the accident and assured the operator that no one had been injured.

"You may have to treat a bruised ego," she added too quietly for the dispatcher to hear.

Her declaration that no one was hurt was factual, for Dr. NipTuck immediately hopped out of his wrecked car, bellowing in rage as he examined the damage to his Corvette. He gesticulated and cursed with such vigor that Olivia knew he was sound of body, if not of mind. The fake tan on Blondie's face had paled a bit and she stood on the sidewalk, making mewing noises reminiscent of a hungry kitten, but she was fine too.

Pouring some water into Haviland's travel dish, Olivia transferred the poodle to the spacious rear of the Rover and put all the windows down so her dog would be comfortable. Only then did she examine the front end of her vehicle, noting that a few scratches to her metallic blue paint were the extent of the damage. Her steel bumper, which was covered by a protective rubber guard, had taken the brunt of the low-speed impact and was now striped with the Corvette's electric orange paint.

Olivia was just reflecting that the black and orange pattern resembled a tiger's pelt when Dr. NipTuck marched over and began to vent his rage. Red-faced and spluttering, he called her a host of offensive names.

"I'm terribly sorry," she responded with absolute calm. "I saw the light turn green and I just gunned my engine. I've already called the police and they're on their way. Let me gather my insurance information." Olivia hesitated and pointed at Blondie. "Is your wife okay?"

"What? Who?" The man's jowls inflated until he resembled a spooked puffer fish. "Forget about *her*. Look at what you did to my *car*!"

Blondie's mewling grew a little louder as proof of her lack of importance hit home.

Ignoring another stream of insults, Olivia collected her vehicle registration and insurance card from the Range Rover's center console and then called State Farm to report the accident. She sat on the curb and talked to her agent, who was local and promised to be at the scene in ten minutes.

A crowd had gathered on the sidewalk but Olivia shouldered past the gawkers and made her way to the stroller bearing the crying toddler.

"Is she all right?" she asked the child's mother.

The woman nodded and pointed to the small red mark on her daughter's arm. "It's just a surface burn. My husband ran to the pharmacy down the street to get a topical ointment. He should be back any second now."

The little girl took a final sniff and fell silent, looking up at Olivia with distrust.

"Would you allow me to buy her a frozen yogurt?" Indicating the shop across the street, Olivia said, "Their Peach

Perfection is delicious. It's completely natural and they serve pint-sized cups for kids your daughter's age. They also have sorbet and regular ice cream if she'd prefer another flavor."

The mother hesitated, casting a brief glance at the periwinkle awnings and front door of The Big Chill. "That's not necessary, but thank you for the offer."

"Actually, this is one of those times when ice cream is totally necessary." Olivia smiled and turned back to the little girl. "I think you deserve a treat."

The child knew a bribe when she heard one and nodded in eager agreement. Olivia jogged across the street and ordered the kid's cup and two shakes for the parents. By the time she reemerged from the shop, the police had arrived.

The doctor spotted her carrying a tray of frozen treats and became apoplectic with indignation. He lunged toward Olivia and the closest cop instinctively threw out an arm to stop him. The doctor instantly shouted for the bystanders to witness what was a clear case of police brutality. He told the flummoxed officer that he would definitely be filing a lawsuit against the department, Olivia, and the entire dump of a town.

To the officer's obvious relief, a second cop car pulled into the loading zone farther down the street, its rotating light bar blazing. Olivia watched as Sawyer Rawlings eased out of the passenger seat, taking a few seconds to survey the scene.

The police chief cut an imposing figure in his uniform. On his days off, he paired Hawaiian-print shirts covered with sharks, pineapples, or palm trees with tattered khaki shorts and a pair of paint-splattered sandals. But he was a different man when he was dressed in his police blues. His posture was rigid, his clean-shaven jaw set, and his eyes were masked behind a pair of mirrored sunglasses. Radiating authority, he walked briskly toward the irate physician, and Olivia felt a quickening of her blood. This man, this middle-aged cop with the salt-and-pepper hair, wide shoulders, slight paunch, and a fondness for chocolate milk, moved her in ways she could not comprehend.

Rawlings walked over to the doctor and held out his hand in introduction. Olivia couldn't hear him speak, but she knew he'd address the civilian in a pleasant, courteous voice. The chief's soft-spoken, almost humble manner didn't diminish his authority, however. In fact, it often increased it.

Olivia never tired of watching Rawlings take command of a situation. He did so now by giving the doctor his full attention, listening to the angry physician as if no one else existed. Rawlings didn't take a single note and remained completely calm while the other man gesticulated, spat, and cursed.

After a few moments, the chief approached Olivia, his face unreadable. She nearly looked away, suddenly discomfited by her rash behavior.

"If you wanted to see me, you could have just called," Rawlings growled.

"But this is more unpredictable," she quipped. "Keeps things spicy. I was just following one of *Cosmo*'s recommendations."

Rawlings pulled off his sunglasses and jerked a thumb at the trashed Corvette. "Somehow, I doubt I was on your mind when you stomped on the gas pedal."

Shrugging, Olivia said, "He deserved it. I'd do it again given the chance."

With a slight shake of the head, Rawlings peered over Olivia's shoulder and she was warmed by the realization that he was checking on Haviland.

She nearly smiled at him, but then had a strong feeling that half the town's population was studying them. The junior police officers had ceased writing reports or shooing bystanders away from the intersection and were staring at their chief with unconcealed interest.

Olivia didn't like it. She was an extremely private person

and had kept her burgeoning relationship with Rawlings under wraps. The only places they'd shared meals or drinks in public had been at one of her restaurants. She'd convinced the chief to spend most nights at her place instead of his house in town, and was rarely seen with him during the day.

"We're like a vampire couple," he'd observed one evening as they drank cocktails on her deck and watched the surf curl onto the shore beneath a sickle moon.

"Not really. Vampires are always young and beautiful," she'd countered.

Rawlings had taken her hand. "You're the most beautiful creature I've ever seen."

Olivia had left her chair and settled onto his lap, her long legs curling around his waist. She'd kissed him and he'd run his strong fingers through her hair, which was the same white gold as the moonlight. Eventually, he'd led her inside and up the stairs to the bedroom.

Now, in the bright summer sunshine, Olivia didn't know how to behave around the chief, especially since her lack of judgment had brought him here. She'd exposed them both to public scrutiny and she began to regret her decision to punish the obnoxious tourists.

Glancing around again, Olivia noticed that the stares of the locals were mostly well meaning. These were not the calculating looks of the paparazzi who'd trailed after her throughout her twenties and early thirties, snapping countless photos of Olivia with her latest beau. She'd dated models, actors, a minor royal, and several Fortune 500 executives, but no one ever lasted beyond a month or two. No one had ever taken her breath away. Not until she'd met Sawyer Rawlings.

"Excuse me, sir." The toddler's mother tapped Rawlings on the arm. "I think I know how this accident happened. You see, my daughter's arm was burned when the woman in the Corvette threw her cigarette toward the sidewalk." She was deliberately sticking to the facts. "Catherine, my little girl, is okay. It's just a tiny surface burn, but when it happened she screamed really loud. She's not even two and the pain took her by surprise," she added apologetically. "Anyway, I think this lady saw the cigarette butt hit my daughter and got distracted." She smiled at Olivia. "Sorry, but I didn't catch your name before."

"I'm Olivia Limoges. And this is Chief Rawlings."

Rawlings was studying the woman with concern. "Are you certain your daughter is all right, Mrs. . . . ?"

"Cimino. Lori Cimino. Yes, Cat's fine. But I wanted you to know that I don't think this would have happened if that woman hadn't tossed her cigarette butt into the street."

"Thank you, Mrs. Cimino. Would you be willing to fill out a report on the incident? I believe this individual needs to be taught a lesson about littering."

The woman nodded, a slight smile playing at the corners of her mouth. Olivia understood exactly how she felt and examined her nails before Rawlings could see how satisfied she was over how things were turning out. But he was shrewder than she thought.

After asking Mrs. Cimino to wait in the shade until he interviewed the Corvette's passenger, Rawlings pointed a stern finger at Olivia. "I cannot condone your behavior, Olivia. I suspect you saw the child get injured and, acting impetuously and without consideration for anyone's safety, used your vehicle as a battering ram." His eyes flicked over the front of her Range Rover and he seemed amazed by the lack of damage, but his look of disapproval quickly reappeared. "I'm going to have to write you a citation."

"Fair enough," Olivia said and lowered her voice to a soft, husky whisper. "Is that all you'll do to punish me?"

If Rawlings was taken aback by the question, he didn't show it. "Next time I come over, I'm bringing my shackles." He winked, slid his sunglasses back on, and headed over to speak with the doctor and his mistress.

Olivia returned to the sidewalk and exchanged small

talk with the Cimino family. They were just discussing the best way to enjoy a filet of flounder when the doctor marched around the front of his car and slapped the blonde across the face. The sound reverberated and the crowd held a collective breath, stunned.

The blonde covered her cheek with her palm and began to sob. Rawlings rushed to her side with the alacrity of a much younger man. He had the physician on the ground and his wrists cuffed before the other cops moved a muscle. Kneeling on the asphalt, Rawlings murmured to the doctor until the man became docile and still. Passing him off to one of his officers, the chief approached the blonde and offered her his hand. She grasped it, sagging against his wide chest.

Olivia's previous aversion toward the woman vanished, and she pitied the doctor's mistress. She'd changed her body, her face, her hair, and her style of dress to please her companion. He'd rewarded her with a weekend trip to a seaside hotel, a string of belittling remarks, and at least one slap in the face.

"Poor thing," Lori Cimino echoed Olivia's thoughts. "Jerks like that are everywhere. I almost ended up with a guy like that. You get trapped into thinking you can't do better, that you aren't worthy of respect. Or happiness. It takes a strong woman to just walk away, to believe that you can make it on your own." She glanced at her husband, who was holding their daughter in his arms and planting loud, smacking wet kisses on her neck and shoulders while she giggled in delight. "By the time I met Tony, I knew who I was and what I wanted, but some women never get to that point."

Olivia considered Lori's words. She too had known women who'd deliberately invited destructive men into their lives and then spent their days bemoaning their situation. It had once been impossible for her to comprehend why these women didn't leave the louts, but she now knew that people were often anchored to negative relationships by fear.

Her fingertips reached for the starfish pendant. Was it fear that kept her from responding to the witch's summons? Olivia shook off the notion. She was scared of nothing.

Picking Rawlings out of a group of policemen, she knew that this was no longer the truth. What she felt for him truly scared her.

Back at her low country–style house overlooking the ocean, Olivia showered and changed into a navy sheath dress and a long Paloma Picasso silver chain necklace. The starfish pendant was tucked underneath the neckline of the dress, but as Olivia stood in front of the bathroom mirror applying bronze-tinted eye shadow and a ruddy beige shade of lipstick, she pulled out the gold starfish and stared at her reflection.

"Mother," she whispered and closed her eyes. She sensed that the images she'd stored of Camille Limoges were romanticized, and she didn't dwell on the rose-colored memories too often, but there were moments when a montage of pictures would play across the movie screen of her mind and she intentionally got lost in them.

Right now she was remembering having been caught by a late autumn thunderstorm when she was six years old. In the aimless, dreamy manner of a lonely child, she'd walked far down the beach, all the way around the Point where she could no longer see the roof of the lighthouse. A squall had swept in from the Atlantic, soaking her within seconds. Her pigtail braids had funneled water down her thin chest and skinny legs and her sneakers had squelched as they sank into the boglike sand.

When she'd finally returned home, her mother had run her a hot bath, plied her with hot chocolate brimming with plump marshmallows, and then wrapped her in a towel warmed by the living room fire. She'd then brushed Olivia's hair until it gleamed a pale gold while she sang *"Ballade à la Lune"* in French.

Standing in her bathroom, decades later, Olivia could smell the lavender of her mother's favorite hand cream. She could almost believe that her mother was there, an invisible force, still promising love and protection. Love and protection. These were things, thanks to her mother's sudden death and her father's disappearance a few years later, that Olivia knew little about.

"I'll go," Olivia spoke to her reflection, knowing how much she favored Camille Limoges, though her mother hadn't lived long enough to earn laugh lines around the eyes or a pair of parentheses around the mouth. Camille had been like Edna St. Vincent Millay's candle. She hadn't lasted the night, but she'd been a beautiful light to many while she'd lived.

Loading Haviland into the Range Rover, Olivia headed off to The Boot Top Bistro. In the quiet, air-conditioned cabin, she sang the first verse of her mother's lullaby.

> *C'était dans la nuit brune*
> *Sur le clocher jauni,*
> *Sur le clocher la lune*
> *Comme un point sur un i.*
> *Ho la hi hi, ho la hi ho*
> *Ho la hi hi, ho la hi ho.*

Haviland made a keening sound in the back of his throat and Olivia switched to English for the second verse, which sent him into a full-fledged howl.

> *Moon, whose dark spirit*
> *Strolls at the end of a thread,*
> *At the end of a thread, in the dark*
> *Your face and your profile?*

Ho la hee hee, ho la hee ho
Ho la hee hee, ho la hee ho.

Unable to compete with her poodle's singing, Olivia fell silent, allowing the last two verses to float through her head in her mother's voice, which was far more melodious than Olivia's.

Memories of Camille Limoges were swept aside the moment Olivia walked into the kitchen of her five-star restaurant. Michel, her head chef, rushed to meet her, grasping a cleaver in one hand and piece of raw chicken in the other.

"Whoa!" Olivia made a sign of surrender. "If you want a raise, you could just ask."

Michel glanced at the cleaver as though wondering how he came to be holding it, tossed it and the chicken in the nearest sink, and said, "You'll never believe who called!"

Knowing Michel's flair for the dramatic, Olivia replied, "Must be someone special to have you in such a state."

It wasn't Michel's appearance that indicated something significant had happened. The kitchen, which Michel ruled over with an iron hand, was a mess. The worktables were covered with fruit and raw vegetables, flour was strewn across the butcher block, there was a tower of dirty mixing bowls and frying pans in the deep sink, and the sous-chefs were unusually edgy. They shot nervous glances at Michel and plaintive ones at Olivia. Her chef wanted something and he wanted it badly. If she didn't give in, he'd pout, rage at his underlings, or unwittingly add too much salt to the entrées.

"Someone special?" Michel scoffed. "How about an executive producer of the Foodie Network? He wants us to act as the celebrity judges at the Coastal Carolina Food Festival."

Olivia made it clear that she wasn't impressed.

"That's just the beginning!" Michel added breathlessly. "If we agree, they're going to tape an entire segment here at The Boot Top. Do you know what kind of name recognition that will bring us?" He was so excited that he was speaking in a high whisper.

"It would be good for business," Olivia agreed, and her head chef performed a little jig of triumph. Olivia watched him in amusement. "But they're asking us at the last minute. Is there more to this story?"

"There *is*. They want us to step in because the original celebrity judge had a massive heart attack and isn't well enough to travel. I've shed many tears for him since I heard the news." The last phrase was delivered with biting sarcasm.

"Ah, the ailing judge must be the rich and famous Pierce Dumas, your nemesis," Olivia guessed.

Michel's face darkened. He and Dumas had attended culinary school in Paris together. They'd been in competition for top chef positions in the finest American restaurants until Michel had fallen for a married woman. Despite the cost to his career, he'd moved to Raleigh to be near her, and while he was mooning after someone who had no intention of leaving her husband, Dumas went on to garner national acclaim for his epicurean skills. He worked in Manhattan, Vegas, and Los Angeles and constantly appeared in culinary magazines and on food-related television shows.

Dumas had fame, wealth, and a gorgeous A-list actress wife. Michel, on the other hand, had been unceremoniously dumped by his married girlfriend and, battling a serious depression, decided to relocate. During his interview for the chef's position at The Boot Top, he'd prepared several dishes for Olivia and she knew right away that Michel was the man for the job. Within months of hiring him, she came to realize that he had two destructive obsessions: married women and a deep-seated envy of Pierce Dumas.

"You haven't mentioned Dumas in over a year," Olivia reminded Michel. "You're happy where you are. Look at the result of his high-stress lifestyle. A heart attack at his age?"

Michel smiled with delight.

"You live in paradise and have complete control of this kitchen. You're the master of your realm, the money is good, and you're healthy. You're not famous, but fame is a curse, believe me."

"Well, I'd like my fifteen minutes and I'm going to get it. My mind is stuffed with menu ideas that will dazzle the producer." Michel rubbed his hands together with glee. "And I've heard Shelley Giusti will be at the festival. We met in a pastry chef class a million years ago. I was in love with her of course, but she married some health nut as soon as we graduated. Even back then, she was a true sorceress with desserts."

"Was she your first crush?" Olivia asked. Michel was constantly falling in and out of love.

"First *love*. And if she looks anything like her photo on the jacket flap of her new cookbook, *Decadence*, then she has aged *very* well. I wonder if she'll remember all the good times we shared. We used to meet for drinks after class and talk about everything and anything. I remember how she'd throw her head back when she laughed . . ." Michel trailed off, a dreamy look entering his eyes.

Olivia was all too familiar with the signs that he was about to embark on a new infatuation. "Does this mean that you're not going to pursue Laurel anymore? I thought she was the butter to your grits, the salsa to your tortilla chips, the vanilla ice cream to your apple strudel?"

"Stop it! Enough with the food clichés," Michel pleaded. "Part of me will always care for Laurel. She is an angel among women and her husband isn't worthy of her, but she doesn't see me as a potential lover. She never will."

Putting a hand on Michel's shoulder, Olivia spoke with rare tenderness. "I don't know why you chase people who aren't free to love you, but you deserve someone to call your own. You're a fine man, Michel. You could make the right woman very happy."

Moved by her words, Michel simply nodded.

Olivia took the piece of paper from his hand and flattened it on the nearest countertop. "I'll speak to this producer. I want certain things in writing before a film crew invades my restaurant."

Michel knew that his employer was wary of the media, regardless of what form it took.

"I know you're doing this for me," he murmured quietly. "Not for the business. It doesn't need the Foodie Network. I do."

His eyes grew moist and for a moment it looked like he might throw his arms around Olivia, but he recognized that she wouldn't welcome a grandiose display of emotion.

He wiped his eyes with the cuff of his chef's jacket and cleared his throat. "Thank you," he said simply. And then, unable to resist a bit of theatricality, added, "Everything you said to me about love is true. I'm getting older. It's time for me to have a grown-up relationship. It's time for me to be happy. And it's time for you to be happy too."

Olivia looked up sharply.

"Oh, yes," Michel continued softly. "You've had enough loneliness to last two lifetimes. Let the past go."

Her fingertips moved to where the starfish pendant was concealed beneath the fabric of her dress. Michel knew the history of the necklace. He knew that Olivia's mother had died during a hurricane and that the loss still haunted her.

Michel grabbed her gently by the wrist, preventing her from making contact with the starfish. "You don't need that anymore. You have a new family. Me, your writer friends, Dixie, Rawlings."

Olivia gave Michel a small, grateful smile, squeezed his hand once, and then let it go. After calling Haviland, who'd been waiting for her signal by the back door, she disappeared into the sanctuary of her tiny office.

Soon she heard Michel begin to hum a tune in a robust and merry tenor. The sous-chefs had obviously relaxed and the rhythms of the kitchen resumed. Olivia could once again hear The Boot Top's unique melody: the hiss of steam, the blades of knives kissing the wood cutting board, the entwining of Spanish, French, and North Carolina accents.

Olivia sighed in contentment. This was the music of her here and now. And it was beautiful.

Chapter 3

*A town is saved, not more by the righteous
men in it than by the woods and swamps that
surround it.*

—HENRY DAVID THOREAU

The little Boston Whaler bounced across the harbor,
leaving a narrow trail of white foam in its wake. Flecks
of salt water speckled Olivia's face, hair, and hands, but
she didn't mind. Neither did Haviland, who licked at the air
and smiled widely. The poodle enjoyed a boat ride even
more than a car trip because he could stand on the deck. He
was so content that he appeared to have forgiven Olivia for
strapping him into a canine life jacket.

For her own part, Olivia had refused the boatman's offer
of a life jacket. She wanted to feel the wind ripple her clothing and gently chafe her skin. Besides, the harbor was calm
today and the man working the shift and throttle levers
handled them deftly, his alert gaze constantly sweeping
from east to west in search of approaching vessels.

She'd found her ride to the creek that ran alongside the
eastern boundary of the Croatan National Forest by asking
questions at the docks on Friday afternoon. After the shrimp
boats had tied up their trawlers for the day, she purchased
a generous amount of fresh seafood for both The Boot Top

Bistro and The Bayside Crab House and then made subtle inquiries on how to reach a recluse named Munin.

The shrimpers knew Munin only as "the witch" and none were interested in taking Olivia within a mile of her swamp, but one of the captains knew someone who would.

"Fellow by the name Harlan Scott knows how to find her," the grizzled seaman said. "But look out, girlie. There are wild things in that swamp. Things you won't see comin', things that'll creep out of the shadows like a shark risin' from the deep water. Bring a big stick. Maybe even the kind that fires bullets."

Olivia had disregarded the fisherman's advice and left her Browning BPR rifle in the coat closet. Instead, she'd packed insect repellant, a canteen of water, Haviland's travel bowl, a granola bar, a bag of dried beef strips, and something that was precious to her into a sturdy knapsack.

Yesterday, she'd felt prepared to face the witch, but now, as the sun-bleached shore of the parkland grew closer and Harlan eased off the throttle, dulling the motorboat's roar to a low rumble, she wasn't so sure.

She and Harlan hadn't exchanged a single word during the crossing, but Olivia suddenly wanted to speak with her guide. She stood and moved next to him, her body close to the steering wheel. "How did you come to know Munin?" she called over the sound of the engine and the wind.

Harlan kept his eyes fixed on the water. "I used to be a park ranger. Knew every inch of this place." He encompassed the land before them with a sweep of his arm. "I was clearing one of the trails when I lost my footing and stepped on a fallen log. The eastern diamondback rattlesnake hiding underneath didn't appreciate the intrusion. He bit me twice before he ever made a noise. Couldn't radio for help because I hadn't bothered to check my battery before heading out that morning. I hollered as loud as I could, hoping against hope that someone would hear me."

"And Munin did?"

He nodded. "She saved my life."

Olivia hadn't expected this. "How? I thought the venom from an eastern diamondback was lethal."

"She had antivenom. She's got vials of the stuff from a bunch of different snakes. We've got copperheads, cotton-mouths, and rattlers in the forest. Munin milked all of the poisonous ones and injected a bit of venom into her goat. Don't know how that works, but without that goat I'd be six feet under."

"Antibodies," Olivia murmured, impressed by Munin's ingenuity. "The goat produced antibodies as a response to the venom."

Harlan shrugged. "Yeah, I guess. Anyhow, I make deliveries for her now and then and I'll run folks out to see her if they want to go. It's the least I can do."

"How often do people seek her out?"

The shore was closer now and Harlan slowed the boat until it was barely coasting forward. Olivia could see the mouth of the creek opening up before them. It resembled a wide river now, but she knew enough about the waterways of the North Carolina coast to predict that the shallow banks would draw close together without warning and then continue to narrow until even the diminutive Whaler would be unable to progress any farther.

Once Harlan had set his craft on a course favoring the right side of the creek, he pushed his faded baseball cap back on his head and scratched his brow. "Less and less," he said, answering Olivia's question. "And they all look the same. Full of fear and hope and a little desperation. Sometimes she has answers. Sometimes not."

"Do I seem desperate?" She kept her tone light, but there was a hint of hesitation in her voice.

Harlan's gaze took in the thick underbrush of the salt marsh and the cypress trees rising in the distance. "Everybody is at one point or another. That's when folks seem to need Munin most."

His reply silenced Olivia and she felt less confident as the open water dropped away behind them. The land seemed to be gathering them close, squeezing the small craft deeper into a world ruled by insects and birds. It didn't take long for the noises of these creatures to over-power the sound of the boat's motor. Haviland barked once as a blue heron took flight from the creek's edge. Other-wise, he was quiet, as if sensing that they were heading toward a strange and possibly hostile destination.

Eventually, the water became tinged with eddies of mud, and Harlan tilted the motor toward the boat deck and coasted toward the left bank. He waited until the bow nearly kissed a slope of grass-speckled dirt and then jumped to the shore. A wood gatepost had been set into the ground and he secured the Whaler's line to it using a figure-eight knot and then offered Olivia his hand.

She hopped onto the ground, feeling ungainly in her high waders. Haviland leapt with more grace beside her and immediately began to track an interesting scent in a clump of tall grass. The air was dense with the sawing of cicadas and the buzz of flies and mosquitoes, and the ground was teeming with armies of ants and beetles.

Harlan shouldered a heavy canvas bag and then grabbed a walking stick from inside the boat and made a final adjustment to his baseball cap. "We'll follow the creek for a spell and then turn inland."

Olivia fell into step behind him, her eyes on his walking stick. It had been hand carved and featured a rattlesnake winding along the shaft. The head formed the stick's han-dle and Harlan's fingers fell over a black marble eye, leav-ing the other to stare at the outside of his right thigh.

"Did you carve that?" she asked over the din of the insects.

He didn't turn around to answer. "No, I don't have the knack for it. I bought this from a Lumbee Indian who sells his carvings to raise money for his lodge."

"Is he local? I thought most of the Lumbee tribe lived in Robeson County."

"They do, but they migrated from this neck of the woods once ages back. I went to one of their powwows a few years back, but I won't have to travel if I want to go this year. They're having a big one in the forest in two weeks." He darted a quick glance at her over his shoulder. "You should go. They sell all kinds of crafts and there's story-telling and dances too."

Olivia had no intention of going, but out of politeness asked Harlan when the event would take place.

"Two Saturdays from now. There's some food festival going on at the same time. It'll be a real circus around here."

Olivia knew about the Coastal Carolina Food Festival. "My brother signed up to run a food tent on Saturday. He thinks it'll bring our restaurant lots of new business."

Harlan shrugged. "There'll be a crowd, that's for sure. Thank Christ I'm retired. I'll be at home watching a fishing show while the rangers show folks where to park and hand out maps."

Haviland trotted in front of Harlan and Olivia called him to heel. The grass they were passing through had grown dense and a canopy of tree limbs shaded the ground, creating a perfect hiding place for snakes. The trail Harlan was following had been little used and Olivia only recognized it as a trail at all because no mature vegetation grew where they walked.

Amazed by how quickly she felt completely removed from civilization, Olivia glanced back over her shoulder. The water was no longer visible and she felt slightly claustrophobic by its disappearance. "Isn't it unusual for Munin to be living on public park land?"

"She doesn't. A little stream runs between her place and the park. I doubt the latest crop of rangers even know she's there."

Olivia wanted to pepper Harlan with a dozen questions. Where did Munin come from? Had she just materialized in the swamp one day? What did she eat? How did she keep clean?

But it wouldn't be long before she'd discover these answers for herself, so she kept quiet, watching Harlan swing his carved stick out before him, creating a steady *swoosh, swoosh* as it moved through the grass.

They kept on like this for some time. The trees grew denser, the cypress giving way to loblolly pines, black walnuts, and red oaks. The ground was now leaf covered and firmer underfoot and Harlan picked up his pace.

They rounded a bend and Olivia saw a narrow creek and then a building that reminded her of a cross between a frontier cabin and a crude wigwam. The walls of the structure were made of logs, but the roof was rounded and had been covered with pieces of sheet metal. There was a corrugated metal door and a single window covered by a rectangle of dirty canvas. A pair of rain barrels was positioned beneath the round roof and a goat was standing near the open front door, as if waiting to be invited in.

"Let me go first," Harlan said and rapped against the metal. He paused for a heartbeat and then stepped inside. Olivia heard an exchange of hushed voices and placed her hand on Haviland's neck. He was staring at the goat with interest, but he didn't bark.

Never one to remain still, Olivia walked around Munin's house, examining a large garden where tomatoes, cucumbers, strawberries, beans, carrots, squash, and a variety of lettuces grew in abundance. A mesh fence formed a protective perimeter around the neat rows of plants, and aluminum pie plates dangled from the fence top, catching glints of fractured sunlight.

Beyond the garden was a lean-to sheltering a potter's kick wheel and a primitive kiln made of stacked bricks. Turned black by wood smoke, the kiln was empty, as was the overturned produce crate used as a drying rack. A crust of clay had been left on the wheel and a few crude tools protruded from a metal pail.

"She's ready." Harlan's voice startled her.

Olivia swung around quickly, tensing. "How will you know when it's time to take me back?"

He held up a burlap sack. "I'm going to check on her traps. I expect you'll be done by the time I'm done."

And with that, he marched into the woods, making almost no noise.

Olivia took a deep breath, stood a fraction taller, and walked toward the witch's house. She knocked on the metal door, received no answer, and after waiting another moment, entered.

Her feet encountered a creaky wood stair and then another, leading her down into the near darkness of Munin's home. Haviland followed, his nails clicking against the planks, nose quivering with interest. Olivia noticed how cool the air was in the dimly lit space. It took a moment for her eyes to adjust to the near darkness, but she found the scents—the rich sweetness of damp soil and of clusters of dried herbs hanging from the rafters—most welcoming.

The witch was standing in front of a bookshelf loaded with jars, the glow from a single candle illuminating her face. She was small framed and slightly stooped, with weathered skin and white hair shot through with strands of black. She wore a shapeless blouse over baggy trousers, and when she moved, the jewelry on her ankles rattled. Her feet were bare and brown with caked mud, but her hands were clean, with beautiful, slender fingers. Munin looked terribly fragile and incredibly strong all at once. Her eyes, dark as a crow's, studied Olivia in return.

Haviland approached her cautiously and sniffed at the hem of her pants. The witch didn't even acknowledge his presence.

"I'm here," Olivia said, not knowing what else to say.

Munin nodded and placed a jar on the shelf. In the weak light, Olivia could see preserves, pickled vegetables, and other foodstuffs on the middle shelves. On the top shelf, almost out of the old woman's reach, were jars of miscellaneous objects like buttons, soda can tabs, nails, bottle tops, shells, beads, arrowheads, and colorful rocks.

"Where do you put the gifts the ocean sends you? In jars like these?" Munin's voice was low and raspy from lack of use.

Olivia tried to conceal her astonishment. Had Munin known that she kept all the sundry items she and Haviland dug out of the sand in jumbo pickle jars neatly labeled with the year?

The crone smiled over Olivia's discomfort, revealing a mouthful of chipped, yellow teeth, and said, "Tea first. Then, we'll talk."

She filled two mugs with boiling water from a kettle hanging over a pair of burning logs. Olivia hadn't noticed the hearth before. The wood was glowing orange in an alcove of stones and a wide pipe funneled most of the smoke outside.

Munin opened an ancient tea tin and filled a steel strainer with leaves. After steeping the tea, she opened another jar, and dropped something thick and syrupy into both mugs.

"The bugs won't bother you after you drink this." With a harsh chuckle, she handed Olivia her tea and eased her body into a lawn chair. The frayed material whined as she settled back against the seat and gestured for Olivia to take the remaining chair. Olivia complied and then reluctantly sipped her tea. It was strong and bitter, but Munin had added a hint of refreshing mint and a dollop of honey for sweetness. Olivia was pleasantly surprised by the tea's complex flavors.

"Thank you. It's delicious," she said.

Munin dipped her head in acknowledgment and brought her own mug to her lips.

"You are taller than Camille, but otherwise, you could be her sister."

Olivia nodded. "I don't favor my father at all."

Munin's eyes narrowed. "Oh, I see him plain enough."

"You met Willie Wade?"

"I've seen your daddy many times," she answered cryptically. "But it was your mama I came to know. An unhappy woman, to be sure. A sad and lonely woman. Lovely too. From her face right down to her soul. Uncommon that. You don't warm to people like she did. I can see that plain enough."

Though she knew this to be true, Olivia felt slighted. But she said nothing, choosing to study the rest of the interior instead. Opposite the bookshelves of jars were tall stacks of newspapers. They occupied the entire wall and had been divided into six towers. Olivia suspected these papers were the source of Munin's knowledge.

"It's here, girl. What you came to see." The witch pointed at a lump near her feet, which was roughly the size and shape of a gallon milk jug. Munin pulled off the burlap sack covering the object with a slow flourish. Her face was unreadable.

It was a jug made of ruddy brown clay. Nearly every inch of its surface had been covered by the commonplace items Munin stored in her glass jars. However, in between the buttons, nails, and bottle caps were more valuable items. Olivia saw a pearl ring, a Cameo brooch, a gold chain, a silver cross, and a framed daguerreotype.

"It's a memory jug," Munin said. "Some say the slaves made them to put on the graves of their loved ones. Others say the Victorians came up with the idea since they were so keen on preserving the past. And there are those who think the early settlers made them on dark evenings to fight off boredom." She gestured at the jug. "Go on, I can see that you wanna touch it."

Olivia drew the piece closer. It was heavier than she'd

expected. Carefully balancing it on her knee, she tilted it toward the candlelight.

"The boredom theory holds the most water with me," Munin continued. "I've made them for half a century now. Harlan takes the jugs to town and mails them off to some gallery on the West Coast. The lady who owns the gallery sends him money and he buys me the things I need. Like my papers." She waved at the stacks of newspapers without looking at them. "Harlan told me they call me the Gypsy Potter of North Carolina in that gallery. I'm right fond of that name."

Casting a glance at Munin's rattling ankle bracelets, Olivia said, "Are you a gypsy?"

Munin shrugged. "I'm a mix of things, just like that pot." She raised the hem of her trousers an inch, allowing Olivia a clear glimpse of her bracelets. They were made of the teeth and bones of small animals.

Forcing herself to not recoil, Olivia met the old woman's dark gaze. "Why did you want me to come?"

Reclaiming the jug, Munin put it back in the burlap sack. "Because the last jug I'm ever gonna make is for you. Because your mama cared for me once when I was real sick. She brought medicine from town and spent the night here. Not many would do that."

"How did you come to meet her in the first place?" Olivia demanded.

"Same way I meet most folks. She needed help no one else could give her." The witch held out her hand, palm up. She wasn't going to answer any more questions. It was time to collect her payment. "What have you brought me?"

Olivia's fingers reached for her backpack, closing over her treasure. In the witch's gloomy hole, surrounded by the rows of dusty jars and the disintegrating newspapers, she was reluctant to bring it forth, let alone hand it over to the crone.

"Ah, it pains you to think of me having your prize."

Munin's face wrinkled in delight. "Then it's a worthy sacrifice. Give it to me."

Unzipping the backpack, Olivia stalled a moment by offering Haviland a dried beef stick. She hated being controlled by the strange woman, and all because she claimed to have known Olivia's mother. But every story of Camille Limoges enriched Olivia's own memory of her, rooting her orphaned daughter to a family tree, to the town of Oyster Bay, to a special place in one person's heart. She knew she'd trade nearly anything in exchange for information on her mother, the person she had loved the most. The only person who'd truly loved her in return.

Her hand closed around the witch's payment and she passed it over without further hesitation.

Munin unwrapped the protective layer of tissue paper to reveal an exquisite wood carving of a young girl standing in the lee of a lighthouse, her hand shielding her eyes as she stared outward in search of something.

"It's you," the witch said. "Looking for your daddy, right?" She touched the wooden girl's skinny arm with a hooked fingernail. "And you think your search is over, but it's not."

Anger flared within Olivia. "Enough riddles. What do you want?"

Munin leaned closer, her dark eyes locking on Olivia's. "Death is coming to this forest. It doesn't want you, but it'll take you if you get in its way. Be wary. Protect your friends. You will all be close to danger."

Olivia pointed at the newspaper on Munin's bookshelf. "Did you read about the food festival? That's how you know I'll be in the forest." She made a derisive sound. "Is that all there is to your hocus-pocus?"

"In part." Munin grinned, unfazed. "I am Memory. I collect memories and I put them on my jugs. The past helps me see into the future. And I use other methods too. The land is rich with plants that aid my visions. Jimsonweed, heliotrope, passion flower."

Eying her tea suspiciously, Olivia set the mug aside, causing Munin to laugh. The sound was like the rustle of dried leaves. "I haven't drugged you, girl. I mean you no harm, which is a good thing, for harm seems to find you. Death is attracted to you."

"I assume you're referring to the murder that happened a few months ago? Again, you read about my involvement in the paper." She narrowed her eyes at the old woman. "And if you knew it would happen, why didn't you send a warning?"

"I don't see in straight lines, child. I knew that the man calling himself Plumley would pay a steep price. There is always a price, as there was for your friend—the one who's in jail now. He has peace for the first time in his life. You don't have to grieve for him anymore."

Olivia felt the tiny hairs on the back of her neck stand up. Only Dixie, Rawlings, and the Bayside Book Writers knew how she felt about the events of the past spring. How she'd mourned the loss of a friend and how her guilt over helping the authorities bring him to justice had weighed her down for months.

"Many of my visions are filled with nightmares," Munin suddenly hissed. "Ugly things that will come to pass. But that does not mean I should interfere. I stay away from such things unless I have a debt to pay. I have survived by staying away." The fire in her eyes died as quickly as it had flared and she settled more deeply into her chair and drank her tea. "I kept others safe for a long time by removing myself from the world, but even I cannot hide forever."

There was a scuffing noise outside the house. "Harlan's emptied my traps. Would you like to stay for supper? If there's quail, I can roast them on a spit and make you a bracelet from their bones. Or would you prefer fresh squirrel?" She cackled.

"Thank you, but, no. Please go on. I've paid you," Olivia reminded her. "I am waiting for my story."

Picking up the carving Olivia's father had made, Munin studied it again. A flicker of sadness crossed her weathered face.

"For your gift, I will tell you two things. The first is that I met Camille Limoges when she was carrying you." She stopped suddenly and stared at Olivia. "Did you never wonder why such a woman—beautiful, kind, wise—would marry an uneducated fisherman who loved whiskey more than any living being?"

"Of course I have!" Olivia snapped, growing tired of the witch's enigmatic manner of speaking. "A million times over. My grandmother couldn't explain it. No one could."

Munin looked exceedingly pleased. "But I can. She had no choice. Consider that, girl. The man who should have raised you couldn't claim you. Couldn't claim your mother either. Poor, sweet fool." She slowly raised herself out of the chair. It creaked in protest until her weight was transferred to her dirty feet. "Soon, many paths will cross in this forest. People who have carried anger around with them too long will meet. People who have swept too many secrets into a dark corner will see them exposed to the light. Death is coming and you'll be in the middle of it all. Again. Be wary. That is all I have to say." She turned toward the door. "Harlan!"

Harlan pushed open the metal door and poked his head inside. "You all set?"

Olivia was on the verge of protesting when Munin said, "I am tired. The jug on the ground is ready to be mailed, Harlan." She looked at Olivia. "The one by the foot of the bed is for you, girl. It holds all of the answers you seek as well as those you might not want to know. My gift can protect you in the days to come. It can also undo you. The truth waits inside." She stroked Olivia's carving, her eyes distant. "I do this for your mother. My debt to her is paid. Go now."

Suddenly, Olivia saw Munin not as a witch, a crazy hag, or a malicious crone, but as a tired, lonely old woman who'd lived without companionship, without laughter for far too long. When had she last shared a meal with another human being? When had she been given a scrap of comfort during times of sorrow or illness? Was Camille Limoges the only person to show her kindness?

Shadows from the candle flame played across Munin's face, and as Olivia studied the creases and the lines, mapping out the old woman's solitary existence, she realized that it had either taken incredible strength or immense fear or a combination of both to live this woman's life.

Before she lost the courage to do so, Olivia reached both hands behind her neck and unclasped the gold chain holding her starfish pendant. She gently placed the treasure in Munin's hand and closed the old woman's fingers around it.

"This is my most precious possession," she said. "It always made me feel like my mother was near. Maybe you'll feel her too."

Munin accepted the gift with a grave nod. "Thank you, child. I will be in need of comfort soon. I should have known that Camille's daughter would be the one to offer it to me. I should have known that there is hope in the next generation . . ."

And with that, she turned away.

Olivia gathered the burlap sack containing her jug and stepped from the gloom of Munin's home into the harsh midday light. She winced, her eyes filling with tears, and motioned for Haviland to heel.

Harlan forged ahead, his walking stick brushing idly against the carpet of leaves until it gave way to the tall grass once again.

"You did a good thing back there," he said when the Whaler came into view again. "Will you come again?"

Feeling the solid weight of the jug in her backpack, Olivia paused on the muddy bank, watching a cloud of gnats descend toward the water. "Maybe," she said, but doubted it. There was something final about her parting with Munin.

After helping her aboard, Harlan started the motor and coasted toward the mouth of the creek. As the warm wind pushed strands of Olivia's pale hair into the air, she stared at the desolate underbrush and blank sky and recalled a poem by Katherine Mansfield. It might have been written for the woman she'd just met.

Olivia spoke a few lines in a soft murmur, sending the words aloft on the salty breeze, unaware that, in her own way, she was delivering the witch's eulogy.

> *Through the sad dark the slowly ebbing tide*
> *Breaks on a barren shore, unsatisfied.*
> *A strange wind flows . . . then silence. I am fain*
> *To turn to Loneliness, to take her hand,*
> *Cling to her, waiting, till the barren land*
> *Fills with the dreadful monotone of rain.*

Chapter 4

I write for the same reason I breathe—because if I didn't, I would die.

—ISAAC ASIMOV

A week after Olivia's trip to the swamp, the Bayside Book Writers assembled in the comfortable living room of the lighthouse keeper's cottage and helped themselves to beer, wine, or, in Olivia's case, a tumbler of Chivas Regal. There was also a selection of tasty tidbits from The Boot Top to sample, including lemon and garlic grilled shrimp skewers, fried crab wontons with a ginger soy dipping sauce, roasted avocado and asparagus wraps, and prosciutto rolls stuffed with goat cheese and dates.

"Anyone else going to the Coastal Carolina Food Festival next weekend?" Laurel asked as she poured herself a generous glass of chardonnay. "I volunteered to cover Saturday's events for the *Gazette*."

Olivia was delighted to hear that Laurel would be attending, especially since Michel no longer had a crush on her. "I'll be there. Michel too. We've been asked to serve as celebrity judges for some of the cooking competitions. Apparently, the Foodie Network will be filming several segments over the weekend. And Hudson's going to run a Bayside Crab House tent on Saturday."

Harris pointed a shrimp skewer at Olivia. "You get all the glamorous jobs. I have to go because my company wants to develop a new game called Koko's Kitchen. It's supposed to appeal to five- to eight-year-olds and there are a bunch of kid-focused cooking demonstrations at the festival, so guess who has to watch all of them to get a feel for the graphic design? Why can't I go to Comic-Con to check out the outfits worn by barbarian warrior maidens instead?"

Millay dunked a wonton into the bowl of ginger-soy sauce and grinned at Harris. "Hey, at least you're getting paid to hang out at a fair. I mean, do you really need to conduct much research to design cyber spaghetti or chicken tenders?" She turned to Laurel. "That's pretty much what kids eat, right?"

Laurel nodded glumly. "I used to cook the twins all kinds of things. Their plates were colorful and oh so healthy, but now I hardly bother. All they want is mac and cheese, pizza, or Happy Meals. And I give it to them." She sighed. "I won't be winning a Mother of the Year award anytime soon."

"Getting kids to try new foods is the whole point of this game!" Harris exclaimed. "There've been all these studies showing that kids are more likely to eat unfamiliar food if they cook it themselves. Especially vegetables."

"In that case, I'd like to preorder a copy," Laurel said. "Or do you need a few test subjects? My kids are all yours if you do. In fact, they could just move in with you for a weekend. What do you say?"

Harris blanched.

Olivia savored the exchange of easy conversation, imagining the words floating through the house on currents of cool air and eventually coming to rest in the cracks of the old pine floorboards. She liked the idea of the entire structure being filled with talk and laugher—the writers coating every surface with a patina of friendship.

Not so long ago, the cottage had felt uninviting, haunted. Olivia had avoided the painful memories lingering within its walls by completely ignoring its existence. But then her friends had given her a reason to exorcise its ghosts and she had renovated it from the roof down, turning it into the perfect meeting place for small groups.

Now, as she stood by the window overlooking the ocean, she marveled over how her life had changed for the better since she'd become a member of the Bayside Book Writers. They'd rescued her from decades of loneliness and neglect, just as Olivia had rescued her childhood home.

"Can I interrupt your space-out session?" Millay asked, breaking into Olivia's reverie. "I really need a napkin."

Seeing the dribble of soy sauce on Millay's chin and the brown splotches on the counter, Olivia laughed and handed her friend a paper towel. "Are you working at Fish Nets or will you be at the festival?"

"I'm only going if there are free samples," she said. "If there aren't, I might as well walk around Costco. If I go around the whole store three times, that's lunch."

Olivia settled into one of the plush club chairs facing the water and gave Millay a bemused look. "I think the food you can taste at the event will top the corn dog bites and protein bars you'll be offered at Costco. If nothing else, Hudson will feed you. The Bayside Crab House is setting up a tent in the vendor area."

"In that case, I'm in," Millay said and Olivia caught the gleam of happiness in Harris's eyes. She studied her ginger-haired friend. Had his boyish, Peter Pan appearance changed since he'd been shot? Yes, he did look different. He was still as smooth faced and bright eyed as ever, and his cheeks still dimpled when he laughed, but he seemed bulkier and much more confident than the lean, uncertain young man she'd first met over a year ago. He was coming into his own.

Olivia couldn't help but wonder whether Millay was seeing him through new eyes too, or if Harris would end up being just another man she dated for a spell before growing bored and moving on to the next bad-boy type. Harris was nothing like the surfers, punk rockers, bartenders, or mechanics

Millay was typically attracted to. It was clear that he was in love with Millay, that he'd been in love with her since the first meeting of the Bayside Book Writers. Whether Millay was capable of returning those feelings was another story. However, Olivia had no interest in getting involved in someone else's romantic drama. Having one of her own was enough.

Rawlings' name surfaced in her mind, making Olivia acutely aware of his absence. She glanced at her watch. The critique session would start within minutes. Laurel already had her copy of Harris's chapter on her lap, the notes she'd taken in green pen clearly visible in the margins.

"Am I ever going to stop being nervous about handing a chapter over to you guys?" Harris asked, trying to catch a glimpse of Laurel's comments.

"Probably not," Laurel said. "And that's a good thing. It shows that you want to improve—that you care what your readers think."

Harris smiled warmly at her. "Even if you ripped me to shreds once a month, I'd still write. I've scribbled sci-fi stories since I could hold a pencil. I think we were all born with the writing chromosome. We can't stop. It's a part of our genetic makeup."

Millay snatched the bottle of beer from Harris's hand and headed to the sofa. Flopping onto the soft cushions, she kicked off her trademark black boots and put both feet on the coffee table. She gave her toes, which were encased in pink and green argyle knee socks, a satisfied wiggle and then pulled a stack of papers out of her messenger bag.

"Okay, Harris 'Watson-and-Crick' Williams, just promise not to turn into a total sellout when you finally get published. Half of the authors on the bestseller list don't give a crap about the quality of their writing anymore. They discover a profitable formula and wham!" She snapped her fingers. "All they do after that is pump out the same book over and over again."

"That's still an accomplishment. I can't imagine what it

would be like to write more than one book," Laurel said. "The whole process is so unpredictable. I was cruising along on *The Wife*. It was practically writing itself until, at about sixty thousand words, I hit a wall."

Olivia gave her friend a sympathetic look. "You're trying to sort out some big issues right now, Laurel." She paused and then gently asked, "How are you and Steve doing?"

Laurel shrugged. "Okay, I guess. Better." She took a sip of chardonnay. And another. "We're being so polite to each other now. So careful not to hurt each other's feelings. It's weird. I hate all the tiptoeing."

"You just need to have a huge fight followed by drunken make-up sex," Millay said. "Smash some plates, rip off some clothes, and you'll be good to go. You can say please and thank you *after* you've done the horizontal tango."

For a moment, Laurel's eyes went wide, but then she laughed. "Actually, you've given me a great idea for my next chapter. Thanks for curing my case of writer's block."

"I won't charge you. This time," Millay said wryly and then glanced at Olivia. "So what gives? Where's the chief?"

"Late again," Olivia said. She'd been wondering the same thing. "But he knows the deal. We start on time as long as the author's here. Ready, Harris?"

Harris devoured the last prosciutto roll on his plate and nodded. "Fire away."

Olivia looked down at her notes. Harris's science-fiction novel featured a complex heroine named Zenobia. Following the tragic death of her parents, this young woman had unexpectedly become the ruler of the entire Zulton race and was tasked with relocating her people from their dying planet to a more viable one.

In the first half of Harris's book, Zenobia had successfully maneuvered through a political minefield and honed her skills as warrior. However, she refused to bend to the customs of the nobility and spent most of her free time alone in a simulation room.

During Harris's last critique session, the Bayside Book Writers had pointed out that they knew very little about Remus, Zenobia's new planet, and he'd responded by having Zenobia lead a team into a vast cavern system in search of a valuable mineral. In one of the deeper caves, Zenobia's party had been attacked by a creature unlike any Zenobia or the Bayside Book Writers had ever encountered before.

Olivia thought he did a good job with this scene, though she still had difficulty picturing the beast in her mind. Apparently, so did Millay.

"Is it part dragon or part alligator?" she asked. "I get it that's it big and drools and has four eyes, but I can't really see it."

"But it's sci-fi," Laurel argued. "He can't compare it with things on Earth. If he says it had the head of a crocodile, it takes away from the sense that everything is alien."

Millay offered suggestions on how Harris could describe the beast more effectively, while Laurel insisted that too much detail would detract from Zenobia. "She's the star."

Olivia told Harris that she liked both the pacing and descriptive detail, but didn't understand why Zenobia was disappointed over being hailed as Hunter, a rare and special title given to only the bravest of leaders. "You show us her emotions, but don't explain why she feels the way she does. And what about the mineral they went to mine in the first place? Are they going back for it or are there more creatures in those caverns?"

Harris was about to reply when a ping came from Olivia's cell phone, indicating she'd just received a text message. "I'd better see if that's Rawlings," she said, getting up from the club chair and moving into the small kitchen. Scooping her phone up from the counter, she glanced at the text box and read the enigmatic message from Rawlings.

"Is it the chief?" Harris asked. "I hope he shows up. I need a guy's take on this chapter. No offense to the ladies, of course."

Millay hit him in the face with a throw pillow. "Offense taken, loser. Your book features a female protagonist! If you want to resonate with female readers, then you should count yourself lucky to have three savvy chicks reviewing your drafts."

Harris protested until Laurel cut him off by saying, "I hear a car."

"That's Rawlings." Olivia held out her phone and pointed at the text window. "He asked me to meet him outside. Alone."

Millay's brows rose. "Oooooh! A tryst? Right in the middle of our critique session?"

Olivia glowered at her. She had done her best to act casual in Rawlings' presence, to understate her relationship with the chief whenever anyone else was around, and she didn't like Millay calling attention to it. "He didn't text me a bunch of *x*s and *o*s," she said tersely. "I don't know what he wants, but it can't be good if he won't talk about it in front of everyone. Be right back."

Haviland jumped up from his position next to the sofa and joined Olivia as she made her way outside. Rawlings, who was dressed in uniform, was talking on his cell phone. When he saw Olivia, he quickly finished his conversation and tossed the phone onto the driver's seat.

"Am I under arrest?" Olivia teased, holding out her wrists. The chief's mouth narrowed to a grim line and he stiffened his shoulders, making it clear that he was in no mood for jokes.

Rawlings gave Haviland's head a cursory pat and then moved closer to Olivia.

"We need to talk," he said, and in his voice Olivia heard an unmistakable command. He hadn't asked her to step outside because he wanted to have an intimate personal exchange, but because he had something to tell her. Something unpleasant.

She folded her arms defensively over her chest, as if to

shield herself from whatever Rawlings had to say. "What's going on?"

Casting a quick glance at the house, Rawlings took Olivia's elbow. "Let's go down by the water."

Sensing that Laurel, Millay, and Harris were watching them from the living room window, she nodded and turned toward the beach. Haviland darted ahead, eager to chase the few shorebirds wading through the shallows before day gave way to night.

The approach of twilight had painted the sky with strokes of pink and orange. The colors shimmered on the surface of the glassy ocean and the pastel hues seemed to be coming in on the tide. Olivia longed to hold on to this picture of beauty, to delay Rawlings for a moment or two.

"I know," he said as if she'd spoken aloud. "It's stunning. The end of a summer day. The citrus shades will be replaced by soft purples and blues. The first star will appear out there, low on the sky, and a breeze will move through the dune grasses. It's my favorite time of the day, Olivia, and I'd love to take your hand and walk on the beach until the moon rises, but this can't wait. I have to ruin this moment. I'm sorry."

Olivia heard the regret in his voice. Steeling herself, she said, "Go ahead."

"Did you pay a visit to Munin Cooper last Saturday?"

Of all the questions Rawlings might have asked, Olivia had expected this one the least. She relaxed. Hudson, Kim, and the children were safe. Her restaurants hadn't burned down. Except for Dixie, her friends were all here in the lighthouse keeper's cottage. Haviland was in plain sight. She could let go of the fear.

"I did," she said. "Why?"

Rawlings was studying her intently. "Tell me about it."

Olivia paused to consider why she didn't want to talk to Rawlings about Munin. Yes, she'd found the experience unnerving. It was something she wanted to shelve and analyze later, in the quiet hour before sleep came. She still hadn't examined the memory jug she'd carried home that day. It was in her bedroom closet, waiting until Olivia's time was no longer consumed with preparations for the upcoming Foodie Network taping.

But Rawlings wasn't making a request. He might have asked her gently, softly, but it was still an order.

"We might as well sit. This will take a few minutes." She found a patch of sand unmarred by scraggly grasses or jagged shells and sat, pulling her knees to her chest.

Rawlings remained standing. He was all cop now. Not Olivia's lover or a member of the Bayside Book Writers. He wasn't going to sit cross-legged on the sand as though they were going to trade stories around a campfire.

Olivia began by telling Rawlings that she'd first heard Munin's name from Dixie. She recounted as much of her conversation with the witch as she could remember, including Munin's ominous warning, and only faltered when she came to the moment when she'd given her treasured starfish necklace to a stranger. She did not want to put that exchange into words. It belonged to her and no one else had a right to it.

Her fingers went to her throat and Rawlings caught the movement.

"There's more, isn't there?" he prompted.

"I gave her my necklace," Olivia admitted with a trace of irritation.

Now Rawlings squatted down next to her, touching her chin and forcing her to meet his eyes. "Why? I know what that meant to you."

Olivia could hear the clamor of insects. She saw the crude shack and felt the moist, humid air of the swamp pressing down on her. Again, the old woman's keen loneliness enveloped her. The terrible isolation. The yellowed newspapers. The jars of knickknacks. Munin's gnarled hands pouring tea into chipped mugs. "I just did," she whispered hoarsely. "It doesn't matter why. I just wanted to."

"It does matter," Rawlings said, surprising Olivia.

Her patience at an end, Olivia got to her feet, dusting the sand from her shorts. "Why do you care that I crossed the harbor and spent an hour with this woman? How do you even know about it?"

Rawlings sighed and stood up. "Because that woman is dead."

Hearing this, Olivia dugs her toes into the sand, suddenly needing to feel the gritty grains pressing against her skin, to anchor her body to the soft ground.

Her mind drifted back in time. She recalled Munin's wrinkled face in the dim light. Had she seemed unwell? No. Weary perhaps, but not ill.

"What are you thinking?" Rawlings asked gently.

"I was wondering if she died of natural causes."

Rawlings cast his gaze out over the ocean. A pair of gulls swooped low over the waves and then lifted skyward again, crying in disappointment after discovering that the shadow on the water was a piece of seaweed and not an injured fish. "The medical examiner said she'd been bitten by an eastern diamondback rattlesnake, but the cause of death was drowning."

Olivia's throat constricted. "Where?"

"The stream behind her house. The park ranger who found her thinks she stumbled down the bank and fell in. That she couldn't think straight because of the pain."

Shaking her head in protest, Olivia said, "Munin wore noisy anklets to spook the snakes. And my guide, Harlan, told me she kept stores of antivenom, which she made using her goat's antibodies. This . . . It doesn't sound right."

The memory of the gratitude in Munin's eyes as the starfish necklace settled against her weathered palm washed over Olivia. It didn't seem possible that the old woman was gone, and Olivia was distressed by how she'd met her end. This wasn't the death Munin was meant to have. Olivia was certain of that.

"The case isn't in my jurisdiction," Rawlings said, pulling a folded piece of paper from his pants pocket and handing it to her. "And the Craven County Sheriff's Department plans to rule it an accidental death. As soon as the deputy in charge has spoken to you, that is. He's already tracked down Harlan Scott and you're the only loose end. When I heard that you'd be called in for an interview, I asked to take a look at the case file." He gestured at the paper in Olivia's hands. "You'll see why I'm concerned."

Olivia unfolded the sheaf and gasped. It was a color copy of a dirt-encrusted hand. The fingers were milky white and bloated to the size of sausages. A thin, muddy chain was looped around the middle finger and the pendant at its end had come to rest on a stainless steel table. The mud had been wiped off the starfish so that its golden surface gleamed beneath the bright, searing light.

Olivia stared at the image. Why was the necklace in Munin's hand? Had she been carrying it around in her pocket? Had she clung to it as the rattler's venom wreaked havoc on her body? Or was it possible that she was trying to send a message using Olivia's gift?

Rawlings took Olivia's trembling hand in his. Gently, he reclaimed the paper and put it back in his pocket. He stroked the skin of her palm with his thumb, his eyes filled with tenderness.

"She said that death was coming. That many paths were about to cross in the forest. Her forest," Olivia said quietly. "I thought she was referring to next weekend's events—the powwow and the food fest—things she could have read about in the paper . . ." She trailed off, not quite knowing what she wanted to say.

"But you think she felt threatened?" Rawlings asked.

Olivia shook her head. "No, not threatened. She acted . . . resigned. Prepared. She summoned me, Sawyer. It was important to her that I come right away, even though we were complete strangers. She needed to see me, to give me advice and her last memory jug. She told me that jug had all the answers I'd need to keep death at bay."

"This gets more bizarre by the minute." Rawlings frowned. "I don't like it. With two highly publicized events coming up, the sheriff is going to want to wrap up this case as quickly as possible. He won't want any media attention."

"So if I tell him about my visit and explain that I'd given Munin the necklace, then she'll just disappear?" Olivia asked, though she already knew the answer. "There's no logical reason why I should have a problem with that, but I do." She searched the chief's face and saw her concern mirrored there. "I can't let her fade away like that, Sawyer. Like she never existed."

Rawlings swept his gaze over the water and then pivoted to look at the lighthouse. As if summoned, Haviland appeared from around the corner of the tower, paused to investigate an interesting scent in a clump of sea oats, and then trotted toward them. Olivia held out her hand and he pressed his nose into her palm and then gave Rawlings a brief nuzzle before heading back up the path to the cottage.

"We need to examine that jug," Rawlings said. "And find out the rest of Munin's story. There's a reason she removed herself from the world. Very few people live like that by choice. She was connected to someone once. A mother? A father? Siblings? Someone."

Olivia nodded. "I think she's been in hiding for so long that being alone became her way of life. After enough years had passed, her past, whatever it was, must have seemed like a dream." She reached for her necklace, her fingertips meeting only naked skin. "But after all this time, something from the past must have found her. I believe she knew it was coming, that there was no place left to run."

They stood in silence listening to the waves whisper onto the shore. And when the first star began shining through the canvas of deep blue, they didn't bother wishing upon it. Instead, they walked toward the cottage, turning their backs on the beauty of the night.

Chapter 5

*Because we focused on the snake, we missed
the scorpion.*

—EGYPTIAN PROVERB

"We have to call it an evening," Olivia told the rest
of the Bayside Book Writers apologetically. Chief
Rawlings remained outside, kicking chucks of gravel as he
made another phone call.

Laurel was the first to recognize that something grave
had occurred. She tucked Harris's chapter back into a folder
and clutched it against her chest. Olivia's eye was drawn to
the red and pink bubbly hearts on its cover. She imagined a
working human heart, sinewy and slick, its powerful muscle
contracting. She saw the same heart falling still, the blood
pooling in the four chambers. How had this mighty muscle
reacted to the venom of an eastern diamondback rattlesnake?
Had it beat double-time? Or had it burned in those last
moments of life as the poison coursed through its valves?

"Are you okay?" Laurel's voice brought Olivia back
from her gruesome reverie.

"A woman I met for the first time last week has passed
away," she said. "I'm reeling a bit over the news because . . ."
She trailed off, unsure of how much to tell the other
writers.

Millay, sharp as ever, drew her own conclusions. "Because something's off about her death? Is that why the chief's in uniform?"

Harris glanced at her in surprise. "He probably just wanted to tell Olivia in private."

Millay shook her head. "I doubt it. Olivia said she just met this woman. There's more to it than that." She looked at Olivia closely, her expression softening. "Can we help?"

Normally, Olivia would have refused the offer, determined to solve any and all problems without assistance, but the memory jug was a complete enigma and she decided that a few extra sets of eyes could be useful. Not only that, but by talking to her friends about Munin, she kept the old woman in the here and now. Kept her from disappearing.

"I hope so." Olivia explained who Munin was and how she'd been found dead, half submerged in the stream behind her home.

"How awful!" Laurel put her hand over her mouth and shuddered. "To die from a snakebite all alone like that. Isn't it horribly painful?"

Harris nodded. "Yeah. It's not a good way to go. No wonder you're upset, Olivia."

"Millay was right. There's more to it than that," Olivia said. "Munin was known as a fortune teller of sorts. During my visit, she spoke of death coming to the forest. The Croatan National Forest." She spread her hands. "Normally, I wouldn't pay the slightest attention to that kind of mumbo jumbo, but now I'm wondering if she knew she was in danger."

"Munin, huh?" Millay pulled her boots back on and began to slowly lace them up. "I've heard all kinds of stories about her, mostly after midnight during a weekend shift at Fish Nets. That's when the real drunks are just getting their second wind. They start one-upping each other with tall tales at about one thirty in the morning, and her name's been dropped more than once. People said she was a witch."

"A witch?" Laurel's eyes opened wide.

Millay shrugged. "The fishermen say she could predict the season's weather better than Doppler radar. Warned one of them about Ophelia turning into a hurricane and bearing down on Oyster Bay before she was still a tropical storm in the Caribbean." Millay paused, and a moment passed as the group recalled the havoc Ophelia had wreaked upon their town. "Back when computers weren't around," she continued, "the wives would go to see Munin before letting their husbands go out on long and risky trips. If the witch said they shouldn't go, the women would pitch a fit until the men stayed put, even if it meant going hungry. 'Hungry's better than dead' is a phrase I hear all the time from these guys."

Harris had closed his spiral notebook and slid it into a black laptop case. He glanced up at Olivia from his place on the couch. "Why did you visit her, Olivia? I can't see you traipsing through the swamp to get a weather forecast."

Reluctantly, Olivia told them the truth. "She asked me to come. I wouldn't have gone but she claimed to have met my mother once. I guess she also wanted to give me the jug, but I don't know why she gave it to me." She hesitated and then, in a very low voice, amended the latter phrase. "Well, she told me why, but it's going to sound really strange."

Millay snorted. "This dysfunctional little group has seen plenty of strange. Lay it on us."

"The jug is supposed to provide clues," Olivia said, moving toward the door in preparation to leave the cottage and walk the short distance to her house.

"To what? The witch's own death?" Harris furrowed his brows in confusion.

Olivia shook her head over the absurdity of it all. "She said death would come to the forest and that I'd find answers I was seeking on the jug. I told you it was bizarre."

"Why you?" Laurel asked.

"Apparently, my mother had been kind to her once and she wanted to repay that kindness through me. There's an object stuck to that piece of pottery that she knew I'd want."

Millay stood up and carried her empty beer bottle into the kitchen. "The guys at the bar mentioned her weird jugs. They said no one went to the witch without paying a price. Sometimes she asked for their wedding rings or photographs or some other trinket. I stopped listening when Crazy Charlie said she collected fingernails and baby teeth."

Laurel squealed in horror.

Olivia took her by the arm and steered her to the front door. "Don't worry, I didn't give her any DNA samples, but she did have a glass jar filled with animal teeth. Probably from possums and raccoons. She'd have come across plenty of skeletons in the forest over the years and she trapped animals for their meat too."

Harris followed on their heels. "Not to sound callous, but you should write about this woman, Laurel. She sounds like no one I've ever met. It would make a great article."

"There's nothing to report!" Olivia said with more heat than she'd intended. "As of this point, it's all gossip and hearsay. No one knows her story. Not yet."

"We know how it ended," Millay murmured and closed the door to the lighthouse keeper's cottage.

Haviland nosed his way into the closet ahead of Olivia and came back out with a tennis ball clamped between his jaws.

"Sorry, Captain. No time to play tonight," Olivia said and gave him a bone to chew on as a consolation prize.

Cradling the burlap sack containing the memory jug in her arms, she carried it into the kitchen, where Rawlings and the other members of the writers' group had gathered around the large pine table. She pulled the sack down and away from the sides of the jug, like a woman shimmying out of a tight dress, and then unwound layer upon layer of protective newspaper.

"It seems like you're unwrapping a mummy." Laurel let loose a nervous giggle.

No one answered her, for the jug had instantly become a presence in the room. All eyes were riveted on the shrouded piece of pottery, and when Olivia removed the last sheet of newspaper, there was only an astonished silence.

The jug was about the size of a table lamp base. It had a barrel-shaped belly and a pair of sloped shoulders that eventually narrowed into a stumpy spout. The spout's opening was half an inch wide and the jug could probably hold two gallons of liquid. Its brown river clay had been fired in Munin's wood-burning kiln and then covered with a gray-hued epoxy. Lastly, the old woman had covered every available surface with a seemingly incongruent group of objects.

"Whoa," Harris breathed. "It's totally ugly at first glance, but when you really look at all the stuff on here, it stops being ugly and starts being really cool."

Olivia's gaze traveled up and down the jug's surface. Nestled among buttons, marbles, animal teeth, shells, bottle caps, beads, pennies, and marbles were several unique decorations.

There was a gilt-framed mirror the size of a ladies' compact, some kind of gold medal whose emblem had been filed or melted away until it was unrecognizable, a class ring, which was so buried in epoxy that only half of the ruby-colored stone and the letters "IGH SCHOOL" could be read, an old skeleton key, and a starfish necklace. Camille Limoges's necklace.

Millay put her fingertip on the pendant and Olivia had to quell the urge to swipe it away. "Is this yours?" She turned to examine Olivia's bare throat.

"No. It was my mother's." Olivia laid her left hand over the hollow between her collarbones.

Harris whistled. "Oh, man. Did you know that you and your mom had matching necklaces?"

"I don't remember seeing her wear this." Olivia stared at the gold starfish and the delicate gold chain, which curved around the top half of the tiny mirror.

Rawlings cleared his throat, eager to get to the business at hand. "Okay, folks. Let's assume the bones, shells, bottle caps, and the like won't tell us much about Munin other than she was a dedicated scavenger. Many of these things could have easily been found in the forest, especially around the recreation areas. What significance might the other items have?"

Laurel retrieved a notepad and pen from her purse and studied the jug. "I'll make a list. Then we can brainstorm theories about what connects them to Munin or to each other."

"We can start with the three pennies," Olivia said. "Are they unusual in any way?"

Harris pulled the jug closer and squinted at each coin. "Yeah. They were all minted in 1958."

"Munin's date of birth?" Millay guessed.

Rawlings shook his head. "No. She was at least twenty years older. But 1958 must mean something. She deliberately added three coins from that year." He looked at Olivia. "Did that date mean anything to your mother?"

Olivia drifted back in time until she saw herself curled up in the window seat in the library at her grandmother's sprawling country estate. Leaning against a plump silk pillow, she turned the pages of a scrapbook. There were dozens of photos of Camille Limoges.

Whether the images were of a chubby toddler, a thin, freckled adolescent, or a tall, strikingly beautiful young woman, Camille's expression was always the same. She smiled with her whole being—a smile that radiated from every pore and created sparks of light in her eyes. She never seemed to pose, but had simply been caught by the camera in the middle of private joke, a pirouette, or a song. Whether holding a blue ribbon in a horse show or a Christmas gift, Camille Limoges made it clear that she found joy in every moment.

Olivia, who was driven by loneliness to the scrapbook every day after tea, had a hard time understanding this joie de vivre. She'd memorized all of her mother's expressions, the tilt of her chin, the pattern of her freckles, and the way her body lengthened and softened as she matured. She studied her report cards and awards, her summer reading lists and her birth certificate. Knowing everything there was to know about Camille Limoges might keep Olivia from forgetting her. And despite the pain of having been separated from her by tragedy, she did not want to forget a thing.

Coming back to the present, Olivia shook her head and said, "'Fifty-eight doesn't match her birth date, high school or college graduation dates, or the year she got married. The pennies must relate to Munin, not to my mother."

Rawlings rubbed his chin. "Maybe there's a link to the forest. We'll have to do some research on the park's history."

Harris held up his laptop case. "I'm on it."

"What's next?" Rawlings looked at Laurel.

She slid the jug away from Harris until it sat directly in front of her. "One old key. Reminds me of the kind that could open the front door to a big old house. It's iron or steel. Nothing fancy, and I can't see any writing on it."

Millay frowned. "Oyster Bay isn't exactly overflowing with historic mansions. Even the oldest homes were fairly simple. This key seems like it would open a heavy door. Maybe a warehouse or something?"

Harris pointed at his MacBook's screen. "According to this website, this type of key was most popular in the late 1800s but was still made well into the twentieth century. Most were used in homes and on pieces of antique furniture."

"This is too big to unlock a chest of drawers," Rawlings

said. "And the house could be anywhere. Unless I can find out where Munin lived before she moved to the forest's edge, this isn't a big help."

Harris put the jug on the flat of his palm and held on to it by the spout. Slowly, he pivoted it to the left and right. Some of the beads and bottle caps winked in the light. "Maybe there's an identifying mark on the back of the key. And half of this class ring is buried in clay." He glanced at Olivia. "Would you consider breaking this thing?"

"No!" Olivia snatched the piece from his hands, catching a glimpse of her face in the jug's tiny mirror. Her sea blue eyes had grown dark with indignation.

Relieved to feel the weight of the piece of pottery, she ran her hands over its curved side, her fingertips touching the ridges of a seashell, the bump of an animal tooth, and the smooth surface of a plastic button. "I hope it doesn't have to come to that. This was her last one."

Then the memory of Harlan tucking a second sack into a box in the prow of his boat came back to her. "Actually, it's not. There was a second jug." She told Rawlings that Harlan was supposed to send the other jug to an art dealer on the West Coast.

"I'll let the sheriff's office know," he said. "I doubt they'll be interested, but I can get the dealer's address from Harlan. I'd like to see images of that piece."

Together, the five friends spent another hour exchanging ideas about the objects. They searched for connections on Harris's laptop, debated possibilities, and ended up without a single, tangible link between the articles and the jug's maker.

"Let's call it a night," Rawlings suggested. "I'll do a background check on Munin. Maybe we can make a connection after we take a closer look at her life before she moved to the swamp."

Olivia tapped her chin, her expression thoughtful. "An antique store opened near The Bayside Crab House two weeks ago. I wonder if the owner could shed some light on this piece."

"Couldn't hurt," Rawlings said. "We can stop by in the morning after your interview."

"What interview?" Laurel asked suspiciously. "This isn't media related, is it?"

Assuring her that it wasn't, Olivia escorted her friends to the door. Millay let Laurel and Harris precede her. Pausing in the doorway, she turned and looked over Olivia's shoulder at the jug. "I'll ask around about 1958 at the bar tonight. Nothing came up on Google, but if anything juicy happened in these parts during that year, my guys will remember. They may not be valedictorians, but I've never known people with better memories."

Olivia had always admired the respect Millay paid to the fishermen and laborers who gathered at Fish Nets every weekend to drink, smoke, and play a game of billiards or darts. These grizzled, sun-and-salt-weathered men and women had welcomed Millay into their fold. They grudgingly accepted her rule when she refused to pour them another drink, opened the back door for her whenever she struggled to carry out an empty keg or heavy trash bag, and confided in her.

"Good idea." Rawlings gave her shoulder a paternal pat.

"What should I tell them about Munin?" Millay asked the chief.

"Just that she's passed away. Don't tell them how. Pay attention to the gossip that flies after you deliver the news," Rawlings replied. "Like you said, those folks have long memories. Who knows what kind of dirt will be shaken loose?"

Nodding, Millay stepped out from under his hand and disappeared down the slope of the driveway.

Olivia lingered by the closed door, watching a trio of moths flutter wildly against the panes. They were desperate to get inside, to reach the light that was so tantalizingly near. The dust from their wings left faint marks on the glass, and even though Rawlings was standing by the sink, Olivia flicked the switch, plunging the kitchen into darkness.

"Why'd you do that?" he asked quietly.

Tapping her fingertips against the pane, Olivia said, "I didn't want them to die of exhaustion."

Rawlings moved closer to her, his breath warm on her neck, his hands on her waist. "They don't realize that they're better off outside. If they reached the light, they'd only get burned."

Olivia didn't like Deputy Bauman of the Craven County Sheriff's Department one bit. He spoke to her as if she didn't understand English and made it perfectly clear that collecting her statement was a formality. The sheriff's department was prepared to rule Munin's death as accidental. All they had left to do was file the paperwork and wait for someone to claim the old woman's remains. If no one did, she'd be cremated and buried in a potter's field.

"Did you find antivenom among Munin's effects?" Olivia asked after Bauman was finished. Ignoring her, he closed his manila folder and slid his silver pen into the pocket of his uniform shirt. "I understood that she made her own," Olivia continued. "Doesn't it seem strange that she'd die of a snakebite within easy reach of a cure?"

Bauman ran a hand over his military-style crew cut and frowned. "Harlan Scott asked us the same thing, but the deceased didn't even own a refrigerator. Antivenom's got to be kept cool. If she had any, we don't know where she kept it."

Having conducted an Internet search on antivenom over breakfast, Olivia had already developed a theory on how Munin kept things cold. "She probably dug a hole in the floor of her house or stored vials in a watertight container at the bottom of the stream. She lived primitively, but she was clever enough to survive in isolation for decades. Did you notice any chains or ropes leading from the stream bank into the water?"

Bauman guffawed. "Somebody's been watching too many cop shows on TV."

Olivia bristled. "Did you look? Because her death doesn't make sense and if you're just trying to brush it aside to avoid bad press before the Coastal Carolina Food Festival kicks off, then you're making a mistake. I have a good friend on staff with the *Oyster Bay Gazette* who'd like nothing better than to poke under the rocks you refuse to turn over."

"Listen, lady," Bauman said, angry now. "We know how to do our job. We checked out the site and the ME went over the corpse. We've collected facts and we're making a ruling. You want to stir up a handful of locals with some piece-of-crap story on how we weren't thorough enough, go right ahead." He stood up, scraping his chair against the floor, and tapped his name badge. "Got the spelling down?"

Refusing to let the deputy see how mad she was, Olivia shouldered her purse and rose to her feet. She walked around the conference table and put herself between Bauman and the door. Slightly taller than the cocksure deputy, she straightened her spine and did her best to look down at him. "What if that had been your mother or grandmother left to die in agony? Alone. No one to hear her cries for help." She spoke gently now, pleading with the man. "Please don't let Munin fade into nothingness. She must have ties to someone, somewhere."

Bauman held her eyes. "You'd be surprised how many remains are unclaimed these days. Sometimes people don't want to come forward if their relative is a known felon, sometimes they don't want to pay the burial costs, and sometimes they just don't want to deal with the hassle of it all. It doesn't happen as much around here as it does in the cities, but it happens. We investigated this case and we've put out the word on this woman. I bet there's even a death notice in your friend's paper. That's as far as it goes." He gestured at the door. "Now if you don't mind, I've got work to do."

During the ninety-minute drive from the Craven County Sheriff's Office to downtown Oyster Bay, Olivia let her anger simmer. She complained to Haviland about Bauman's attitude, but the poodle was far too interested in sticking his head out the passenger window to pay her much attention. Eventually, she put her own window down and let the end-of-summer air whisk away some of her frustration.

She was calm by the time she met Rawlings outside of Circa, the recently opened antique store. Olivia hadn't met the proprietor, Fred Yoder, but his name was familiar because he leased space in the revitalized warehouse building she owned.

As was her habit, Olivia left Haviland in the car until she could determine whether Mr. Yoder would welcome a standard poodle in his shop. Rawlings held the memory jug in one hand and opened the door with his other. They were immediately greeted by the sound of barking.

"Duncan!" a man's voice called with the barest hint of a reprimand, but the blur of white fur racing to the front door did not reduce speed.

Olivia smiled and knelt down to say hello to an adorable terrier. "A Westie," she said and held out her hand, palm up, for Duncan to sniff. He accepted the invitation, gave her a lick, and then moved in closer to get a good whiff of her shoes.

"Duncan!" A man in his mid-sixties with glasses and pink-tinged cheeks rushed forward. "Give the lady some space!"

Laughing, Olivia ran her hand through the Westie's fur, pressing her fingertips through the wiry topcoat until she reached the soft undercoat. She gave Duncan a gentle scratch and he gazed up at her with adoration. When she stood upright, he tried to follow. He raised himself on his haunches and grinned, giving her a full view of his bubble gum pink tongue.

"Sorry about that." The man Olivia took to be Fred Yoder pulled Duncan away. "He's a big dog in a little dog's body."

"No apology necessary. I'm a dog lover too. In fact, Captain Haviland, my poodle, is right outside in the car."

Fred didn't hesitate a moment. "Feel free to bring him in."

Olivia glanced around at the display shelves stuffed with porcelain plates and figurines, cut glass, and delicate sterling bud vases.

The spacious interior had been divided into several themes. To the left was a masculine office complete with campaign desk, bookshelves, hunting prints, and antique weapons. To the right was a woman's parlor whose showpiece was a fainting couch. Hundreds of Victorian knick-knacks and a collection of ivory-handled fans and perfume bottles had been arranged on side tables and stands. Straight ahead was an English dining room with a heavy Empire sideboard covered by crystal decanters and a sterling silver punch bowl. A dazzling chandelier hung above the Chippendale table and an Oriental runner led the way across the hall to an early American bedroom.

"This is wonderful." Olivia was impressed. "I'm already writing a big check in my head."

Fred laughed. "My favorite kind of customer." He held out his hand and introduced himself first to Olivia first and then to Rawlings. "I see you've brought me something."

"It's a memory jug," Rawlings said. "Know anything about them?"

Opening his hands, Fred smiled. "I know a little bit about everything. Usually just enough to confuse folks." His eyes twinkled with a boyish mirth and he waved at the front door. "Before we unveil your piece, invite your fellow inside. He and Duncan can hang out in the back room while we talk. I'm about ready for a coffee break."

Duncan seemed to like the suggestion. He wagged his tail and shot quick, hopeful glances between Fred and Olivia.

A few minutes later, Fred, Rawlings, and Olivia were seated at a game table exchanging pleasantries, sipping Fred's excellent coffee, and watching the two dogs get to know each other.

During a lull in the conversation, Rawlings placed the jug on the table and removed it from the bubble wrap. Fred immediately focused on the piece. He began his inspection by looking at all of the objects, his powder blue eyes taking in every detail. Next, he touched several of the items embedded in the clay, smelled the jug's surface, and then turned it upside down in search of a maker's mark. There wasn't one.

"Judging by the clay and the shells, I'd say this was a local piece," he said, raising his brows in search of confirmation.

"It is," Rawlings agreed. "But we can't seem to find a connection between the objects."

Fred seemed surprised by this. "Is there supposed to be one?"

"The potter, a woman, told me there was," Olivia said. "The problem is that we don't have any background details on her and have no idea what story this jug is trying to tell us."

Clearly intrigued, Fred returned his attention to the jug. "That's the function of most memory pieces. They're like a scrapbook made with found objects. And if this jug was meant to serve as a record of a person's life, then it's not being obvious about that life. This key could open any old door, the pennies aren't rare, and the mirror's contemporary. I can't tell where the ring's from either. But this . . ." He pivoted the jug, his index finger probing the surface of the circular medal. "This gold medal—it's got lines on it.

They've been filed or melted down, but . . ." He trailed off and got up to rummage around in a kitchen drawer.

"Is it a sports medal?" Rawlings asked.

"I don't think so," Fred replied and there was a sudden wariness to his voice that hadn't been there before. As Haviland and Duncan settled onto the floor for a group nap, Fred rubbed the medal's surface with a sheet of thin paper and a pencil riddled with teeth marks. Lines resembling sun rays appeared on the paper. Fred studied his drawing and grunted. "I'll need to research this a bit more. How quickly do you need an answer?" He gave Rawlings a shrewd look. "Is this a police matter?"

Rawlings shifted in his chair. "Not exactly, but if you have a hunch, I'd like to hear it now."

Fred shook his head. "You're the chief of police." He turned to Olivia. "And you're my landlady. I'm not going to identify taboo memorabilia without being sure. It would be like pointing the finger at somebody without any evidence."

"Fair enough," Rawlings answered after a pause.

Olivia touched Fred's hand, briefly. Her dark blue stare met his sky blue one. "The case we're working is technically unofficial, but it's important nonetheless. To be honest, it's personal and I'd appreciate anything you could do to help." She handed him her business card. "If you discover anything at all, please call me. I'd love to welcome you to Oyster Bay by treating you to a meal at The Boot Top. Duncan can hang out with Haviland in my office while we drink cocktails and talk."

Fred accepted the card with a grin. "I'd be a damned fool to refuse that offer."

After thanking him for the coffee and his time, Olivia wrapped up the jug and softly called for Haviland. She and Rawlings showed themselves out, the poodle reluctantly parting from his new friend.

"What was that about? His hesitancy?" she asked as they walked to her Range Rover.

"Depends on what Mr. Yoder considers taboo. Could be racial, sexual, political, religious . . . Who knows?"

Olivia slipped on her sunglasses, her gaze drifting toward the placid harbor. What could Munin have embedded into the jug to make the affable Fred Yoder uncomfortable?

Like the water behind the warehouse, the medal's smooth, golden exterior seemed harmless and pretty. But if it was anything like the ocean, there could be all kinds of dangers lurking beneath its shining surface.

The image of the green serpent drawn on the western edge of one of Fred's antique maps appeared in Olivia's mind. Staring at the water, she held the jug just a little bit tighter against her chest and whispered the warning conveyed by the map's fearsome symbol, "Here be dragons."

Chapter 6

The television crew from the Foodie Network descended
upon The Boot Top Bistro Monday morning. The first
to enter was a man wearing a T-shirt and black jeans holding a take-out coffee cup. He was followed by several har-
ried assistants on cell phones and a group of unshaven
cameramen and sound and light technicians.

The man in the T-shirt, who ignored The Boot Top's
staff until he'd walked around the restaurant's bar and dining areas, turned out to be the director, Noah Wiseman. He
stood the middle of the dining room in complete silence for
several minutes, sipping his coffee and studying the space.
Then, he abruptly turned and strode back to the entrance.
He introduced himself to Olivia while examining her from
head to toe. "You've got a good look. Not sure that dress is
going to work. We might have to shoot you in the bar." His
eyes roved around the restaurant, assessing and eager, and
his fingers tapped an energetic rhythm against his take-
out cup.

"Would you like to see the kitchen?" Olivia asked.
"Michel has prepared a special treat for you."

Noah smiled at her like she was the village idiot. "I only eat raw foods, but I'm sure the rest of the crew will be delighted." His eyes glazed over and he began to stroke his chin. "We'll do your interview first, then Michel's, then film some action in the kitchen, and if there's time, we'll get some local color shots and . . ." His fingers fell still. "There's a lighthouse, right? People love lighthouses. And beach scenes." He looked over his shoulder. "Candice? My notes?"

A bony girl bustled forward and handed Noah a clipboard. He looked at it, flipped a sheet over, and then handed it back to her and began to dictate a time line for the day's filming. Olivia listened patiently until the director began discussing the rearrangement of the dining room in order to accommodate additional lighting. He pointed at wall outlets and gestured across the carpet, and one of the male crewmembers came forward with a trio of electric orange extension cords.

"Excuse me." Olivia positioned herself directly in front of Noah. "While I'm honored to have The Boot Top featured on *Talk of the Town*, this is still a place of business. You asked for us to carry on as if this were any other day, and in order for us to do so, our customers and servers need to be able to move about without fear of tripping. Why don't you tell me how you'd like to stage the dining room and we can work together to make everything flow smoothly?"

Candice's mouth hung open in surprise but Noah didn't seem to mind Olivia's directness. "Yes, let's do it!" he said and gestured for Candice to hand Olivia his clipboard.

Instead of taking it, Olivia beckoned Noah to follow her. "Come to the bar. Gabe will fix you a virgin Bloody Mary that adheres to your diet."

Noah held out a warning finger. "Only if there's no Worcestershire sauce and the horseradish is fresh." He pursed his lips. "Does he make a good Bloody Mary? Could help me get over this jet lag."

Olivia smiled knowingly. "I think you'll be pleasantly surprised."

As it turned out, Gabe's sister had gone on a raw-food diet six months after becoming a vegan and he was thereby well versed in which ingredients were acceptable and which were not. He presented Noah with the perfect Bloody Mary, and while the director was sipping happily away, showed him The Boot Top's wine list, pointing out all the choices that were sulfite free.

"We need to shoot a segment of Gabe at work," Noah said, turning to Olivia. "He oozes charisma from every pore. What are the house cocktail specialties?"

"Right now we're featuring The Boot Top Bellini and an Oyster Bay Breeze. I'll let Gabe tell you about them while I invite your crew to sample Michel's fare. He came in very early to make something special and I don't want him to think his efforts were wasted."

In truth, she wanted him to be in a good mood for what looked to be a very long day, so she waved at the men and women who'd be calling The Boot Top home for the next eight to ten hours and asked them to join her in the kitchen.

Michel had laid out an exquisite breakfast buffet of scallion goat cheese muffins, chorizo frittatas, applewood smoked bacon, poached apricots, and rum raisin sticky buns. The table was festooned with citrus-colored orchids, and a French press filled with coffee stood at the ready.

The Boot Top's head chef was industriously chopping carrots at the butcher block when Olivia and the TV crew entered the kitchen. He looked up as if he were pleasantly surprised by their arrival, wiped his hands on his apron, and spread his arms wide in a gesture of welcome. He was beaming.

"Welcome to my kitchen!" he called out happily, his faint French accent more pronounced. His smile wobbled slightly. "Where's Mr. Wiseman?"

"Being spoiled by Gabe," Olivia assured him. "Let these folks indulge before your magnificent dishes grow cold, and in the meantime, you can introduce yourself and the rest of the kitchen staff."

Taking her advice, Michel described the dishes he'd prepared and then served coffee with steamed milk to the crew, asking their names and pausing to exchange brief biographical tidbits with each and every person. He was so gracious and charming that the crewmembers nearly forgot they were there to work.

Noah Wiseman quickly put an end to the relaxed atmosphere. Waltzing into the kitchen he announced, "No, no. This won't do at all!"

Michel looked stricken, the sous-chefs offended. Even the dishwasher frowned and quickly dried his hands on a towel as if he might be called upon to defend The Boot Top's honor by stepping outside and throwing a few punches.

Candice immediately put her fork down and hastened to Noah's side, clipboard at the ready.

He turned to her. "How am I going to get a wide shot? I need to see this kitchen in action. I want curtains of steam and flames leaping from sauté pans. This space is too, too narrow." Throwing out his hands, he said, "It'll be like shooting in Manhattan all over again!"

"And look what magic you were able to create there," Candice said in a honeyed voice.

Noah brightened. "It was exciting, wasn't it? Where's my chef?"

At last, Michel was able to present himself to the director and the pair fell into an easy conversation over the proposed menu. Meanwhile, the crewmembers had second helpings from the breakfast buffet and began to wander around the restaurant to search for outlets, test the lighting, and pile up equipment in the bar.

Leaving them to their tasks, Olivia disappeared into her office. She walked around Haviland's sleeping form and sat down in front of her computer. The poodle opened his eyes briefly, only to shut them again after receiving a cursory pat on the head. Accustomed to the clanging of pots and pans and the sound of Michel shouting to his underlings, he was unfazed by the additional noise created by the TV crew.

Olivia decided to use the time before her interview researching the class ring embedded in the memory jug. Though the name of the school was hidden from view, it was still possible to see a sliver of green stone poking out of the epoxy. Last night, Olivia had studied the exposed side of the ring with a magnifying glass and had discovered a small symbol inside a shield. It looked like a bee or wasp, but she had yet to find a high school whose mascot was an insect.

Unable to sleep, Olivia had taken her laptop to bed and had surfed until she'd found several companies who produced class rings. Since then, she'd gone through online catalogues until the bright gemstones, embossed crests, Latin mottos, and school names blurred together.

None of the catalog samples matched the shield found on the jug's ring, but Olivia refused to give up. Hoping the piece of jewelry came from North Carolina, she now began to systematically look up each and every high school in the state, scrolling through page after page of material before locating the school colors and mascot.

She had just finished looking at New Bern High's website and was about to cross its name off her list when someone knocked timidly on her door.

"Come in," Olivia said without turning around.

"Ms. Limoges." Candice spoke in a deferential whisper. "Noah's ready to interview you now."

Following Candice to the bar, Olivia was amazed by the network of power cords crisscrossing the carpet and the blinding brightness of the lights directed on Gabe as he prepared a Boot Top Bellini for the camera.

Olivia didn't need to be a director to see that Gabe was a natural. Completely at ease in the spotlight, he smiled and spoke in the relaxed conversational tone that encouraged customers to show up at the bar well before dinner. With his all-American-surfer-boy good looks and the devotion with which he performed his job, Gabe was sure to coax droves of female *Talk of the Town* viewers into visiting the Carolina coast.

Delighted by Gabe's performance, Noah asked him to wrap up by serving a glass of red wine and an Oyster Bay Breeze to a well-dressed tourist couple Candice had plucked from the streets. This simple sequence was filmed at least five times before Noah was satisfied. Finally, the cameras and the powerful lights were turned off and the tourists returned to their vacation, a gift certificate for a free meal in hand.

"We're in the kitchen in five, people!" Noah shouted and sank into one of the bar's leather club chairs. He held out his hand, palm up, clearly waiting for Candice to fulfill an unspoken demand.

She was ready with a pack of cigarettes and a lighter, but when the director went to light up, Olivia grabbed his wrist. "Not in here, please. You can smoke out back. That's where the staff goes."

Noah's cigarette dangled from between pursed lips, his expression incredulous. But then he shrugged, said, "Sure thing," and headed through the swing doors to the kitchen.

Fifteen minutes later, Olivia grew tired of waiting for her interview and returned to her office. She clicked on the next high school on her list, searching their website until she discovered that the school's colors were gold and white and their mascot, a wild mustang. Thus far, she'd encountered bulldogs and devils, pirates and horses, eagles and rams, warriors and cavaliers, but not a single bug.

"No bees," she muttered and moved on to the next school.

From his spot on the floor, Haviland yawned, stretched, and nudged Olivia in the thigh, indicating his need to be let outside. They headed through the kitchen and opened the back door to find Noah and one of the sous-chefs in deep conversation.

Noah turned to Olivia and exclaimed, "This man is a treasure! We're going to have to expand this segment to include his story." He pointed at Olivia. "I need you at the bar in five."

Noah disappeared and the sous-chef, whose name was Willis Locklear, peered at his employer from beneath long dark lashes. He seemed embarrassed by the director's interest and quickly stubbed out his cigarette on a loose brick near the door. "Sorry, Ms. Limoges."

She waved off the apology. "Don't be silly. I know you haven't been with us long, but Michel said you'd bring something unique to the kitchen staff. I guess Mr. Wiseman saw it too."

Willis shrugged, his young face relaxing. "I'm part Lumbee Indian. I was telling Mr. Wiseman that Michel let me have time off to do a Native American cooking presentation at the festival this weekend and now that director guy wants me to talk about how my Lumbee background adds flavor to this kitchen. On camera."

Olivia watched Haviland trot behind the shrubbery lining the parking lot. "Isn't your tribe having a major celebration at the national forest?"

He nodded, his dark eyes filled with eagerness. "Yeah, a powwow. Good thing I've got most of Friday and all of Saturday off. We're gonna have dancing and stories and cool music. And food, of course. My sister is setting up a craft tent and I'm going to help her out." He flashed Olivia a quick smile. "You should come. Our site isn't too far from where you'll be judging, and if you've never hung around a bunch of Lumbee before, then you don't what fun is."

Was I ever this young and full of life? Olivia wondered

silently, listening as Willis described his tribal costume. "I've never been to a powwow, but how could I resist after hearing you describe it? My friends and I will head over to your part of the forest as soon as we're done at the food festival."

The door to the kitchen opened and Candice emerged into the bright sunlight. "Ms. Limoges, we're ready for you. Melanie will do your hair and makeup while I prep you for the interview."

It took over an hour for Olivia to respond to Noah's questions to his satisfaction. She refused to discuss anything about her past other than that she'd spent the first ten years of her life in Oyster Bay and had returned nearly three decades later to move within sight of her childhood home and open The Boot Top Bistro. Her affection for the town and its people shone through most clearly when she spoke of the area fishermen and farmers, the local merchants, and the Bayside Book Writers.

Once the filming was complete, she thanked Noah and the crew and escaped to her office. It was finally Michel's turn to strut his stuff. Knowing her head chef would be preparing some of the best dishes of his career and that Noah wanted to capture real patrons enjoying Michel's fine cuisine, Olivia had decided to keep The Boot Top's regular hours. Last week, she'd told the hostess taking reservations to alert future diners about the presence of a television crew. As a result, the reservation book had been filled days ago.

"I have a waiting list a mile long," the pretty hostess said when Olivia emerged from her office. "We could have charged our customers double for this meal. They're all dying to be on TV."

Olivia shook her head, perplexed. "I will never understand the allure of reality shows." Then she grinned and tapped the reservation book. "But I love a full ledger and am over the moon with the menu Michel's chosen for tonight. He'll dazzle them all."

She walked into the kitchen to watch Michel in action and saw a cameraman waiting to zoom in on the first entrée. Michel slid a filet of cornmeal-crusted flounder from a sizzling frying pan onto a pool of lemon mustard sauce. He then drizzled more sauce on top and garnished the dish with clover sprouts and twisted slivers of lemon.

"More entrées!" Noah mouthed and Willis rushed forward balancing three dinner plates. Olivia smiled in pleasure as she watched the sous-chef present a filet of beef sautéed in white wine and rosemary, Thai spareribs, and shrimp paella. He quickly stepped back, allowing Michel to return to the counter. The head chef garnished a plate of chicken with asparagus and fried capers and then hurried to fill a wide bowl with Asian noodles tossed with barbecued duck confit. Noah beckoned a cameraman to get a close-up of a plate of scallops and bacon with port reduction and then instructed another crewmember to take shots of waiters delivering the entrées to the dining room.

Michel didn't break stride for a second. As the filming continued, Olivia found the process repetitious and rather dull, so when the dinner orders increased in number and the kitchen fell into its customary rhythm, she decided to go home. Her business would flourish because of today's events, but the success was marred by her inability to identify the class ring. Having gone through the entire list of North Carolina high schools, Olivia had yet to find one whose mascot was a bee or a wasp.

And though she planned to leave, she didn't. She tarried at the restaurant long enough to feed Haviland and have a drink, and thirty minutes soon turned into an hour. Then two. She ended up chatting with some of The Boot Top's most loyal customers, including the mayor and his wife, until it was well past her own dinnertime.

Back in the kitchen, Olivia had an array of delectable dishes to choose from. She opted for the scallops and ate the succulent dish at one of the long counters, contentedly watching her employees wash, chop, toss, tenderize, sauté, flash fry, mix, plate, and garnish the evening's menu items. This was one of her favorite places to sit, and she smiled as Michel barked orders like a drill sergeant, his demeanor unaffected by the presence of the *Talk of the Town* crew.

Noah, who'd snacked throughout the day on mixed nuts, carrot sticks, and strips of dried fruit, was being treated to beef carpaccio with Parmesan, a mango and avocado salad, and tuna tartare. He'd also decided to dine in the kitchen and sat down next to Olivia, looking tired but content. "We've wrapped for today," he said. "Got some really good stuff, but we'll be back tomorrow. I want to film desserts and do a sidebar on Willis."

Olivia didn't want the crew to invade her restaurant for a second day, especially since she'd planned on spending a few hours at The Bayside Crab House, but after glancing at Michel's flushed and happy face, she nodded in acquiescence.

"I have to admit," Noah said after swallowing a bite of tuna. "I had my doubts about what kind of talent we'd find here, but I am seriously impressed." He gestured at the plates in front of him. "Michel could open a raw food restaurant in LA and make a fortune."

"He could make a fortune anywhere, but he's content in Oyster Bay," Olivia said, hoping she spoke the truth.

"Then he's found his place." Noah polished off his meal and left the kitchen in search of Candice and his cigarettes. He was back minutes later, complaining that Candice was nowhere to be found.

"Willis! Can I bum a smoke?" he shouted amicably to the sous-chef.

To his credit, Willis finished steaming a pot full of vegetables and dumped them into a colander before offering Noah his entire pack.

The director shook out a single cigarette and then asked Willis for a lighter. "Want to take a break?"

Willis shook his head. "Sorry, I've got sides to plate."

Noah gave the sous-chef a thumbs-up and proceeded outside. At that moment, Olivia happened to glance over at Michel. She saw something dark flit across the chef's face and realized that he wasn't watching the director. He was glaring at Willis.

He's jealous, Olivia thought. At any other time, she might be amused by Michel's juvenile behavior, but the dining room was filled with customers and a negative mood could affect the chef's cooking. When he was truly miserable, he tended use too much salt or was heavy-handed with sauces, ladling them on until they threatened to overpower the entire dish.

"I'm going home," she told him as he drizzled soy sauce over a tangle of Asian noodles. "You've outdone yourself today, Michel. Shelley Giusti is sure to sit up and take notice."

Upon hearing the name of the lovely pastry chef, Michel perked up immediately. "You think so?"

Olivia nodded. "The whole crew's been talking about how great it was to watch you do your thing." She gestured at Willis, who was busy arranging the steamed vegetables on two dinner plates. "He works for you, Michel, and he happens to have an interesting heritage. If Noah ends up filming his story, a five-minute interview focusing on your sous-chef's American Indian background won't diminish your segment. In fact, anything Noah films from this kitchen enhances your reputation. Isn't this your domain? Aren't you the king of this castle?"

She smiled, perfectly aware that she was laying it on thick, but Michel's face smoothed over and the shadow she'd seen cross his features vanished.

"Dodged that bullet," she told Haviland as they got into the Range Rover.

At home, she changed into a nightgown and sat in the living room, the memory jug on the coffee table. Despite The Boot Top's success, Olivia felt deflated. The meaning behind the jug's decorations remained elusive, and though she stared at it and talked to it and touched it, it refused to divulge a single secret.

When the moon rose above the ocean, painting the water with a soft, white glow, she turned away from the jug, climbed up the stairs, and went to bed. It didn't take long before the sound of Haviland's breathing, mingling with the sigh of the waves, lulled her to sleep.

Olivia was reluctant to spend another day with the *Talk of the Town* crew, preferring to wile away the morning walking on the beach followed by breakfast and a writing session at Grumpy's Diner.

However, she wasn't about to leave Noah Wiseman on his own in her restaurant. If they could just make it through today's filming, the director would take his cameras elsewhere. He'd head to the docks to shoot the fishermen unloading their catch of fish, shrimp, oysters, muscles, and crab, drawing a crowd of curious onlookers and suspicious glowers from the vessels' captains. Early the next morning, he'd capture the colors and energy of the farmers market and then wander around downtown until lunchtime, searching for the quintessential summer moment, such as a child licking an ice cream cone, or two lovers sharing a milkshake.

But right now, he was at The Boot Top, nibbling almonds and making demands of Candice.

As the crew got to work, Michel and the rest of the kitchen staff prepared a stunning array of desserts. By the time the dishes—chocolate soufflé with a side of hazelnut ice cream, lemon cheesecake with cherry compote, Grand

Marnier crème brûlée, apricot and candied ginger pie, white chocolate espresso torte, peach sorbet with sesame brittle—were lined up on a white tablecloth to be filmed, the kitchen was redolent with the caramelized scent of warm sugar and melted butter.

"Brilliant!" Noah declared and gave Michel a pat on the back. "I love it! All of it!" He then mimed a smoking motion to Willis and the pair disappeared outside.

Michel came into Olivia's office and flung himself down on the extra chair. He looked exhausted. His eyes were bloodshot and his skin wan.

"You'd better go home and put your feet up for a few hours," Olivia suggested.

"What, and have Willis get picked up for his own show while I'm gone? Not a chance." Michel wasn't too tired to sulk.

Olivia hid a smile. "You were a triumph. Pierce Dumas will see it, as will Shelley Giusti and a million television viewers. This is what you wanted. Try to enjoy it." She reached over and touched his arm. "Have you ever worked this hard before? Weren't the dishes you made over the past two days some of the finest of your career?"

He nodded.

"Then be happy! You'll be on camera again this weekend as a celebrity judge. Before long you'll be a media sensation and I'll have to worry about you leaving me."

"Never," Michel said solemnly. "Who else would put up with my artistic temperament?" His forehead creased as he frowned. "But if Willis Locklear makes one move to take my place in the sun this weekend, I will kill him."

Olivia knew Michel was merely being dramatic, but the person standing in her threshold didn't know Michel the way she did.

Candice glanced at Michel, her expression that of a spooked animal. Olivia took note of the young woman's wide eyes and then her glance moved to the crewmember beside Candice. His handheld camera was pointing at Michel and the red record light was on.

Olivia smiled and calmly assured Candice that Michel was only kidding. Then, she stood up and gently closed her office door in their faces.

On the other side, she distinctly heard Candice say, "Didn't sound like he was kidding to me."

Chapter 7

Every heart sings a song, incomplete, until another heart whispers back. Those who wish to sing always find a song. At the touch of a lover, everyone becomes a poet.

—PLATO

On Friday morning, Olivia woke slowly, swimming to consciousness from a lovely dream that slipped away the moment she tried to hold on to its memory.

Without opening her eyes, she moved closer to Sawyer Rawlings' body. She listened to him breathe, to the slight sawing noise that rose from low in his chest whenever he slept on his back. She longed to touch him, to slide her hand across his collarbone and let it come to rest on his shoulder, but she didn't want to wake him, so she settled for laying her cheek against his upper arm.

At the foot of the bed, Haviland stirred, his paws twitching as he chased imaginary shorebirds. Olivia heard him whine once and then sneeze and knew the poodle would soon press his moist nose against her palm, silently asking to be let out. The moment she opened the deck door, he'd take off like a racehorse out of the starting gate, tearing over the dunes until he reached the water line. In the peach light, he'd send crabs scuttling into their burrows and force the gulls to take to the air, his caramel brown eyes shining with such unadulterated joy that he often made Olivia wish she were a dog.

A soft gurgle sounded from the kitchen. The coffee machine was brewing twelve perfect cups of coffee. Olivia sighed. She'd have loved nothing better than to spend the morning in sweatpants and a T-shirt, drinking cup after cup as she and Rawlings read the paper and then took a lazy stroll on the beach. But they'd have little time to dawdle today. They had to be on the road by midmorning in order to make it to the Croatan National Forest for the opening of the Coastal Carolina Food Festival.

Thinking of the presence of television crews, festivalgoers, and the hours she'd committed to judging made Olivia want to linger in this moment even more. She lifted her hand and laid it gently on Rawlings' chest. She could feel his heart beating, its pace steady as a clock's, and she suddenly yearned to feel it leap beneath her touch.

Using the pad of one finger, she made circles around his nipple and then traced the outline of his pectoral muscles. Goose bumps erupted over his skin and he shifted, his breath becoming shallower as he was pulled toward wakefulness.

Without making a sound, Olivia eased her nightgown over her head. She tossed it on the ground and then draped a long leg over Rawlings' leg, pressing her bare stomach and breasts against his body. His hands reacted instantly, curling around her back and traveling down over the curve of her buttocks. His fingers dug into the soft flesh of her thighs, pulling her naked body more firmly against him.

Olivia rolled on top of Rawlings, erasing the space between them. She felt him grow hard under her and his response quickened her own yearning. Kissing his neck just below his ear, she tugged at the waistband of his boxer shorts with one hand and buried the other in his thick hair.

Fully awake now, Rawlings kicked off his shorts and flipped Olivia onto her back. He pinned her hands above her head and kissed her deeply. She closed her eyes as his lips moved down her body, moaning softly, and then with more urgency as he entered her. He kept her hands captured, forcing her to surrender control. She gave in to his will, letting him manipulate her until desire threatened to burn her from the inside out. Without warning, she became a supernova, a mass of white light and intense heat, exploding into the quiet darkness of space.

Afterward they lay panting, their bodies entwined like a pair of twisted roots. Wrapped in each other's arms, Olivia and Rawlings silently watched as sun rays painted their skin pink and gold.

Haviland, who'd left the room when Olivia had thrown her nightgown on the floor, returned wearing such a disdainful expression that Rawlings had to laugh.

"I'll let him out," he offered.

"No, you've already outdone yourself." She leaned over him to examine the clock on the nightstand. "And it's not even eight."

"I could get used to being woken up like this," he said, giving her another long kiss before letting her go. "Sure beats an alarm clock."

Olivia got out of bed and crossed the room to her closet. Pulling on a silky robe covered with dogwood blossoms, she paused in the doorway and smiled at Rawlings. "You were good, but I'm not serving you breakfast in bed. Coffee's ready whenever you want to come down."

Rawlings stretched his arms and yawned. "I'll be there in a bit. I'm going to wallow in the afterglow a little longer." Grinning, he grabbed Olivia's pillow, hugged it against his chest, and closed his eyes.

Olivia followed Haviland downstairs to the sliding glass doors in the living room. After the poodle darted outside, she headed into the kitchen to make him breakfast and pour herself some coffee.

She'd just added a splash of cream to her cup when the phone rang. It was too early to be a business-related call, so she examined the caller ID box before answering. The name and number belonged to Fred Yoder.

Olivia felt a thrill of excitement. Had he confirmed his hunch about the gold medal embedded in the memory jug?

Picking up the phone, she said, "Hello," as brightly as possible, but her voice was still husky from lovemaking.

"Uh, Ms. Limoges? I hope I'm not disturbing you," Fred said and Olivia's mouth curved into a small smile, thinking that it was a good thing the antique store proprietor hadn't called fifteen minutes earlier.

"Not at all. Haviland rarely lets me sleep in."

Fred chuckled. "Tell me about it. Duncan is capable of producing some of the most noxious odors known to man between the hours of five and six in the morning." He cleared his throat. "Anyway, I called because I believe I've located a photograph of the medal on your jug. It's a rather unique item, and as I mentioned the other day, it's . . . controversial. The kind of thing only a few dealers will sell. I'd be glad to explain everything in more detail, but I need to show you a photograph to do so. I'll be at the store by nine thirty if that suits you."

"I'll be there. Thank you, Fred." She cast a glance at the memory jug, which continued to occupy a prominent place in the center of her kitchen table. "No matter what you've found, I'd be grateful to have one of Munin's riddles solved."

Fred hesitated and then said, "I wouldn't count on that, Ms. Limoges. You'll understand when we meet, but I suspect I'm only going to increase the jug's mystique. In any case, make sure to bring Haviland along. Duncan would love to see him again."

Olivia assured the shopkeeper that she rarely went anywhere without her poodle and, after thanking Fred again for his help, hung up. Pouring Rawlings a cup of coffee, she forgot all about her claim that she wasn't going to serve him in bed and hurried upstairs.

She found him standing in front of the oversized window facing the ocean. Setting the coffee cups down, she moved to his side. He put his arm around her waist and pulled her against him.

"Why do I get the sense that a phone call is about to ruin my chances of getting you back into bed?" he asked, frowning.

"Because you have a cop's instincts." Olivia loosened the sash of her robe, lifted one of his hands, and invited him to slip his fingers beneath the silky material. Pivoting, she pressed her bare breasts against his chest. "We do have someplace to be," she whispered. "But there's still time . . ."

Rawlings didn't need any further encouragement. He lifted Olivia into his arms and carried her to bed, laying her down on a rectangle of yellow white light. "There's still time," he repeated, lowering himself until his lips met hers. He kissed her, his hands moving over her body until she forgot about Fred, Munin, and the memory jug. There was only Rawlings, the heat, and the shooting stars behind her closed eyes.

Fred unlocked Circa's front door and invited Olivia and Rawlings inside. Rawlings carried the memory jug while Olivia held the door for Haviland and presented Fred with a small gift bag.

"Organic treats for Duncan," she said. "These are Haviland's favorites."

Fred peered into the bag. "Oh, these look fancy. I'll give one to each of the boys so they have something to chew on in the back room. I want to show you some images on my computer."

With Duncan and Haviland happily settled in the kitchen, Fred sat down at an old desk with a cracked leather blotter and gestured for Olivia and Rawlings to take a seat in a pair of Victorian side chairs upholstered in rose-colored brocade. Placing the memory jug on the desk, Fred swiveled his computer screen so that it faced his guests and then pointed at a photograph.

"This is a Ku Klux Klan medal," he said. "They're also called tokens. This is a very rare item that it was only available for purchase during the Klan's march through Washington, DC, in 1926."

Olivia was stunned. "The Klan?" She moved to the edge of her seat to get a closer look. "Are you sure?"

Fred touched the PC's screen. "This image shows the reverse side of the medal. A triangle sits atop a cross that's surrounded by sun rays." His eyes met Olivia's. "The rays are what first tipped me off. You don't see this many on coins." His finger moved to the lower half of the onscreen medal. "The Klan motto, 'One Country, One Flag, One Language,' curls around the bottom edge. "

"What does the acronym, the AKIA, inside the triangle stand for?" Rawlings asked.

"'A Klansman I Am,'" Fred said, maintaining his professional neutrality. "These other initials in between the rays are KIGY, and mean 'Klansman, I Greet You.'"

Olivia glared at the medal. "I almost hate to ask what was on the front."

Fred scrolled to the top of the screen and pointed at another image. "In the center is a blood tear and the year 1866, which is probably when the Klan was founded, but don't quote me on that. The tear is set inside a hero's cross and the mottos on each side read, 'Without Fear' and 'Without Regret.' Along the bottom edge is the date and place of the march. See?" He indicated the text. "Washington, DC, 1926."

"I'm not familiar with the Invisible Empire's demonstrations," Rawlings said, failing to keep the disgust out of his voice. "What was the Klan doing in Washington?"

"Having their sheets dry-cleaned?" Olivia asked snidely.

Fred pulled up another website. "Look."

When the black-and-white photograph filled the screen,

Olivia gasped. Hundreds of Klansmen, dressed in white robes and peaked hoods, marched down Pennsylvania Avenue in a calm, orderly fashion. The costumed men carried banners bearing the names of states. The two states depicted in the photograph were Connecticut and Rhode Island, and Olivia was shocked by the sight of so many white-robed figures. Row after row stretched all the way down the avenue.

"There were so many," she breathed, both horrified and fascinated. "My God. So many."

Rawlings looked from the image to the memory jug, his forehead furrowing. "So Munin's medal is a KKK token?"

Fred nodded. "I believed it the moment I made the rubbing, but I wanted to take measurements and compare it with the real thing. I know the dealer who posted these photos online and he helped me confirm my hunch." Brushing the gold medal with his fingertips, he cast a sidelong glance at Olivia. "Of course, the only way to be sure is to break the jug. I'm willing to bet the token's obverse side is in better shape than the reverse."

Olivia put a protective hand over the jug's spout. "No. The real question isn't about this being a genuine Klan medal or not," she said. "The real question is why Munin put it on the jug at all."

Rawlings stroked his chin and stared off into the middle distance. Olivia could see that he was searching his memory for a clue. When his eyes came back into focus, she knew that he'd come up with a hit.

"Do have a copy of yesterday's *Gazette*?" he asked Fred.

Jerking his thumb over his shoulder, Fred said, "In the kitchen. I'd just spread it out on the table when you knocked. Would you like to see it?"

"I can probably find this needle in a haystack on the *Gazette*'s website instead. There was teaser on the Coastal Carolina Food Festival in yesterday's paper and a few lines about the Lumbee Indian powwow. I remember seeing a sentence or two about an event the tribe was celebrating."

He shook his head, as if willing the memory to sharpen. "I could have sworn it had something to do with the KKK."

Olivia had looked through yesterday's paper too, but without the same attention to detail. She always read Laurel's articles word for word, but often passed over other pieces if she had a busy day ahead of her.

Fred vacated his chair and invited Rawlings to sit in front of the computer. Within seconds, the chief found what he was looking for. "Here it is. Saturday evening at the Cedar Point campground—that's where the Lumbee events are being held—will feature songs, dancing, and storytelling to celebrate the tribe's victory at the Battle of Hayes Pond."

"What's that?" Fred wanted to know.

"I'll read you a direct quote," Rawlings said. "'The Battle of Hayes Pond occurred after Klan leader James "Catfish" Cole decided to put the Indians in their place. Calling his fellow Klansmen to arms, he gave them instructions to gather in the small town of Maxton. Very few responded, while the Lumbee showed up en masse, sending the KKK packing and turning their rally into a night of shame and regret. The Lumbee typically commemorate their victory during the month of January, but due to a history of inclement weather, tribal elders voted to hold the event in conjunction with the annual powwow.'" He looked up from the screen. "If we want more details, we can read about the battle on the Lumbee's official website."

Olivia sighed. "I don't get it. What does this have to do with Munin?"

"The battle occurred in 1958. According to the medical examiner, Munin was in her early seventies at the time of her death. She could have been at the rally." Rawlings reached for the computer mouse. "Maxton's in Robeson County, about a hundred and seventy miles from her house at the edge of the Croatan Forest."

"Maybe she had roots in Robeson County," Fred

suggested. "Everyone's from somewhere. I don't know this lady from Eve, but she must have seen something terrible to have ended up living all alone in a swamp."

"Was the battle very violent?" Olivia wondered aloud.

Rawlings let loose an uncharacteristic snort. "Hardly. The Klansmen were outnumbered ten to one and there was a single gunshot. The bullet knocked out the only source of light, which had been rigged up in the middle of the field. The bad guys scattered, and Cole, the KKK leader who started the whole thing, ran off. If this source is credible, Cole's right-hand man departed in such a hurry that his wife was left behind to fend for herself."

Olivia shook her head. "What a gem."

Rawlings kept his eyes on the screen. "The lady ended up driving her car into a ditch. Ironically, it was the Lumbee who came to her aid."

Fred whistled. "Damn, I bet things were pretty chilly between her and her man for a long time after that."

Olivia glanced at her watch. She and Rawlings needed to leave if she was going to make it to the food festival's opening. "Thank you for everything, Fred. I'll take the jug and show it to the people at the Cedar Point campground this weekend. If Munin has a connection to the Battle of Hayes Pond or to the Lumbee tribe, someone will know her name or recognize one of the items on the jug."

"I hope so," Fred said. "I'm going to lend you a milk crate I've attached to a dolly. With a little cushion of bubble wrap, you'll be able to wheel that jug across the state without so much as a chip." He smiled. "And when you return the dolly, you can tell me what you found out." He gestured around the shop. "I haven't been involved in such an intriguing mystery since Duncan got into a customer's car. The young couple drove all around town without knowing he was in the backseat. Nearly crashed when a fire truck went by, sirens blaring, and Duncan started to howl like the world was coming to an end."

"I promise to fill you in," Olivia said. "It's the least I could do."

Fred began to rewrap the jug and then paused. "That high school ring is a solid clue, you know. The rest of the school's name is buried in the clay, but I'd bet the shop that it's perfectly legible."

Olivia knew what he was implying. "I can't break it. Not yet. Smashing that jug won't change Munin's fate and I . . . I just can't destroy the last thing she created." She swallowed, trying to find a way to explain her reluctance. "Munin won't be buried under a marble angel or a grand tombstone. She'll be cremated and stuck in a potter's field. To me, that's no tragedy. When you're dead, you're dead. But what bothers me is that there's no one to mourn her. To keep her memory alive." She laid her hand lightly on the jug. "In a sense, this is her grave marker. Her epitaph. And she gave it to me."

Fred touched her hand, his kind eyes filled with understanding. "I get that. Believe me, I do. I've seen families come to blows over a loved one's treasure. Sometimes, by possessing a thing someone else made with the strength of their hands and the sweat of their brow, we become bound to the maker. I've seen how the stories told in a needlepoint sampler, or oil paintings, or piece of pottery can change a person. Usually, it's a wonderful thing to witness, but there are times when the story a piece carries does more harm than good."

Olivia didn't want him to go on, but despite her misgivings, she had to ask, "Such as?"

"I used to have a shop in Greensboro. One of my regular customers was a wealthy woman who collected Victorian mourning jewelry. She only wanted pieces showing a child's portrait or silhouette or containing a kid's lock of hair. After being in business for fifteen years, I eventually learned that this lady had lost both of her children in a house fire. She never learned to live with her grief. Instead, she became obsessed with collecting jewelry that belonged to the grieving mothers of another century."

"How sad," Rawlings said.

Nodding, Fred gazed intently at Olivia. "Your potter, Munin, obviously felt connected to you. She gave you clues to her story. Go on and run the clues down, but keep your distance. You don't know what kind of insects are hiding under the rocks you're going to turn over."

He pointed at the image on the computer screen, at the hundreds of figures in white robes and pointed hoods marching through the nation's capital. To Olivia, the dark eye slits transformed the hoods into sinister masks. She felt like she was staring at a parade of soulless wraiths. And that they were staring right back at her.

Chapter 8

*Murder is commoner among cooks than
among members of any other profession.*

—W. H. AUDEN

The Coastal Carolina Food Festival was being held in an
area of the Croatan Forest called Flanners Beach.
Olivia, Rawlings, and Haviland joined a large crowd of
attendees heading toward the campground by the Neuse
River. They walked up a wide path cut through the trees
where hundreds of vendors were hawking culinary-themed
merchandise. From chef's knives to homemade jams to per-
sonalized lobster bibs, festivalgoers were lured into stall
after stall by the promise of free samples.

"Kudzu jelly?" Rawlings said after waving away a platter of jam-covered crackers being offered by a pretty girl in
a floral skirt. "Doesn't sound very tempting."

"At least someone's found a use for that awful vine."
Olivia elbowed him. "There won't be any chocolate milk
here, Chief. You're going to encounter more exotic foods
today."

He shrugged. "As long as no one offers me a grilled,
candied, or chocolate-covered bug, then I'm willing to try
anything. It's all I see on TV. People eating bugs."

Olivia laughed. "Don't forget the shows about women

giving birth or following the antics of a gang of cretins from the Jersey Shore. After being exposed to that crew, I'd rather watch a good-looking man eat a centipede."

Rawlings shook his head. "Not this man. I'll have to find other ways to entertain you."

"You know how to do that already. You proved that this morning." Olivia grinned.

The couple strolled deeper into the forest. The soft ground was sun-dappled and the August morning air was deliciously cool. A breeze drifted in from the Neuse River, carrying scents of burning wood chips and charcoal as well as more enticing aromas like sizzling butter, grilling meat, and the saltiness of fried fish.

"There's the Foodie Network tent," Olivia said. She examined the map she'd been given at the park's entrance. "Looks like they've set up a stage and a cooking platform closer to the beach. That's where my judging job will take place. I bet Michel is beside himself. He lives for this show."

"*Chefs Gone Wild*?" Rawlings read the banner above the seating area. "Never heard of it."

"Four chefs have to create a gourmet meal using local ingredients and relatively primitive cooking methods. In this case, they're obviously going to be given a grill and a camping stove. But I have no idea what the food items are." She craned her neck, searching for Michel's white chef's coat amid the audience members and the dozens of crew-members in Foodie Network T-shirts conducting last-minute sound and lighting checks.

As the scent of cooking food intensified, Haviland's nose quivered and his eyes darted about the campground-turned-television-studio. He then gave Olivia his most expectant stare.

"You've just had a bag of treats," Olivia scolded. "You'll have to hold on until lunchtime."

Rawlings put his hand on the poodle's head. "Don't

worry, my man. You won't be eating bugs. I'm sure there's a nice hunk of meat with our names on it. I plan to start with some pulled pork and chase that down with a tower of onion rings, an ear of grilled corn, and maybe some root beer . . ."

"This isn't a carnival." Olivia gestured at the chief's hot dog and hamburger print Hawaiian shirt. "Though you're dressed for one."

"I know you love my Hawaiian shirts." Rawlings winked at her. "Ah, here comes Michel."

The Boot Top Bistro's head chef was all smiles. He kissed Olivia on both cheeks and gave Haviland's neck an exuberant ruffle. "The network is going to kick off the new season with this episode! By next summer, people will be lining up for a seat at one of our tables, *ma cherie!*"

"Excellent news," she said. "And what about Shelley Giusti? Have you seen her yet?"

Michel put both hands over his heart. "She is even more beautiful now than she was in school. And how I missed her voice! Words flow from her mouth like melted chocolate. We've spent the last hour together and I'm in heaven. *Heaven!*"

Rawlings arched his brows. "Who is this sweet-talking muse?"

"An enchantress and a world-class pastry chef of her own right," Michel said, his eyes dreamy. "She's also one of the celebrity judges, so you'll see for yourself that she is *très magnifique.*"

"I look forward to meeting her," Olivia said as they made their way to a seating area cordoned off by bright yellow rope and a sign reading "*Chefs Gone Wild*—Authorized Personnel Only."

Rawlings pointed at the sign and smirked. "Sounds like a spring break special. One of those featuring girls in bikinis. Or in bikini bottoms at any rate."

Olivia didn't have a chance to reply because Noah

Wiseman spotted their little group and sent Candice running over to collect Michel and Olivia.

"We need to get your mics on!" she cried, her face flushed with exertion. Rawlings took this as his cue to leave and rolled the dolly holding the memory jug over to a small seating area to the left of the stage. Haviland followed and Olivia paused a moment to search for the familiar faces of the Bayside Book Writers, but she didn't see Laurel, Harris, or Millay anywhere.

"I hate these off-site episodes," Candice complained. "When we get back to Manhattan, I'm going to ask to work for a director who never leaves the studio!" She handed each of them a clip-on microphone. "Feed that under your shirt and through your top button hole. We'll test them when you're seated. God, what I'd give for an iced latte."

Noah called her name and she pasted on a chipper smile and hurried off, leaving Olivia and Michel to exchange perplexed shrugs.

"She doesn't know paradise when she sees it," said a woman with a silky voice.

Olivia turned to find Shelley Giusti standing beside her. She recognized the chef's trademark auburn locks and the sparkle of intelligence and humor in her nutmeg-colored eyes.

"That's fine by me," Olivia said. "Someone's got to live in the skyscrapers."

Shelley shuddered. "Not me. I'm done with the urban grind. I need a break from traffic jams and television shows. I want to open a dessert shop in the perfect small town. Pastries, baked goods, and fine chocolate. I already have a menu and a name picked out, but I haven't found the right—" She stopped midsentence and held out her hand. "Sorry. Here I am, gabbing merrily away and I haven't even introduced myself."

As Olivia took Shelley's hand, she couldn't help but

notice the thin gold band on the chef's ring finger. *Not again!* Olivia thought. *Can't Michel ever fall for a single woman?*

Despite this unpleasant discovery, Olivia asked Shelley if she'd had a chance to visit Oyster Bay. There was a vacancy in one of Olivia's downtown buildings and she'd love to see a dessert shop occupy the prime retail space.

"Not yet." Shelley reached over and linked her arm through Michel's. "But I hear there's an amazing restaurant there. I also heard that a devastatingly handsome and talented chef slaves away in the kitchen from dawn to dusk." She gave Olivia a conspiratorial wink.

"His hours aren't quite that bad," Olivia replied with a laugh.

Shelley and Michel walked arm in arm to the judges' table, heads bent as they talked, and Olivia paused for a moment to wonder why a married woman would act so openly flirtatious. Having never been married, she'd have to ask Laurel what triggered this type of behavior. Was Shelley trying to make her husband jealous or was she actually interested in Michel?

Olivia couldn't dwell on the pastry chef's motives because Noah directed her to take a seat, her mic was tested, and then Candice reviewed the parameters by which the contestants were to be judged. By the time she was done, every space in the standing-room-only audience area had been filled and the cameras were pointed at the black curtain erected in the front of a large white tent.

Craning her neck, Olivia scanned the faces one more time but was disappointed to find that her friends still hadn't arrived.

"Welcome to *Chefs Gone Wild*!" The host, a trim, well-coiffed man in his mid-fifties named Allen Murray, beamed at the audience. They responded with a roar of applause. Allen waited a beat for them to quiet before introducing the judges. Olivia and Shelley both received a few whistles and catcalls, and Michel's face lit with joy when the crowd clapped and hollered upon hearing his name.

Next, the black curtain was whisked aside and the contestants were invited to come out. Two men and two women dressed in chef jackets and aprons jogged to their places in front of the judges. Allen spent a little more time on the chefs' introductions, emphasizing that the contestants worked in some of the nation's best restaurants in Las Vegas, Napa Valley, Chicago, and New York.

"And now, let's show the chefs what they have to work with in their first challenge." He moved to a table on which a large stainless steel bowl was covered by a black cloth. Whisking away the cloth, he waited for the camera to zoom in on the items. "You must use the following local ingredients in your dish: peaches, molasses, shrimp, garlic, tomatoes, kale, and barley." He gestured at the grills and camp stoves set up behind the chefs. "You have twenty minutes to prepare your dish. Go!"

Olivia noted that in addition to the ingredients set out in the steel bowl, the chefs had access to an array of spices, butter, and olive oil. She relaxed, taking pleasure in watching the culinary masters at work. The camera feed was relayed to a large screen above the audience, and Allen provided a stream of exciting commentary while the chefs worked. He also asked the judges how they'd like to see the ingredients combined.

"I'd use the barley and molasses as a breading and fry the shrimp in olive oil," Michel said. "Then I'd sauté the kale in garlic and make salsa from the tomatoes and peaches."

Allen nodded and held the microphone near Shelley. "How about you? How would you handle this challenge?"

"I'd surrender to Michel!" She raised her hands in a show of defeat. "I could make a dessert dish with the barley, peaches, and molasses, but the kale? No way."

The twenty minutes passed quickly and the judges were

presented with four dishes to taste. Olivia's favorite was the barley-breaded shrimp salad.

For the second course, the contestants were given sweet potatoes, pork, cornmeal, endive, and celery root. This task completed, they were asked to round off the meal by preparing a dessert using cherries, honey, pecans, mint, and wheat flour. Despite being given a thirty-minute time allotment, one of the chefs presented the judges with a treat that stood out among the others: a pecan and cherry brittle drizzled with a sweet mint sauce. It was one of the best desserts Olivia had ever tasted.

"I can see why people like this show," she whispered to Michel, covering her mic with the palm of her hand. All too soon the judges were faced with the difficult task of choosing a winner.

After a great deal of civilized arguing, they agreed that the female chef from Napa Valley was the victor. She received a big check and the opportunity to appear on the network's *Celebratory Chefs* show. The other chefs were given smaller checks but didn't seem the least disappointed. Winning the contest didn't seem to matter as much as being given the chance to cook in front of a crowd. They exchanged handshakes and hugs and then walked to the Foodie Network's merchandise tent to sign cookbooks.

Because she had authored several cookbooks, Shelley accompanied the other chefs and Michel disappeared to sneak a cigarette behind the tent. Olivia tried to rejoin Rawlings and Haviland but was waylaid by Noah Wiseman.

"What did you think?" he asked.

"Honestly, I had a ball. It's a great show."

He smiled. "It's fun to shoot too. And the segment of The Boot Top will appear following this one, so you'll have a large viewing audience. The producers have given me the slot after that to do a special piece on the Lumbee Indians and the foods prepared by the Lost Colony."

"If I remember what my fourth grade history teacher

told us, those colonists suffered from malnutrition," Olivia said.

Noah nodded absently. "I'll show the viewers examples of a balanced Indian diet, and raise the theory that they might have taught the colonists how to survive. It's good drama." His voice changed, and when he spoke next, it was with the deep timbre of a radio announcer. "If only they'd been aware of the bounty within their grasp. Forests filled with venison, rabbit, nuts, berries, and roots and an ocean teeming with fresh fish and shellfish!"

Olivia laughed. "I can see you've thought this through."

"And I've got another card up my sleeve," Noah went on. "There's a theory that the Lost Colony sought refuge with the Lumbee Tribe. Intermarried and relocated to Robeson County. Your sous-chef told me all about it. He's a fascinating kid."

"Have you filmed his demonstration yet?"

Noah tapped his watch. "Next on my list. He's cooking in the campground area over an open fire. He'll make *Chefs Gone Wild* look like a day at a Beverly Hills spa, but it'll be worth it." Glancing toward the tent, his eyes went wide. "Here he is now! Look at that awesome getup!"

Willis Locklear was truly resplendent. He wore a knee-length scarlet trade shirt, a tan vest embellished with geometric patterns, fringed buckskin boots, a beaded finger sash, and a partial turban covered with multihued feathers. As colorful as a rooster, he wore his costume with confidence, seeming more comfortable in it than he did in a chef's jacket and loose pants.

Olivia gave Willis a thumbs-up and then paused, surprised to see Michel trailing behind the sous-chef, a bag of supplies in each arm.

Excusing herself, she turned away from Noah and closed the distance between herself and The Boot Top's two chefs. "Willis, you look incredible," she said.

His cheeks pinked. "Thanks, Ms. Limoges. I didn't want

to cook in my costume, but Mr. Wiseman really wanted me to. I just hope I don't set it on fire."

"You'll be great," she assured him. "And Michel? Are you . . . involved in this segment too?"

"Today, *I'm* the sous-chef!" Michel smiled brightly at Willis. "Our kitchen is a team, after all."

Olivia studied him. Michel was hardly a democratic head chef. He was more of a benevolent dictator. And not always so benevolent at that. "How sweet of you," she said, her eyes betraying her disbelief.

"Willis? Could I borrow you for a few minutes after you're done?" she asked. "There's a piece of pottery I'd like to show you."

Willis was clearly confused by her request, but replied with a cheerful, "Sure thing," before heading over to Candice to be fitted for his mic.

Giving Michel a lingering look of warning, Olivia joined Rawlings and Haviland. She took her phone from her bag and noticed that Millay had sent her a text message. Laurel was at the Cedar Point campground conducting an interview and they'd meet Olivia and Rawlings there at two.

Pleased to finally hear from her friends, she watched Willis build two fires close to the audience section. He made a teepee out of wood and then set some dry grass alight with a match. Only after both fires had been ignited did the cameras begin to roll. Olivia assumed that Noah didn't want the presence of the match to ruin the sensation that Willis was cooking as his ancestors once had. And yet, as the good-looking young man with the dark hair and elaborate costume set up a spit over the fire pit to his left, Olivia had no trouble picturing him emerging from the dense forest, a leather pouch filled with fresh game slung over his shoulder.

Over the next thirty minutes, she watched Willis prepare a summer squash soup and a salad made of apples, nuts, and collard greens. The Lumbee sous-chef then fried corn pone on a flat pan over the first fire while a rabbit stew loaded with beans and carrots bubbled in a cast-iron pot hanging over the second fire. Willis explained how to make each dish and described why each food item was significant to the Lumbee. He was a humble and engaging performer and completely overshadowed Allen Murray and all of the contestants of the previous show.

"I'm going to finish up by making some pumpkin seed candy for dessert," he said, giving the audience a winsome smile.

"They're going to steal this kid and take him back to New York," Olivia whispered to Rawlings. "He's a natural. I can easily picture him hosting a multicultural cooking show."

Olivia looked over Willis's head to where Michel was squatting near the tent's entrance, well out of camera range. His mouth was pinched and his eyes were dark. Olivia recognized the expression. Her head chef was consumed by envy. Again. "Michel is going to be impossible to be around after this."

But after Willis finished his demonstration to a round of hearty applause, Michel jumped forward to help his underling collect his pots and utensils. Olivia, Rawlings, and Haviland followed both chefs inside the tent.

"I am never cooking in this outfit again," Willis said and dropped into a folding chair. He unscrewed the cap from a bottle of water and drank it down in one go. When he was done, he wiped his forehead with a dishtowel and sighed. "I was totally worried that drops of sweat were going to fall into the stew pot."

"You seemed perfectly comfortable working over an open fire wearing eight layers of clothing," Olivia told him.

Michel snorted and then pointed at the dolly, clearly hoping to shift the focus away from Willis. "What's that?"

Rawlings lifted the memory jug onto the table.

"I'm trying to find out something about the woman who made this," Olivia said, her eyes on Willis. "Have you ever heard the name Munin Cooper?"

Willis shook his head, his expression neutral. He reached for the jug with eager fingers and then hesitated. "Can I touch it?"

"Of course." Olivia watched him carefully as he examined the jug, but he didn't seem to connect with any of the objects on it. He was merely curious. She directed his attention to the KKK medal. "This is what I wanted to talk to you about. The *Gazette* mentioned something about the Lumbee celebrating a victory over the Klan at the Battle of Hayes Pond, right?"

Willis nodded, his eyes flashing briefly with pride.

Olivia pressed on. "Have there been any other incidents between your tribe and the KKK? More recent ones, perhaps?"

Now a shadow crossed the young man's features and his eyes flashed a darker shade of brown, turning nearly black for a second before he shrugged his shoulders and fought to appear impassive. "I guess, but nothing as big as Hayes Pond. I wasn't even born then, but I've heard that the Klan hated us even more after that night. They got their asses handed to them and they never really got over it. Still harassed my people whatever way they could, but it was all small stuff."

"Like what?" Rawlings asked.

"Rocks through windows. Slashed tires. That kind of crap," Willis said, shifting in his seat. Olivia didn't know if it was the heat or the subject of conversation that was making him uncomfortable.

Rawlings subtly morphed into cop interview mode. He began by establishing a rapport with Willis by telling him some boyhood memories of how the minorities in Oyster Bay had been mistreated. He leaned close to Willis, lowering his voice as though he were sharing a special secret. Then, ever so gently, he turned the focus back on Willis. "Did anything like that ever happen to your family?"

Willis squirmed in his chair. He reached for the dish-towel again and hid his face behind it. "Not really," he said after dragging the cloth from his forehead to his neck. The movement made it appear like he'd been trying to erase his own expression, but fear lingered in his eyes like tiny white sparks glowing in the wood of a quenched fire.

"Look, I gotta run. My sister's waiting for me at the other campground." He stood and cast a brief, anxious glance at the memory jug. "I hope you'll come watch some of the dancing. And my sister's a crazy good storyteller. She performs at two."

"We'll be there," Olivia promised. It was obvious that Willis wasn't going to open up to them about whatever he was frightened of and she didn't want to put pressure on him in the middle of the festival. Resolving to speak to him again once he was back at The Boot Top, Olivia waved good-bye.

Michel watched Willis leave and then shook his head. He'd begun to sulk. "I'm French. My ancestors were cooking five-star meals before his even crawled out of the ocean. *We're* the reason there are foodies in the first place. We *invented* gourmet. Even the word is French!"

"Willis hasn't eclipsed you," Olivia said. "And Shelley Giusti seems to like you just the way you are. Though I'm sorry to see that she wears a wedding ring."

"I haven't asked her about that," Michel said. "Maybe I'll invite her to Indian Story Time and she can tell me why her husband isn't doing it for her."

Olivia scowled. "I know you're fond of crossing lines, Michel, but leave Willis alone. He's only being himself and poses no threat to you."

"He'd better not." Michel glared and stomped out of the tent.

Rawlings slid the memory jug back into the crate on the dolly. For a second, the little gilt mirror caught a stray sunbeam and threw diamonds into the air. Rawlings put his hand out as if to capture the splinters of light. "This is no good, Olivia," he said. "I've seen that look before—usually right before a man is about to do something he'll regret."

The Cedar Point campground was an explosion of color. Lumbee Indians in ceremonial dress moved about the clearing like a flock of exotic birds. Olivia suddenly realized she had no way to communicate with all of them. She'd have to appeal to the chief or find someone who could e-mail photos of the memory jug to the rest of the tribe.

Echoing Olivia's thoughts, Rawlings said, "This is a tough place to talk to people. We need to put this on display."

"That's exactly what we'll do!" Olivia exclaimed. "I'll rent a booth space and ask festivalgoers to identify the mystery objects."

Rawlings was skeptical. "Really? And will you offer a prize in exchange for information?"

"Maybe I will," she snapped, annoyed that she hadn't already come up with a plan to approach the Lumbee.

Walking in stony silence, the couple followed a stream of people heading toward the picnic area. Here, the aroma of cooking food was just as prevalent as it had been at the other campground, but these scents were greasier, hinting of sausage and funnel cake.

Olivia spotted Willis engaged in what appeared to be a serious conversation with a man in his early fifties who was not, judging from his light skin and fair hair, a Lumbee. The man nodded gravely and, after Willis had finished talking, spoke a few words of his own and then put a reassuring hand on the sous-chef's shoulder.

Looking relieved, Willis pulled a pack of cigarettes out of the pouch hanging from his sash and lit up, earning him an admonishing finger wag from the older man. He smoked for a while and they shared a few laughs until a drum began to beat. Abruptly, both men turned their attention to the raised platform at the end of the picnic area.

A beautiful young woman stepped onto the stage. She had a river of jet-black hair that shone with ribbons of blue in the fractured light. The hem of her daffodil yellow dress, which was covered by a long white apron, whispered as she moved to the edge of the platform. A multicolored medallion had been stitched on the front of the apron and she wore a crownlike headdress. Barefoot, she walked in regal silence and then stopped, gazing intently at the audience.

They instantly fell quiet.

She raised her hands in the air. Elegant and slender, her arms closed slightly, coaxing her listeners to draw closer together and closer to her. In a strong, deep, singsong voice, she began her tale. "Let me tell you how the snakes got their poison."

And then she stared straight at Olivia.

Olivia thought her heart might stop. This girl, who had to be Willis's sister, reminded her of someone. Olivia was certain she recognized the angles and planes of her face, the distinctive slope of her nose, and the proud tilt of her chin, but she wasn't sure which of her acquaintances the girl favored. And then, this beautiful, self-assured young woman looked at Olivia. She regarded her as if she could see right to the bottom of her soul. The wisdom of her gaze was unsettling. So was the fact that she was gazing out through a pair of very familiar eyes.

Munin's eyes.

Chapter 9

*Time is the coin of your life. It is the only coin
you have, and only you can determine how it
will be spent.*

—CARL SANDBURG

Olivia was rooted to the ground, hypnotized by the girl's
dark brown eyes and the lulling cadence of her storyteller voice.

"'If Man bothers me I will rattle my tail until he leaves
me alone,' said Diamond Snake." The girl began to shake a
rain stick, creating a sound like a snake's rattle. "'And if he
doesn't leave me alone, I will sssssstrike!'" She leapt forward in a low crouch, thrusting the hand with the rain stick
toward the audience. Several people jumped back, startled,
and then covered up their embarrassment with a chuckle.
Haviland issued a low growl, but Olivia stilled his disquiet
by placing her palm on his head.

Next, the girl pulled a scarf from inside the sleeve of her
dress. The thin strip of material was made of red, black,
and yellow stripes and looked like a coral snake.

"The Grand Council asked the third snake, 'How will
you let the People know you are poisonous?'"

Raising the scarf above her head, she let it wriggle
between her clenched fists. It rippled and undulated like a
real serpent. "'If Man does not take my colors as a sign of

danger, then I will ssssstrike!'" She whipped the scarf toward the audience. A little girl screamed and pressed her face against her mother's belly.

Olivia suspected many of the Lumbee gathered around the stage had heard the tale before. Yet they listened on tenterhooks, their gazes never leaving the face of the captivating storyteller.

"The fourth snake lived by the shores of the water. When he opened his white mouth, it was a sign to leave him alone." From behind her back, the girl drew forth a gray snake puppet with an oversized head. "'If Man does not heed these signs, I will ssssstrike!'" She drew the puppet's mouth open, revealing a set of deadly looking fangs.

The tips of the fangs had been covered with glitter glue, and when the girl pivoted the mask so that the cottonmouth's unhinged jaw caught the light, the upper fangs appeared to be slick with venom.

Olivia saw the glistening fangs and shuddered. Without warning, she was once again in Munin's shack, studying the strange old woman over the rim of a chipped pottery mug. That image quickly dissolved and was replaced by a picture of Munin's bloated body half submerged in the stream behind her house. In her mind's eye, Olivia searched the imaginary scene for the snake, but she refused to believe a reptile had killed Munin. She thought it much more likely that someone had carried the snake's poison in a syringe, tiptoeing through the quiet forest with the stealth of a leopard.

An overpowering scent of cloves brought Olivia out of her reverie. She turned to find Willis standing to her right.

"That's Talley, my sister," he whispered reverently. "She's good, isn't she?"

Olivia nodded. She wanted to ask Willis a dozen questions. Most importantly, she wanted to know why Talley bore a resemblance to Munin—a woman he claimed not to know. But the question could wait, for Olivia was unwilling to break his sister's spell.

Onstage, Talley finished her story by showing how glad Vine was to have given her poison away to the four snakes. "Now she could play with the People again!" Talley began to dance about the stage, lifting a vine made of artificial plants and green glitter into the air. She wrapped it around her body and waltzed in circles, her face filled with joy.

"The People were not like the newcomers from across the Great Water!" she shouted proudly. "The newcomers were mean to Vine and to the snakes. But the People were kind and gentle. They respected the poison in these creatures and knew that if they listened to the warnings, they would not get hurt."

Tally placed the vine on the stage where she had already laid the symbols of the four snakes. Carefully, she picked her way around them. She moved slowly, soundlessly, until she came to stand in the center once again. She raised her hands to the sky, thanked the Creator, and wished the crowd a day of peace and harmony.

After the applause died down and the crowd began to disperse, Olivia drew in a deep breath of clove-scented air. "Is that you I'm smelling, Willis?"

He looked chagrined. "Yeah. I smoked a clove cigarette. Never had one before and I wasn't wild about it, but I left my Camel Lights in the truck, so I went ahead and tried it."

"I smoked like a fiend when I was your age, but I had to quit," Rawlings said. "I couldn't be a cop if I didn't pass the physical."

Willis used his palm to wipe his forehead, which was glistening with perspiration. "Did you go cold turkey?" His voice came out as a rasp and he seemed surprised by the sound of it. Swallowing, he tried to speak again, but nothing came out.

"Willis?" Olivia put a hand under the young man's elbow. Haviland began to whine. He shifted anxiously, sniffed, and whined again. Something was wrong.

"Can't . . . breathe . . ." Willis whispered hoarsely before teetering over.

Rawlings lurched forward to catch the sous-chef, but he was caught off balance by the suddenness of the younger man's fall. He slowed Willis's descent, but ended up on the ground too.

"Willis!" Olivia shouted, sinking to her knees and pushing the multihued turban off his head. Willis's black hair was slick with sweat, and when Olivia touched her fingers to his cheek, she flinched. "He's burning up," she said to Rawlings, who had Willis's wrist in his hand and was checking his pulse. Haviland sniffed the air and whined again.

Rawlings dropped his ear to Willis's mouth. "He's breathing. Fast and shallow." And then he had his cell phone out and was calling for help.

Olivia scanned their surroundings, hoping someone had noticed Willis fall and was rushing off to find an EMT. With two significant events occurring in the forest, Olivia expected a park ranger, physician, or paramedic to show up within seconds.

"Stay with us, Willis," she pleaded softly. "Help is on the way."

Moaning unintelligibly, Willis turned his head and vomited into the grass. Olivia recoiled from the acidic odor, a knot of helplessness forming in her gut. While she was averting her face, she saw Talley emerge from a small tent behind the stage. She took one glance at the sight of her brother and sprinted to his side.

"What happened?" she cried, bending over him.

"He just collapsed," Olivia said. "Does he have a medical condition?"

Talley shook her head. "No! Nothing! I have asthma, but Willis is healthy as a bear! Did you call anyone?"

"EMTs are on the way," Rawlings said.

"He's so hot! What's wrong with him?" Talley's eyes

filled with tears and she put her lips against her brother's forehead. "Willis! It's me, Talley. Can you hear me?"

Willis curled the fingers of his right hand upward and Talley grabbed on to them. "We've got to get him help!" she shouted, wiping the vomit from her brother's chin and neck with the red bandana she'd been using to hold back her hair. "Where's the freaking ambulance?"

"They're coming. It won't be long now," Rawlings promised and Olivia was thankful to have him there. He sounded so calm and reassuring while she sat uselessly by Willis's side, unable to utter a word of comfort.

Willis, who'd kept his eyes closed since he fell, now opened them and looked around. The whites showed, reminding Olivia of the desperate gaze of a frightened and confused animal. Garbled sounds came from his throat and Talley leaned closer to him, frantic to understand.

"His arm feels weird," she mumbled, touching the exposed flesh near his wrist.

Olivia mirrored Talley's movement and was disturbed to find that the muscles in Willis's forearm were rigid, as if he were struggling to lift a heavy object. Hesitating, she wrapped her palm over his bicep. It was also hard and taut.

"Rawlings," she whispered. She'd never seen anything like this before and she was frightened. Sensing her fear, Haviland nudged her with his head, whining so quietly that he was barely heard.

The chief's eyes flicked toward Talley before meeting Olivia's, as if willing her to stay composed for the girl's sake. But Olivia had no bedside manner. She needed to act, to do something to stop from feeling like the world was spinning too fast.

"We need to get him out of the sun," she told Rawlings. To Talley, she said, "Let's carry him into the tent. Keep talking to him while we move him. Keep him in the here and now." When Talley responded with silence and a glassy look, Olivia gently squeezed her shoulder. "Tell him a story. Anything. Just talk to him."

Talley nodded, bent close to her brother's ear, and began to speak. "In the beginning, the Great Spirit gave the birds and the animals the knowledge and the power to talk to men."

Rawlings grabbed Willis's shoulders and Olivia took hold of his feet. Together, they managed to shuffle across the brittle grass and crisp pine needles toward the tent Talley had used as a dressing room. They'd almost made it inside when Olivia's foot caught on a tree root and she stumbled.

Thrown off balance, Rawlings fought to hold on and Talley thrust her hands under her brother's waist, dislodging his sash and the buckskin pouch attached to it. She kicked the bag aside and the three of them entered the cool tent, laying Willis on Talley's yellow dress. They'd barely eased him down when the sound of an approaching siren filled the air. Haviland began to howl and turn in nervous half circles.

"Finally!" Talley sobbed.

"I'll wave them over." Rawlings darted out of the tent.

Olivia picked up Willis's hand. His breath was coming faster now and his skin had turned a frightening shade of dull gray. The tent was close with the scent of cloves and dread.

She scuttled out of the way when a pair of paramedics entered, watching in silence as they placed an oxygen mask over Willis's mouth and nose, fit a blood pressure cuff over his arm, and spoke to one another in hushed, rapid speech.

Amid a flurry of medical talk and deft movements, Willis was placed on a gurney and loaded into the ambulance. A ring of spectators surrounded the vehicle and Olivia was glad to see a few familiar faces among the crowd.

"Olivia?" Laurel called out, hugging a notebook to her chest. "Are you okay?"

Gesturing for Laurel, Millay, and Harris to come closer, Olivia drank in the sight of Harris's ginger-colored hair, Laurel's wide, blue eyes, and Millay's trademark frown. Along with Rawlings, these were the people who kept her anchored to Oyster Bay. The pull of childhood memories, which had called her back to the area several years ago, were not as powerful as these bonds of friendship. The Bayside Book Writers were always there when she needed them. They were here now. And she needed them.

"How do you know him?" Harris asked.

Olivia struggled to find her voice. "He's a sous-chef at The Boot Top."

Millay glanced at the ambulance in time to see the paramedics slam the rear doors shut. "What happened to him?"

"I have no idea," Olivia said. "One minute I was talking to him and he seemed perfectly normal. And then, he couldn't speak or breathe freely and he keeled over."

"He looks so young!" Laurel exclaimed, her gaze following the emergency vehicle as it eased forward.

"Only twenty-one," Olivia said. "The girl who went with him is his sister. Rawlings and I had just finished listening to her recite a Lumbee folktale when Willis collapsed." She ran a hand through her hair. Damp strands clung to her neck and forehead and her throat was dry. "Do any of you have water?"

Laurel immediately produced a plastic bottle. "Take this. Drink it all. You look . . ."

"Like you're in shock," Millay finished and then jerked her thumb in the direction the ambulance had gone. "Is it serious? Will he be all right?"

Olivia paused. Judging from the weakness of Willis's breathing, his muscle rigidity, and the color of his skin, he was gravely ill. She had no medical training, but Willis seemed to have slipped away right before her eyes. And from beneath her hands. It was as if she could feel parts of his body shutting down. He wasn't dead. He wasn't even unconscious. But the Willis she recognized was gone and she didn't think he was coming back.

She hated to voice this thought.

"Olivia?" Laurel prompted.

Bending over to retrieve Willis's leather pouch, Olivia rubbed her fingers over the smooth buckskin. "It doesn't look good."

Silence descended on the group. They watched Rawlings as he spoke to a fresh-faced park ranger and a bearded sheriff's deputy.

"I think something fell out of that bag," Harris said, reaching for a scrap of paper near Haviland's front paw. He examined the paper, his brows knitting together, and then handed it to Olivia.

Four lines had been typed on a field of plain white:

The voice of that fitful song
Sings on, and is never still
A boy's will is the wind's will,
And the thoughts of youth are long, long thoughts.

"What is it?" Millay stood on her tiptoes, trying to catch a glimpse of the note's contents.

"A metaphor." Olivia passed it on to Millay.

Laurel frowned. "Is your sous-chef a writer?"

"I don't think so." Olivia opened the bag and, pulling out the items one by one, dropped them into Harris's cupped hands. There was a cheap lighter, a cell phone, keys on a dream catcher key chain, and twenty-six dollars in cash.

The friends stared at the contents for a long moment and Olivia sensed they were all thinking the same thing. Could the objects people carried in a bag or a pocket define a life? Family photos, keys to a car or a house, a good-luck charm, credit cards and cash—could each of them be reduced to a handful of similar articles?

Rawlings finished talking, shook hands with the two

men in uniform, and walked over to join the Bayside Book Writers.

"Willis's effects?" he asked Harris.

Olivia didn't care for the sound of the word "effects." It was too clinical. Too removed from the vibrant young man she was just beginning to know. "They came from his pouch," she answered before Harris could. "As well as that slip of paper." She passed it to him.

The four friends watched as Rawlings' eyes darted over the lines several times. "Sounds like poetry," he said. "But I don't recognize it. Does anyone know the author?"

A collective shake of heads.

"I'll google it." Harris brandished his smartphone and began to type while Millay held out the paper for him.

Rawlings touched Olivia on the arm. "I told the uniforms what happened. There's a deputy at the hospital already—some kid set off fireworks inside a convenience store and ended up with mild burns—and he's going to radio an update on Willis's condition. Do you want to talk to someone about the memory jug while we wait?"

"I guess we have time to kill," Olivia muttered darkly. Her fingers curled around the dolly's handle and she nodded. "Sorry. We did come here with a purpose. Maybe one of the craft vendors can help."

Harris put Willis's things back in the pouch and Laurel stored the whole bundle in her cavernous shoulder bag. She pointed at a booth up ahead. "I'm going to photograph those adorable Lumbee dolls. You should get one for your niece, Olivia. They make me wish that I had a sweet little girl at home instead of my hang-from-the-chandelier boys."

"I'll be there in a minute," Olivia said, drawn to a booth across the path. While the rest of the Bayside Book Writers paused to examine a vendor's exquisite needlework, Olivia admired a collection of oil paintings. Most of the subjects were Lumbee women in ceremonial dress, but there were also black-and-white portraits of elderly Lumbee men.

These were close-ups of weathered faces, showing every furrow and wrinkle. The subjects gazed at some point in the distance, their proud, dignified features tinged by a hint of sorrow. Or perhaps regret. Olivia wasn't sure which emotion the artist was aiming for, but she found his work stirringly beautiful.

"Can I help you?" a plump woman wearing a tight T-shirt and cutoffs inquired. She smiled at Haviland and then, after asking Olivia's permission, reached out to stroke his curly fur.

"Are you the artist?" Olivia asked.

The woman laughed at the idea. "Heavens, no! I can barely draw a circle. My grandfather made these. He's sitting in the shade over there." She pointed to a copse of trees where a group of men sitting in folding chairs were chatting and sipping from beer cans tucked inside paper bags.

Taking note of the signature in the corner of the closest portrait, Olivia eased the memory jug from the crate and approached the men. "Graham Wright?"

She was surprised when a man with fair skin and gray eyes raised his hand. "That's me. You interested in my art?"

"I am, yes. I particularly like the black-and-white portraits, but I also need your help. May I join you?"

At this, all of the men gave her their full attention.

"You'd best sit down." Graham gestured at the large cooler to his left and Olivia perched on its plastic seat. Haviland trotted a few feet away and settled down on a carpet of pine needles.

Olivia held out the jug. "I was wondering if anything on this piece was familiar to you?"

The old man grasped the jug tightly, almost reverently around its base. "Well, now, I haven't laid eyes on one of these for years." He began to rotate the jug, his eyes glimmering with delight.

"The pennies are from 1958," Olivia said. "Does that year have special meaning to the Lumbee?"

Graham nodded. "Only because of the Battle of Hayes Pond."

"Anything else?" she asked.

The old man thought for a moment. "Nothin' comes to mind, but when you get to be my age, it's hard to pick apart the years. They lump together, kind of like that clay this jug was made from. You could talk to the chief. She put our whole history on the computer. Folks can look up all sorts of things. Pictures and stories and newspaper clippin's from way back when."

"Your chief's a woman?" Olivia was surprised.

The men nodded proudly.

"She's a warrior, that one," the old man next to Graham said and cackled. "We set her loose on those jokers up in Washington and she helped get the government to admit that we're a real tribe. Took a hundred years for that to happen."

"That gal's tough as nails," another man agreed.

Olivia was impressed. She sensed this group was sparse with their praise. "She sounds like a force to reckoned with. So what's her name and where can I find her?"

Graham checked his watch. "Her name's Annette Stevens and she'll be crownin' the winner of the beauty pageant. The boys and I have a little wager on who's gonna be Miss Lumbee, but I know who's sure to win."

The man to his left spluttered. "Talley Locklear's not the only pretty girl in the tribe. My granddaughter will give her a run for her money."

At the sound of Talley's name, Olivia had a flash of the young woman's anguished face as she climbed into ambulance.

"I don't think she'll make it," she said and hurriedly added, "To the pageant, I mean. Her brother's sick."

Graham cocked his head. "Willis Locklear? I just saw the boy an hour ago. He couldn't be too poorly."

Olivia hated to be the bearer of bad news. "I'm sorry,

but he collapsed after Talley's performance. An ambulance was called. I don't know what's wrong with him."

"Probably heatstroke," said a man with a long, silver braid and a gold tooth. "These kids run all day without drinkin' a drop of water. Then they pass out. We see it happen every year." He waved a finger at Olivia. "You look a bit worse for the wear yourself, young lady."

Olivia hadn't been called a young lady for decades, and she couldn't help but smile at the man. His face was similar to those in Graham's portraits, etched with deep lines and loose skin, but his eyes didn't reflect the same mixture of sorrow and hope. They were bright and inquisitive and Olivia was certain very little escaped his keen gaze.

As if to prove her point, he pointed at something over Olivia's shoulder and said, "I think that fellow's lookin' for you."

She swung around. Rawlings was pocketing his cell phone and walking toward her. She didn't like the set of his jaw. She didn't like the sweat shining on his forehead or how he motioned for Laurel, Millay, and Harris to stay where they were. She didn't like his resolute stride.

"I . . ." Olivia began, rising slowly to her feet. "I need to go."

Graham glanced up at her. "Somethin' wrong, hon? He botherin' you?"

But Olivia couldn't answer. Part of her mind registered the concerned looks being exchanged among the old men. The other part plotted an escape route. There, to the right was a narrow gap between the trees. She and Haviland could vanish deep into the forest. They could run to the heart of the woods, to a spot where light barely penetrated the dense canopy overhead.

"Olivia." Rawlings took hold of her arm.

She kept her gaze fixed on the narrow trail leading away from the campground.

"Look at me," Rawlings commanded gently.

She knew what he needed to tell her. It was too late to flee from the knowledge. Slowly, she met his eyes. The splinters of gold she often saw in his muddy green irises weren't there. They'd been replaced by shadows.

"Willis is gone, Olivia." He held tightly on to both of her arms and she dug her fingertips into his flesh. "He died on the way to the hospital."

The old men cried out. Rising to their feet, they hammered Rawlings with questions and shouted their disbelief, but when he told them who he was, their protests gave way to shock. In the dappled light, they reached out to each other with gnarled and trembling hands, trying to make sense of the senseless.

Olivia drifted away, returning to the stall filled with Graham Wright's portraits. She stood in front of a drawing of a majestic old man and allowed grief and anger to wash over her. Her fingers curled into fists as she stared and stared at the image of a man who'd walked the earth for at least eight decades.

And then she began to cry.

She cried because Willis Locklear would never have the chance to attain such a beautiful, timeworn face.

Chapter 10

The news of Willis's death moved from tent to tent like electricity, rocking the Lumbee tribe to the core.

Olivia watched people leave their booths, moving with the hesitant gait of those who don't want to believe what they've been told. Holding on to each other's hands, they slowly made their way to the place where Willis had collapsed. It looked like some invisible force was pulling them to the spot and Olivia felt compelled to follow.

The Lumbee made a loose circle around the patch of grass where Willis had fallen, crying quietly and shaking their heads over the senselessness of his passing. Men and women of all ages seemed to be waiting for someone to explain what had happened. A hundred pairs of dark eyes cast about for an authority figure, for someone to calm and assure them. But no one came. No one had any answers.

Finally, the park ranger Rawlings had spoken with earlier came forward and addressed the distraught group. He told them that there were no updates from the hospital regarding the cause of death and that it might be hours before that information was released to Talley. He advised them to return to their respective booths.

"I realize what a horrible shock this is . . ." he began and then stopped, uncertain of what else to say. He put his palm on his walkie-talkie, perhaps wishing a more competent voice would emit from the speaker and release him from his unpleasant task.

At that moment, the middle-aged man who'd been talking to Willis prior to Talley's performance appeared, his fair skin looking nearly translucent with shock. A portly man dressed in a white polo shirt and pressed slacks walked by his side, dabbing at his cheeks and forehead with a blue handkerchief. He was older than the first man by ten years and the crowd immediately fell silent, waiting for him to speak. He thanked the park ranger and held his hands out as if to embrace the entire assemblage.

"My dear friends, I've heard the terrible news," he said in a languid drawl tinged with sadness. "Judson and I will go ahead to the hospital and get some answers. I know you're torn to bits by this awful, awful thing, as are Judson and I. There's nothing I can say to lessen your heartbreak, but Willis would want this celebration to go on. He loved days like these. Am I right?"

There was a murmuring of agreement. "That boy was one of the finest dancers I've ever laid eyes on," the man continued. "But the rest of those excellent performers are here in front of me. Dance for him today, folks. Make his spirit smile."

Olivia wondered if the speaker was a tribal elder, but he was as blue eyed and fair skinned as the man named Judson. The two men began to walk away and Olivia and Haviland rushed after them.

"Excuse me!" she called, causing both men to turn. "I'm Olivia Limoges. Willis worked for me," she said breathlessly.

"We've heard of you, of course. Willis was thrilled when he was hired to work at your restaurant. Fletcher

Olsen, at your service." The man in the pink shirt held out his hand. "And this is Judson Ware, my associate."

Judson stepped forward and Olivia squeezed his hand, moved by the grief she saw in his face. He gave Haviland a sad smile but didn't speak.

"The Olsen law firm has represented members of the Lumbee tribe for over seventy years. We attend all the powwows." Fletcher mopped his forehead again. "Never has this celebration been marred by such a tragedy. Willis was a fine young man."

"I can't wrap my head around it," Olivia said in a low voice and then turned to Judson. "I saw you and Willis talking before Talley's show. Did he seem okay to you then?"

Judson nodded. "He was the same exuberant Willis I've known since he was a kid. He was smoking more than usual. Said he'd been through a whole pack already, but I guess he'd been on edge over an argument he'd had at the other campground."

An argument? Olivia felt the air rush out of her lungs. She could already picture the face of Willis's enemy. "With whom?"

"He said the fellow was his boss," Judson replied after a slight pause.

Olivia fought to mask her anger. "He was probably referring to Michel, The Boot Top's head chef. I own the restaurant, but Willis works"—she corrected herself—"worked under Michel."

"Willis said the guy's bark was worse than his bite—that he was used to him," Judson said. "But I told him that he shouldn't have to accept disrespect in or out of the kitchen. No one should put up with—"

"Well said, Judson," Fletcher interrupted smoothly. "However, that doesn't matter now. We need to find out what happened to Willis, call the tribal chair, and get to Talley's side as quickly as we can. Willis was the only family she had left and we don't want her to go through this nightmare alone. So if you'll excuse us." He gave Olivia a little bow.

She handed the attorney her business card. "Please call me if there's anything I can do. As Willis's employer, I feel a responsibility to his sister."

"That's mighty kind of you. I'll be in touch," Fletcher promised.

Judson gave her another sad smile and then the two men strode up the trail toward the exit.

Olivia headed back to the copse of trees where she'd left Rawlings and the memory jug. The Bayside Book Writers were waiting for her there. They looked at her with a mixture of concern and curiosity.

"The chief told us that you think Talley looks like Munin," Millay said, the question in her tone evident.

Relieved that she could focus on something other than Willis's death for the moment, Olivia nodded. "They have the same nose, face shape, and eyes. But it's more than that. The way Talley carries herself reminds me of Munin too. She has Munin's piercing stare."

"Willis didn't react at all when you mentioned Munin's name," Rawlings reminded her.

"No, but he certainly reacted to the Klan token." She turned to Harris. "Can you do some research this afternoon? Find out if there are any documented hate crimes against the Lumbee following the Battle of Hayes Pond?"

Harris checked his watch. "I can, but not until after the kids' cooking demonstration. I'm supposed to be working, and if I don't show up on Monday with ideas for the company's new game, I'll lose my chance to take the lead on the project."

Olivia glanced at Laurel. "I know you have to stay. You've got a bigger story to cover now."

Laurel sighed. "I'm not looking forward to gathering quotes on Willis while people are still trying to digest the news. At least I can bring the jug with me. Maybe someone will recognize one of the mystery objects." She shook her head. "I'm going to be home late again. Guess I should grab a snack before I get started. Be right back."

Millay picked at her chipped purple nail polish as though standing still were causing her physical pain. "I don't have to be at the bar until nine, so if you need help, just say the word."

"We need to get a complete picture of the Locklear family," Olivia said.

"Sure. I can surf a few of those genealogical sites. Harris isn't the only one who can find stuff on the Internet. I can be a wicked cyber geek too."

Harris scowled. "The only sites you have bookmarked on your laptop are soft-core porn featuring a bunch of half-naked vampires."

"There's nothing *soft* about them," she protested. "And they're totally naked. I mean, who needs clothes when you can't feel the cold?"

"What makes dead guys so damn hot?" Harris grumbled. "It'd be like sleeping with a six-foot ice pack."

Olivia put out her hands to stop Millay from continuing the conversation. "Enough. Why don't we all meet again for dinner at The Bayside Crab House? I'm sure by seven we'll all need a margarita or a tall glass of beer."

"Order me a pitcher," Millay said, pivoting on her heel. "Of each."

Rawlings, who'd been noticeably quiet during this exchange, shook his head in frustration. "Don't you think you're jumping to conclusions?" he asked. "You met Munin once. You met Talley once. And suddenly they're related and possibly the victims of a hate crime?" He moved to touch her and then abruptly changed his mind. "It's all right to be upset about Willis. That's what death does to us. It throws us off balance, makes our world tilt. But you can't restore order by involving everyone in an investigation. This thing with Munin, it's a long shot at best."

Wounded, Olivia brushed past Rawlings and eased the memory jug back into its crate. When she looked at him again, she knew her eyes were angry. "Don't you want justice for her? Or were you just pretending so I'd be more compliant? Invite you into in my bed more often?"

"That's ridiculous and you know it," Rawlings retorted, moving directly in front of her. "And compliant is that last word anyone would use to describe you." He grabbed her by the arms. Haviland was instantly at Olivia's side, watching Rawlings warily. The chief ignored the poodle. "I want to find out what happened to Munin just as much as you do, but I have no jurisdiction, so we need to be discreet. It's one thing to show the others the jug, but asking them to poke around in the Locklears' past? What do you expect to find?"

Olivia shrugged him off. "I don't know, but the jug won't give up its secrets easily and Munin put that KKK token on it for a reason. She put my mother's necklace on it for a reason. She said that I'd be involved in a death and here I am, involved in two of them!" Kicking at a pinecone, she sent it skittering across the ground. "Now I'm repeating her predictions as if they were fact. Just shoot me, Sawyer, before I start buying tarot cards and following my horoscope."

"Don't disregard the jug." Rawlings' voice was gentle. "Let Laurel have it for the afternoon, and if she comes up dry, then you'll have to consider doing something you don't want to do."

Gazing over his shoulder, she could see Laurel heading toward them, a grease-marked brown bag in her right hand. Olivia wheeled the dolly out from under the trees. "I'll break it, but not until tomorrow. Enough damage has been done today."

Olivia dropped Rawlings off at his house and drove straight to The Boot Top to confront Michel.

Flinging the back door open, she was surprised to hear the sound of a woman's laughter reverberating from within the kitchen. Haviland darted inside, no doubt anticipating a tasty treat from his favorite chef.

It was too early for dinner preparations, yet Olivia knew that Michel liked to be alone in the kitchen for an hour before the rest of the staff arrived. He was here now, perched on a stool at the counter and watching in fascination as Shelley Giusti made herself at home in his realm.

"Hello," Olivia said, unable muster a smile. Her mouth simply wouldn't curve upward. It drew down at the corners in a clear sign of disapproval.

Looking abashed, Shelley wiped her hands on her borrowed white apron. "I heard about what happened to the young man who worked here. I'm so sorry." She gestured helplessly at the mixing bowls and soufflé dishes set out before her. "When I want to comfort people, I cook them things, so I asked Michel if he'd allow me to make dessert for the entire staff. Chocolate always makes me feel better when I'm upset."

Olivia inhaled the aroma of rich chocolate and melted butter and nodded in agreement. "That's very kind of you. Don't mind me. I just need to borrow Michel for a few minutes."

Michel was immediately nervous. "Let me make you a drink first. Gabe's not in yet, but I know my way around the bar well enough."

Olivia signaled for him to leave the room. "I'll meet you there in a minute."

Shelley gave Michel an encouraging smile and Olivia couldn't help but wonder if the pastry chef was always so positive. She decided to find out. "Are you traveling alone or did your husband come along?"

"My husband?" Shelley was flustered enough to drop the spoon she was holding. "How—"

"Your ring." Olivia pointed at Shelley's finger.

"Right. Of course. Sometimes I forget that I still wear this." Pivoting her hand, she examined the gold band with a grim expression. "I was married. My husband passed away three years ago. It was very unexpected."

Olivia felt like a heel. "I'm sorry. I had no right to pry."

Turning her attention to the ramekins, Shelley began to fill them with the soufflé mixture. "The doctors told me it was an arrhythmia. There's nothing we could have done to prepare. One day he was fine. The next, he was gone." Her gaze grew distant. "He had the most beautiful hands. Michel's are just like them. The hands of a passionate man. They make for great artists and even greater lovers."

"I'll take your word on that." Olivia hid her discomfort by excusing herself and ducking into the walk-in refrigerator to gather ingredients for Haviland's supper. Pausing before the crates of fresh fruits and vegetables, it struck her that Willis wouldn't be at his station tonight. He wouldn't stand hour after hour, dicing onions, julienning carrots, or carving radishes until they resembled delicate orchids. His orange peel flowers wouldn't grace the edge of the dessert plates. One of the other sous-chefs would be tossing salads, steaming rice, and mashing potatoes, reluctantly occupying the space that had once been Willis's small domain.

"I need a cocktail," Olivia said to a shelf filled with plump tomatoes and waxy cucumbers. She closed the door against the cold, left the kitchen, and headed for the bar.

Michel was pacing around the lounge's sitting area. He'd made himself a gin and tonic and was sipping greedily when Olivia approached.

"I am a terrible man!" he cried as she reached for the tumbler of twenty-five-year-old Chivas Regal. Michel had poured generously, adding a splash of water to the smooth Scotch whiskey.

She sank into one of the leather club chairs and looked up at her head chef. "Sit, Michel. You'll wear a path in the carpet."

"You know already, don't you?" he asked shrilly. "That my last words to poor Willis were horrible!"

Shaking her head, she placed a cocktail napkin on the table in front of her and set her drink on it. "I heard that you two were arguing, but I don't know what was said."

Michel's eyes glistened with tears. He brushed them away with the sleeve of his white coat. "Noah wanted to film him again on Sunday—something about the history of Lumbee cuisine—and Willis told me he needed more time off. He didn't ask, Olivia. He just told me. He had this swagger about him that just made me see red."

"Really?" Olivia didn't bother to conceal her skepticism. "He seemed totally normal to me. Enthusiastic and happy. Right up to the moment he collapsed."

Taking a fortifying gulp of his drink, Michel nodded. "I was probably seeing something that wasn't there. I told Willis that he was only on TV because he was a Lumbee and that Noah never would have noticed him if I hadn't wanted him to be in my kitchen in the first place. He said he could leave at any time—that he'd wanted to learn from me, but he wouldn't cook with me if I didn't treat him with more respect."

"Good for Willis," Olivia said. "And then what happened?"

"I made some stupid joke about poisoning his tasting spoon and he walked away." Michel dabbed at his eyes again. "And now he's dead. I can't apologize. I can't tell him that I was jealous of his youth and his talent. If only I had the chance to say what I really believed—that he had all the right ingredients to make it big. I would have helped him too. You know I don't stay jealous for long. You know I'd have come around!"

Olivia was aware that Michel wanted her to agree with that statement, but she couldn't. "You've been on edge since that TV producer called. You've been moody and juvenile and even petty in the past, but you've never been cruel."

Michel swallowed hard. "It's true. My hunger for

recognition has driven me insane. Now I know that I couldn't have kept up with Pierce even if I'd had the chance. I can't handle the pressure."

"That's *Pierce's* life, Michel. It's the path he chose. You don't need national acclaim. You're content here. In this town. In this kitchen. What more do you want?"

"Shelley," Michel said simply. "But I don't deserve her. If she'd seen my behavior over the last few days, she wouldn't be making soufflés in my ovens. If she'd heard how I spoke to Willis . . ."

Olivia picked up her drink and nursed it in silence. Finally, she lowered the glass and gazed at the ice cubes crowded at the bottom. "We all make mistakes, Michel. Try to learn from this one and move forward."

He sniffed and put his hand over hers. "I'm sorry for behaving like a threatened alpha male."

"More like a middle school girl." She smiled at him. "Of course I forgive you, but I hope you know what you're doing with Shelley. She doesn't strike me as the kind of woman to have flings. I like her. So be careful."

He grinned. "I knew you would. She's been a shining light in my memory since culinary school. What I'd give for a second chance to woo her. Unfortunately, she's still married."

Olivia's eyebrows shot up. "You haven't asked her about that? Get in the kitchen, you fool. She's more available than you think. God help her."

An hour later, Olivia and Haviland entered The Bayside Crab House and were greeted at the hostess station by a smiling kindergartner. Caitlyn, Olivia's niece, was a quiet child with molasses-colored eyes and hair. She was very fond of Haviland and hugged him fiercely. Then she shyly held out a piece of paper for her aunt.

"It's you, me, and Haviland," she said in her high, little-girl voice. "At the beach."

Olivia examined the drawing. In front of a sea made of green, blue, and grey waves, Olivia and Caitlyn held hands while Haviland sniffed at a bright red crab. Bubbly hearts floated around the frame and a rainbow stretched across a sky filled with fat purple clouds. Most children Caitlyn's age would have created a very two-dimensional scene, but Caitlyn was already demonstrating advanced skills as an artist and she'd infused her drawing with light, shadow, and depth.

"I love it." Olivia smiled at her. "May I keep it?"

Caitlyn nodded, pleased.

"Is your mom here with Anders?" she asked, hoping to catch a glimpse of her nephew, the only baby Olivia had ever wanted to hold.

"She's outside, talking to your friend. The man with the pineapple shirt." Caitlyn waved her arm. "I'll show you."

Rawlings was at a table on the spacious deck overlooking the harbor. He had a frosted pint glass of beer in front of him and was bouncing Anders on his knee. Kim, Olivia's sister-in-law, was gazing at Rawlings indulgently. Seeing Olivia, she stood and gave her a quick hug and said, "Hudson is in a state over something that happened at the food festival today. Would you go back and talk to him when you have a sec?"

Olivia's half brother would be setting up a Bayside Crab House tent at the Coastal Carolina Food Festival the following morning, and Olivia assumed he had an issue with the tent's location or another irksome detail. "Sure. Let me say hello to my handsome nephew first."

Olivia eased Anders from Rawlings' arms. The baby focused his dolphin grey eyes on her and produced a wide, gummy smile. As she drew him close to her chest, he cooed and gurgled. She drank him in, enchanted by his hair, which smelled like sunshine, and his cheeks, which were smooth as peach skin.

Pressing a kiss on her nephew's forehead, Olivia could feel a loosening inside. The solid warmth of her nephew's body lessened the weight of sadness she felt over Willis's death. When Anders reached out to grasp her starfish neck-lace and, finding his aunt's neck bare, went for her shiny earring instead, she kissed his plump wrist, laughing in delight as he kicked his bare feet into space.

"Aren't they a picture?" Kim said to Rawlings.

"Beautiful," the chief replied, his eyes filled with ten-derness.

Olivia looked at him, momentarily wondering if Rawl-ings regretted not having a child of his own, but she pushed the thought aside and smiled at him. "Nice threads," she said, ogling his Hawaiian shirt with amusement.

He glanced down at the yellow and green pineapple print. "Anders likes it."

"Well, that's all that matters," she said and everyone laughed.

The ocean breeze wafted over the tables and rippled the furled sails and mast flags of the boats anchored in the har-bor. Olivia watched them gently bob and sway as shallow waves rolled under their hulls. Gulls perched atop wooden pylons and the sun sank into the water, leaking a wash of orange across the horizon. Diners talked and ate heartily while bluegrass music danced from the speakers. Olivia soaked in the sights and sounds and scents and took strength from them.

Eventually, Anders shoved his fist in his mouth and grew fussy.

"He's hungry," Kim said.

Olivia passed the baby to his mother. "I'll be back to check on Hudson in a minute," she said.

"I'm going to the office to draw." Caitlyn collected her Shirley Temple and then looked at Haviland. "Wanna come?"

Haviland wagged his tail and Olivia knew the poodle would do anything to get closer to the kitchen. She told him to follow Caitlyn and Kim inside and he trotted off, flash-ing the other diners a toothy smile.

Rawlings and Olivia sat in companionable silence, soaking in the tranquility while it lasted.

And it didn't last long. Rawlings had just taken a sip of beer when his pocket buzzed. He pulled out his phone, examined the screen, and frowned.

"What is it?" Olivia asked.

"The deputy texted me the cause of death. He wrote: 'Docs weren't sure. Are calling it arrhythmia. Sister was taken back to her hotel by lady chief.'"

Olivia rubbed her temples. "Arrhythmia? That's twice I've heard that word today. Shelley Giusti's husband died from arrhythmia. What is it exactly?"

"Let me pretend to be Harris." Rawlings typed on his phone's tiny keypad and then squinted in order to read the results. "It's an irregular heartbeat that messes with the heart's electrical signal. Many people have this condition and still lead normal lives, but it can kill healthy people. According to this website, too much stress, exercise, nicotine, or caffeine can cause premature or extra beats. Those throw off the heart's electrical signals."

"Willis smoked like a fiend," Olivia mused quietly. "And his stress levels have probably been elevated since the Foodie Network rolled into town. But he was so young, Rawlings. It seems unbelievable to me that the heart of a twenty-one-year-old kid can just . . . wink out."

Rawlings scrolled his phone screen. "It's not common, but it happens. Oh, wait, here's another text from the deputy. He says Talley's agreed to an autopsy. The doctors want to be sure the cause wasn't genetic."

"They'd like to protect Talley from the same fate." Olivia gazed at the saffron- and persimmon-colored sky. After a moment, she pushed back her chair. "I need a drink. Be right back."

She wove her way around the tables, stepped inside, and walked past the crowded bar and into the kitchen.

Steam billowed in clouds around Hudson's head as he

upended a deep stockpot filled with crab legs into a metal colander. He looked up as Olivia entered, and wiped his hands with a dishtowel. Plucking one of the sous-chefs on the sleeve, he gestured at the crab legs and then led Olivia into the walk-in.

"Hey," Hudson said, always a man of few words.

Olivia gestured at their surroundings in confusion. "Did you really need this level of privacy?" she teased.

Hudson looked at his shoes. "You're going to think I'm crazy as it is. I don't need them to think it too." He jerked his hand in the direction of the bustling kitchen.

Crossing her arms against the cold, Olivia studied her brother. When he wouldn't meet her eyes, her befuddlement changed to concern. "Did something happen at the campground today?"

He nodded but wouldn't speak.

"You went to view the site where The Bayside Crab House tent will be, right?"

Hudson grabbed an orange from the shelf and began to work at its peel. "Yeah, and when I was there I saw . . . I don't know . . . a ghost. A hallucination. I don't know what."

Olivia had been expecting Hudson to say that he'd had an altercation with another vendor or was irate about the tent's location, but his statement took her completely by surprise. Her mouth opened and then closed again.

"It's crazy, but I know that I saw . . ." He began to separate the peel from the fruit in one long curl. He still wouldn't look at her.

"What?" Olivia put her cold hand on his arm and drew a little closer. "What did you see, Hudson? What's got you so rattled?"

He looked at her now, his dark eyes wide and frightened. Her brother, who was tough as nails, was trembling. "I saw him, Olivia. I saw our father."

Chapter 11

*In gambling the many must lose in order that
the few may win.*

—GEORGE BERNARD SHAW

The cold seeped into Olivia's bones. She shook her head in
denial, but the movement did not lessen the chill or
alter the expression on her brother's face.

"That's impossible, Hudson. We watched him die. He's
gone."

"I know!" Hudson growled. "That's why I can't make
sense of it. I thought that if you could . . . arrrrh!" He
slammed his elbow into a cardboard box on the shelf
behind him. "If only you'd seen him too! If only you'd been
there!"

Olivia had seen Hudson this agitated only once before,
when he'd been told that his newborn son had come into
the world with a birth defect and needed emergency heart
surgery. He'd reached out to her then, pleading for her to
intervene on behalf of his family. He was reaching out to
her again now.

Olivia knew that there was nothing fanciful about Hudson Salter. He was devoted to work and family above all
other things. He didn't believe in the supernatural and had

no use for organized religion. Mentions of the hereafter—of angels, spirits, or ghosts—were met with a dismissive grunt.

"Think back on what you saw." Olivia spoke very gently. "Do you really believe that our father's ghost appeared to you at a food festival?"

Hudson rubbed his face with his hands and then balled them into fists. "Listen to me. I *saw* him. He wasn't the same. He was better dressed. Had better hair. Nicer teeth. Maybe ten more pounds of muscle on his bones, but it was him. He looked right at me, Olivia. Felt like he was looking right through me." He took a quick breath. "I was so scared that I dropped my drink. Spilled Dr Pepper all over my shoes, damn it. And I don't scare easy."

"Okay, okay." Olivia held out her hands, hoping to mollify her brother. "There's only one logical explanation. You saw a man who looks so much like Willie Wade that it gave you a genuine shock. Hudson, your reaction to this guy could be some form of grief. Have you been thinking about our father lately?"

Hudson snorted. "Are you kidding? I've got a new baby, a new house, and a new restaurant. The man's barely crossed my mind since I stepped into this kitchen." He examined the orange peel in his fist and then stuffed it into his apron pocket. "I'm not being haunted. I don't believe in that crap. But I know what I saw."

"What do you want from me?" she asked. "How can I help you?"

Her offer seemed to be what Hudson needed. His shoulders relaxed ever so slightly. "Keep your eyes open tomorrow. Maybe you'll see him too and then I won't feel like such a nutcase. If not, then I'll just let it go. It'll take a few days to forget, that's all."

She smiled and squeezed his arm. "I'll be as observant as possible. Promise. Can we get out of here now?"

"Yeah." He pushed open the thick door and then paused.

"Don't mention this to anyone, okay? Especially Kim. She's got enough on her plate."

"I won't," Olivia assured him. "But right now I need to get to the bar. This day seems to be going on forever, and trust me, that's not a good thing."

Now it was Hudson's turn to look concerned. "You wanna tell me about it?"

Olivia hesitated. She wanted to be closer to her brother. They'd made small strides in the right direction, but in many ways, he was still a stranger to her. He was so quiet and reserved that she often found herself talking with Kim and Caitlyn more than with him. He poured all his energy into The Bayside Crab House, and while the restaurant was a safe subject and one they could discuss at length, the half siblings rarely touched on more personal topics. Olivia knew that reviewing menus and supply lists weren't going to help strengthen their bond, so she took a breath and said, "A sous-chef from The Boot Top died today. I was talking to him when he collapsed. I just can't accept what happened. I don't want to believe it."

Hudson didn't say a word. Instead, he pulled her to him and embraced her tightly. It was a brief hug, but Olivia felt renewed by it. When Hudson released her, he said, "The world doesn't always make sense, does it?"

"No," she agreed. "And today, for both of us, it's been especially off kilter."

"Go get that drink," he commanded softly. "And I'll fix you something to eat."

Hudson would try to comfort her by cooking her something special, so even though she wasn't very hungry, she gave him a grateful smile and left the kitchen.

A few minutes later, she returned to the deck area with a tumbler of Chivas Regal in hand. During her brief absence, the rest of the Bayside Book Writers had arrived and were making quick work of an appetizer platter of fried calamari, grilled shrimp wrapped in prosciutto, salmon spring rolls, and mini crab cakes in a curried yogurt sauce. Two pitchers of beer had also materialized and Millay was busy filling pint glasses until the rims were moistened by white foam.

"Are you going to join the commoners or are you sticking with your Scotch?" she asked Olivia, the pitcher hovering over the last glass.

"I'll pass," Olivia said. "I need something stiffer than our local microbrewery can provide."

"The chief told us how Willis died." Harris helped himself to more calamari but ended up staring at his food with a guilty expression. "It seems totally impossible. He was so young."

Olivia didn't want their gathering to turn morose, so she nodded and then gazed expectantly at Laurel. "Any luck with the jug?"

Laurel pulled out her notebook and began flipping through the pages. "One woman thought she'd seen the insect on the high school ring before. She said it wasn't a bee, but she couldn't remember the right name."

"A wasp?" Millay guessed.

"No," Olivia said. "I looked up every high school in the state with a wasp or bee mascot. They don't match the green stone."

Glancing at her notes, Laurel said, "I asked the woman about wasps too. It wasn't the bug she was thinking of."

Rawlings rubbed his chin pensively. "Could it be a hornet?"

"I suppose," Olivia said. "I never checked for a hornet mascot."

Harris took out his phone and gave it a little shake. "You guys keep talking while my fingers do the walking."

Millay rolled her eyes and then focused on Laurel again. "What did people say about Willis?"

"Only good things. In fact, I heard the same descriptions over and over—that Willis was energetic, fun loving, hard working, and devoted to the tribe and his sister."

"Nothing more personal?" Olivia asked in surprise. "Did he have a girlfriend? What happened to his parents?"

Laurel's shoulders slumped. "I tried to find out. Believe me, I did my best to dig deeper, but that's all I got. I know most of the tribe is still in shock, but I didn't hear one silly story from childhood or teenage antics or anything."

"There's something weird about that. Why would people want to paint him in such a perfect light? That's not how I want to be remembered," Millay said, dumping her messenger bag on the table. Beer sloshed over the side of Harris's glass and puddled next to his plate. When he protested, Millay told him to drink faster. She then removed a pad of paper from the bag and tapped her handwritten notes. "There's a reason why everyone knows Willis and Talley. In the tribe, they're, like, famous. They were about to become rich too. In a few weeks, Willis could have told Michel or you to 'take your job and shove it.' Now, Talley will get an even bigger piece of the pie. If the deal goes through, that is." She took a gulp of beer and gazed at her friends through hooded lids, enjoying the moment of suspense.

"Since we know you won't continue until one of us of asks, I'll ask," Rawlings said. "What deal?"

"Willis and Talley own a piece of land that's going to be the future home of the Golden Eagle Resort and Casino." Millay's mouth curved upward into an impish grin. "Forget Vegas, baby. What happens in Lumberton stays in Lumberton."

"A casino?" Laurel was stunned. "Is that even legal?"

Harris held out his finger, signaling that he was in the process of searching for an answer to that very question. He swiped at his phone's screen a few times and then read a dense block of text. "A Cherokee casino in the western part of the state was recently granted permission to have poker tables and to serve alcohol. Before that, they were more like a glorified bingo hall."

"Lumberton's right off I-95," Rawlings said. "Tons of travelers could be lured into a casino."

Millay refilled her empty beer glass. "According to the newspaper article I read, the people from Maxton are totally on board with the whole thing. To them, the Golden Eagle means new jobs, a new life for their town. Right now, Maxton is just some dot on the map. If this casino goes up, they'll have something going for them."

Olivia jumped at the mention of the town's name. "Maxton?" She looked at Rawlings. "Isn't that where the Battle of Hayes Pond took place?"

"Whoa! There's a heavy dose of poetic justice for you." Harris chuckled. "First the Lumbee make the Klan look like the Caped Cowards of Carolina and now—because of legalized gambling—they are going to become the most influential people in Robeson County! Eat your heart out, Sopranos."

Laurel, who'd been writing furiously in her notebook, paused and tapped her lips with her pen. "I can't explain it, but I think Olivia's onto something. There must be a connection between the Locklear family, the Battle of Hayes Pond, and Munin's jug."

"Why? None of the objects link Willis or Talley to Munin," Rawlings argued agreeably. He then looked at Harris. "Did you find a match for that class ring?"

"Oh, yeah, let me go back to that window."

The Bayside Book Writers ate and chatted about their Saturday plans while Harris worked his magic. A pair of waitresses removed the appetizer platters and passed out glasses of ice water and a fresh supply of napkins. They returned carrying dishes loaded with Hudson's specialty: a surf and turf entrée of grilled beef tenderloin and lobster tails served with a side of spicy garlic-shallot butter.

Olivia's friends clapped in delight, but she didn't welcome

the sight of such heavy food. For some reason, the mound of grilled meat made her think of her father and of Hudson's conviction that he'd seen Willie Wade's double walking around the Croatan National Forest.

"This is for you." A waitress placed a dinner plate in front of Olivia. "Hudson made you a lighter entrée. This is a filet of orange roughy in a ginger and scallion sauce with a side of greens."

"Thank you." Olivia smiled at the waitress and then put a forkful of the flaky fish in her mouth and sighed in contentment. The sauce was subtle and soothing and the fish was so tender that it practically melted on her tongue. She imagined Hudson taking pains over her entrée, willing her to be nourished and comforted by his food, and she was. Every bite felt infused by warmth and affection and she was silently grateful for the bizarre chain of events that had brought Hudson Salter into her life.

"Ha!" Harris shouted and brandished his phone in the air. "Here we are. The hornet was the mascot of Littlefield High School in Lumberton." His self-satisfied grin quickly faded as his eyes met Olivia's. "Lumberton again, huh? This can't be coincidence. Munin must have been trying to get across a message about that place, but what was she trying to tell you?"

Rawlings frowned. "You said the hornet *was* the mascot. Why?"

Harris pointed at his phone. "Littlefield stopped being a high school in the nineties. Looks like it became a middle school instead. Kids go to Lumberton High now and their mascot is a nasty-looking pirate. Check it out. He's even got a dagger clamped between his teeth." He titled the screen to allow Millay a glimpse.

"So this ring belongs to someone who graduated from Littlefield when it was still a high school," Olivia said. "Someone who loved his or her school, because giving the ring to Munin would have been a sacrifice."

"Who loves high school?" Harris spluttered. "Hell is made of dental offices and high schools! No offense, Laurel."

She smiled. "None taken. The sound of Steve's drill is worse than nails on a chalkboard." She shuddered in distaste.

Ignoring the exchange between her two friends, Olivia put her fork down and pushed her plate away. She was frustrated. Too many facts cluttered her thoughts. The Lumbee, the KKK, a casino, a class ring, and a young girl left with a valuable inheritance in the form of a desirable parcel of land. The word "inheritance" struck a chord. Where was the rest of Talley's family?

"Millay? What about Willis's and Talley's parents? Did you find anything more specific about them?" Olivia asked.

"Not a thing on the dad. Not even his name," Millay replied. "As for the mom, she apparently died from postsurgery complications."

Olivia stared at her friend. "That's it? There were no more details on what caused her death?"

Millay shrugged. "Most of my info came from old newspaper articles. I tried to hunt around for more on the mom, but all I came up with was a photo of her winning the Miss Lumbee title back in the day. Her name was Natalie Mitchell and she was drop-dead gorgeous." She flinched over her choice of phrase. "I mean, she was smoking hot."

Wondering if Natalie also resembled Munin, Olivia asked Millay if she'd brought a printout of the image.

"I was at the library and the pay-per-page printer was busted." Millay's tone was apologetic.

"Don't worry, I'll look on the computer later. There can't be too many pictures of a Miss Lumbee named Natalie Mitchell," Olivia said.

Laurel dabbed at her mouth with her napkin and checked her watch. "I'd better get going. Steve's parents are watching the boys and they want to be back at their place in time to watch reruns of *30 Rock*."

"Man, I love that show. Alec Baldwin is a genius." Harris glanced at Millay. "Do you want to hang out before your shift starts?"

"Only if you're willing to let me kick your ass again at Don King Boxing," she said and he instantly agreed.

Seeing that their party was breaking up, Olivia experienced a fleeting moment of panic. With her friends gone, she'd also have to go home. There, in the quiet house, she'd throw open all the windows and listen to the murmur of the surf curling into the shore. She'd flop on a deck chair and wait for the moon to climb higher in the indigo sky. And, whether she wanted to or not, she'd picture Willis's face over and over again. She'd see him talking, laughing, gesticulating. And inevitably, she'd relive his fall, the feel of his burning skin, his final whispers.

Pushing the memory aside, she told her friends she'd see them tomorrow night and waved off their attempts to pay for their meals.

Rawlings didn't leave with the others, but his body language betrayed his restlessness. Olivia watched his fingers drum against his beer glass as his gaze flickered between the boats and her face.

"What are you thinking?" she asked him.

"That I'd like to know exactly what happened to Natalie Locklear." He scooted his chair closer to hers and reached for her hand. "I've been trying to piece together a connection all day. I've got nothing and I'm tired, Olivia. The Nick Plumley case wore me out. Wore me down. I can handle petty crime, like women ramming into tourists driving orange Corvettes"—he gave her a sly smile—"but I'm man enough to admit that I'm not ready to see this town and the people I care about torn apart again."

She nodded. She felt fragile too. And now she had Hudson's bizarre vision to add to her list of concerns.

"On the other hand," Rawlings continued, "I think we're being pulled into the middle of something. The coincidences are piling up and you know I don't believe in coincidence. For my own peace of mind, I need to be sure that a healthy, twenty-one-year-old man truly died from accidental causes. I need to read the facts relating to his mother's death. And I want to know everything there is to know about this casino deal."

Olivia ran her fingertips over the knuckles of his hand, tracing the ridges and the fine lines crisscrossing the skin. "Are you going to the station?"

"I am." He finished his last swallow of beer and brought her hand to his cold lips, kissing the soft flesh of her palm. "Will you be all right?"

"I will. I'll talk to you tomorrow." Olivia gave him an encouraging smile as he stood up. She didn't watch him leave, preferring to keep her eyes locked on the sky. All traces of orange and gold were gone, replaced by a luminescent shade of blue purple. A bright star hung just above the tallest boat mast, and Olivia stared at it until fatigue washed over her. Suddenly eager to escape the din of the restaurant, she paid the bill in cash and went inside. Haviland was dozing in the manager's office.

"Home, Captain," she whispered to him. He rose slowly, yawning, and followed her to the Range Rover.

Entering her quiet house, Olivia opened the back door and gave Haviland the go-ahead to run to the beach and revel in the night air. She sat on a deck chair with her MacBook on her lap and searched for a photograph of Natalie Locklear née Mitchell.

It didn't take her long to find a website link devoted to former winners of the Miss Lumbee title. Olivia began scrolling back in time, starting with the full-color image of last year's crown holder, and carefully examined each of the dark-eyed, dark-haired girls. As their photographs passed by, she noted how the straight hair and subtle makeup of the nineties gave way to the highly teased hair and sequined gowns of the eighties. Then the winners from

the seventies appeared, looking younger and more innocent than those from the twenty-first century.

Olivia was discouraged to find that the photos became
grainy and rather out of focus as the years descended. By
the late sixties, the quality was so poor that the girls, with
their long, black hair and white dresses, looked more like
ghosts than beauty queens.

"I must have passed her," Olivia mused aloud and scrolled
the page until she could see the winners from the late seventies again. She found Natalie's picture all the way to the left.

She's a Lumbee Charlie's angel, Olivia thought, studying the girl's feathered hair and shiny lipstick. Her dark
eyes had been rimmed with black eyeliner and were framed
with a sweep of curled lashes. She wore a liberal amount of
blush and her shiny lip gloss captured the light.

Olivia couldn't stop staring at the stunning young woman. Natalie held her chin high and her gaze was both wary
and challenging. She didn't have a beauty queen's smile.
Her face didn't glow like the other girls' and her expression was more serious, conveying a blend of pride, strength,
and determination. She reminded Olivia not of a pageant
princess but of a warrior maiden.

It was easy to see where Talley's good looks had come
from. But while Talley resembled Munin, Natalie did not.
Natalie had a softer mouth, a sharper nose, and a less
intense stare. Perhaps Talley's father was related to Munin.

"How do you fit into this puzzle?" Olivia asked the
beautiful woman wearing a rhinestone tiara. As she stared
at the Natalie of long ago, Haviland bounded up the stairs
to the deck and sniffed at the door. He was ready for bed.

"One more minute," Olivia promised the poodle.

Opening a new window on-screen, she tried to discover
more about Natalie Mitchell both before and after she
became Natalie Locklear, but came up dry. She then searched
for Munin Cooper and struck out. Olivia closed the laptop's
lid with an irritated sigh.

She was too tired to sort through more clues, and the rows of lovely, unlined Lumbee faces on her computer screen made her think of Willis.

As she washed her face and brushed her teeth, Olivia wondered what would have become of Willis had he lived. Would he have stayed at The Boot Top while the casino was being built? Did he dream of becoming the head chef of the Golden Eagle's restaurant? She could easily picture him doing just that—running a kitchen built on the piece of land that had belonged to his family. He might have even incorporated traditional Lumbee dishes into the menu.

After pulling on a soft nightgown and slipping between her crisp, cotton sheets, Olivia ran her fingers through Haviland's curls. Eventually, her eyes closed and her thoughts became random and disjointed. She fell asleep to an image of Talley Locklear holding the cottonmouth puppet aloft, its giant mouth glowing and its long fangs slick with venom.

More than once, Olivia's hand reached out, seeking the comforting warmth of Rawlings' body. And though Haviland slept in a ball by her feet, he could not soothe her when she cried out in the night as oversized serpents and men in white hoods invaded her dreams.

Chapter 12

*All our progress is an unfolding, like the
vegetable bud, you have first an instinct, then
an opinion, then a knowledge, as the plant has
root, bud, and fruit. Trust the instinct to the
end, though you can render no reason.*

—RALPH WALDO EMERSON

Olivia woke to a cloudless, heron blue sky.

After opening the deck doors to invite the sea-
scented air inside, she brewed coffee and transferred four
cups' worth into a small thermos, served Haviland breakfast, and stuck a peach and a granola bar into her backpack.
Pulling her metal detector from the storage closet beneath
the deck, she climbed over the dunes, her fingertips reaching out to touch the tufted heads of the sea oats as she and
Haviland made their way to the water's edge.

Though it hadn't rained for the past few days, the Carolina coast was often hit with an afternoon thunderstorm
during the summer months. Heavy banks of fierce gray
clouds would amass with surprising speed, and within
minutes, a hard rain would fall, pockmarking the sand and
sending people scurrying for cover. Sheets of lightning
would illuminate the sky, and the sound of water falling
from the rooftops and splattering against the roads and
sidewalks was nearly deafening.

But then, as if someone flipped a switch, the storm
would stop. The skies would clear, the sun would reappear,

and the tourists would breathe a sigh of relief. These brief storms kept the gardens of Oyster Bay green from March until November. They also stirred up the ocean, coaxing the sand from the lightless bottom to roil and shift. Other things would move then too. Shells, seaweed, trash, and trinkets would become dislodged from the wet sand's possessive grasp and find their way onshore.

There were dozens of treasure hunters in Oyster Bay, but Olivia had a stretch of beach virtually to herself. She owned a significant portion of the spit of land called Tern's Point. The other residents were older couples who rarely ventured over the uneven dunes, so she usually had the run of the beach.

Today, Olivia was happily alone again. With the exception of a few scuttling crabs and waterfowl, the shoreline was deserted. She walked until the lighthouse shrank behind her and then switched on her Bounty Hunter Discovery 3300. Adjusting the headphones, she slowed her pace and listened to the device's familiar clicks, whirrs, and beeps.

The mechanical conversation was one-sided, but Olivia found it comforting. For an hour, she could shut out the rest of the world and focus on the warmth of the sun on her shoulders, the kiss of the breeze on her face, and the flashes from her metal detector's display.

She was just about to stop for a breakfast break when the machine alerted her to the presence of precious metal. Easing her pack to the ground, she removed a sieve and a trench shovel and called for Haviland.

"Time to dig, Captain!"

The poodle bounded out of the surf, shook himself thoroughly, and trotted over to join Olivia.

According to her Bounty Hunter, the metal object wasn't buried deep, so she only dug out a few shovelfuls of sand before using her hands to scoop piles of it into the sieve. Haviland, who was well trained in the art of searching for small items, dug slowly and deliberately with his front paws, pausing every now and then to sniff the edges of the expanding hole.

Less than ten minutes later, something rattled around in the sieve.

"What do we have here?" Olivia asked, brushing the sand away from surface of a thumbnail-sized piece of yellow gold. Unable to recognize the shape, she walked to the water, bent down, and washed off her find.

"Looks like a pendant," she told Haviland, drawing the piece of jewelry closer to her face. An androgynous, curly haired angel reached its arms out to hold on to a sphere. The top of the sphere was fashioned into a loop, but the pendant's chain was no longer attached.

Olivia ran her fingertip over the cherublike child's face and then realized that a second pair of hands was fastened to the sphere. These hands were identical to the first, and she assumed that another angel, a mirror image of the first, had broken off.

Wondering if the pendant had belonged to best friends, sisters, or a pair of twins, Olivia studied the lone angel, feeling inexplicably sad that it had lost its other half.

Sighing, she slipped the piece of jewelry into her pocket and took the peach out of her backpack. Returning the trench shovel and sieve to the bag, she switched the metal detector off, and turned toward home.

The peach was ripe and delicious. She bit into it and sticky juice ran down her chin. For a moment, the fruit's sweetness was marred as Olivia thought about Willis Locklear and how he would never eat a peach again. He wouldn't walk on the beach or see a sunset or dive into the cool water. Such simple pleasures were beyond his reach.

Olivia wallowed in these morbid thoughts until she stepped into the shadow cast by the lighthouse. She looked at the cozy keeper's cottage and remembered that she hadn't finished editing Sawyer's chapter, which would be up for review that evening.

Shoving the granola bar into her pocket, she turned to Haviland and said, "I'd rather have blueberry pancakes anyway. Are you up for breakfast at Grumpy's?"

Haviland barked his assent and Olivia had no doubt that the poodle was envisioning a plate piled high with plump sausages and thick strips of bacon.

Without bothering to change out of her loose linen pants or faded navy T-shirt, Olivia drove into town and skillfully maneuvered the Range Rover into a tight spot between two minivans. Commandeering her favorite window booth, she took her laptop from its case and waved at Dixie.

Dixie skated over, her purple and blue tutu bobbing like a buoy. She kissed Haviland on the nose and then gave Olivia an assessing stare. "You've got bags under your eyes. Good Lord, 'Livia, tell the chief to ease off a bit. You gotta get *some* sleep!"

"I was alone last night, thank you very much," Olivia growled. "How about some coffee?"

"Right away, your highness," Dixie retorted and zipped off, her tutu flouncing in indignation. Haviland watched her disappear into the kitchen, his mouth curved into a smile and his eyes hopeful.

When Dixie returned carrying a carafe of her wonderful coffee and a clean mug, Olivia apologized to her friend. "I'm all out of sorts because of what happened yesterday, but I shouldn't take it out on you. Did you hear about Willis Locklear?"

Dixie perked up immediately. There was nothing she liked better than a fresh piece of gossip. "Don't know the name. Should I?"

Adding a splash of cream to her coffee, Olivia watched the white liquid spiral outward, lightening the deep brown to a warm shade of tan. She told Dixie everything and her friend listened without interrupting or paying the slightest heed to the couple in the *Tell Me on a Sunday* booth who had pushed their empty plates to the edge of the table, signaling their desire to pay for their meals and leave.

"Ah, hon." Dixie made a sympathetic face. "You can't seem to catch a break. Maybe you and your man should take a little trip. Get out of here for a spell."

"Because death follows me?" Olivia asked. She'd meant to sound glib, but her near whisper betrayed her anxiety.

Dixie swatted at her with the dishtowel she kept in her apron pocket. "No, 'Livia! Because once trouble comes around, you can't walk away from it. I know you love this place—every buildin' and dock and grain of sand, but enough already. Let go for a bit. You're wound tighter than a fishin' reel."

Olivia had to admit that the idea of driving to the mountains and holing up in a cabin with Sawyer had its appeal. She could imagine spending hours in a rocking chair with a good book. Or she and Sawyer could both work on their novels while Haviland pursued a host of woodland animals.

"None of this mess happened in Oyster Bay, so there's a limit to how much I can be involved." She gave Dixie a reassuring smile. "But forget about all that, I'd do anything for a plate of Grumpy's blueberry pancakes."

Dixie nodded. "I'll put in two orders. Millay's crossin' the street and she looks as wrung out as you do." She leaned down and whispered to Haviland, "And I won't forget a tasty morsel for you, you handsome devil."

Haviland licked her hand in a show of gratitude.

Olivia looked out the window and grinned. Millay was standing on the double yellow line, glaring at the oncoming motorists until they stopped and waved her across the lane. Dressed in a lime green miniskirt, a black AC/DC T-shirt, and her trademark patent leather knee-high boots, the black-haired bartender certainly stood out among the crowd of tourists and locals.

Shoving the diner door open, Millay slid into the vacant

seat in the window booth, grabbed Olivia's coffee cup, and without waiting for permission, drank the entire contents in several gulps. Slamming the cup down, she looked around for Dixie.

"Rough night?" Olivia asked, trying not to grin.

"I didn't sleep much." Millay touched a strand of hair dyed the same lime green as her skirt. "But I know who wrote that poem we found in Willis's bag."

Olivia caught Dixie's eye and held up her empty coffee cup. Dixie winked and then handed the disgruntled *Tell Me on a Sunday* couple take-out boxes containing pecan pie and assured them she was terribly sorry for having kept them waiting. The couple walked out of the diner wearing satisfied smiles.

Millay unfolded a piece of paper and pushed it across the table. "The poem's called 'My Lost Youth.' It's by Henry Wadsworth Longfellow. Apparently, he was a master of metaphor and this piece is chock full of them. I read an analysis on this website for English geeks, and Longfellow was supposedly writing about this idyllic place near the sea, where a boy could be happy and totally carefree. So part of the poem is like this golden childhood memory. Longfellow is celebrating a boy's ability to imagine and dream, and then the War of 1812 comes along and changes everything."

Scanning the first two stanzas, Olivia quickly became absorbed in Longfellow's coastal imagery. As one who'd grown up alongside the sea, she admired the poet's ability to evoke its beauty and mystery. "Anything else?"

"At the end, the speaker or whatever he's called, wants to go back in time and capture his lost youth, but of course he can't. He hears this song he's heard since he was a boy and it tells him that his childhood has passed him by. It feels sad to me, like he really misses who he once was."

"The verses Willis had in his bag described him well," Olivia said, moving her gaze to the seventh stanza. "The line that says the song will sing on and never be still. Willis was like that. He was so full of life, so full of energy. But now that I'm reading the whole poem, that line feels negative. Like the song is a restless spirit. A ghost that can't find peace." Her hands curled around the edge of the paper and she swallowed hard. She wanted to rip it to shreds, but that would do nothing but relieve her of a fraction of her anger.

Millay sighed in relief when Dixie skated over with the coffee carafe and an extra mug. "Your food will be out in a sec." She held up a warning finger and wagged it at Millay. "And don't tell me you're not hungry, missy. Your face is almost as green as your hair. You need to fill up that flat belly and get some pink in your cheeks."

"I hate pink," Millay grumbled.

Dixie covered her ears in mock horror and zipped off to the kitchen.

Olivia poured coffee for Millay and refilled her own cup. "Did you research this after giving up on sleep?"

"Yep."

Olivia studied her friend. "Were you upset about Willis?"

Millay was quiet for a long time. She sipped her coffee and gazed out the window. Without turning to face Olivia, she began to speak softly, almost inaudibly. "What happened to Munin really got to me. I didn't even know her, so it doesn't make sense, but this stuff with the KKK makes me so angry I can't see straight . . ." She drew in a deep breath. "Look at me. I'm a mutt. A potpourri of races." She snorted. "That will be the only time you'll hear me use the word potpourri in a sentence."

Sensing she needed encouragement, Olivia said, "Do you think Munin was an outcast? Do you identify with that?"

At first, she didn't think Millay would reply, but she finally met Olivia's eyes and nodded. "Do you know what it was like to be in a southern school with my skin tone, my eye shape, and my hair color? Harris had it right when he said high school was hell."

Olivia was stunned. "But you're gorgeous. You could be on the cover of any beauty magazine. Are you telling me that being exotic caused you pain?"

"Yeah, and you nailed the reason why. Exotic isn't in when you're a teenager. Tall, blond, bouncy, and white is in. I've been called everything from a gook to a spick to a towel head. Those dumb-ass bitches in my school actually thought I was Middle Eastern. To them, anything different was bad. Worthy of punishment. I got notes in my locker, had people get up and move if I sat at their lunch table, and heard my name whispered seconds before the whole class bust out laughing. This lasted for four years. I wasn't invited to parties, I had no date for the prom, for homecoming, for anything. That's why I ended up with older guys. They didn't seem to mind that my skin was the color of café au lait or that I could curse in Filipino. Of course, my being with those men provided the blondies with fresh fodder. They added 'slut' to my long list of flattering nicknames."

"That's awful, Millay," Olivia said. After her grand-mother had whisked her away from Oyster Bay and placed her in an elite boarding school, Olivia found herself on the social fringes too. In the eyes of both the teachers and stu-dents, a family's lineage carried the upmost importance, so when it became known that Olivia's father was a lowly fish-erman, her classmates excluded her from activities and complained about the presence of rotten fish odor when-ever she was around.

She shared this with Millay. "I guess that's why we get along," Olivia said to her friend.

"And I guess that's why we write." Millay moved her coffee cup to make room for platters of blueberry pancakes and sausage and watched as Dixie put a dish of eggs scram-bled with ground sirloin on the floor for Haviland.

"Get that down your throats, gals," Dixie ordered and skated over to the *Cats* booth.

Olivia doctored her pancakes with butter and syrup and

then began to cut them up into bite-sized pieces. "After I finish critiquing Rawlings' chapter, I'm going to call the Locklears' attorney. I'd like to see if there's anything I can do for Talley, but I also want to find out more about their family. Especially Natalie. And then I'll track down the Lumbee chief. If there were any hate crimes directed toward her people, she'd know."

Millay swallowed a mouthful of sausage. "The chief's a woman? That is so cool. But why would she tell you anything? You're a total stranger."

"True, but I have a feeling that Munin wasn't. I'll use the memory jug as my ice breaker if need be."

The two friends finished breakfast in silence. Lost in their own thoughts, they watched townsfolk and tourists pass by the window, looking carefree and unhurried on the picture-perfect late summer morning.

"I'm going to bounce," Millay said, gazing forlornly into her empty coffee cup. "Now that my stomach's full, I'm turning into a zombie. It's nap time." She reached down and gently scratched behind Haviland's ears.

"Go to bed," Olivia said. "I'll call you if there's any news."

"Just let me know when you're heading out to the festival. I'll come with. And I know Harris and Laurel want to go too, so we might as well go green and carpool." She gestured at her skirt and Olivia laughed.

Every man in the diner turned to watch Millay's departure. Olivia knew that Millay believed she drew stares because of her Goth clothing, facial piercings, and dyed hair, but she could do nothing to obscure her unique beauty.

Olivia briefly reflected on the damage teenagers were capable of inflicting upon one another and then pulled Rawlings' chapter from her bag. Millay's chapter was up next for the group critique, but Rawlings had asked Olivia to take a peek at his if she had the time. Since she'd already finished with Millay's, she'd been happy to oblige.

She flipped through pages in which the protagonist, an

eighteen-year-old boy named Pete, was in danger of failing his second semester of college because he spent too much time researching North Carolina's most infamous pirates. Pete's grandfather had spent a lifetime collecting books, maps, and documents about Blackbeard, and on his death-bed, had whispered to Pete about buried treasure. No one had listened the old man. They thought he'd squandered his savings on a fruitless hunt. He was pathetic. Pitiful. And thanks to Alzheimer's, his family also believed he'd gone completely mad by the end.

But not Pete. At least not after he'd unearthed an old captain's log in his grandfather's dinghy describing a spe-cific location along the banks of the Neuse River. Accord-ing to legend, a small cache of Blackbeard's gold had been buried under "Teach's Oak," near this spot.

Olivia had read up to the part in which Pete was perus-ing the diary of a young woman who'd almost been seduced by Edward Teach, aka Blackbeard, beneath a massive oak tree. As she continued with the chapter, she scribbled notes in the margin. Rawlings was treading a fine line between writing a novel and a history text. At some points, the voice sounded too young and at others, too mature. She wanted to circle specific passages, but found that she couldn't focus on Pete or Edward Teach anymore.

With a waitress's keen sixth sense, Dixie suddenly ap-peared, cleared the table, and placed the check next to Olivia's coffee cup. "Where you headin' next? You've got that look. The one that says, 'Don't mess with me. I'm on a mission.'"

Taking her phone and wallet out of her purse, Olivia said, "I'm going to track down the Lumbee chief and Wil-lis's lawyer. I've got questions for both of them."

"Is *your* chief comin' along?"

Olivia hesitated. "No. They might not talk openly in front of him. But the rest of the Bayside Book Writers want to tag along and that's fine by me. We work well as a team."

Dixie put her hands together in a gesture of prayer. "A miracle has just occurred in my diner! Olivia Limoges would rather be with her friends then go it alone." She swiveled on her skates and shouted, "Praise Jesus!"

A few customers echoed her sentiment and then turned back to their food. Scowling, Olivia slapped a few bills on the table and stood up.

"Come on, Haviland. We'll make our calls from the car. We wouldn't want to interrupt Dixie's moment of rapture."

Dixie's theatrical cries of "It's a miracle!" and "Hallelujah!" followed her all the way outside.

Thirty minutes later, with every seat in the Range Rover occupied, Olivia headed to a coffee shop in the town of Havelock. Fletcher had graciously invited her to join him, Judson, and Annette Stevens at a place called Uncommon Grounds before they all returned to the powwow.

Leaving Haviland in the car, the Bayside Book Writers exchanged determined glances and entered the small café.

Olivia wasn't interested in more coffee, but for the sake of appearances she ordered a café au lait and then introduced her friends to Fletcher and Judson, ignoring the baffled look on the senior attorney's face.

"We're quite a party now, aren't we?" he said, recovering quickly. He pulled a vacant table over and gestured at a black-haired, middle-aged woman with a round face and dark, intelligent eyes. "This is the Honorable Tribal Chair Annette Stevens."

The woman shook hands with Olivia. "Most people call me Annette." She indicated the empty seat beside her. "Please, join us."

Olivia sat down and Annette openly studied her. "I hear you were with Willis when he . . . fell."

"Yes," Olivia replied softly. She cupped her hands around her warm mug. "How is Talley?"

"I stayed in her room at the Hampton Inn last night." Annette shook her head sorrowfully. "She can't accept that he's gone. To tell you the truth, none of us can. Who could have foreseen something like this happening? Willis was full of life. He had so much to look forward to."

"Like selling his land?" Olivia asked, fully aware that she was being crass.

Laurel jumped in. "I heard about the Golden Eagle deal through a colleague. I'm a reporter." She gave Annette a disarming smile. "It must be really exciting for your tribe. For the whole town of Maxton."

A flicker of alarm crossed Annette's face before she pasted on a politician's smile and said, "It will certainly give our local economy a boost."

"How did two kids younger than me end up with all that land?" Harris asked, sounding completely innocent.

Annette and Fletcher exchanged a brief, anxious look. Judson fidgeted with an empty sugar packet, twisting it with his fingers while he kept his eyes fixed on his coffee cup.

"The land belonged to their father, Bo Locklear," Fletcher said after a pregnant pause. "Land has always been treasured by the Lumbee Nation. But until Annette came along and made sure the tribe was recognized by the federal government, there was no hope of opening a casino. Now, thanks to her efforts, things are about to change for the better."

"I'm not surprised that a woman finally forced the politicians to pull their heads out of their asses," Millay said. "I hope Talley is as tough as you."

Annette rewarded her with a smile. "I believe she is. In fact, she insists on dancing this afternoon. She said that she needs to be onstage and that Willis would want her to perform, but right now, she's still asleep. She finally took the sleeping pills the doctor gave her."

"Willis told me that she planned to sell crafts this weekend as well," Olivia said. "What will happen to her booth?"

"I don't know," Annette said. "Frankly, I hadn't thought about that."

"We can run it for her," Laurel offered. "We'd love to do something to help."

My friends are much slier than I realized, Olivia thought, smiling inwardly.

"That would be really nice," Annette said. "Talley is proud of her baskets and rightfully so. She does some of the most intricate weaving I've ever seen."

"Maybe you can find something for your house, Harris," Millay said. "Add a splash of color to all those drab grays and browns."

Harris turned to Judson. "Every woman I know wants to mess with my bachelor pad. Last week, my mom mailed me curtains. *Gingham* curtains."

Judson's laugh sounded forced.

Fletcher asked if anyone wanted a refill and, receiving no takers, got up to order another Café Americano.

"You want them?" Harris continued bantering with Judson as if he hadn't noticed the tension in the air. "Just write down your address and I'll box them up for you."

"I practically live at the office," Judson said. "The glamorous life of a paralegal. I only go home to eat and sleep. If I have any free time, I spend it volunteering at an animal clinic. I like to walk the dogs."

Olivia tried to sound apologetic. "Oh, I assumed you and Fletcher were partners."

Judson shrugged. "I could barely afford community college, let alone law school. Fletcher was groomed to run his daddy's practice, while the only thing I inherited from my parents was a pile of debt. Anyway, Fletcher doesn't treat me like I don't count just because I don't have a bunch of framed diplomas over my desk. He was more interested in where I was going than where I came from. He's a great guy."

"And you work harder than a dozen lawyers put together."

Annette gave Judson an affectionate pat with her right hand. And that's when Olivia noticed the chief's ring.

It was gold and had a bright green stone and block letters encircling the stone.

Olivia leaned over to sip from her coffee cup and stole a glance at the lettering. She could see only the first half of the school's name, but it was enough.

The tribal chair had gone to Littleton High.

Her ring matched the one on the memory jug.

Thinking furiously on how to broach the subject, Olivia watched Fletcher return to the table. He didn't sit, but tore open a sugar packet and poured it into a take-out cup.

Olivia nearly gasped when she noticed the wink of gold on his right hand.

Fletcher Olsen also wore a class ring from Littleton High.

It's like we've stumbled on some secret society, Olivia thought, recalling the strange looks passing between Annette and Fletcher. The tension in Judson's fingertips. *But what do they want to keep secret?*

Chapter 13

The heart will break, but broken live on.

—LORD BYRON

"We'd better move along," Fletcher said. He hadn't returned to his seat after getting his refill and his closed expression made it clear that he wasn't interested in prolonging their conversation.

Annette quickly agreed. "Yes, there's so much to do before the parade begins."

"If I could just ask you both one more question," Olivia said. "It concerns the Battle of Hayes Pond. Willis told me that the Lumbee will be celebrating their victory at today's powwow. Is that right?"

The chief's shoulders relaxed and she smiled proudly. "We certainly are. There'll be storytelling, dancing, and we're presenting special medals to the tribe members who were there that day."

"Wow," Harris breathed. "I'd love to watch that."

"I was curious about the tribe's interaction with the Klan in the years following that event," Olivia continued as if Harris hadn't spoken. "But when I broached the subject with Willis, he got very quiet. It seemed to upset him. Can you tell me why?"

Judson raised a finger. "I can. After his mom died, Willis became the head of the family. Talley was still in high school and Willis was taking classes at Robeson Community College when their house was vandalized." He stopped, clearly unwilling to elaborate, but Millay wasn't going to let him off that easy.

"What was it? Graffiti? Racial slurs?"

Fletcher put a hand on Judson's shoulder and the paralegal immediately fell silent. "Oh, it was more like baseball bats to the mailbox and that sort of thing," the attorney said breezily. "Probably a bunch of kids testing their limits. They'll do anything to be on YouTube. Now, if you don't mind, we need to get going."

"Of course." Olivia stood up. "I hope you'll forgive me for prying. It's just bothering me that I might have contributed to Willis's stress level yesterday by bringing up the KKK." She lowered her voice. "He looked scared when I mentioned the subject. Like he'd been recently frightened. Was he being threatened? Was someone out to do him harm?"

Fletcher's mouth drew into a tight line. "Are you suggesting murder?"

Annette sucked in a quick breath, her eyes going wide. "That's ridiculous. We know what happened to him!"

Olivia couldn't help but wonder why Fletcher had brought up the idea of murder, but now that he had, the word hung in the air like a thundercloud, robbing the space of light and conversation.

The chief put both hands on the table and pushed herself out of her chair. With trembling fingers, she reached for the purse hanging from the back of her chair. Catching it by one handle, she tipped it forward and its contents spilled out onto the hardwood floor.

"Let me help you." Laurel jumped out of her seat and began to pick up pens, a glasses case, a set of keys, and a tin of mints. "What time should we meet you at Talley's booth?"

An orange pill bottle rolled under Olivia's chair. She bent over and closed her fingers around it. Giving the label a cursory glance, she saw the name "A. Stevens" and the word "olanzapine" before returning the bottle to Annette.

"No more caffeine for me today." Annette issued a hollow laugh and handed Laurel a sheet of paper. "This is a map of the booths. I circled Talley's. The woman selling quilts in the next booth has Talley's petty cash box and receipt book. She'll fill you in on what to do. Thank you for your help."

Abandoning his take-out cup, Fletcher took the chief by the elbow and steered her to the exit. Judson trailed behind, looking more like a penitent child than a man in his fifties.

"That went well," Millay said after they'd gone.

"You're being sarcastic, right?" Laurel asked and then turned to Olivia. "What were those pills, Olivia? The ones Annette had in her purse?"

Olivia made a hurry-up gesture at Harris. "Can you look up the name before I forget it?"

He whipped out his phone. "Hit me."

She spelled the drug and Harris found a useful result within seconds.

"It's prescribed for people with bipolar disorder," he said, raising his brows. "The chief's taking an antipsychotic?"

Olivia shrugged. "I can't say for sure. The label did say A. Stevens."

Millay tugged on Harris's sleeve. "What does it do? The drug?"

"It's basically a mood stabilizer."

"Do you think this is relevant?" Laurel asked. "To Willis or Munin or anything?"

"I don't know," Olivia admitted. "But both Annette and Fletcher were wearing rings from Littleton High."

"I noticed that too!" Harris exclaimed proudly. "Their graduation years are safely stored in my massive brain.

Now we just have to see if they match the year on the ring on the memory jug."

Laurel bit her lip. "That means breaking it, doesn't it?"

Ignoring her, Olivia's gazed into the middle distance. "Why did Fletcher raise the possibility that Willis didn't die because of an arrhythmia?" She blinked and turned to Harris. "What are the side effects of this olanzapine stuff?"

Harris squinted as he read the tiny font on screen. "There's the usual list: dizziness, restlessness, drowsiness, dry mouth, weight gain, constipation, and lack of sex drive." He elbowed Millay. "Bummer, huh?"

Millay said, "Depends on who your sex partner is."

"Go on," Olivia said impatiently.

"Okay. According to this website, there's a chance that these meds can cause something called neuroleptic malignant syndrome. This can result in some super fun symptoms like muscle rigidity, high fever, irregular pulse rate, sweating, and irregular heartbeat." He pushed out his chest. "Man, I feel like Dr. House."

Olivia didn't hear his last comment. She'd gone back in time to the previous day and was kneeling beside Willis again, feeling his fever-hot skin and the strange tautness of his arm muscles.

"So the official cause of death was an irregular heartbeat." Laurel's voice shook a little. "But what if someone . . . ?" She trailed off, looking at her friends. No one completed her thought.

Harris shoved his phone back into his pocket. "We'd better talk to Rawlings. If we're considering the possibility that Willis was murdered, he needs to know."

"I agree, but whatever went down—and I'm not sure anything did—it went down outside his jurisdiction," Millay said. "He can't walk around the campground interrogating people."

"Maybe not," Harris replied. "But I'd rather be investigating with the chief than selling baskets. There might be a killer on the loose." He hesitated. "Then again, there might not be. We have no idea what's going on."

Laurel opened her notebook. "So far, I've got these key words written down: Munin, KKK, Lumbee, Locklear deaths, land deal. We still need a better picture of the Locklear family."

Olivia's phone buzzed. She examined the new text message and touched Laurel on the shoulder. "We're about to learn all there is to know. Rawlings is waiting for us at the Cedar Point campground entrance with a folder's worth of info on the Locklears. And we've got our own news to share with him."

Millay held out her hand. "Don't back out of the parking lot just yet. If I have to stay awake for the rest of the day *and* have our meeting tonight, then I'm gonna need a double espresso." She looked thoughtful. "And maybe a six-pack of Red Bull."

Rawlings was pacing around the campground entrance when the rest of the Bayside Book Writers arrived. Olivia carried the memory jug in her arms, eschewing the crate and dolly. Even though the bubble wrap stuck to her warm skin, the press of the jug's curve against her chest and stomach felt good. She liked being able to hold on to something solid, especially when her thoughts seemed as vaporous as fog.

"There's a picnic table down this trail to the left," Rawlings said after greeting his friends. "It'll give us the privacy we need."

Her curiosity piqued, Olivia tried to elicit information from the chief as they walked, but he wouldn't say a word until they were away from the rest of the public. Haviland jogged by the chief's side and gazed up at him with smiling eyes.

"I don't know what you fed him yesterday," Olivia said, pointing at her poodle, "but he's obviously hoping for more."

"That's a secret between us guys." Rawlings gave Haviland an affectionate pat.

The moment they reached the picnic table, Rawlings' demeanor abruptly changed. His body stiffened and his shoulders and jaw tightened as he transformed from friend and fellow writer into Oyster Bay's chief of police. Opening a manila folder, he pulled off his sunglasses and focused on the top sheet of a thick stack of papers. "You know this already, but let me just review it. Natalie Locklear died from complications that arose during surgery. She slipped and fractured a bone in her leg and died on the operating table."

"Does that report list her symptoms?" Olivia gestured at the file folder. "'Complications' is a vague term."

"Not in much detail," Rawlings answered and looked at Olivia. "Why are you interested in her symptoms?"

Olivia told him about Annette Stevens' prescription.

"That's troublesome," he mumbled.

Laurel took her notebook out. "What happened to Mr. Locklear?"

Rawlings searched for another piece of paper in his file. "Car accident. He was driving under the influence and plowed into a tractor-trailer. The truck driver wasn't injured, but Bo Locklear died upon impact. Willis and Talley would have been fairly young when this happened. They probably don't remember him much, if at all."

"This is a seriously unlucky family," Harris pointed out.

Millay sighed in exasperation. "Come on. Do you actually think the Locklears are cursed? That Munin was a real witch who had a set of Locklear family voodoo dolls? Or *maybe*"—she tapped her chin, her voice dripping with sarcasm—"these *unlucky* deaths have something to do with the piece of land they own?"

"I spent half the night trying to put together a picture of this family," Rawlings said. "Therefore, I don't have much info on the land. But I can tell you this much. Grandpa

Calvin Locklear never married. And when Bo was five years old, Calvin disappeared. He just up and vanished and no one ever heard from him again. Bo was raised in another county by a childless Lumbee couple. Right before he disappeared, Calvin bought a piece of land and eventually Bo came back to Maxton to live on it." He tapped the stack of papers. "That's not all, folks. No matter how hard I looked, I couldn't find a birth record for Bo that listed his mother's name. The Locklear family really is shrouded in mystery."

"Weird." Laurel was about to add to her sentence when the sounds of drums and a chant of "Go, Diego, go!" emitted from her cell phone. "The boys picked my ringtone." She said, looking at the incoming caller's number. "This is a colleague of mine from the *Robesonian*. I asked him to check into the casino deal. Ugh, I only have one bar." Grabbing her notebook while answering her phone, she edged toward the main path, and then stopped, listening raptly. Two minutes later, she rejoined her friends.

"Whatchya got, Brenda Starr?" Millay asked.

"Lots. The land once belonged to the Dawson family. They ran a large, successful farm for many years, but fell on hard times in the early sixties and ended up selling the acreage and the house to Calvin Locklear for less than its appraised value. Here's the kicker." Laurel's light blue eyes were dancing with excitement. "The Dawsons received offers from two other local parties prior to the sale. The Olsen and Stevens families."

Harris ran his hands through his ginger-colored hair. "I need one of those Red Bulls just to keep up with all of this."

Rawlings ticked off the names on his fingers. "Locklears, Olsens, Dawsons, Stevenses. What's the connection? And why would the Dawsons undersell their land? With no income, they'd have to live on the money from the sale of their farm for years to come."

"There's more." Laurel paused to make sure she had their full attention. "My guy at the *Robesonian* heard rumors about Calvin. Said everyone was shocked when he bought the Dawson farm. Turns out he never got the chance to live there because he took off with another man's wife. The farm was abandoned until Bo came of age and moved in."

Millay winced. "That had to piss the Dawsons off. They sold their place only to see it go to pot? Ouch."

Laurel nodded. "Now fast forward another fifteen years and you've got Bo carrying his new wife Natalie over the threshold. According to the Robeson County rumor mill, the marriage was doomed from the start. Bo was lazy and Natalie was a go-getter. And even though they had two kids together, they were always fighting over money and how badly Bo ran the farm. Natalie actually seemed happier after Bo's death."

"Was anyone in that family normal?" Millay thumped the table in frustration. "We need to talk to Talley. If the lady chief and that smooth-talking lawyer have anything to hide, they won't tell us a damn thing. Maybe they want the land to themselves—to make up for their families not getting it the first time. Who knows? Talley could be feeling scared and alone. I want to make sure she's okay."

Olivia put a hand on Millay's arm. She knew that her friend was having a strong reaction to the possibility that a young woman of color was being targeted and that this same young woman had no family to protect her. "I think we should talk to her too, but she's probably still at the hotel. We'll have to be patient."

Millay crossed her arms over her chest and sulked. For a moment, she looked like a vulnerable child.

"Let's find her booth and get to work. She's bound to stop by eventually," Harris suggested and then turned to Rawlings. "We volunteered to sell her baskets for a while."

"Good," Rawlings said. "You can put the memory jug on display."

"Wouldn't that be awesome?" Harris asked quietly, his hand resting on the bubble wrap enveloping the piece of pottery. "If someone just walked by and said, 'Hey, this must be one of Munin Cooper's pieces. Yeah, I know her. We go way back. Want me to tell you about all the objects on this jug?'"

"Dream on," Millay murmured and the group headed toward the main path.

Once again, the smell of fried food wafted through the trees. Haviland raised his nose, his nostrils flaring in interest. Laurel consulted the vendor map and led the Bayside Book Writers past tables of dream catchers, wood carvings, leather bags, etched copper jewelry, dolls, yarn hair accessories, bead medallions, pottery, and paintings of Lumbee in ceremonial costume. Next to a tent filled with a rainbow of quilts was Talley's stall.

The first of Talley's works to catch Olivia's eye was a large hearth basket. It had been woven with reeds dyed a rich, forest green and was sturdy enough to hold several pounds of kindling. She picked it up and examined the tight weaving.

"These are cool," Millay said, pointing at a berry basket decorated with pink reed strawberries growing from a vine of pale green reed tendrils.

"Thanks." Both women turned to find Talley standing behind them. "That berry basket's my bestseller. I don't make enough profit to cover the hours of work these things take, but it's what I do at night while I'm watching TV." She looked down at Haviland. "Hey, sweetie."

Haviland moved forward, inviting her touch, and Talley seemed grateful to be able to run both hands through his fur.

Olivia glanced over her shoulder, relieved to see that Harris, Rawlings, and Laurel had paused at a booth across the aisle. Rawlings was showing the jug to an old man whose mouth was filled with a plug of chewing tobacco.

"Who taught you how to do this?" Millay asked Talley,

pivoting the berry basket. She pointed at the taut under-side. "If you told me it was watertight, I'd believe you."

Talley rewarded Millay with a small smile, but there was no trace of pleasure in her eyes. They were filled with shadows instead. Gone was the radiance that had animated her features during yesterday's performance. Now her skin was dull and her face was puffy from sedative-induced sleep. Her hair fell down her back in tangled, unwashed strands and her nails had been chewed until they'd bled.

"My mom had lots of talent," Talley said in a low, frag-ile voice. "She had my brother and me doing all kinds of things by the time we were ten. We could sew, weave, chop wood, do our own laundry, and cook. Willis was way bet-ter than me in the kitchen but I had him on log splitting. Mine would go right down the middle every time." Her eyes had grown glassy and Olivia knew Talley was miles and years away from them.

"Talley," she whispered, gently pulling the young woman away from her memories. "We're so sorry about Willis. My friend Millay and I have come to work in your booth today. Is that all right?"

She looked lost. "I don't know. What would I do then? I need to keep busy until the dancing starts or I'll . . . I'll . . ." She put her hands out in a gesture of helplessness.

"I understand," Olivia assured her. "Why don't you show us how to write receipts?"

Relieved to be able focus on her business, Talley showed Olivia and Millay where she kept the cash box, receipt book, and shopping bags. She then dug an inhaler out of her purse and gave herself a quick dose of medicine.

"The air's terrible today," she murmured. "It'll be tough to dance later."

While festivalgoers looked over the baskets, Millay sat next to Talley in a folding chair at the back of the booth. "I wish I could make something that reflected my cultural heritage," Millay said. "Both my parents are from mixed-race families, so they could have shown me all kinds of things, but they never did." She continued to hold the berry basket in her hands. "This must feel so good. It's like a cord tying you to generations of Lumbee."

Talley nodded. "I don't know what my life would have been like if I didn't have my people. We take care of each other. That's why I couldn't stay away today. I need this. I need *them*."

Seeing Talley choke up, Millay grabbed the younger woman's hand and squeezed. "It's okay," she murmured. "I've got you."

The booth suddenly became crowded with customers, and soon all three women were too busy collecting money and putting baskets into shopping bags to talk.

After they'd sold half a dozen baskets, Talley turned to Millay. "Do you have brothers and sisters?"

Millay shook her head. "Nope. No tough guys to stand up for me or an older sister to warn me how nasty the other girls were going to be because I look different." She paused. "Speaking of different, we met your chief this morning. She seems like a very cool chick."

Talley nodded. "She looked in on us all the time after my mom died. And she totally helped us navigate this crazy land lease deal."

"The whole tribe will benefit from this thing, right?"

"Our tribe's pretty big," Talley said. "Some of us will get jobs from the deal; some, like the chief, are investors, so they're hoping to make a profit. The bottom line is that once Golden Eagle opens, there'll be more money in Maxton. Most folks are pretty happy about it."

"Are there non-Lumbee investors?" Millay asked casually.

"Sure. Fletcher Olsen, a lawyer most of us know, and other local businessmen. The biggest loan is coming from the bank."

Millay rearranged a few baskets. "You said most folks are happy about it. Who isn't?"

Talley averted her glance. "People who don't like seeing my tribe flourish." She began to organize the receipts, making it clear that she didn't wish to elaborate.

Olivia sidled closer to the pair of dark-haired women. "Annette mentioned that your house was recently vandalized. Do you think it had something to do with this deal?"

Talley pinched her lips together.

Millay leaned closer to her. "Hey, it's happened to me too." She listed some of the offensive names she'd been called in high school and told Talley how much it had hurt to be ostracized by her peers. "So tell me about what they said to you."

"It's happened a few times—graffiti, a busted mailbox, toilet paper in the trees—but most of that was when I was a little kid. Things were quiet for so many years that I forgot about being targeted or whatever you want to call it. But while Willis and I were at the bank signing papers, someone visited our house." She paused, steeling herself. "Our cars were spray-painted." Talley locked eyes with Millay. Her gaze was haunted. "Nit, half-breed, pie face, squaw humper, redskin, scalper, filthy Injun, dirty crow." Pink spots had bloomed on her cheeks. "And bush nigger. All written in big, black letters. Looking at them felt like . . ."

"You'd been punched in the stomach," Millay finished for her.

Talley nodded and then sought relief from her inhaler again.

Horrified by Talley's revelation, Olivia stared at the young woman. She could picture a deranged white supremacist spraying graffiti on the two cars, incensed over the idea of two Native American kids making good, of the tribe opening a successful business during tough economic times. The Lumbee would run the casino, forcing the non-

Indian locals to make nice in order to get a piece of the pie. Were remnants of the Klan still active in Robeson County?

At that moment, several customers entered the booth and Talley and Millay stopped speaking to help them.

Rawlings was there too, holding the memory jug in his arms. "The gentleman with the impressive walking stick was at the Battle of Hayes Pond," he said, indicating the man with the mouthful of chewing tobacco. "He didn't recognize anything on the jug, and though Munin's name sounded familiar to him, he couldn't remember why. He's going to introduce us to the other Lumbee who were present at the battle. Laurel and Harris are asking him a few follow-up questions and we may pull something from Laurel's notes later, but so far the guy hasn't told us anything new."

"Millay's been great with Talley," Olivia whispered. "But I think the two of us being here is all she can take. I'll ask her about the jug while you guys talk to the Hayes Pond folks."

Rawlings picked up a cutlery basket and examined the yellow and green floral pattern woven around the handle. "My sister would love this." He handed Olivia some cash. "Would you put that aside for me?"

She smiled at him, knowing that he was buying the basket more for Talley than to brighten his sister's kitchen. "Of course."

When she swiveled to tuck Rawlings' purchase under the table, she hit a basket woven into the shape of a teacup with her elbow. It bounced off Haviland's back and landed between his paws. Startled, the poodle grabbed it between his teeth and trotted out of the booth, prancing in the middle of the aisle. He was ready for a game of chase.

"Captain!" Olivia scolded.

Talley put a hand on her arm. "It's okay. Even if he slobbers all over the basket, he's going to attract lots of attention."

She was right. Within minutes, people gravitated to Haviland. When they reached out to pet him, he'd dance to the side, swinging his head around so that they'd be looking directly at the basket in his mouth.

"Aren't you the cutest thing?" a woman wearing a fanny pack and an enormous sun hat exclaimed. "And what a sweet basket!" She marched into the booth and purchased two items.

An hour later, Talley's stock was so depleted that Olivia decided to place the jug at the end of one of the tables. "Do you mind if I display this?" she asked Talley. "I'm trying to identify the objects on here and I was hoping a passerby would recognize one of them."

Talley was instantly curious about the piece. "I've seen jugs like this before, but those pieces were mostly covered by bottle caps or other junk. This one has real valuables on it. Look at this starfish necklace." She carefully spun the jug. "And somebody's class ring? Where did you get this?"

Olivia watched Talley carefully. "Have you ever heard of a woman named Munin Cooper?"

Straightening, Talley considered the question, but her expression was totally blank. She shook her head. "No. Is she a famous potter or something?"

Stroking the smooth lid of a picnic basket, Olivia wondered how much to say. In between customers, Talley had been shedding her tears into a paper napkin, but her red-rimmed eyes and blotchy skin betrayed her grief. Was it right to talk to her about Munin now?

"She lived on the other side of this forest," Olivia said after a long pause. "I only met her once, but it was a memorable interaction." Studying Talley, she added softly, "She was an old woman, but I swear there's an undeniable resemblance between you two. I know that sounds ridiculous, but the moment I saw you onstage, I felt like I was looking at a much younger version of Munin."

Talley didn't seem to find Olivia's confession strange. In

fact, she pretended not to notice the customer searching for a price tag on a hearth basket. "Maybe we are related. My mom's parents moved to Florida when I was a baby and they passed away before I was three. I never knew my dad's folks. And both he and my mom were only children, so I have no aunts or uncles. No cousins." Her eyes filled with tears and her fingers shook. She curled them around the jug, hugging the clay with her hands. "And no brother. I have no one. *Willis!*" she cried. "How could you have left me alone?"

Millay was at Talley's side in seconds. She put an arm around the distraught young woman and led her out of the booth and away from the crowd.

As Olivia watched them disappear into the trees, she noticed a pack of children racing down the path directly toward Haviland. The poodle clearly didn't like the speed with which he was being approached and began to retreat for the safety of the booth.

Dropping the basket at Olivia's feet, he stood behind her, anxiously shifting his weight from one leg to another.

The children didn't slow their pace, but turned the corner into the booth screaming, "Here, doggie!" and, "I saw him first!"

Before Olivia could react, one of the bigger boys gave his brother a powerful shove, careening the smaller boy backward into the table's edge. The memory jug wobbled and then disappeared from view, falling to the ground on the far side of the table.

Olivia heard a muted crack and felt a surge of sadness course through her. The children backpedaled slowly, clearly wary of Olivia's reaction. Spying something else of interest farther down the row of booths, they turned and rushed off, calling out apologies.

Slowly, Olivia walked around the table and stared down at the broken jug. She sank to her knees, feeling that something inside her had broken as well, and reached for one of the larger shards.

Its flat, undecorated shape indicated that it had once been the jug's bottom. Turning it over in her hands, she drew in a sharp breath. There was a key embedded in the ruddy clay.

Glancing around in hopes that Rawlings and the others had returned, Olivia's heart skipped a beat. And then another. She forgot to breathe.

For there, gazing at an oil painting of a Lumbee warrior, was her father.

Her father.

A man who'd died right in front of her. Months ago.

Chapter 14

For many men that stumble at the threshold
are well foretold that danger lurks within.

—WILLIAM SHAKESPEARE

Olivia stood on rubbery legs, the piece of broken pottery clutched in her hand. She wanted to run after the aberration but couldn't move. As she watched her father melt into the crowd, a small cry escaped from between her clenched lips. Haviland nudged her with his nose, whining in concern.

"I'm okay, Captain."

Glancing around the empty booth, Olivia knew she couldn't just leave. She'd have to take the cash box with her and gather up the clay shards before chasing after the hallucination.

Her gaze swept the crowd, but the ghost of her dead father had vanished. None of the Bayside Book Writers were within sight either.

Grabbing a plastic bag from Talley's supplies, Olivia squatted near the broken jug and collected the pieces. She then dropped into a folding chair at the back of the booth and dialed Hudson's cell phone number.

"I saw him," she croaked when her brother answered.

"Hold on, I can't hear a thing!" Hudson yelled over

shouts, clanking utensils, hissing steam, and laughter. "Okay, start again," he said a minute later, the background noise somewhat faded.

Olivia looked across the aisle, staring at the exact place where her father had been standing. Except that it couldn't have been her father. "I saw what you saw," she blurted, before she lost her nerve. "He was here."

Hudson sighed, and Olivia couldn't tell whether the sound reflected relief or resignation. "I knew I wasn't crazy," he said. "Or maybe we both are. What the hell is going on, Sis?"

She gripped the phone so hard that its edges dug into her palm, but the discomfort allowed her to think, to process the impossible. "No, no, no. It can't be. This guy walked like a man with no troubles. Our father was as tense as a spring. He moved like a wounded animal, always ready to lash out at a potential threat, always looking for a fight."

"How many troubles can you have if you're dead?" Hudson asked, a lame attempt at wry humor.

Ignoring him, Olivia went on. "And his clothes were all wrong. Willie Wade in Italian loafers? An ironed dress shirt? No way." Her voice became steadier. "This guy was squeaky clean. No filthy jeans, no chin stubble, no ratty baseball cap, no greasy fingernails. In fact, I'd dare to suggest that this man uses hair product."

Hudson wasn't convinced. "Forget the clothes and the hair, Olivia! Did you see his eyes? Did he look at you?"

"No."

"Then you haven't seen him. Not really. When you do, he'll look right through you."

He always did, Olivia thought. After all, she'd spent ten years with a man who rarely spoke to her, let alone showed her affection.

"Well, I can't go chasing him now," she said testily, standing on tiptoe in order to get a glimpse of the festivalgoers heading toward the exit. She didn't see her father's look-alike, but she did spot Fletcher, Judson, and Annette heading in her direction. "How's The Bayside Crab House tent going?"

Hudson seemed to welcome the change of subject. "We're slammed. People are lined up all the way down to the beach and we've handed out three hundred take-out menus already. I'll have to send someone back to the restaurant for supplies or we'll never make it through the dinner rush."

"Wow, you're knocking it out of the park, Hudson. All those competing vendors and you're running out of food? Nice job."

"Thanks," Hudson mumbled and Olivia could practically see him scuffing the ground with the toe of his sneaker, smiling with pleasure over the compliment. "Michel stopped by earlier. Bought a sampler platter to share with his pretty chef lady. She asked me a bunch of questions about Oyster Bay. Guess she's thinking of moving."

Olivia raised her brows. "Oh? And what did you tell her?"

"That it's a good place with good people. You've got your fair share of annoying tourists, but those folks'll fill your piggy bank. Schools are decent. There's stuff to do. Cost of living isn't too steep and there's plenty of beach to go around."

Laughing, Olivia said, "What a romantic picture you've painted."

"Must have been enough to whet her whistle," Hudson said. "She's going to ask to see that space you've got for lease."

"Well, well." Olivia could already picture the dessert shop opening on Main Street. She was certain it would be a success, and no one else had expressed an interest in the storefront up to this point. Then again, how would Shelley Giusti becoming a permanent resident of Oyster Bay affect

Michel? Would he moon after her night after night, the dishes he prepared for The Boot Top suffering as a result of his fickle passion?

"I gotta go," Hudson said suddenly. "A pissed-off customer at the front of the line is making a scene."

He rang off and Olivia slid her phone into her purse just as Millay and Talley returned to the booth.

"Sorry." Talley sniffled. "I've got to pull it together before the dancing starts." She noticed Annette Stevens approaching and raised her hand in the air. Her whole being seemed to be willing the tribal chair to walk faster. Olivia could see how desperately Talley wanted Annette by her side. Her yearning to be comforted was so strong that it was almost palpable.

Annette Stevens didn't say a word, but strode into the booth and enfolded Talley in her arms, rocking her back and forth and stroking her long hair. Talley's shoulders relaxed and she sighed. Olivia knew that for a few precious seconds, the heartbroken girl felt safe and loved. She could only hope that the chief wanted to do right by Talley, because Talley obviously trusted her. If Annette Stevens were abusing that trust, she'd be sorry. Not only would she have Olivia to answer to, but she'd also have to face Millay, who had obviously adopted the role of Talley's protector.

"This is a Hallmark card in the making," Millay muttered under her breath as she sank down on the chair next to Olivia. "Annette had better—" She stopped abruptly, taking note of the bag on Olivia's lap.

"The memory jug broke," Olivia said. "A couple of kids bumped into it. Guess they saved me the trouble of having to do it myself."

Millay's expression turned sympathetic. "Yeah, but still . . . that sucks. I would have rathered it was your choice." She gestured at the bag. "Was anything, like, revealed?"

Having been derailed by the vision of her father, Olivia hadn't yet examined the shards, so she passed the bag over to Millay. "Why don't you take a look? I feel like I'm going to need several shots of whiskey before I can move from this chair."

"Did I miss something?"

"I'll tell you later. Here comes Rawlings and the rest of the gang."

By this time, Fletcher and Judson had joined Annette in the booth. Fletcher handed Talley a plastic dry-cleaning bag containing a brightly colored dress. "Ms. Talley, you're going to be the belle of the ball."

"Thanks, Mr. Olsen." Talley took the dress and managed a small smile for Judson. "And thanks for sitting with me yesterday. I know I was a wreck." Her eyes filled with tears again.

Judson wiggled his finger. "None of that, young lady. You need to get your game face on. Your fans are waiting for you and I know you're going to dazzle them just like you always do."

Talley hugged the dress, looking very young and very lost. "Should I close my booth? I'd like Millay and Olivia to be able to take a break and watch me dance."

Fletcher shook his head. "Judson and I will take over here. Why, I bet we sell every basket you've got."

As Rawlings, Harris, and Laurel drew near the booth, Olivia and Millay moved to the center of the path to meet them, ensuring their conversation remained private.

"Did you learn anything useful?" Olivia asked.

Laurel shrugged. "It's hard to say. There's quite a bit of bluster and bravado with that group. Don't get me wrong—I think they're all heroes for standing up to the Klan, but the stories of courage grew more and more elaborate with every person we spoke with."

"And Munin?" Olivia sent an involuntary glance at the bag in Millay's arms. "Was her name familiar to anyone?"

Rawlings frowned. "No. Just with the old-timer behind us. He's got ten years on everyone else we interviewed and I asked him to keep thinking about her name. He has my card, so all we can do is hope he can shake off a few mental cobwebs over the course of the day."

Harris pointed at Millay. "Is that . . . ?"

She nodded and Olivia told her friends how the jug had been knocked to the ground.

"Can we see the pieces?" Harris asked eagerly.

"Not now. I need to be with Talley," Millay said, gesturing at Talley, who was now walking arm in arm with Annette toward the stage area. "She'll be alone with Annette and I'm not sure I trust the woman. After all, if the lady chief wants the land for herself, it'll go back on the auction block should anything happen to Talley."

Rawlings nodded. "I think it would be wise for us to keep watch over Miss Locklear for the remainder of the day. Especially since many of the elderly members of the tribe view her mother's death with suspicion." He indicated that they should get moving. "I can fill you in while we walk."

The friends kept close to each other like a school of fish heading for open waters. Danger waited in the depths and they moved hurriedly, sensing it close in around them like a dark shadow.

Olivia was glad to be sandwiched between Rawlings and Haviland. As they progressed, the chief's gaze swept over the faces of festivalgoers. Back and forth, back and forth he looked, as if the answers to all the riddles they'd encountered could be revealed in a suspicious glance or hostile stare.

"Tell me about Natalie," Olivia prompted.

Without ceasing his observations, Rawlings reviewed what he, Laurel, and Harris had learned. "We met a few women who knew Natalie. Their stories reinforce what we've already heard—that she slipped on a patch of ice in the grocery store parking lot. A cashier saw it happen, raced outside, and noticed that her shinbone was sticking through her pants. He covered Natalie with a blanket and waited until the ambulance came. At the hospital, she was put under while a doctor repaired her leg and she died during the surgery."

"Why?" Olivia demanded. "From blood loss? Shock? Drug allergies?"

"According to her file, I'd say it was the latter. She had an adverse reaction to general anesthesia."

Olivia noted the diverse faces and body types of the people in the crowd. "Some things are still a mystery. The human body isn't a simple machine."

"That's true," Rawlings agreed. "We're complicated. As unique as snowflakes. Or stars."

She smiled at him, loving that he could still pause to appreciate life's wonders despite all that he'd witnessed in his twenty-plus years as a cop. He caught her smile and gave her a little wink.

"Go on," Millay said, sounding exasperated. "There's got to be more to it or you wouldn't have brought Natalie's name up again."

"There is!" Laurel jumped in. "Apparently, Natalie had been put under once before—when she was giving birth to Talley."

Millay turned to her. "And what happened?"

Rawlings gave Laurel the go-ahead. "This is more your field than mine. Whenever the women around the station start swapping labor stories, I high-tail it out of the room as fast as my legs will carry me."

"Men are such wimps." Laurel snorted with mock disgust. "Natalie had an umbilical cord prolapse, which means the cord was being delivered before the baby. That's no good because the baby's oxygen and blood supplies can be cut off. The hospital staff had to move quickly, so they gave Natalie general anesthesia and her doc delivered the baby by C-section. Talley turned out just fine, but Natalie nearly died."

"If she had an adverse reaction to general anesthesia once, why would anyone in their right mind put her under a second time?" Olivia was astounded.

Rawlings shook his head. "I'm not sure, but it would appear that the hospital didn't have a record of the complication that arose during Talley's delivery. I'll have to speak with someone on the hospital staff."

The stage where Talley had performed yesterday came into view and Olivia's pace involuntarily slowed. The midday sun was bleaching the patch of grass where Willis fell with a yellow white light. Without the forest's shade, the air felt thick and cloying.

Rawlings touched her on the elbow. "Steady now," he whispered so that only she could hear.

Talley is amazingly brave, Olivia thought as they joined the rest of the spectators gathered around the semicircular stage.

"I'm going to poke my head in the tent," Millay said and strode off.

Harris followed her with his eyes. "She's really taking this personally," he said. "I've seen her angry before, but this is different."

At the mention of anger, Olivia silently wondered if the person or people who'd covered the Locklears' cars with racial slurs were here at the powwow. Were they in the crowd, waiting for Talley to begin her dance? Would they attend the evening's celebration of the Lumbees' victory at the Battle of Hayes Pond if only to inflame their rage?

Her musings were disturbed by the eruption of multiple drumbeats. Lumbee men of all ages formed a perimeter around the base of the stage, thumping out an infectious rhythm in perfect unison. A few seconds later, dozens of women clad in multicolored dresses burst onto the stage and the crowd released a raucous cheer.

Olivia was just lifting her gaze to search for Talley among the women when Millay elbowed her way through the crowd and grabbed Rawlings by the arm.

"Someone's after Talley!" she shouted, frantically waving a piece of paper in front of the chief's face. "Look, another time metaphor! It was in her purse!"

Rawlings took the paper and quickly read it. He then passed the small sheet to Olivia. She held it out for both Harris and Laurel to see.

Olivia scanned the typewritten lines and then read them a second time, trying to absorb the poem's meaning over the noise of the drums and the spontaneous hoots and hollers coming from the audience.

Gather ye rosebuds while ye may,
Old Time is still a-flying;
And this same flower that smiles today,
Tomorrow will be dying.

"The language sounds old fashioned." Laurel had to raise her voice to be heard over the drums.

Harris reached for his phone, but Rawlings waved for him to stop. "I know this poem. It's by Robert Herrick and is called 'To The Virgins, To Make Much of Time.'" He turned to Millay. "And I think you're right. I believe this is meant to be a threat. Or worse. A promise of suffering. Today, the flower, who's got to be Talley, is smiling. But tomorrow? She could be dead. Isn't that what this poem is meant to convey to whoever finds it?"

"Oh no!" Laurel squeaked.

Rawlings ignored her and locked a steely gaze on Millay. "I want you, Laurel, and Harris to go back to the tent and wait for Talley there. Olivia and I will watch the crowd. If someone makes a move, Haviland can react faster than we can."

Millay touched the poodle's head. "Don't let anything happen to her, Captain. I don't care if you sink your pearly whites halfway through some guy's calf. Just don't let go if you get hold of the bastard. Got it?"

Haviland sniffed and gave Millay a lick on the hand.

After the rest of the Bayside Book Writers disappeared into the tent, Olivia pointed at the poem. "I don't get it. Is this meant to reflect Talley's suffering or the sender's?"

Rawlings didn't look at the paper. He was already too busy studying the spectators. Olivia copied his lead.

"Let's move around to the left a little," he said. "I want to be able to see who has eyes only for Talley. And I want a clear view of people's hands."

Once they'd repositioned themselves, Olivia did as Rawlings suggested, but it was difficult to focus on so many people at once. All of the audience members looked enthralled, and because the dancers were constantly changing positions onstage, she couldn't tell whether someone in the crowd was fixated on a particular woman. It was just as challenging to keep an eye on hundreds of hands. For the most part, people were gripping water bottles, drink cups, food items, or the handles of shopping bags. If they weren't, they were clapping or snapping their fingers in time to the drumbeat.

Facial expressions were of no help either. People smiled, made comments to friends or family members, scolded children, and shouted encouragement to the dancers. Olivia openly observed them, feeling particularly exposed because she and Rawlings had their backs against the stage.

"We're not being very subtle," she said.

The chief nodded. "I know. I want this person to realize that we're taking the offensive. I want them to see that we're prepared to defend Talley—that we've got our fists raised and we're ready for a fight should it come down to that."

A fight. That was exactly what Olivia wanted. She longed for a confrontation, for a chance to act, to grab hold of their foe and demand an explanation. She spent several seconds indulging in a fantasy in which she and Haviland brought down a hulking creep whose pockets were stuffed with time metaphors, but then the sight of a familiar face startled her from her reverie. There, on the fringe of the crowd, stood Harlan Scott.

Olivia hadn't seen Harlan since her fateful visit with Munin. They'd barely spoken on the trip home and Olivia had been too emotionally spent to do more than mumble a hasty "thank-you" and "good-bye" to her hired guide upon disembarking from his boat.

Harlan was a retired park ranger, and there was nothing unusual about his attending a well-publicized event in the Croatan Forest. However, something about the tightness of his jaw and the way his arms were folded over his chest bothered Olivia. He wasn't smiling or showing any outward sign of enjoying the performance, and his gaze was too intense for her liking.

Turning to follow his stare, she saw that Talley had taken center stage. The young Lumbee woman was mesmerizing the audience with her beauty and the graceful movements of her body.

Everyone watched her with a mixture of awe and admiration.

Except for Harlan Scott.

There was a darkness in his eyes, a shadow of anger that transformed his entire being. Olivia no longer saw the quiet, gentle man who'd tended Munin's traps, brought her supplies, and took care of her pottery sales. She didn't see the courteous but reserved guide who'd agreed to transport her across the harbor and up the creek leading to Munin's shack, or the cautious nature lover who'd warned her to watch out for snakes. Forgotten were all of these attributes. The man Olivia was looking at was a complete stranger.

Even children knew that strangers weren't to be trusted. And sometimes, they were to be feared.

Chapter 15

Medicine sometimes snatches away health,
sometimes gives it.

—OVID

O livia touched Rawlings on the arm.
   "Harlan Scott is here. Eleven o'clock, near the back.
He's in jeans and a Cheerwine T-shirt. Look at his expres-
sion."

Rawlings quickly located the retired park ranger. "Let's
move," he said after a brief glance.

The chief surged forward and Olivia and Haviland followed on his heels. The trio reached Harlan just as the
drumbeats ceased and the dancers lined up to take their
bows.

"Harlan!" Olivia called out before Rawlings could speak.
Because Harlan knew her, she believed he was unlikely to
dash off upon seeing her. "What a surprise! I thought you
were going fishing this weekend."

"I slept too late to get a good start," Harlan said, offering his hand to Olivia. "Nice to see you." He nodded at the
poodle. "And you too, Haviland."

Haviland, who clearly didn't feel threatened, sniffed
Harlan's shoes and then sat back on his haunches and peered
around. Seeing the poodle completely at ease gave Olivia

pause. Haviland would have either uttered a low growl or kept his distance if he'd sensed the slightest bit of aggression coming from Harlan.

"Are you all right?" she asked him. "I saw you watching the dancers and you seemed upset."

After a long pause, Harlan jerked a thumb at the stage. "There was a girl . . . she looked just like Munin. I swear—they've got to be related. And if that's true, then Munin didn't have to be alone. She had people. So why did they cut ties with her? They left her—to be found by strangers. To be in that stream for who knows how long. I—" He stopped abruptly and reined in his anger. "Sorry. Your friend's going to think I'm crazy."

Olivia turned to Rawlings. "I'm sure he's seen worse. This is Sawyer Rawlings, Oyster Bay's chief of police."

Harlan shook the chief's hand. "I thought I recognized you. I've seen your picture in the paper a time or two."

Rawlings inclined his head. "And I've heard about you too. From Olivia. But I also read the statement you provided the Craven County Sheriff's Department." He averted his eyes, feigning interest in a pair of Lumbee drummers who were laughing loudly at some private joke. "You don't believe Munin died of a snakebite."

Harlan didn't respond. He studied the chief and eventually nodded as if he'd come to a decision. "She lived among those snakes for decades. Made her own antivenom. And she was found by the riverbank. Not exactly eastern diamondback territory. It doesn't sit right with me. Not at all."

"Then that makes three of us," Rawlings confided.

Harlan released a long, pent-up breath. He was obviously relieved that his opinion mattered to Rawlings. "What can be done?"

The chief pointed at the stage. "The girl who bears a resemblance to Munin Cooper? Her name is Talley Locklear. Ever heard the name before?"

"No."

"I see." The chief looked pensive. "I've got to admit, Harlan, that with such an age gap between the two women, I'm a little amazed that you were so certain they were related."

Harlan's shrugged. "There's no mystery here, Chief. I've seen a picture of Munin from when she was young. She and this Talley girl could have been sisters."

Olivia couldn't remain quiet a second longer. "What was Munin wearing in the photo? Was there anyone else with her? Did she tell you where or when it was taken?"

"That old woman wouldn't have given me a straight answer about that picture or anything else," Harlan scoffed. "I gave up asking her questions years ago. I did things for her and I got paid for my work. We'd chat about her traps and what was in the paper sometimes, but neither one of us were big on talking. I suspect it's one of the reasons we got along."

"So that's all?" Olivia couldn't mask her frustration and disappointment. "It was just a candid shot showing a young woman who looked like Talley?"

Harlan's eyes were sympathetic. "She wasn't in tribal getup, if that's what you were hoping. But if that girl is Lumbee, then so is Munin. At least part Lumbee anyway. I know she was a blend of races. Called herself a gypsy all the time and I don't think she was referring just to her way of life. She said there was gypsy blood in her veins."

"But if she was Talley's grandmother or great aunt or whatever, why would she choose to separate herself from her family?" Olivia was thinking aloud, but Rawlings answered her question.

"To protect them. That's the only theory I can come up with that would explain her living in isolation. Yet she was still close enough to keep tabs on folks through the local papers."

"That's true enough," said Harlan. "She had me pick up several of them every week. She read every word."

"Of course, we can only assume there's a family

connection between Munin and the Locklears," Rawlings said. "We have no proof."

Olivia studied Harlan. He was clearly troubled by Munin's death and his disappointment over having nothing useful to offer to help Rawlings discover what really happened to her was written all over his face.

Harlan Scott posed no threat to the Locklears. Of that, she was certain. She was just about to open her mouth and tell him about the puzzling objects on the memory jug when Harris came sprinting toward them hollering, "Chief! Chief!"

The speed with which he moved and terror in his eyes told them that something horrible had happened.

"It's Talley!" he shouted breathlessly. "She took a few hits off her inhaler and then passed out." He grabbed Olivia's hand and squeezed it desperately. "It's exactly like your description of Willis's collapse! Hurry!"

Without hesitation, they ran back to the tent. Inside, Olivia had to hold back the cry that rose up in her throat when she saw Talley lying on the ground, her long black hair fanning out around her inert torso.

"We've already called for an ambulance." Laurel's voice was hoarse with dread. "But I don't know what else to do."

Millay was on her knees next to Talley, murmuring to her and stroking her hair. Tears fell from Millay's chin and dripped onto Talley's dress.

Harlan moved to her other side, checked her pulse, and then bent over her chest, listening intently. "Her breath is shallow," he said as he stood. "We've got oxygen at the ranger station. I'll go get it."

Olivia and Rawlings locked eyes. They were both experiencing a horrible sense of déjà vu, but this time, their helplessness was more acute. And this time, their surprise and shock was tinged by a white-hot anger.

"Where's her inhaler?" Rawlings asked Harris.

Harris pointed to where Talley's purse sat on top of a rubber storage bin. "We haven't touched it."

That's when Olivia noticed Fletcher and Annette standing in a corner of the tent. Fletcher had a cell phone pressed against his ear and Annette was leaning heavily against him, as if the only thing keeping her upright was the attorney's sturdy shoulder.

"What happened?" Olivia addressed the tribal chair.

Annette shook her head. "I don't know! She came in here after the last dance and was having a hard time breathing, so she grabbed her inhaler and seconds afterwards she just dropped." Her voice trembled. "Judson ran off to find a doctor. There are a few from home here at the powwow." She looked doubtfully at her cell phone screen. "Fletcher's been trying to reach them but no one's answering."

At that moment, Harlan burst into the tent followed closely by a uniformed ranger carrying an oxygen tank. Harlan placed the mask over Talley's mouth and nose and everyone fell silent, listening as a hiss of oxygen flowed from the tank. "Her pulse is irregular," Harlan told the ranger. He then placed his palm on her forehead. "Skin's hot to the touch."

Olivia felt her panic rising. She turned back to Annette. "Is there some kind of medical condition in the Locklear family? A predisposition that could explain why first Willis and now Talley have collapsed?" She was shouting at the tribal chair, but she didn't care. "Could that inhaler have caused this?" Gesturing at Talley, she moved forward until she was inches away from Annette. Towering over the smaller woman, she balled her hands into fists. "You *must* know something!"

"I'm not a doctor!" Annette cried, her lower lip quivering. "I don't know what's happening to Talley! There are genetic issues in almost all native populations, but I don't know which one this could be! I—"

The ambulance sirens cut her off and Olivia was suddenly struck by an idea. Last spring, when she'd needed more information on North Carolina's prisoner of war camps, she'd made contact with a history professor named

Emmett Billinger at the University of North Carolina at Chapel Hill. He'd given her his cell phone number and they'd chatted a few times since her visit to UNC's campus. Perhaps Billinger had a colleague who'd studied the Lumbee and could tell the paramedics why a young woman was dying for no apparent reason.

Retreating to a corner of the tent, she dialed Billinger's number, praying that he'd answer. On a late summer afternoon, he could be anywhere. Golfing, playing tennis, or taking his beloved greyhounds to the dog park. When she heard him say hello, she nearly cried in relief.

Wasting no time on formalities, she told him exactly what she needed, and when he assured her that in fact, the department's chair had done extensive research on the Lumbee and he would call him immediately, she had to bite the inside of her cheek to keep her emotion in check.

"What is it?" Rawlings was suddenly at her side. He stroked Haviland, trying to soothe the agitated poodle.

"Hope," she whispered, her voice catching. "A long shot, but it's better than nothing."

By this time, the paramedics had strapped Talley to a stretcher and were loading her into the ambulance. Olivia's phone rang seconds before the gurney disappeared into the back of the vehicle.

"It could be malignant hyperthermia," Billinger said and rattled off a list of symptoms.

"That's got to be it!" Olivia's exclamation sounded more like a sob. "Can she survive?"

"Yes, if she's given a particular drug very quickly." Billinger sent a text containing the name of Dantrolene, a muscle relaxant, and Olivia rang off. She'd thank him later.

"WAIT!" Olivia dashed after the paramedic who'd just climbed into the passenger seat. She told him why Talley was suffering and showed him the text message. "Remember the name of this drug and go!" Slamming the door, she watched the ambulance pull away in a cloud of dust.

Millay jogged after it for a few paces and then her shoulders drooped and she slowed, momentarily hiding her face in her hands. Roughly brushing the tears from her cheeks, she swiveled and scanned the faces of her friends until her gaze landed on Olivia.

"What did you tell that EMT?" Her eyes shone with anger. "What do you know?"

Olivia took Millay's hand and told her about her conversation with Emmett Billinger. When she was done, she handed Millay the water bottle from her purse. "Drink that. We've got to keep it together for Talley's sake. We can dissect this whole thing at the hospital, okay?"

"She can't die," Millay said in a very small voice.

It was highly likely that she would, but Olivia refused to consider the possibility. "No, that won't happen. Not this time."

There was no need to round up the rest of the Bayside Book Writers. Harris had already grabbed Millay's messenger bag, and without another word, he, Laurel, and Rawlings hurried toward the parking lot. Fletcher, Annette, and Harlan were also in motion.

"I hope there's a quiet corner in the ER's waiting room," Rawlings said after the five friends had piled into Olivia's Range Rover. "It's time for the lawyer and the tribal chair to spill their secrets. I don't care if I have to drag in every sheriff's deputy, every cop, and all the park rangers in the state of North Carolina to make those two realize I mean business. They're going to tell us everything. Or else."

From the back of the car, Haviland growled his agreement.

At the hospital, Rawlings remained in the ambulance bay and immediately contacted the Craven County Sheriff's Department about collecting Talley's purse and having her inhaler tested. He offered the full resources of the Oyster

Bay Police Department and asked to be included in the investigation. Olivia didn't know what was decided, but left Haviland and the keys to her car with the chief. She needed to be in the waiting room, sharing in the wordless dread that had rendered everyone silent.

Fifteen minutes later, the sheriff himself arrived. Watching through the front windows, Olivia saw the sheriff hand Rawlings a take-out coffee cup. The two of them sat on a bench facing the parking lot and talked for the better part of an hour. Then Rawlings put Haviland in the back of the Range Rover and he and the sheriff made their way inside the hospital.

The two law enforcement officers entered the waiting room at the same moment Fletcher appeared through an entrance at the other end.

"She's going to pull through!" he announced, his relief evident. "The doctors don't want us celebrating just yet because they don't know what the full effects of her ordeal will be, but for now she's stable and that's excellent news."

The Bayside Book Writers jumped up and hugged each other and then included Annette and Fletcher in their embraces.

"Let me call Judson," Fletcher said after detaching himself from a teary-eyed Laurel. "I know he's worried sick."

Rawlings hadn't participated in the rejoicing, opting to watch Fletcher and Annette from a distance. Olivia knew that he was now 100 percent cop. His feelings over Talley's prognosis were carefully camouflaged, and the moment Fletcher pocketed his cell phone, the chief and sheriff gestured for the attorney to join them at a small table in the far corner of the room.

Without waiting for an invitation, Olivia took a seat next to Fletcher. It wasn't long before the rest of the Bayside Book Writers had trailed over to the private nook.

"This is Sheriff Poole," Rawlings introduced the stout, round-faced man to his left. "If a crime was committed against Talley, the case falls under his jurisdiction. Together, with assistance from the Oyster Bay police and the park rangers of the national forest, we hope to get to the bottom of this." He looked at Fletcher. "Mr. Olsen, the sheriff and I would like to ask you and Mrs. Stevens some informal questions about the Locklear family. In light of Ms. Limoges's discovery that there might be a predisposition to malignant hyperthermia in the Locklear family, we now need to take a second look at the cause of death for both Willis and Natalie Locklear."

Fletcher was nonplussed. "Malignant what? I'm a lawyer, sir, not a doctor."

Rawlings gestured for Olivia to handle the explanation. Having already told her friends about the medical condition on the car ride over, she now gave the attorney a clear and concise summary. When she was done, she stared hard at Fletcher. "None of your Lumbee clients have mentioned malignant hyperthermia before?"

"No." Fletcher sounded sincere, but Olivia didn't trust the man. With all that had happened within the last forty-eight hours, she couldn't take that chance. She flicked her gaze to Rawlings and knew that he was studying the attorney very closely.

"We're going to need to get our hands on Natalie Locklear's complete medical records, of course," the sheriff began in a disarmingly pleasant drawl. "But I wonder if you have anything locked away in your office that could shed a little light on this mess. Chief Rawlings tells me that Mrs. Locklear nearly died in childbirth. Can you provide specific details about that event?"

Annette interjected. "I remember hearing that it was a close call. My mother was still alive then and she told me what happened. The cord came before the baby and Natalie was rushed into surgery. She nearly died on the operating table." She turned to Fletcher. "It was Talley's birth, right?"

"Yes, and I have loads of documentation on the event,"

he said proudly. "You see, Natalie considered filing a suit against the hospital, but later dropped the idea. Said she had enough battles to fight and didn't want to get drawn into another one. By that time, however, I'd gathered enough information to scare the hospital board into paying her bill. Without that big bill hanging over her head, Natalie decided to move forward and focus on her kids instead of suing the hospital."

Sheriff Poole put a hand under his doughy chin and leaned his elbow on the table. "I'm going to need to see everything you have on that incident."

Fletcher didn't seem surprised by the request. "Oh, here comes Judson, my assistant. He'll drive to the office this afternoon and fax over the necessary papers. I can't leave Talley. Not now, knowing what we know."

"What do we know?" Judson asked, his eyes anxious, his hands clenched tightly by his side.

"That someone might have tried to kill Talley, but she's going to pull through." Fletcher shook his head mournfully. "Judson, Willis may have been murdered. Maybe Natalie too." Before Judson could demand an explanation, Fletcher pointed behind him. "You'll have a man keeping watch over Talley, won't you, Sheriff?"

Poole examined his watch. "I've got a pair of deputies on the way. I'll be right outside her door until they get here."

Fletcher touched Judson on the sleeve and quietly told him why he had to leave for Lumberton immediately. The sheriff handed Judson a business card with his cell phone and fax numbers. Judson accepted the card but seemed unable to leave the waiting room.

"What about Talley?" He was obviously distraught over being sent away in the face of the shocking events. "What if she needs something when she wakes up?"

Annette smiled at him. "I'm not going anywhere. Fletcher and I will make sure she gets the best care possible. And we'll tell her why you had to go. She'll be grateful to you for trying to find out what happened to her and her family."

Judson seemed to be on the verge of voicing another protest, but he finally nodded and turned to face Poole. "I'll get those files to you before suppertime."

Millay, who'd been unusually quiet throughout the discussion, turned to Olivia and asked, "How could someone drug Willis? You were with him. He didn't have an inhaler, so how—"

"He'd just smoked a cigarette," Olivia said, facing Sheriff Poole. "I'll never forget the smell. Someone had given him a clove cigarette to try. That someone must have been the murderer."

Both Poole and Rawlings were taking notes. "We'll have to talk to a doctor about the nitty-gritty details," Poole said. "See if it's possible to load this kind of medicine into a cigarette filter. This stuff is way above my pay grade."

"I bet it's possible," Harris said. "All you'd have to do is soak the tobacco with a drug that triggers malignant hyperthermia. Even if it tasted funny, Willis wouldn't know why. He'd think he was just smoking a funky clove cigarette when he was really sucking a bunch of toxic drugs into his lungs."

"And what kind of drugs could have been made into a trigger? Could you use the pills in the lady chief's purse, for example?" Millay was practically snarling. "Did you grind them up and use them to murder innocent people?"

Annette's face turned ashen. "W-What? That's insane! I've given my life to the people of my tribe!" She dumped the contents of her purse on the table and grabbed the pill bottle before it could roll off the edge. "This is olanzapine. It's a prescription for my son, Andrew. He has bipolar disorder." She handed the bottle to Rawlings. "Count them if you want. There were thirty pills and Andy's taken two." A tear slipped down her cheek. Fletcher put a protective arm around her and offered her a handkerchief.

Harris was gazing intently at his cell phone's screen. He looked up, locked eyes with Millay, and shook his head. "Those pills wouldn't do it. I found a much more detailed medical site than I'd been on before and this one says that the catalyst would have to be an anesthesia inhalant."

Rawlings returned the bottle to Annette. "Thank you, but I'm sure it won't be necessary to examine these." He spoke very gently. Annette sniffed and returned the pills to her purse. Millay helped her gather up the rest of her possessions and was clearly surprised when Annette grabbed her hand and held on to it.

"It's okay," the older woman whispered. "I know you were just trying to help Talley and I'm grateful that she has you in her corner."

Poole observed this exchange impassively and then focused on Olivia once again. "Did Willis Locklear mention a name, Ms. Limoges? Did he give an indication about the person who gave him the clove cigarette?"

"No. If he had, this whole thing would be over already," Olivia's said regretfully.

Annette looked at Olivia. "You're not to blame. I don't know why someone has it in for the Locklear family. They've never harmed anyone. People have only become familiar with Willis and Talley because of the casino deal. A deal everyone's happy about. I know I've said this before, but I can tell you don't believe me." She scanned the faces of the Bayside Book Writers and then her gaze came to rest on Rawlings. "The tribe voted unanimously to build the Golden Eagle and the residents of Maxton have smoothed our way at every turn, every town meeting. This is a good thing for all of us." She tucked a strand of dark hair behind her ear and sighed. "I can't see the rhyme or reason behind hurting the Locklears."

"My guess is that someone's unhappy about the deal and is well practiced at hiding it," Rawlings answered. "And since it appears that the casino will be built no matter what, if the crime against Talley is truly attempted murder, then the killer's anger is burning brighter than ever. He or she has nothing to lose, because they believe they've already lost. If that's the case, these are payback killings. This is a matter of revenge."

"Thus the time metaphors?" Harris wondered aloud.

"If Natalie was murdered too, then the killer is extremely patient," Olivia said, reflecting on the morose nature of the Herrick poem. "He or she has suffered for a long time and is therefore willing to wait, to *suffer* a little longer because, in the end, the Locklears will pay. For what wrong, we still don't know."

Laurel wrung her hands together. "Then the murderer won't stop. As long as Talley's alive, there's still a Locklear who'll live to see the casino's success."

Millay rose to her feet, her dark eyes ablaze. "She'd damned well better live." She gestured at Harris, Laurel, and Olivia. "We need to look at those memory jug pieces and solve Munin's riddle. Now. We can't sit around and wait for this maniac to strike again." She then pointed at Rawlings and Poole. "The rest is on you two. Protect and serve. Keep Talley safe and find the bastard who did this to her." And with that, she shoved her chair backward with such force that it toppled over.

Ignoring the overturned furniture, Millay strode from the room.

Sheriff Poole raised a shaggy eyebrow and looked at Rawlings. "Are all the women from Oyster Bay that feisty?"

"They most certainly are," Rawlings said and met Olivia's gaze. "And I wouldn't have it any other way."

Chapter 16

Fiction is the truth inside the lie.

—STEPHEN KING

Following her departure from the waiting room, Millay had tried to bully her way into seeing Talley, but she was firmly rebuffed by the duty nurse and told to come back during visiting hours the following morning.

"I need to check in at home before we reconvene for our critique session," Laurel said after glancing at her watch. "Are we still meeting tonight?"

"It's a waste of time to talk about my dumb book when all of this is going on," Millay muttered. "Why don't we focus on the memory jug instead?"

Olivia steered Millay toward the exit. "We will. Over supper. After that, it's back to the business of critiquing. You're almost done with your novel, Millay. You're the closest of all of us to beginning the agent query process. Don't give up on your book now."

Harris slung an arm around Millay's shoulders and sniffed her neck. "You need a shower anyway. You smell like funnel cake, fried fish, and sausage grease. Personally, I find it very attractive, but the rest of—"

Millay walloped Harris in the gut, preventing him from

further speech. Over her head, he winked at Olivia and Laurel and then pretended to stumble out of the ER.

Rawlings promised to show up for the critique session if he could, but he was intent on obtaining blood samples from Munin and Talley to see if they were related, and he was already dreading the red tape that task would entail. Once he had that ball rolling, he planned to join Sheriff Poole's deputies in canvassing the powwow. They hoped to track down a needle-in-the-haystack witness—to find someone who'd seen a man or woman give Willis a clove cigarette or sneak into the tent behind the stage to tamper with Talley's inhaler.

As for Olivia, she felt completely wrung out. She drove her friends home and then headed straight to The Boot Top, where she asked Gabe to fix her a coffee laced with whiskey. Only when she'd taken several invigorating sips did she make her way to the kitchen.

It was too early for the sous-chefs to be prepping for the dinner service, so Michel was alone in his stainless steel kingdom. Perched on a stool near the butcher block, he was drinking tea and studying the evening's menu. Without greeting him, Olivia crossed the room and let Haviland out the back door.

"Well, hello!" Michel trilled merrily. "Are you done powwowing?"

The light in his eyes and the dimples in his cheeks irritated her. Michel's cheerfulness was unwelcome at the moment, and though she knew it was unfair, she felt an uncontrollable urge to wound him. "Where's your chocolate enchantress?"

Oblivious to the note of sarcasm in Olivia's voice, Michel raised his mug in a toast. "Visiting your favorite Realtor, Millicent Banks."

"Oh?"

"She saw your leasing agent this afternoon, fell in love with the space, toured every inch of the town, and is now scoping out neighborhoods." Michel was beaming. "I think she'll be hanging up a sign in Oyster Bay by Christmas."

"Fa-la-la," Olivia groused and drank more spiked coffee. Feeling dog tired and unkind, she sat opposite Michel and pursed her lips. "She was married, your Shelley. Her husband bit the dust. I hear his death was quite unexpected— that he was as robust as an Olympian. Suddenly developed an irregular heartbeat." She snapped her fingers. "Gone! Just like that."

"Shelley told me all about it," Michel said. "It must have been horrible for her. She really loved him."

"That's how Willis died, you know. Dropped like a stone. Death by irregular heartbeat."

Michel cast his eyes down. "I know. And maybe it's wrong for me to be happy, to be hopeful after what happened to him, but I can't help it. Whenever I'm around Shelley, I feel like anything's possible. I feel at ease in my own skin. Do you know what a relief that is?"

Olivia did. It was how she felt whenever Rawlings was around, but she wasn't in the mood to congratulate Michel on finding a woman who could truly make him whole. "And it doesn't bother you that he and Willis died from the same accidental death?"

"Why should it?" He frowned in confusion. "It's not like Shelley murdered them both." Suddenly, his face flushed with indignation. "What's wrong with you, Olivia? Not everyone is a psychopath. Not everyone has closets stuffed with deep, dark secrets. Are you seriously implying that Shelley Giusti had something to do with Willis's passing?"

Shame washed over Olivia and she shook her head. "You're right, it's an absurd notion. Forgive me." She rubbed her temples. "I'm coming unraveled, Michel."

He took her hand. "Tell me everything."

When she was done and her coffee cup was empty, Michel disappeared into the walk-in and came back out a

few minutes later with his arms loaded. He placed tomatoes, heavy cream, an assortment of cheeses, and a mound
of fresh basil leaves on the cutting board. "Go home," he
told her. "Take a walk. Have a hot bath. Put on a pair of
sweatpants and an old T-shirt. A waiter will show up at the
cottage at half past five with food for all the Bayside Book
Writers."

"But—"

Michel began to sharpen a paring knife. "Go! That's an
order. You need some time to let everything sink in. Kick
off your shoes, go down to the beach, and get your feet wet.
The ocean always helps when you're off kilter."

He was right about that. She could almost feel the
water's pull, a silent call that could be heard only by the
heart. Longing to gaze upon its blue expanse and to make
contact with the cool waves, Olivia rounded up Haviland
and drove home.

Taking Michel's advice, she walked slowly over the soft
sand, her hair still damp from the shower. Haviland sprinted
ahead of her until he was only a black blur against the horizon. With every step, the riot of thoughts in Olivia's mind
became less frenzied. On the isolated stretch of beach, she
listened to the murmur of the waves until their steady rhythm
calmed her to the core.

By the time Harris, Millay, and Laurel showed up at the
lighthouse keeper's cottage, Olivia was relaxing in a wing
chair, a tumbler of Chivas Regal in her hand.

"What smells so good?" Laurel exclaimed when she
entered the tiny kitchen.

Olivia gestured at the pot simmering on the stove.
"Michel made us creamy tomato soup and there are grilled
cheddar and asiago cheese sandwiches on herb focaccia
bread warming in the oven. He thought we could use some
comfort food."

Harris opened the oven door and inhaled. "He nailed it.
This is exactly what I need."

The friends ladled soup into bowls and carried plates of grilled cheese sandwiches into the living room. Harris popped the caps off four bottles of beer while Laurel passed out napkins and Olivia spread out the shards from the memory jug across the coffee table.

"So the only thing we haven't seen before is this little key," Laurel said after she'd swallowed a spoonful of soup.

"I think it'll open a safety deposit box at the Oyster Bay Federal. I have an account there and my key looks just like it," Olivia said and then took a long pull of beer, surprised to find it the perfect complement to their meal. She wasn't very fond of beer, but tonight, the bready heartiness of the local microbrew was soothing.

Millay frowned. "Then you'll have to wait until Monday to see what's in the box. Unless you have some kind of 'in' with the bank manager."

"Forget it," Laurel interjected. "He's a deacon at my church and would never bend the rules. You're not getting in on a Sunday."

"God-fearin' folk are no fun," Millay grumbled and Olivia was pleased to see that the humorous glint had returned to her friend's eyes.

"Come on, I thought you lived for hellfire and damnation," Harris teased Millay.

She raised her bottle and clinked it against his. "Damn straight."

The friends discussed the memory jug as they ate, but no one came up with a useful conclusion. Just as Olivia was confessing that the presence of the starfish necklace among the rest of the clues troubled her deeply, Rawlings walked in. He looked weary and dejected, and the Bayside Book Writers knew better than to ask whether he'd made any headway in the investigation.

The chief accepted a bottle from Millay and drank half of it down, eyes closed and head tilted back. "Man, I hadn't realized how thirsty I was."

"There's food too." Olivia gestured at the soup pot and oval platter containing the remaining two sandwiches.

Rawlings loaded a plate, and in between bites of grilled cheese, told them the bad news. No one had seen anything suspicious at the powwow, lab work on the blood tests wouldn't commence until Monday at the earliest, and the inhalants used to spike Talley's inhaler—and undoubtedly Willis's cigarette too—could have been stolen from any number of places. "A doctor's office, for example," Rawlings said. "A hospital. Even dentists and veterinarians have this stuff on hand." He sighed and sank down in his favorite club chair. "All we know for certain is that Talley's inhaler was tampered with. However, we have no leads."

"What about Natalie's medical file?" Olivia asked.

"There's a tiny notation on her chart reading 'MH' followed by a question mark. That's all." Rawlings took an enormous bite from his sandwich and chewed mechanically, gazing at some point in the middle distance.

Millay's eyes narrowed. "So one of the doctors suspected Natalie had malignant hyperthermia during Talley's birth, but he scribbled some note in the margin and went on with his day? She nearly died and he was probably thinking about being late for his tee time."

"And years later, it did kill her." Harris looked at the chief. "Right?"

Rawlings nodded. "Natalie was given general anesthesia after fracturing her leg. Neither Fletcher, Judson, or Annette were within miles of that grocery store the night in question. I believe it was a genuine accident. A case of bad luck."

"Well, Willis's death had nothing to do with luck," Olivia said very softly. "Look, I want to go back to Munin's place tomorrow. We might find an answer in those newspapers or tucked away in one of her glass jars." She silently pleaded for Rawlings to agree with her decision. When he didn't respond, she squared her shoulders and raised her chin, making it clear that she wasn't asking for permission.

"Okay," he eventually said. "Ask Harlan to take us over and I'll run it by Sheriff Poole. But it'll just be the three of us. Munin's home is a crime scene now."

Laurel waved him off. "No worries. If I don't spend the day with my family, my boys are going to start calling the nanny mommy. But I'll type up my interview notes after church. Maybe there's a useful nugget hidden in those scribbles."

"I'm going to the hospital," Millay said. "Make sure those deputies are staying sharp."

Harris sulked. "What about me? What can I do?" He directed the question to Rawlings.

"Research." The chief handed Harris a folder. "I made a list just for you."

Puffing his chest out with pride, Harris tucked the folder into his laptop case. He then put a packet of papers on the coffee table and uncapped his green ballpoint pen. "Shall we commence with the critique?"

"You're practically drooling," Millay growled. "Did you hate it that much?"

"Au contraire!" Harris protested. "When Tessa was captured by the Wyvern Warriors, I thought she was toast. Then I thought the imprisonment scenes would get old quickly, but being inside Tessa's head, *really inside* for the first time, has fleshed her out in a way that makes me believe she exists. I totally have a crush on her."

Olivia laughed. "A gryphon-riding, tough-as-nails hottie? No surprise there." She glanced at her own copy of the chapter and scanned her favorite part, which described a growing attraction between Tessa and her captor, a handsome, magnetic prince who ruled over the people who'd been her race's enemies for millennia.

Looking up from the pages on her lap, Olivia said,

"Millay, you always leave me hungry for more. Take the end of this chapter, for instance. I don't know if you're going to use this newfound romantic tension to bring these warring races together or if the prince will end up betraying Tessa."

"He'd better not!" Laurel cried. "And what about that boy from Tessa's village? The one she grew up with? I thought she'd end up with him. She thinks about him all the time when she's homesick."

Harris sighed in frustration. "None of that matters if both races are in danger." He turned to Millay. "Tessa can't let the injustices to her people go unpunished. As a reader, I feel like I know her by now and I don't think she can move past what happened to her family. It ticks me off to think some hot prince could make her forget what defines her."

Rawlings nodded. "I see what you're saying, Harris, and I don't believe Millay's going allow Tessa to move ahead without obstacles. Change is difficult. However, this is a young adult novel and there's something in me that wants to see peace between these clans. Isn't that what we've struggled to achieve in our own world? Isn't that our hope?"

"But that hasn't happened for us either," Harris argued. "What about the racial slurs on the Locklears' cars? And the way people treat Millay? The hate and the bullying didn't end for her in high school. Not everyone in Oyster Bay thinks she belongs in our town, and she's put all that anger in here, into this book. Tessa's choices have to mesh with what Millay feels or it's going to be so transparent to the reader."

Laurel patted Harris on the leg. "But this is fiction, Harris. Millay can create whatever outcome she wants."

"It's done, actually," Millay said before anyone else could speak. "The whole book is done." She glanced at Rawlings. "I want to believe it's possible to leave the things that haunt us behind. I'm sick of thinking about that crap. I want to be over it, but after being near Talley—after what they did to her—I know I'm not over it. I'm as pissed as I ever was. Maybe more. And I can't believe in peace for Tessa or anyone else unless we make what happened to the Locklears right."

The Bayside Book Writers fell silent, nodding in mutual agreement. On Monday, they'd all return to their regular schedules. They'd go to work, run errands, and try to act normal. The powwow would be over with nothing left to show that a young man had lost his life, nothing to mark the moment when his sister nearly died too.

"Let's call it a night," Olivia suggested. "We need to come at this fresh and clear-headed tomorrow."

"We're running out of time, aren't we?" Laurel said, speaking to no one in particular.

Harris sighed in exasperation. "There's that word again. Time, time, time. The killer's used time to their advantage, but it's totally working against us. And we have to use that word now. Killer."

"We still have a trump card," Rawlings said before Harris could get too worked up. "Talley's alive. The killer's plans for her failed."

"And we won't give the bastard a second chance." Millay raised her bottle in a toast. "To Talley. A fighter. A survivor."

They all looked at Millay, who'd risen to her feet and, for a moment, had transformed into the warrior maiden from her novel. Fierce, beautiful, and brave.

"To Talley!" The friends clinked bottles, cleaned up after their meals, and disappeared into the night.

Alone with Rawlings, Olivia relocated to the couch and patted the cushion next to her. The chief got up from his club chair with an exaggerated groan and joined her. They pressed against each other, drawing strength from each other. Rawlings' arms wrapped around Olivia's waist and their fingers intertwined. They sat like that for an hour, listening to the surf and watching stars bloom in a field of indigo through the cottage's windows. And then Rawlings lifted Olivia's palm to his lips and kissed it softly.

"I have to go," he whispered, explaining that he couldn't sleep without reviewing his notes another time and that he needed to be at his own place if he wanted to focus on his work.

Olivia knew he'd read every fact, random note, and wild theory over and over again—that he'd finally nod off sitting up in his bed, the lamp on the nightstand burning, papers scattered across the blue comforter. She thought of how his glasses would slip down his nose as his head sank against his chest and he'd begin to snore, his hands refusing to let go of the pen, which he'd been using to circle names or dates.

She pictured all of this and loved Sawyer Rawlings for it. And yet, she didn't tell him so. With the words sticking in her throat, she kissed him and let him go.

Harlan was more than willing to ferry Olivia, Haviland, and Rawlings across the harbor. He'd been eager to search Munin's place himself, but hadn't had the heart to return to the site of her death.

Both he and Olivia were eager to leave as early as possible, but Rawlings had stayed up most of the night and needed a few hours of sleep, so Olivia and Haviland decided to grab a bite at Grumpy's and fill Dixie in on all that had happened over the weekend.

Olivia settled in at her customary window booth, surprised to note the amount of empty tables.

"Folks are either at church or out fishin'," Dixie said when Olivia asked what Dixie had done to scare away her customers. "We've got a big storm comin' in this afternoon and it's supposed to last through 'til tomorrow. I already told Grumpy to whip up some chowder. A heavy rain makes people crave soup."

"Michel made us creamy tomato for our meeting last night," Olivia said. "It was the best part of my day."

Dixie poured Olivia coffee and then perched on the end of the vinyl booth cushion while Olivia recounted her tumultuous Saturday. When she was just about finished, she noticed Fred Yoder seated toward the back at the *Starlight Express* booth. He looked up, caught her eye, and waved.

A minute later, he made his way to her booth, coffee cup in hand. "Howdy," he said with a cheerful smile. "I'm not even going to pretend that I didn't come over here to pry." He put his cup on the table and reached down to greet Haviland. "About the mystery jug. Did you make any progress?"

Olivia motioned for Dixie to slide over. "Join us."

Fred hesitated. "What about your other customers? I don't want to pin you in."

"Handsome fellow such as yourself? Feel free to pin me anytime you want," Dixie teased. "And don't worry about that couple in the *Cats* booth. They're cuttin' coupons from the paper. They'll be there another hour and I've already topped off their coffee twice. I give 'em any more and they're going float away."

"Where's Duncan?" Olivia asked once Fred was comfortably seated.

"He's worn out. He and I hit the beach at first light. He'll be in a canine coma until lunch after all the seagull chasing he did this morning." Fred smiled. "How about you? Has Haviland gotten his paws wet already?"

Olivia shook her head. "There's no playtime for us today." She filled him in on recent events and then pulled the bag containing the pottery shards from her purse and showed him the safety deposit key. Fred examined all the pieces with a collector's curiosity, but didn't comment on any of them.

"The only thing that the Locklears had going for them was their land," Olivia said. "That's why we're assuming that the casino deal somehow triggered the murders."

Dixie whistled. "And some white supremacist whacko's involved? An ugly business, Olivia. I hope you're watchin' your step."

Olivia ignored her friend and traced the outline of the Klan token.

"What about the ring?" Fred asked. "Did the year hold any significance?"

"It says nineteen seventy-something, but we can't read the last digit. It's not the year Fletcher or Annette graduated and it's way too old to have belonged to Willis or Talley."

Fred reached for the piece containing the old key. He stroked the metal with his fingertips and pivoted it toward the light. "Maybe it's not about the land. Maybe it's about a house. Perhaps there's something inside this house—the danger that Munin warned you about." He glanced out the window, unseeing. "The Battle of Hayes Pond started a chain reaction. Therefore Munin selected the token and the pennies for the jug. The land and the house were sold to the Locklears for next to nothing. And two kids were going to become wealthy from selling it to others." He slid the key over to Olivia. "What's on the other side of the door? Why does the house matter?"

"You're a genius, Fred," Olivia said. "I never thought about the house itself. None of us did. We were so focused on the land because of the casino deal."

"The house might be torn down to make room for a shiny new buildin'. Maybe that idea has the killer seein' mad-bull red." Dixie pointed at the ring. "Someone who went to Littleton High School."

Olivia's cell phone buzzed as she received a text from

Rawlings. He planned to meet her at the dock in five minutes.

Placing several bills on the table, Olivia shook Fred's hand. "I'm buying you breakfast. You earned it."

"I'll only accept if you promise to tell me how this story ends." He gave Haviland a fond pat. "We can meet at the park so the boys can race after squirrels."

Haviland's ears pricked at the mention of squirrels and Olivia had to tell him that they were not going to the park. The poodle whined once and stared plaintively at Fred.

"Sorry, fellow. I should've known better than to speak the magic word out loud." Fred did his best to appear penitent.

Dixie gave Fred a playful elbow. "Okay, lemme out. I've got to grab some take-out cups for Olivia and the chief." She wagged a finger at Olivia. "But I'm only gonna give them to you if you promise to fill me in at the same time you're sharin' with Fred here. After all, I've known you longer, and despite my better judgment, I still happen to like you."

Olivia watched Dixie skate off toward the kitchen, slapping a check on the *Cats* table as she passed by. A whirlwind of coupons rose up in her wake, fluttering in the air like colorful pieces of confetti before drifting to the floor.

After sending a text message to Millay and Harris instructing them to research Talley's house and its previous owners in-depth, Olivia looked up in time to see Dixie burst through the kitchen's double doors, once again kicking up a maelstrom of coupons. Savings on peanut butter, laundry soap, cheese crackers, tuna fish, and toilet paper scattered over the tiled floor like fallen leaves.

Olivia started to laugh. The sound surprised her, but it felt good. In fact, it was such a glorious release that she kept on laughing. She knew that stress and exhaustion were behind the giddiness, but she couldn't seem to stop.

"It's finally happened," Dixie told Fred with a resigned sigh. "She's lost her marbles."

Fred opened the front door so that Olivia could stagger

out. "Maybe those folks have a coupon for marbles," he said as Dixie wagged a warning finger at Haviland.

"Watch out for her, Captain," she whispered. The poodle seemed to understand. He sniffed in acknowledgment and trotted outside, his ears and nose raised. He caught up to Olivia, walking so close to her heel that he merged with her shadow.

Chapter 17

*It is a fateful part of human destiny that it is
condemned to wage perpetual war against
ghosts. A shade is not easily taken by the
throat and destroyed.*

—VICTOR HUGO

By the time she reached the docks, Olivia's laughter had died.

Rawlings had already taken a seat in the stern of the Boston Whaler and Harlan was standing by its prow, bowline in hand. He gave Olivia and Haviland a brief smile as the pair stepped over the gunwale and onto the boat deck.

Harlan cast off and slipped behind the wheel in a quick, fluid movement. Maintaining a speed of five knots, the engine purred as they passed slip after slip of luxury sail and motor yachts. For the past five years, Oyster Bay had been dubbed the sailing capital of the East Coast and every dock space and harbor mooring now had to be rented a year in advance.

People were out and about, visiting their nautical neighbors, giving orders to the boat hands, or lounging on their scrubbed decks reading the newspaper while dining on croissants and freshly squeezed orange juice.

Olivia didn't pay much attention to her surroundings. She knew that today's group of boat enthusiasts would be gone by next week, replaced by a similar-looking set. The pattern would continue until after Labor Day. By then, hurricane season would be in full swing and most of the travelers would forego their pleasure cruises until spring.

Something on one of the bridges leading down to the last dock caught Olivia's eye. A momentary flash, like a mirror catching a beam of sunlight. When the flash winked out, she saw that it had come from the lens of a man's sunglasses. He'd lowered them to his waist to wipe them with a cloth and the light had shot toward Olivia like a beacon.

Olivia went rigid.

Not again, she thought. *This isn't possible.*

At that moment, the mirage of her father glanced out over the water. His eyes widened and his mouth dropped open. Obviously stunned, he raised his right hand and cried, "Camille!" in a voice laden with anguish.

Mechanically, Olivia shook her head, refuting the name he'd called her.

Rawlings came to her side, gripping the side rail as he followed her gaze. "Who . . . ?" But he couldn't grasp what he was seeing.

"I saw him at the powwow yesterday too," Olivia said, her eyes fixed on the figure. The man was now jogging along the bridge in order to keep pace with the Whaler. Harlan drove on, oblivious to the drama occurring onshore. In a few seconds, he'd increase his speed and leave the congested harbor behind.

"Camille!" The desperate cry carried across the water. *"Camille!"*

Now even Haviland was paying attention. He barked a few times, warning the strange man that his passionate shouts were unwelcome.

"I'm Olivia," Olivia said in a near whisper and then she lifted her head and called out, "I'm Olivia Limoges! Camille's daughter!"

The declaration seemed to knock the wind out of the man. He stopped abruptly and placed a clenched fist against his chest as if experiencing the preliminary symptoms of a heart attack. Then, he dropped his arm, his whole body going limp as he stared at her.

Harlan turned, studying his passengers. "Everything all right?"

When Olivia didn't answer, Rawlings put a hand on her arm. "Do we need to go back?"

"No time," Harlan said. "A storm's coming in from the southeast. We'll be lucky to get to Munin's and back without getting hit."

He hesitated for a long moment and, when no one argued, eased the throttle up. The engine roared and the boat raced forward, its speed increasing as they moved toward the open water.

The man, Willie Wade's double, receded. Olivia watched over her shoulder until he was just a tiny smudge against the horizon.

"That wasn't your father," Rawlings said, still holding on to her arm. "For a second, I thought I was seeing a ghost, but even I can spot the differences. Did your dad have a brother?"

Olivia was silent for a long time, her brows creased in thought. Finally, she nodded. "That must be it. He had a brother and I never knew it. They look enough alike to be . . . twins." And then, in a rush that knocked the breath from her lungs, she remembered everything Munin had told her. Staggering to the seat in the stern, she sank down and tried to draw in a mouthful of air.

Rawlings squatted down next to her. "Focus on a point in the distance," he said gently. "Keep staring at it until you can breathe again. There." He pointed at a fishing trawler anchored offshore. "Concentrate on that boat."

She watched the vessel until it became a black dot in the distance and then disappeared entirely. Rawlings had returned to his seat but she could feel his eyes on her. Not wanting to shout over the rumble of the Whaler's engine, she pointed at her lips and then at the approaching shore, indicating that she'd explain once they disembarked.

Olivia drew in great gulps of salty air, trying to quiet her mind. But as the wind whipped her hair and tiny grains of salt flecked her skin, she felt more adrift than ever. If a siren were to break the water's surface at that moment, Olivia would be sorely tempted to surrender to the creature's seductive song.

The engine noise suddenly decreased and Harlan steered the boat as far up creek as he could and then cut the motor. As they drifted toward the bank, the instant cacophony of bird and insect noise transported Olivia to her previous visit two weeks ago.

She and Rawlings followed Harlan down the overgrown trail. He swatted at the tall grass with a stick and Haviland jumped at his side, enjoying a game of keep-away with the retired ranger.

Olivia let Harlan get even farther ahead before she spoke. "When I was here, Munin made several cryptic remarks about my father. I gave her the carving he'd made me in exchange for information on my mother, and Munin recognized that the girl standing in front of the wooden lighthouse was supposed to be me. She guessed that I was looking for my father, wondering if he'd ever return."

"The *Gazette* ran stories about that for days," Rawlings said. "The whole town knew about his disappearance and how you were found adrift in that dinghy. It would have been easy for her to glean that information."

Olivia didn't want to dwell on that night of fear and endless fog, when she'd been left all alone on a vast and angry sea. "Munin said that I was wrong to believe that I'd found him. She said, 'you think your search is over, but it's not.'"

Rawlings shot her a worried glance. "And because you caught a glimpse of a man who resembles Willie Wade, you think Munin is right?"

"I had more than a glimpse at the powwow. He was only

a few feet away. Hudson's seen him too. And it's not just a close resemblance. That man from the bridge is my father's identical twin." Olivia shrugged. "Judging from his clothes and the extra fifteen pounds, life was kinder to him. But the way he said my mother's name . . ."

"I heard," Rawlings said softly. "The longing. And the pain."

Olivia clasped her hands together to stop them from shaking. "Munin said that the man who should have raised me couldn't claim me. Or my mother for that matter. She asked me to consider why a woman like Camille Limoges would marry an unrefined, whiskey-loving fisherman. Now I know what she was trying to tell me."

Rawlings slowed. "And what's that?"

"The mirror in the jug was meant for me. I was supposed to look at myself, to see my mother's starfish necklace, and to question my origins." Olivia swallowed hard. "That man cried out my mother's name like a lover would. If that's so, whose daughter am I? Willie Wade's? Or his brother's?"

They rounded a bend and Munin's shack came into view. The forest already seemed to have closed in around it, shielding the crude structures and beginning to reclaim the clearing where she'd worked on her pottery.

Rawlings was clearly torn between rushing off to investigate Munin's possessions and grappling with Olivia's theory. "We'll find the guy when we get back," he assured her. "I promise. Until then, you're taking Munin's word as gospel just because you ran into your father's lookalike." He took her by the hand. "Please, Olivia. I need you with me right here, right now. I need you to be sharp. So does Talley."

"I'm on it." Olivia reached down with her free hand, searching for Haviland, and he quickly moved to her side so that her fingers could connect with his fur. "Trust me, Sawyer. My stuff doesn't matter now. I want justice for

Munin, no matter how much she's still screwing with my head. Let's go."

Harlan needed to disable Munin's traps before joining them in the search, so only Rawlings, Olivia, and Haviland stepped down into the shack's dark, musty interior. Harlan had provided them with a pair of battery-powered lanterns and Rawlings positioned his near the shelf filled with glass jars. Olivia was about to place hers near Munin's stack of newspapers when she realized that they were gone.

Lowering her lantern to the ground, she noticed a trail of ashes leading to the hearth. "The killer came back," she whispered to Rawlings, feeling a chill race up her spine. "The killer returned to burn of all Munin's papers."

Rawlings followed the scorch marks to the hearth. He bent down and poked at the mountain of ash using Munin's walking stick. "Damn! There's nothing left."

"Her memories have been destroyed," Olivia murmured, sinking into the chair Munin had occupied during their visit. Her chipped pottery mug was still on the mantel and Olivia recalled the strange, pleasant taste of the old woman's tea. She had a sudden yearning to smell the leaves, to let Munin spring to life again through the aromas of strong black tea, sharp mint, and sweet honey.

While Rawlings pried the lids from glass jars filled with shells, pennies, buttons, bottle caps, smooth pebbles, pull tabs, marbles, and nails, Olivia opened Munin's tea tin and imagined cradling a warm mug in her hands. Acting on impulse, she took Munin's chipped mug from the mantel and returned to the chair. She stared into the gloom and held the mug as if were made of the finest porcelain.

"What's that?" Rawlings asked.

Only when Olivia glanced down at the mug did she notice a slip of paper nestled inside. "I don't know. Should I take it out?"

"No." Rawlings removed a pair of tweezers and an evidence bag from his kit. He pulled the paper from the mug and placed it on top of the evidence bag, holding the edges down with gloved fingers. "Another time metaphor."

Olivia closed her eyes, trying to force down the rage that seemed to be clawing its way up her throat. It was as if the killer was mocking them. She hated feeling so helpless. She hated the thought of the murderer being in complete control while everyone else fumbled in the dark, always one step behind. "What does it say?"

Time is
Too Slow for those who Wait,
Too Swift for those who Fear,
Too Long for those who Grieve.

They both fell silent, pondering the words of what sounded like another stanza of poetry.

"More time metaphors," Rawlings said after a long moment. "Natalie, Willis, Talley, Munin. Their lives have been defined by Time. It passed quickly for the first three— way too swiftly for the ones who died. And Munin? Time moved slowly for her. She was here, alone, waiting. For what, I don't know, but I believe the killer identifies him or herself with Time."

"Then whatever wrong the killer perceives as having been committed must have originated with Munin," Olivia said. "I think that's why she moved out here. To protect her family. To carry the offense with her, leaving her family to flourish in ignorance. If she was Talley's grandmother, Talley never knew it."

Rawlings slid the strip of paper into an evidence bag. "We need to track down someone from Munin's generation. Someone who was at the Battle of Hayes Pond. Maybe interviewing the older members of the Lumbee wasn't the direction we needed to take. Maybe we should have been talking to the aging Klansmen."

Pivoting, he swung his lantern in an arc around the

room and a beam of light fell on an overturned crate in the corner. Standing on the crate was the carving Olivia had given to Munin. Olivia reclaimed the sculpture of the little girl and the lighthouse and held it against her chest. The movement hadn't escaped Rawlings' notice and he lowered the lantern and took her in his arms. "When this case is over, I can get your necklace back from evidence too," he assured her. "You don't need to lose anything else that matters to you."

"No." Olivia shook her head, her voice hoarse. "I want Munin to have it. She was clinging to it in the end, Sawyer. It meant something to her. Maybe a few seconds of comfort amidst all that pain." She cast her eyes around the cabin, at the pitiful remnants of a woman's life.

Rawlings nodded in understanding. "All right, let's go. There's nothing else we can do here."

Outside, Harlan was squatting on his heels and rummaging through a pile of pottery shards. Haviland was assisting by digging with his front paws. "Anything?" Harlan asked upon seeing them emerge from the shack.

"The killer burned all her papers," Rawlings said. "And left a message behind. We're done and ready to head out whenever you are."

Harlan stood up, a broken jug in his hand. He stared at it for a moment, his eyes filled with sorrow, and then let it fall gently to the ground. "Her cooler of antivenom is gone. She kept it on the bottom of the creek and the rope tied to the handle's been cut. If she died on the bank, then she was just a few feet away from that cooler. Whoever killed her made sure she couldn't reach it. That's why the sheriff's men never saw it, but they should have noticed the posts stuck in the ground."

"Show me, please," Rawlings said and the two men walked behind the shack. They remerged minutes later, silent and angry.

"What will happen to this place?" Olivia asked Harlan.

He gestured outward with both arms. "When the lawmen are done poking around, the forest will claim it." He dusted off his hands and began to make his way toward the path. Then he paused and looked at Olivia. "That would make her happy. She was as much a part of these woods as the trees or the stream or the clay. She belongs to them now."

Olivia liked the thought of that. She gave Harlan a grateful smile before he turned away.

Together, the small party left the remains of Munin Cooper's existence behind, bequeathing her meager possessions to the wilderness.

Rawlings left Olivia at the dock and hurried off to contact Sheriff Poole. Harlan, who had errands in town, tied up the Whaler and said his good-byes as well.

Finding herself suddenly alone, Olivia headed for The Boot Top. Though Hudson needed to know that she'd seen their father's double again, she didn't want to tell him now. Once again, her head was crowded with disjointed thoughts and she didn't want to sort out the question of her paternity at the moment. Instead, she headed straight to her office at The Boot Top to look up the quote she'd found in Munin's mug.

Typing the words into Google's search box produced an instant result. The killer had left the final four lines of a poem entitled "Inscription for Katrina's Sun-Dial" by Henry Van Dyke. Like the other poems the killer favored, this one focused on things lost due to the passage of time. Olivia found it interesting that the poem actually ended with a positive message about the enduring power of love. She had no doubt that killer had omitted those lines because they didn't mesh with his or her distorted view of justice.

She was just about to search for a deeper analysis of the poem when Haviland issued a low growl.

"What is it, Captain? Is someone here?"

Haviland rose to his feet, his ears raised.

"It's me!" Millay called out and Haviland immediately stopped growling.

Millay appeared in the doorway and stopped. "I was hoping to find you here," she said, stuffing her hands in the pockets of a very short and very frayed jean skirt.

"Oh?" Olivia asked, momentarily flustered by her friend's unexpected visit. "Have you been to the hospital?"

Millay tugged at one of strings hanging from her skirt. "Yeah. Talley's awake and talking. Fletcher, Annette, and Judson are there, along with a few other people from her tribe. I didn't feel like I really belonged." She snapped the thread and began to wind it around her fingers. "I'm here because I have an idea." Now she looked directly at Olivia. "But I need Haviland."

Involuntarily, Olivia put a hand on the poodle's back. "What?"

Millay opened the flap of her messenger bag and withdrew a pack of cigarettes from inside. "Clove."

Olivia merely raised her eyebrows, silently inviting her friend to explain.

"I want to find the killer," Millay said with forced nonchalance. "All three of our major suspects are with Talley. All three of them are staying at the same hotel. Haviland can track this scent. If it's on their dirty clothes or sheets or whatever, he can find it, right?"

"Yes, but . . ." Olivia trailed off. It was crazy to even entertain the idea of breaking into three hotel rooms. Rawlings would be livid if he found out. Yet she was tired of feeling useless, of believing that Willis's murderer had rendered every member of the local law enforcement as well as the Bayside Book Writers utterly inept. "How do you plan on getting two women and a poodle into their rooms?"

Millay's smile was blinding. She had an accomplice. "The hotel uses magnetized key cards so I'll either swipe a master key from housekeeping or go with Plan B."

"I'm afraid to ask."

"Last night, I talked to some of my Fish Nets buddies about lock picking and let's just say one of them lent me a very handy tool. I've got it in a garment bag." She gestured at Haviland. "The toughest part will be sneaking him in."

Olivia waved off the idea. "When I'm desperate, I tell people I have a medical condition that Haviland is trained to respond to it." She smirked. "I've only resorted to the lie once or twice, but this is an emergency, isn't it?"

Millay backed out of the doorway to allow Olivia and Haviland to exit. She averted her eyes, overcome by a rare moment of shyness. "You know, I don't admire many people, but you're on my short list." She held out the clove cigarettes.

"Same goes for you," Olivia said and put the pack to her nose. If she'd felt any hesitation over breaking and entering, it vanished the moment the powerful scent hit her nasal passages. She closed her eyes and could almost feel the sun on her shoulders and hear the din of the powwow crowd. Those last moments with Willis rushed through her mind. Not as he lay dying, but of the time beforehand, when he was talking and gesturing animatedly, his face aglow with vitality.

Olivia gripped the cigarette pack hard and opened her eyes. She looked at Millay and found the same quiet rage reflected in her friend's gaze.

Nodding, the two women marched outside, determined to gain the upper hand at last, even if it meant committing a crime.

As Olivia entered the town of Havelock, the storm that had been moving in from the Atlantic made itself known. The sky rumbled with thunder and a hard, saturating rain fell from a wall of charcoal gray clouds. She parked the Range Rover and, eschewing an umbrella, she, Millay, and Haviland ran for cover.

The hotel lobby was nearly deserted when they strode in through the sliding glass doors. A lone desk clerk was preoccupied showing an elderly couple how to reach a landmark on their road map. None of them looked up as Millay, Olivia, and Haviland turned down the first corridor in search of the stairwell.

"Do you know their room numbers?" Olivia asked as they climbed the stairs to the second floor.

"Pretty much," Millay replied smugly. "This morning Annette mentioned that her room had a little balcony that overlooked the pool and she could hear the ice maker going at it in the middle of the night. That means it backs up against her room. The men will either be on the same side or across the hall from her. It's easier for housekeeping that way."

Olivia mulled this over. "And the mention of the balcony versus a patio is why we're headed to the second floor."

"Yep. Hotels save the ground floor for seniors and the handicapped. Couples and families get the higher floors." Millay tapped her head. "Amazing what you can find on the Internet. I even watched a YouTube video on how to use my handy break-in gadget."

Millay had shown the tool to Olivia in the privacy of the Range Rover. It looked like an oversized coat hanger and was meant to slip beneath the door and then curl up on the other side, grabbing hold of the handle.

However, when they reached the niche where the ice maker and a pair of vending machines stood, Millay spied a housekeeper coming out from a room two doors down and decided to appeal to her first. She claimed to have been sent to get an insurance card for her aunt who'd landed in the hospital and made quite of show of being both worried and rushed.

The housekeeper repeated the words "hospital" and "insurance" in English and then murmured to herself in Spanish. She quickly nodded her head and opened what they suspected was Annette's door with her master key.

She then pointed at Haviland and raised her pencil-thin brows in question.

"She needs a dog." Millay jerked a thumb at Olivia and adopted a pained expression. "Very sick."

That was all the housekeeper needed to hear. She gave the two women a tight smile and quickly pushed her cart in the opposite direction, her orthopedic shoes squeaking as she hustled down the hall.

"Now she thinks I have the plague," Olivia said and pushed past Millay into the room. "Check the closet. See if you recognize Annette's clothes."

While Millay shut the door and turned to the closet, Olivia took the clove cigarettes out of her purse and held them under Haviland's nose. "Find," she commanded.

He sniffed the open pack, sneezed, and shook his head in distaste, but then got to work.

"She wore this shirt yesterday." Millay pointed into the closet and then stepped aside as Haviland stuck his head into the space. He backed out again and entered the bathroom. Olivia watched him carefully while Millay spent her time opening and closing drawers and flipping through the pages of the novel on Annette's bed.

After five minutes of deliberate sniffing, Haviland returned to Olivia's side and sat down on his haunches. He hadn't found the scent anywhere in Annette's room.

"Now what?" Olivia asked though she already knew the answer.

"Keep an eye out for the housekeeper and I'll open the room next door."

Olivia moved to the center of the corridor and kept watch as Millay got on her knees, slipped the wire tool from the bag, and slid it under the door. She then pulled back on the wire in a movement that reminded Olivia of an archer nocking an arrow on a bow, and maneuvered the hooklike piece on the other side of the door until it caught hold of the handle. Within thirty seconds, Millay had gained access to the room.

"Damn," Olivia breathed once they were safely inside. "You're way too good at that."

Millay shrugged. "I practiced it like fifty times after work. I want to nail this bastard and I wasn't going to let some locked hotel door stand in my way."

The next room appeared to be Fletcher's. It was easy to identify his clothing, and the leather travel case in the bathroom bore his initials in gold lettering. Millay carefully rummaged through his drawers, Haviland investigated every nook and corner in an attempt to track the aroma of cloves, and Olivia examined the stack of papers on the desk. "There are copies of Natalie's medical records detailing Talley's birth," she told Millay. "Looks like the same stuff the sheriff asked Judson to fax him."

At that moment, Olivia's phone buzzed. She had an incoming call from Laurel. Deciding that it wasn't the best time to talk, she motioned for Millay. "Let's go. There's nothing here."

Once again, she took up a position in the hall while Millay opened the door to the next room. It became clear right away that they'd entered the wrong room.

"No way this is Judson's." Olivia pointed at the pink nightie and floral robe thrown across the unmade bed. A set of hot rollers and an enormous cosmetics bag in the bathroom confirmed their error.

Back in the hall, the women paused. They could try for the last room on the row or pick one of the rooms across from Annette's. Before they could decide, the elevator beep sounded and a couple carrying a sleeping toddler headed in their direction.

Olivia and Millay quickly pretended to be studying something on Millay's phone. The couple entered the room opposite Fletcher's.

"End of the hall it is," Millay said.

Hesitating, Olivia whispered. "What if that family comes back out?"

"Get Haviland to foam at the mouth." Millay tried to sound cavalier, but Olivia could tell she was just as nervous. "We've got to finish what we came here to do."

And with that, she crouched down in front of the last door. The instant they got inside, Olivia's phone vibrated again. Laurel was calling for the second time. "Let me see what she wants."

"Where are you?" Laurel demanded. "I've been calling all of your regular haunts and no one's seen you."

"Millay and I are doing some recon." Olivia crossed the room and began to open the nightstand drawers.

Laurel grunted. "Well, the twins are watching cartoons and Steve's absorbed in some preseason NFL show, so I had a chance to type up my notes from Saturday. I found something, Olivia." After her dramatic pause she continued. "Of course I had to research the Battle of Hayes Pond again to make sure that I wasn't seeing things, but I know what Munin's clues mean."

Olivia waved for Millay to join her by the window. "I'm going to put you on speaker."

"Remember how Rawlings told us about the woman whose husband ran off and left her behind after the Lumbee showed up at the KKK rally and gave the Klansmen what for?" Laurel's excitement practically leapt through the phone speaker.

"Yeah?" Millay drummed her fingers against her skirt.

"Her name was Mrs. Marjorie Dawson, but her maiden name was Ware." Laurel fell silent, waiting for her friends to catch on.

Suddenly, the skin on Olivia's arms erupted in goose bumps. "Jesus. Judson. His last name is Ware."

"You got it!" Laurel cried as if Olivia was her star pupil. "He's the son of Mr. and Mrs. Virgil Dawson. He wasn't even a twinkle in anyone's eye when his daddy dashed off and his mama drove her car into a ditch. But I found out that he was born in 1960 and we're all familiar with where he lived. That is, until his parents ran out of money and sold their place for pennies on the dollar."

"Talley's house," Millay breathed.

Olivia passed the phone to Millay and held the cigarettes out in front of Haviland's quivering nose. "Find," she whispered, unashamed of her shaking fingers or the dread she felt as she stared at a pair of Judson's shoes.

"The school ring. The one from the memory jug," Millay said dully. "It was from the class of 1970-something, right? Did Judson go to Littleton?"

"Yes, but why do you two sound so stressed out?" Laurel's tone was tight with concern. "Where are you?"

From within the small bathroom, Haviland barked once, signaling that he'd located the scent.

Millay and Olivia exchanged a long look.

They were standing in the killer's room.

And by the time Olivia saw the flash of movement reflected in the window glass, it was too late to leave.

Chapter 18

Time is the justice that examines all offenders.

—WILLIAM SHAKESPEARE

The movement Olivia had seen was that of a man's arm being raised into the air. Then, a blunt object made contact with the back of her head. The blow was hard enough for an explosion of white stars to obscure her vision. The pain surged through her entire body, driving her to her knees.

From what seemed like a great distance, she heard Millay scream. From even farther away came the sound of the muffled, frenzied barking of a very agitated poodle.

Olivia fought to stay conscious, but her limbs were as heavy as anchors and her head had filled with a thick fog. She kept her eyes shut, struggling to maintain her balance and to not keel over like a capsized boat.

She stretched her right hand out, tentatively searching for support, and curled her fingers around the edge of the window curtain.

That was all she was able to do. The small movement still made her feel sick to her stomach, so she clung to the coarse fabric, waiting for the pain to abate.

Noises continued to filter through the fuzz in her brain.

Two voices sounded in the air behind her, rising and falling like the swells of a stormy sea. Haviland's barking continued and Olivia could detect the furious scratching of her dog's claws against a door.

Her first lucid thought was, *Judson must have shut Haviland in the bathroom.*

The clarity didn't last long, however, and her body sagged even lower until her right hip was resting on floor. The contact with solid ground helped and the nausea receded. After a few more seconds, the world began to regain its balance. She no longer experienced the sensation that the earth was tilting and if she didn't hold on to the curtain tightly enough, she'd slide right off the edge.

"You can do whatever you want to me, you sick bastard!" Millay growled without a trace of fear. "But it's over. My friend was on the other end of the phone when you came in and she's already called the cops. There's a certain chief of police who's going to enjoy kicking your ass all over town."

Rawlings. Olivia desperately hoped he was on the way and that Millay wasn't merely stalling for time. They needed him, but the only chance of his kicking in the door was if Laurel had been able to recognize that her friends were in danger. Olivia knew that their phone connection had been intact when Judson had struck her, but she had no idea what happened next. Had Millay shouted for Laurel to call 911? Had she yelled that they were trapped in a hotel room with a murderer?

As much as Olivia loathed having to be rescued, she knew that's exactly what she needed. After all, she still couldn't open her eyes, let alone rush to Millay's aid.

"Why did you do it?" Millay's voice rose in a challenge. "Are you in the Klan?"

Judson snorted. "There is no Klan anymore. It's just me."

"But why Willis? Why Talley?"

"Why, why, why," Judson mocked her. "Because the

Locklears ruined my life. I vowed to wipe them off the face of the earth and I'm nearly done. None of you will stop me from finishing the job. I've been planning this weekend for a long time."

Millay was silent for a moment. Olivia wanted to look at her, but the pain was still wracking her body and she needed to wait for it to ebb a bit more.

"When did it start? Your hatred for the Locklears?" Millay asked with surprising gentleness.

Judson immediately responded to her tone. "It began at the so-called Battle of Hayes Pond. When my daddy ran off like the coward he was and left my mama behind. She drove our car into a ditch and was apparently so grateful to one of the Indians who came to her aid that she started sleeping with him. Daddy found out and beat her over and over. Tried to beat the animal out of her. He locked her in the house. He got her pregnant with me, but once I was born, she snuck out more and more. She only wanted *him*. I didn't matter to her. Looked too much like Daddy for her tastes."

"Who was he?" Millay whispered. "Her lover?"

"Lover?" Judson scoffed. "A highbrow word for the loser she spread her legs for. The whore."

Olivia could sense Millay's wheels turning. "If he was a Locklear, then he must have been Talley's grandfather."

Judson didn't respond and Olivia had to assume he'd nodded. He then said, "Calvin Locklear was an Indian gigolo. Not only was he banging my mama, but he was also sleeping with Munin Cooper. He and Munin already had a son together, but they never bothered to get married. Real classy, those two."

I was right, Olivia thought sadly. *Willis and Talley had a grandmother and never knew it.*

"Judson." Millay spoke his name with surprising softness. "Talley told me about the marks on the wall in the root cellar of her house. Your house," she quickly amended. "There was a name she couldn't read. And lots of lines."

Judson expelled a long breath. For a moment, Olivia didn't think he'd rise to the bait. When he did, his voice was low and distant. "That's my childhood, written in stone. A mark for every beating. An X for each time I was locked in the dark—sometimes for the whole day without food or water. That's *my* name on the wall. Sonny. That's *my* blood in the dirt. That's *my* house. It will *always* be my house. I'm a part of it."

Though his words held only a trace of emotion, Olivia was able to picture a little boy cowering in the corner of the lightless cellar, his body bruised and sore, tears running down his cheeks. How many times had he incurred his father's wrath? How often had he been struck for his mother's mistakes? Had his nose been broken or his ribs cracked because of one parent's cowardice and the other's infidelity?

And now it was too late to offer sympathy. The boy Sonny was gone. He'd grown into a vengeful and tortured adult named Judson Ware. And he was a killer.

"What happened to your parents?" Millay was still speaking in a hushed tone.

"Oh, Mama sold our farm to her red-skinned rescuer, but my daddy wasn't about to leave the land he'd worked his whole life. He loaded his shotgun and told Mama he'd give her a head start, but he was coming after her and her man. He vowed to hunt them down and destroy Calvin's seed next." Olivia heard a note of pride in Judson's voice. "They tried to run, Mama and Calvin, but Daddy tracked them to a cabin in the mountains. Buried them there too. No one ever knew except for Munin. That witch woman. Part gypsy, part Injun. Her kind was lower than animals. No wonder her man choose a white woman over her."

Olivia knew this comment would enrage Millay and she dared to open her eyes a crack, hoping to warn her friend with a glance, but the light caused a fresh bout of agony. She fought it, willing her vision to come into focus and, finally, the blurry edges became sharp and she could see a bed, a pair of shoes, the legs of the nightstand.

She lifted her gaze higher and saw that Millay had been tied to the desk chair. Judson sat on the edge on the bed, one leg crossed casually over the other, a wicked-looking hunting knife resting on the coverlet near his hand.

"Why would you want to finish the work your dad started? A man who beat you and locked you up? Because of the casino deal?" Millay asked. Olivia thought her friend seemed amazingly calm considering the fact that her wrists and ankles were bound to a chair.

Neither Judson nor Millay seemed aware that Olivia was coming around. Judson's attention was fixed on Millay and even Haviland's persistent scratching didn't distract him. However, the placid expression on his face changed the moment Millay brought up the casino and now he leaned forward, his hand curling around the knife handle, his body taut with anger.

"I told you. The house and the land are rightfully mine! It all belonged to Mama and she sold it to her Indian. It was meant to be a payoff for Munin and her bastard son, a consolation prize because her man had left her for another woman. And then Munin left it in trust for Bo. But what was my consolation? What did I get out of all of this?" Judson was so mad that his words shot out of his mouth like bullets. Millay flinched as he sprayed her face with spittle. "Yeah, what about *me*? She just *left* me alone with *him*. She knew what would happen to me, but she didn't care. That Lumbee devil worked his mumbo-jumbo on her and she never looked back."

Olivia winced. She knew all too well how it felt to be abandoned by a parent. A hurricane had claimed her mother's life. A few years later, she thought that the sea had taken her father's, only to learn decades afterward that he'd staged his own death and had started his life over again. He'd never contacted her, letting her believe that she was an orphan.

Again, she pictured Judson as a boy, repeatedly paying the price for his mother's betrayal and his father's shame.

He must have been abused for years, Olivia thought, her heart aching for the child who paid for others' mistakes.

"Because you work for Fletcher, you saw Natalie's medical records," Millay murmured, as if she were talking to herself. "You looked up MH and decided to fulfill your dad's vow to wipe out the rest of Calvin Locklear's family."

Relaxing, Judson resumed his casual posture, took his hand off the knife, and smiled. "I was always very bright. I could have been an incredible attorney if I'd had the money to go to law school. But I took the job with Fletcher because I wanted to get close to the Lumbee. I didn't see Natalie's medical records for a long time. Fletcher's a paranoid man and he keeps his old case files locked up securely at home. But when he asked me to watch his place while he went on a golfing trip, I discovered where he hid his keys."

"Some house sitter," Millay said but Judson ignored her. He was too wrapped up in his own story.

"When I saw Natalie's chart, I looked up MH and knew I'd found a way to get my house back. I stole the inhalants from a Lumbee veterinarian. I told you that I like walking the dogs in my spare time." He uttered a single, humorless guffaw. "Willis's went into a clove cigarette and Talley's into her inhaler. Munin got rattlesnake venom in her syringe—easy to buy online, by the way."

Millay had balled her hands into fists. "She wasn't a Locklear. Why punish her?"

"She tried to keep Calvin's son from me, but I got all the old-timer Lumbees to trust me and slowly, over many, many years, I learned that Munin had borne Calvin a son and when she got wind of my daddy's vow, she hid him in plain sight and then took off, just like my whore of a mother." His mouth twisted into a crooked smile.

"So what's with all the time poetry?"

Judson examined his nails. "After Mama sold the farm, Daddy and I rented rooms in a run-down shotgun house facing the highway. That's where he began to drink himself to death. After he succeeded, I got dumped into the foster care system. I only had a few possessions from my old life. A photo of our farm and Mama's favorite book of poems. I was drawn to the ones about time and I needed something to think about while my world went to hell." He held out his finger to silence Millay. "No. No more questions. I'm tired of the sound of your voice."

Olivia quickly closed her eyes and tried to formulate a plan. She could call out a command to Haviland and knew that he'd respond by pulling down on the bathroom door handle with his teeth. Even if it were a knob and not a handle, Haviland could turn it and get out. However, he'd been schooled since puppyhood not to open a door in such a manner and only an emergency could get him to break the ingrained rule. At the moment, he was alarmed and agitated, but if he thought Olivia was in immediate danger, he'd be out of the bathroom in a streak of black fur and bared teeth.

And yet, Olivia hesitated. Judson had a nasty-looking knife and she couldn't risk Haviland being injured. She'd rather tackle Judson herself than have that happen. On the other hand, if she could create a distraction, perhaps Haviland could disable Judson without getting hurt.

She opened her eyes a sliver and saw that Judson was in the midst of gagging Millay. He stuffed a bandana in her mouth as she bucked in the chair, her voice rising in a stifled shout as she twisted her head back and forth, her face full of fury.

Olivia knew that she had to act now. Judson was preparing to leave. And if he escaped, Talley would spend the rest of her life looking over her shoulder. She would never be safe. Perhaps none of them would.

Very slowly, she ran her fingers across the carpet, reaching for the pair of shoes on the floor. She didn't want to attract Judson's notice, and having to move her muscles with such control was extremely difficult. Her head rang and the light from the desk lamp sent little needles of pain into her eye sockets, but she grabbed hold of the shoes and pulled them to her. Then she drew in a deep breath and yelled, "HAVILAND! ATTACK! ATTACK!"

Several things happened at once. The scratching from the bathroom stopped and Olivia knew that Haviland had the handle or knob between his jaws. Judson swiveled, startled to hear Olivia's voice, and picked up the knife. He positioned it loosely in his hand, the gleaming blade pointed right at her, but before he could take a single step in her direction, she launched the first shoe straight at him.

The shoes were leather with a solid rubber sole. The left one hit Judson square in the chest, stopping his forward movement while his mind tried to grapple with what had struck him. Olivia aimed higher and released the right shoe, the pain blooming in her head.

She heard an "umph" as the shoe connected with Judson's chin and then Haviland was there. Mouth open in a ferocious snarl, he leapt onto Judson's chest, knocking him backward onto the floor. The knife came loose and Olivia crawled forward to retrieve it, fighting against the shadows creeping into the edges of her vision. She gritted her teeth and, clinging to the arm of the desk chair, sawed through the rope binding Millay's wrist.

Millay yanked out the bandana and took the knife. A high keening arose from Judson's throat and Olivia could see why. Haviland had his mouth clamped around the man's neck. He hadn't applied enough pressure to sever the skin and was looking to Olivia for instructions.

"Good work, Captain," she whispered gratefully as the black fog drifted in over her vision. "Hold him. Wait for the chief."

And with that, she passed out.

Olivia reasoned that she couldn't have been unconscious for long because when the harsh odor of smelling salts jarred her back to wakefulness, she was still on the hotel room floor. One pleasant change was that a pair of strong arms was supporting her torso and her head was pressed against a man's sturdy chest. Rawlings' chest.

Without speaking, she pushed away the inhalant he'd placed under her nose.

"Sorry," he said, his lips hovering just above her hair. "A blast of ammonia is a nasty way to be brought back, but concussion victims need to stay awake."

Olivia buried her face in his shirt, hoping to escape the acrid smell of ammonia. His scent of sandalwood and coffee helped steady her and she breathed it in greedily. He'd come to her rescue, just as she'd hoped he would.

"I will always come for you," he whispered as if she'd spoken the thought aloud.

"Haviland," Olivia said, turning her head. She tried to take in the crowded room, but there was too much commotion for her muddled brain to process.

Haviland, who'd been standing guard over her, moved forward and nuzzled her with his nose. She kissed him, putting an arm around his neck and drawing him against her. "My hero. You'll be eating like a king for the foreseeable future."

Sheriff Poole approached the trio and, after shooting Haviland a nervous glance, squatted well out of the poodle's reach. "Paramedics are here, Chief. It's time for you to get your head checked, ma'am." He smiled at Olivia.

"Millay?" she asked.

"She's fine," Rawlings assured her. "She's waiting in the sheriff's car."

Poole chuckled. "When the manager let me into this room, I thought I might have a gun fight on my hands. Instead, your dog had Mr. Ware pinned to the ground, his teeth hovering over the guy's jugular. As if that weren't enough, your friend had a knife pressed against his groin. That man was afraid to breathe, let alone move. I've never met anyone so eager to be cuffed and taken away."

Olivia tried to sit up unaided, but Rawlings refused to let her go. With his hands on her back, she was able to turn and look at him full in the face. His expression surprised her. The fear and worry he'd felt for her was quickly giving way to anger.

"It was Judson," she told him. "He killed Munin and Willis and tried to kill Talley."

"Maybe so," Rawlings said in dangerously quiet voice. "But unless he confesses, we'll have a helluva time proving it."

Poole rubbed his expansive chin. "Now that he's out of harm's way, he's full of threats. He's going to sue the hotel, the sheriff's department, and especially you, Ms. Limoges. Said he'll make sure your dog is put down if it's the last thing he does."

"Everything that went on in this room happened because you and Millay committed a B and E," Rawlings said unhappily. "Judson could stand in front of a judge and claim to have surprised a pair of thieves ransacking his room, after which he was attacked by a dog belonging to one of the intruders. He knows the law, Olivia. You and Millay might have compromised the whole case."

Olivia began to shake her head, but the movement hurt too much. "He's proud of what he's done. He'll tell you everything." She wasn't completely certain that this was the truth, but she needed to believe that it was.

"I hope you're right," Rawlings said and Olivia heard the fatigue in his voice. "But we'll talk about it later. Right now, you have a date with an ER doctor."

"No way," Olivia objected, recovering some of her pluck. "I am *not* climbing onto that thing." She pointed at the stretcher parked in the hall. "And if I go to the hospital, they're going to insist on observing me for who knows how long. I can't leave Haviland."

Rawlings gave her an indulgent smile. "I'll take care of Haviland. As for you, you get on that gurney or I'll carry you to the ambulance. And I'm not young anymore, Olivia. I'm not sure my back can take it."

"Then I'll walk. Just hold on to me."

After telling the paramedics that he'd meet them by the front door, Rawlings slipped an arm around Olivia's waist. "You're the most difficult, infuriating, and impetuous woman I've ever known."

Olivia leaned her head against his shoulder and they walked slowly down the hall to the waiting elevator car, Haviland following on their heels. "I'm sorry, Sawyer. It wasn't my intention to screw this up. I could have tried to talk Millay out of her plan, but I have to admit that I found it very attractive. I wanted to act. I wanted this to be over."

"Well, for both of you, it is over."

The elevator doors slid closed and Olivia wrapped her arms tighter around the chief's waist. There were so many things she wanted to say to him, but the brief drop from the second floor to the first made her feel dizzy.

"You should have gotten on the gurney, you stubborn woman," Rawlings chided as he half dragged her through the lobby.

"I love you too," Olivia mumbled and then grudgingly allowed the paramedics to help her into the ambulance. Suddenly, the idea of lying down was very appealing and she settled on the stretcher, relaxing as an EMT strapped her in for the ride. Having the sheet tucked around her feet made her feel like she was in a cocoon of clean, white cotton, and she wanted nothing more than to fall into a deep sleep and wake the next morning with the whole nightmarish event behind her.

"Oh, no you don't." Rawlings gave her shoulder a shake. "They'll hit you up with the smelling salts if you try to nod off."

She opened her eyes and glared at him. "I thought you had a bad guy to work over."

"I do. And don't think that what you said earlier is going

to keep you out of hot water," Rawlings said. "This is Poole's neck of the woods and I don't know how he's going to handle this mess."

"What did I say?" Olivia frowned and then suddenly realized that Rawlings was referring to the "I love you too" comment. "Oh, that." She paused and then reached up and touched his cheek with her hand. "I know you're supposed to say that kind of thing over a candlelit dinner or a walk on the beach, but it just tumbled out. Doesn't make it less true though."

The EMT waiting by the rear doors coughed discreetly, signaling Rawlings that it was time to get a move on.

Rawlings ignored the paramedic and lowered his face so that his lips brushed Olivia's. "Say it again," he whispered.

"I love you," she whispered back and the two of them lingered for a long second, clinging to a moment that belonged to them alone, a tiny oasis of light and warmth in the dark night.

When Rawlings tried to straighten, Olivia grabbed him by the arm. "Judson's pain is connected to the house. If he won't talk, mention the house. The only time he had a family, as screwed up as that family was, was in that house. When his mother sold it to Calvin Locklear, it broke his world apart. He could never pick up the pieces. Life wouldn't let him."

Kissing her hand, Rawlings nodded. He stepped out of the ambulance and she heard him say, "Come on, Captain. We've got to get a signed confession before I can feed you one of your fancy suppers," before the paramedic closed the rear doors.

"So your dog is the hero of the hour, eh?" the fresh-faced EMT said.

Olivia smiled. "He is. He's going to be impossible to live with over the next few days."

"And the police chief? Is he your boyfriend?" the EMT

continued, fitting a blood pressure cuff around Olivia's upper arm.

Olivia laughed and then winced. Laughing hurt. "I'm too old to have a boyfriend. At my age, women have lovers, not boyfriends." Her head throbbed. "What the hell was I hit with anyway?"

The paramedic was pleased to be able to answer her question. "It was a woodcarving. Almost as long as my arm and pretty solid too. One of the deputies said that your attacker must have bought it at the powwow."

It had certainly felt solid. "A carving?"

"Yeah, an eagle perched on a log. Guess the guy was really patriotic or something." The paramedic placed stethoscope buds in his ears, inflated the cuff, and then wrote a note on his chart.

"Not patriotic," Olivia said. "Psychotic."

This got the EMT's attention. He was about to pop a thermometer under her tongue but he paused, his hand in midair. "I heard that he killed people. Is that true?"

"Yes."

"Man, I hope the sheriff and your chief will make sure he's put away for a long time," he said.

"Me too," she said and opened her mouth to receive the thermometer.

After taking her temperature, the paramedic jotted down a few more notes. He let her close her eyes and they rode the rest of the way in silence.

My chief. Olivia repeated the paramedic's words to herself. She liked the sound of it.

As the road passed beneath the ambulance, Olivia pictured the man she loved, the man with the salt-and-pepper hair, the strong hands, and the pond green eyes. She knew that he was already back on the job, probably striding down a corridor at the sheriff's office, a cup of coffee in his hand, preparing to sit in on an interview with a murderer. He would work tirelessly until justice was achieved for Judson's victims. He would work until he had what he needed to put the killer away.

And then he would come to her.

I will always come for you, he had said.

Her chief. The only man who dared to claim her.

Olivia thought about time. She thought about how Judson had used it to exact his twisted revenge. How she had wasted so much of it nursing the pain of her past, by barricading herself behind a wall of loneliness. How it had taken half a lifetime for her to find love.

Better late than never, she thought as the ambulance pulled to a stop in front of the emergency room. The EMT opened the rear doors and light flooded in, the dust motes dancing in the sunbeams like millions of tiny stars.

Chapter 19

*Parents wonder why the streams are bitter,
when they themselves have poisoned the
fountain.*

—JOHN LOCKE

Courtesy of the wooden eagle, Olivia received nine stitches and, much to her annoyance, was forced to remain overnight for observation. To her surprise, she curled up in her hospital bed and fell into a deep, dreamless sleep and awoke feeling refreshed and remarkably clearheaded. By the time her nurse's shift ended at seven the next morning, Olivia was demanding her discharge paperwork.

As she filled out countless forms, her cell phone rang and she scooped it up with unusual eagerness. She'd had no luck getting through to Rawlings last night and was concerned about both the case and Haviland's well-being.

"Are you on the beach?" Dixie demanded tersely. "I already tried calling your house."

The breathless quality to Dixie's voice was unsettling. "What's going on?" Olivia asked.

"The spittin' image of Willie Wade is at my window booth, that's what!" Dixie exclaimed. "Ordered eggs and sausage calm as you please and is sittin' there readin' the paper like he was king of the universe."

"Keep him there, Dixie. I need to talk to him."

Dixie spluttered, "But why? Who is he?"

"I think he's my father's twin brother. Will you tell him who I am and that I'd like him to wait for me at the diner? I have to call a cab and it'll take me at least thirty minutes to get back to Oyster Bay."

"Where in God's green earth are you?"

Olivia sighed. She didn't want to provide Dixie with a lengthy explanation right now. "In the hospital. I had a concussion but I'm okay. I promise to tell you what I can when I get there."

"What you can?" Dixie scoffed. "That means I'll get next to nothin' out of you." She tried to sound disgruntled, but she was too excited to be convincing. "Ah well, I suppose I'll have to amuse myself by grillin' the doppelganger wavin' his coffee cup in the air like it's gonna be refilled by a troupe of flyin' fairies."

Olivia laughed and said good-bye. She'd just dropped the phone back into her purse when she looked up to find Laurel and Harris standing in the doorway. Laurel was carrying a beautiful arrangement of orange and yellow lilies in one hand and a glass vase in the other.

"Why are you dressed?" she asked, nonplussed. "We brought you flowers."

"They're gorgeous," Olivia said, smiling. "It's so good to see you both. How's Millay? What's going on with the investigation? Have you talked to Rawlings?"

Harris held up his hand. "Whoa, whoa. Slow down. First of all, are you cleared to leave? Millay said you got whacked pretty hard."

Olivia showed him her paperwork. "I'm legit. I was just about to call a taxi when you showed up."

"Mom's taxi at your service." Laurel performed a little curtsy. "You can even sit up front. Harris doesn't mind the cookie crumbs, apple juice spills, and cereal debris in the backseat. We'll fill you in on the case on the way to the parking lot."

The three friends headed outside. Olivia felt unsettled to be walking without Haviland at her side. It felt like part of her was missing. Why hadn't Rawlings at least sent her a text message?

"Have you seen the chief?" she asked Laurel. "Haviland stayed with him last night and I'm worried about them both."

"That must have been hard on you," Laurel said. "But we only talked with Millay. After giving her statement yesterday, she insisted on visiting Talley. The next thing we knew, she was in the car and on her way to Maxton."

Olivia paused next to the passenger door of Laurel's minivan. "That's a three-hour drive!"

Harris nodded. "It sure was. I know because I went with her. She was hell-bent on visiting Talley's house. Apparently, Judson refused to confess and Millay swore she had a plan to get him to tell the cops everything."

Laurel unlocked the minivan and they all got in. Olivia breathed in a mixture of Cheerios, juice, and coffee. "Why did she want to go to Talley's house?"

Harris kicked aside a pile of empty juice boxes and buckled his seat belt. "First, she wanted to photograph the walls in the root cellar. Second, she wanted to collect photos of Talley and Willis in the house. Happy ones, you know? Christmases, birthdays, Willis and Talley carving pumpkins, that kind of thing."

"Brilliant," Olivia said. "Did it work?"

"I have no clue," Harris admitted. "Millay brought her camera and Talley's photo albums to the sheriff's office, but neither Poole nor Rawlings invited her to enter the inner sanctum, so she left the stuff with a deputy and went home and crashed. She's still out cold."

Olivia studied the landscape for a moment. "I'm assuming

that she told you what we did." She glanced at Laurel. "And you obviously realized we were in trouble."

"It wasn't hard to figure out!" Laurel exclaimed. "Millay shouted for me to call the cops, that you two were in Judson's hotel room, and that he was there too. I used the landline in my kitchen to get ahold of the chief." She put a hand over her heart. "I've never been so glad to have someone answer on the first ring in all my life."

Laurel put her hand back on the steering wheel and gripped it tightly. Olivia saw her friend's knuckles turn white. "It's all right, Laurel. You did everything you could and I'm sorry we scared you like that."

"If only I'd typed up my powwow interview notes earlier . . ." Laurel left the rest of the sentence unsaid.

"Hey, if anyone missed something important, it was me," Olivia said. "Judson made several comments about growing up poor and having had to deal with hardship. He even mentioned the fact that he volunteered at an animal clinic. That's where he got the inhalants. It was like he was taunting us—dropping little bread crumbs for us to follow and then laughing while they were eaten by hungry birds."

Harris groaned. "This was the strangest weekend I've ever lived through. There were so many riddles, so many things spinning out of control. It felt like time was moving too fast for us to catch up. All I want to do now is chill out for a few days."

"Aren't you supposed to be at work?" Olivia asked.

"I took a sick day." Harris gave Olivia a demonstration of the coughing fit he'd produced for the benefit of his boss.

Laurel laughed. "After I take you home, Olivia, I'm going to spend the rest of the day at my cubicle. I might not be able to tell the complete story on Judson Ware and the Locklears, but I've got enough to wet plenty of whistles."

"Actually, could you drop me off at Grumpy's?" Olivia asked. "I have something to take care of there."

This surprised Laurel. "But the chief had someone

bring your car back to your house. And what about Haviland?"

Olivia felt a twist of guilt in her belly. "I don't even know where he is."

"Haviland's with the chief," Harris assured her. "Rawlings called me at five thirty this morning and asked me to check on you. He didn't want to wake *you* up, but it was totally fine to wake *me* up."

"That's because you don't have a head injury," Laurel said. "And he called me too, remember?"

Harris filled Olivia in on a few more details. Talley was being discharged from the hospital and had accepted Annette Stevens' invitation to live with her and her family for a while. Fletcher Olsen, who was shocked and sickened to discover the monstrous duplicity of his longtime employee, announced that he planned to put his clients' affairs in order and then close his practice for good.

"He's going to move to Hilton Head," Harris continued. "And spend his days getting a golfer's tan."

"Poor guy," Laurel said. "I feel terrible about suspecting him and the Lumbee chief. That woman has done nothing but fight for her tribe. She's worked her whole life to improve things for her people and we actually thought she might have killed one of them."

Olivia nodded. "I know how you feel, Laurel. But what we did was necessary, if not exactly kind. A young woman's life was at stake and time was running out." She saw a road sign for Oyster Bay up ahead and smiled. "In this case, I took the ask-for-forgiveness-instead-of-permission mantra. I know Annette will understand. I just hope Rawlings will too. Eventually."

The three friends rode in silence for a few minutes. As downtown Oyster Bay came into view, Olivia thanked Laurel and Harris for coming to get her and suggested they all meet for dinner at The Bayside Crab House later in the week.

"Do you want me to drop Harris off and come back for

you?" Laurel asked as she double-parked in front of the diner.

"No," Olivia said. "Thanks again for the flowers." She put the lilies to her nose and hesitated for a second before getting out of the car. She hadn't showered and was wearing yesterday's clothes. Her hair had been shaved around the area where she'd received the stitches and she hadn't bothered to dig out either the tube of lipstick or the bottle of Shalimar perfume she kept in her purse. Is this how she wanted to present herself to the man who was in all likelihood her biological father?

Actually, it is, she thought. Clutching the flowers to her chest, she waved good-bye to her friends and entered the diner.

Dixie dumped the plate of waffles she was carrying and skated forward to greet her. "Lord have mercy! You look like you've been to hell and back!"

Olivia darted a quick look at the window booth. Her father's twin was there and he was staring at her. "I've had better nights," she murmured, thrust the flowers into Dixie's hands, and walked over to the booth.

Zipping ahead of Olivia, Dixie performed the introductions. "Charles Wade, this is Olivia. Olivia, meet Charles." For once, Dixie's eyes weren't glittering over the high potential for drama. In fact, her face was pinched with concern. "You want coffee, hon?"

"Please," Olivia said. "And grits with butter. I'm starving."

Charles Wade had been gazing unblinkingly at Olivia from the moment she entered the diner. After Dixie moved off, he clasped his hands together and exhaled very slowly. "You look just like her. When I saw you in the boat yesterday, I thought you were Camille. I knew it wasn't possible, but my heart stopped."

"I saw you at the powwow on Saturday," Olivia said cautiously, studying the man. Up close, it was even more obvious that he and Willie Wade were identical twins. Charles's grooming was meticulous and he wore expensive designer brands from his eyeglasses to his watch to his Italian loafers, but the shape of his face and his tall, wiry frame were the same as his brother's. "I thought you were my father, but he died last spring." She waited for Charles Wade to react to this piece of news, but he didn't. This bothered Olivia. Had he already known or did he just not care?

"Why did you come to Oyster Bay?" she asked. "And how is it that I've never seen or heard of you before now?"

"My company sponsored the Coastal Carolina Food Festival. We own the television network that produces most of the food-related shows, including the one that filmed the feature on The Boot Top Bistro." There was nothing boastful in his manner, which was a relief to Olivia. She wanted to like this man. "Dixie told me that The Boot Top is your restaurant. I enjoyed an excellent meal there last night."

Olivia acknowledged the compliment with a dip of her chin. "Do you usually attend the festivals? They seem rather unsophisticated for a Fortune Five Hundred CEO type."

He smiled. "You got me there. I only came to this one because it was so close to Oyster Bay. To the last place Camille and I—" He halted and then began again. "I looked her up about ten years ago only to discover that she was dead. Until then, I'd forced myself to forget about her. I had a wife and children and a fulfilling career. I told myself I'd never look back, but Camille was a difficult woman to forget."

Suddenly, Olivia understood. "So you were already married when you had an affair with my mother. Did she know about your wife?"

Charles gave her a dark look. He probably wasn't accustomed to being spoken to so bluntly. "Not at first," he said, recovering his affable manner. "Camille and I met at a museum fund-raiser in Raleigh, but even then I knew I wanted to move to New York. My wife's father had promised me a job at his network after I proved myself at the local station. I worked my ass off. I didn't have the advantageous upbringing that my wife or your mother had, so I had to learn how to polish my rough edges and shed all traces of where I'd come from."

"Including your brother?" Olivia asked, feeling a rare pang of sympathy for Willie Wade.

"He and I never got along. He never wanted to be more, to be better than our father or all the Wade fishermen before him," Charles said, his voice rising slightly. "And he wasn't better. He was *worse*. Flunked out of high school, got arrested for a dozen petty crimes, starting drinking at fourteen. How Camille could stand it, I'll never know."

Olivia stared at him. "You got her pregnant, that's how!" she snapped. "And my guess is that you told my mother about your wife and your big career plans at about the same time she discovered she was carrying your baby."

All the color drained from Charles's face. "What? *My* baby?"

Dixie arrived with Olivia's coffee and grits. She shot Olivia a worried glance and then glided away to check on the customers at the *Evita* booth. Olivia poured a splash of cream into her coffee and tried to calm down. "How did my mother meet Willie?"

Charles searched his memory. "She wanted to be introduced to my family, and even though I knew there was no point in it, she could be very convincing and so I brought her to Oyster Bay. I figured once she saw the place, she'd be turned off and would drop the subject of meeting my folks. But she loved it. She fell in love with every inch of this dinky, little town. With *this*!" He made a sweeping gesture. "Unfortunately, we also ran into my brother that day. He invited us out for drinks, probably because he wanted to see me squirm, and he and Camille got along just fine. Still, I never imagined she'd marry him."

Olivia fought to contain her indignation. "She couldn't have you, so she took the closest thing. And your brother accepted her even though she was probably carrying your baby. He was more honorable than you could ever hope to be, high school dropout or not." Olivia's voice was cold and hostile. "My mother tried to protect me from having to grow up a fatherless bastard. She couldn't have predicted that Willie could barely look at me, that he saw his brother's child every time I walked into the room. She couldn't have known that none of us would ever be happy."

Charles Wade rubbed his chin nervously. "I'm sorry. I had no idea she was pregnant, and the last time I saw my brother, he told me never to step foot in Oyster Bay again— that I wasn't wanted here anymore. Believe me, I was glad to leave it all behind. I didn't even come back when my parents died." He looked at Olivia plaintively. "Listen, I love my wife. We have a good life together. I loved your mother too, but . . ." He threw out his hands. "What can I do to make you see that I'm not a bad guy? How can I make amends?"

Narrowing her eyes, Olivia leaned over and said, "You can keep your promise. Leave this town and never come back."

Startled, Charles reached for her hand. "But you're my daughter, aren't you?"

Olivia drew away as if his touch would burn her skin. "Biologically? Maybe. Maybe not. In any case, I had a father. His name was Willie Wade. Now I see that he loved a woman who was in love with his own brother and that he raised a kid who probably wasn't his. Over time, his decision to marry my mother turned him into a mean and bitter man, but he stuck it out as long as he was able. And then, just like you, he took off to lead a different life. A better life."

She pushed her bowl of grits away, no longer interested in eating, and stood up. "I don't know you, Mr. Wade, nor do I care to. Have a safe trip back to New York."

And with that, she left the diner.

Though she was eager to get home, she had no way of getting there, so she headed for the police station, hoping against hope that Rawlings wasn't still in Havelock. Her thoughts were in turmoil and the bruised spot on her head was starting to throb again.

She sat down on a park bench and dialed Rawlings' cell phone number. He answered right away.

"Where are you?" he asked. She told him and he sighed in exasperation. "You had Laurel drop you at Grumpy's? You couldn't just make instant grits at your house? Stay where you are. Haviland and I are minutes away." His voice was leaden with fatigue. "It's been a very long night."

"Let's go home," she said. "And you can tell me all about it."

As displeased with her as he was, Rawlings had driven Olivia home, showered, and told her everything that had happened since their parting in the ambulance the previous night.

Millay's idea to show Judson photographs of Talley and Willis living out a carefree childhood in his former house had been a success. The images of Talley hanging from a tire swing, her mouth stretched into a huge smile, or of Natalie and Willis planting a vegetable garden in the back-yard had sent Judson into a self-righteous rage. Incensed, he'd grabbed for the photos and ripped them to shreds, screaming out his confession. He'd vandalized the Lock-lears' cars, stolen inhalants from the animal clinic, com-mitted two counts of murder and one count of attempted murder. By the end, he was howling and spitting like a wounded animal.

"I'm relieved, but bone weary, Olivia," Rawlings had said, stretching out on the bed and closing his eyes. "The photographs Millay took told us a terrible story. There were so many lines, so many marks in the stone. That poor child."

Olivia had curled up next to him and covered his hand with hers. "The things people do to each other, to those they supposedly love, can be truly unforgivable." She hadn't been thinking of just Judson's parents, but of the twin brothers, Charles and Willie Wade; of two betrayed woman named Camille Limoges and Munin Cooper; of all the times she had stood on the beach and looked out to sea, silently wishing for her loneliness to abate and for the agony of being unloved to be washed away by the next wave.

She'd been about to tell Rawlings that people could save each other too, but his breathing had slowed, the air escaping through his slack lips in the steady cadence of sleep.

Olivia had taken Haviland and driven back into town. She'd freed the safety deposit key from the pottery shard and, after a short meeting with the bank manager, was led to a safety deposit box that had been rented by Olivia's mother over forty years ago.

"She purchased one of our hundred-year leases," the manager had explained. "I wasn't here then, but according to my records, no one has requested access to the box since Ms. Camille first opened it."

Thanking the manager, Olivia had entered the vault, removed the safety deposit box, and stepped into one of the tiny, private rooms in order to examine the contents. Her hands were trembling as she fit the key into the lock. What did she expect to find? Her mother had been disowned by Olivia's grandmother the moment she'd exchanged vows with Willie Wade, so Olivia doubted the box contained anything of value. What if another earth-shattering secret waited within?

"I can't take any more of those," Olivia had mumbled and opened the box.

Inside, she found a single piece of paper. Her birth certificate. And there, on the line indicating "Name of Father," was the name Charles Wade.

Olivia had removed the certificate, stuffed it into her purse, and left the room. On her way out of the bank, she handed the manager the key. "You can rent it to someone else now. It's been emptied."

Returning home, Olivia grabbed a box of matches from the kitchen and paused for a long moment to stare at the woodcarving the man she'd known as her father had made for her.

She then kicked off her shoes and hurried over the dunes, the salt-laden wind whipping her hair around her face. While Haviland danced in the sea foam, she'd taken the birth certificate from her pocket, struck a match, and set it on fire.

Now, she waded into the water, the only place where she and a man named Willie Wade had always felt at home. The same could not be said about her biological father. He hated everything about Oyster Bay while Olivia loved her town and the people in it with all of her heart.

The paper burned until it was nothing but a scattering of ashes. Olivia watched as the ocean pulled the pieces, and her secret, into the deep.

Chapter 20

To go forward is to move toward perfection.
March on, and fear not the thorns, or the
sharp stones on life's path.

—KHALIL GIBRAN

That following Friday, the Bayside Book Writers got together for an impromptu end-of-summer celebration at The Bayside Crab House. The men wore Hawaiian shirts in bold prints and the women wore flirty sundresses and strappy sandals. The hostess led them to a table on the deck laden with appetizers and pitchers of pomegranate margaritas.

"I noticed that the 'For Lease' sign is missing from the storefront around the corner," Laurel said as she and Olivia took their seats. "Does that mean Shelley Giusti is moving in?"

"It does. She plans to have her desserterie open by Christmas." Olivia offered Haviland a piece of shrimp. "Michel is beside himself with glee."

Laurel rubbed her hands together. "Me too. An entire shop filled with chocolate? There goes my paycheck. And my waistline."

Millay poured herself a margarita and lifted the glass in the air. "I'd rather drink my calories."

Olivia smiled at her friend. Millay was beginning to

unwind and behave more like her old self. Olivia knew that the Locklear case had brought some of Millay's most painful memories—the ones she'd hoped to bury forever—to the surface. She'd had to meet those memories head-on and she'd done so with boldness and courage. Now that Judson was in custody and Talley was being looked after by Annette Stevens, Millay could begin to let go of things from her own past that had haunted her for too long.

Harris broke into Olivia's reverie by describing the children's cooking game he was designing. "I'm starting with food they don't actually have to cook, like putting peanut butter and raisins on a piece of celery. Totally healthy stuff."

"Ants on a log," Laurel said. "My boys love that snack."

Rawlings pretended to be confused. "Your kids eat ants?"

They all laughed. Olivia sipped her margarita and gazed around the spacious deck. The overhead trellis was festooned with colorful paper lanterns and nautical flags. Potted plants wound with white lights separated the tables, and the ocean breeze stirred the centerpieces made of red carnations and pinwheels. Soon, the band would arrive and country western music would encourage the crowd to become a little louder and a little rowdier. But that was okay with everyone. It was a Friday night after all.

"I told Steve he'd probably have to come get me," Laurel said, handing her glass to Millay for a refill. "I always get tipsy after one of our adventures."

"It's the relief," Rawlings explained. "Cops feel this way all the time. When you've been on someone's trail, especially someone as clever and evasive as Judson Ware, you put all your energy into tracking that person down. Once they're finally caught, you're utterly drained, but you also want to seize hold of everything that makes you feel alive." He sent Olivia a warm glance. "You probably gave Steve and the boys some extra TLC this week, didn't you?"

Laurel grinned. "I sure did! I hugged and kissed them

every chance I got and I also ate a whole pint of cappuccino fudge swirl ice cream. I *never* eat the whole pint."

"That's what happens," Rawlings said. "As a cop, you try to enjoy as much as you can because it's only a matter of time before you catch a new case. Until then, you live large."

Millay raised an eyebrow. "So what did you do, Chief? Buy two gallons of chocolate milk instead of one?"

He balled up his napkin and tossed it at her. "I started a new painting, stuffed my face with jumbo bags of sour cream and onion potato chips, and took long walks on the beach with my favorite dog." He ruffled the fur on the back of Haviland's neck. "What about you? You've obviously been motivated. Harris told me that you finished your book. Edits and all."

Though she shrugged as if it were no big deal, Millay couldn't stop her mouth from curving upward into a proud grin. "Yeah. I'm ready to tackle the dreaded query letter."

This announcement drew a round of applause from her friends. They clinked glasses and toasted Millay, and while she tried to pretend she didn't enjoy the attention, her eyes were alight with pleasure.

"You're falling behind on your word count, Chief," she teased Rawlings. "You'd better make some progress on your novel."

Rawlings waved off the suggestion. "That's not going happen anytime soon. Sheriff Poole and I have been dealing with a ton of paperwork. We're still trying to tie up a few loose ends."

The chief's statement clearly troubled Millay. "It's nothing serious, right? Tell me that bastard isn't going to get off on some technicality."

Rawlings' tone lost all traces of levity. "No, he's not. But we've had to gather all kinds of statements. For example, when Munin bolted for the swamp, she didn't just abandon her son. She liquidated her assets and gave all the cash to a Mr. and Mrs. Robert Oxendine. They're the ones who raised Bo Locklear as their own. Called him Bobby Oxendine until he came of age. When he turned eighteen, they handed him the deed to the Dawson farm and told him his real name and that his parents were both dead."

"That must have been rough," Harris said. "I get that Munin was trying to protect her kid, but even after Judson's dad was dead, she didn't come back for him. She let him believe he was an orphan."

Olivia pictured Munin's shack at the forest's edge. "I think she knew that he'd found his parents in the Oxendines. I also believe that Munin truly forgot how to be among people. She'd scour the papers, keeping watch on the Lumbee from afar, but she couldn't go back. She'd become a wild thing. A seer. A witch." She shook her head. "It's really sad, because Bo could have helped her heal if only she'd let him."

"Instead, Judson found her," Laurel said and then looked at Rawlings. "How?"

"From one of the Lumbee who drove out to the Croatan National Forest to scout out the campground for the annual powwow," Rawlings said. "He was a client of Fletcher's. Over a lunch meeting, he told Fletcher and Judson that he was pleased by the presence of so many animal spirits in the forest. He also mentioned that a Lumbee medicine woman lived nearby and felt that her proximity to the campground was a sign that the tribe should hold the powwow where their ancestors had once lived."

Harris groaned. "And Judson put the pieces together."

Rawlings nodded. "He did his research first. A phone call to the art gallery selling Munin's pottery supplied him with a name. That's all he needed to confirm his suspicions."

"I don't see why he went after her," Olivia said. "She wasn't a Locklear. She and Calvin weren't even married. And her life was already ruined."

"I believe Judson wanted to punish her for making sure

that his home would stay in the Locklear family. She protected Bo and the deed, and now it all belongs to Talley. He couldn't forgive her for that."

Millay raised a finger to stop him. "Actually, it belongs to the casino now. They're going to raze the house to the ground and that terrible stone wall in the basement will be destroyed too."

"And Munin's going home," Rawlings said quietly. "Talley wanted her grandmother to be buried alongside her parents and Willis."

Olivia's throat tightened. "She finally has a family."

The group fell silent. They watched the boats gently bobbing on their moorings. The gulls and shorebirds soared over the horizon, vacating the docks and shoreline to find shelter for the night as the first stars began to appear in the periwinkle sky.

"I thought this was a party!" came the voice of Olivia's sister-in-law. "Oh, I see what's wrong. Your margarita pitchers are empty." Kim grabbed a waitress and gestured at their table with one arm while bouncing Anders with the other.

"Let me have that baby," Laurel pleaded, holding out her arms. Kim acquiesced, but the moment the transfer was made, Anders began to cry.

Another waitress jogged up to Kim and whispered something in her ear. Kim glanced at a table at the far end of the deck and Olivia sensed that a dissatisfied customer had asked to speak with the manager. "I've got Anders," she told Kim with a smile. "Go work your magic."

Laurel passed the unhappy infant over to Olivia. She cupped her palm around the back of his head and turned him to face her. She gazed into his dolphin gray eyes. "Hello, handsome," she whispered, planting a featherlight kiss on his forehead.

Anders stopped crying and returned her stare. He reached out a chubby hand and closed it around a lock of her hair. He gurgled and drooled, his toothless mouth curving into a cherub's smile.

"I'll be right back," she said and stood up, holding the baby tighter in her arms. She hadn't told Hudson about her encounter with Charles and she knew it was time to put the subject to rest. Her brother had been bringing up "the ghost" for the past few days.

My brother, she thought. *Not by blood. I know the truth and the truth doesn't matter. We belong to each other.* She kissed Anders again. *We all belong to each other.*

"Olivia!" Rawlings called out from behind her.

She stopped and turned, surprised to see that he'd followed her inside.

"I wanted to give this to you earlier but I haven't had the chance." He handed her a small jewelry box.

She eyed the box nervously. "What is it?"

"Nothing scary," he said with a secretive grin. "Just open it."

Shifting Anders to her hip, Olivia popped the lid back and gasped. Resting on a square of black velvet was her starfish necklace. "How . . . ?" She frowned, unable to hide her displeasure. "I told you that I wanted Munin to have this."

"She has yours," Rawlings assured her gently. "This is the one from the memory jug. It was your mother's." He removed the necklace from the box and turned the starfish over. "Look. Her initials are engraved on the back. CL." He undid the clasp and moved behind Olivia, deftly fastening the necklace around her neck. "I had to get a new chain. There was no way to get the other one out of the clay without it breaking, but the pendant came free like it knew where it was going."

Olivia felt the starfish settle in the hollow of her neck. She reached up to brush it with her fingertips, too moved to speak.

"I know you always felt like your mother was near when

you wore the necklace she'd given you. Now you can feel that way again." Holding her by the shoulders, he slowly spun Olivia around to face him.

With the baby in between, Olivia leaned over and gave Rawlings a deep, lingering kiss. She tried to infuse the kiss with all the love and gratitude welling up inside her, sweeping over her like a great wave. "There'll be more of that later," she promised, touching the starfish again.

"Then I'd better go load up on protein," he said with a laugh and headed back to the table.

Olivia watched him until he disappeared outside. Her heart felt like it was too large to fit inside her chest. What had she done to deserve such a man?

Don't ever let him go, she told herself and walked into the kitchen.

Hudson was busy mincing garlic, but he heard the coo of his son over the hiss of steaming pots and the chatter of the kitchen staff. He glanced up from his task and smiled at Anders and Olivia.

She jerked her head in the direction of the side door and Hudson understood. Laying the knife down, he rinsed his hands in the sink and dried them on his apron before joining her.

"Hey, my man," he said to his son, squeezing a rosy cheek. Anders squealed and wriggled in Olivia's arms. Hudson led Olivia outside to a narrow deck on the side of the building where The Bayside Crab House employees took their breaks. Hudson waited for Olivia to take a seat at the lone picnic table and then sat down across from her, smiling widely for Anders' benefit.

"I wanted to tell you that I found the guy who looked like our father," she said without further preamble. "I spoke with him."

Hudson's smile vanished. "Who is he?"

"Our father's twin brother. His name is Charles. He was in the area for the food festival. Apparently, he's some bigwig from New York and his TV network sponsored the whole thing."

"Our dad had a twin? How come we've never heard of him before?" Hudson asked suspiciously.

"He and Willie never got along. And I can see why. The guy's a jerk."

This made Hudson laugh. "Sounds just like Dad."

Olivia couldn't help but grin. "True, but Willie Wade wasn't arrogant. He knew who he was and never tried to be anyone else. He was true to himself, for better or for worse."

Hudson took a moment to consider this. "But this Charles guy is our uncle, right? Shouldn't we, I don't know, keep in touch?"

"I can look up his contact information for you," Olivia said. "He's married and has kids, so we probably have cousins too. Personally, I don't want anything to do with him."

"I guess I should want to meet this new family, but if we're being honest here, I don't," Hudson said. He sighed contentedly and looked up at the restaurant. "I have this place, a wife, a daughter, and a son. I've got a sister now. And a few guys I go fishing with every now and then. I don't need an uncle or a bunch of cousins who don't know me from Adam. I've got everything I need right here."

Olivia thought of her sister-in-law and niece, who were probably in the manager's office. Caitlyn was undoubtedly coloring in her sketchbook while her mother answered the phone. Across from Olivia was the man she called brother. Her adorable nephew was cradled in her arms. Around the corner of the building, her friends Millay, Laurel, and Harris were waiting for her. The man she loved and her precious Haviland were there too.

"I've got everything I need right here too," Olivia said with a smile.

Together, they watched a sailboat glide across the water, its mast light twinkling like a Christmas tree star. The vessel was heading for the open sea, following the path of the moon beneath the cloudless night sky.

Olivia Limoges didn't feel even the tiniest twinge of wanderlust as the boat disappeared into the twilight. She'd traveled the world, but it was only in Oyster Bay that she'd found what she'd been searching for. She belonged to the town and to its people and they belonged to her.

She had everything she needed.

Drawing Anders closer, she leaned over and softly sang a verse of her mother's lullaby.

> *C'était dans la nuit brune*
> *Sur le clocher jauni,*
> *Sur le clocher la lune*
> *Comme un point sur un i.*
> *Ho la hi hi, ho la hi ho*
> *Ho la hi hi, ho la hi ho.*

> *(It was in the dark night,*
> *On the yellowed steeple,*
> *On the steeple, the moon*
> *Like a dot on an i.*
> *Ho la hee hee, ho la hee ho*
> *Ho la hee hee, ho la hee ho.)*

AUTHOR'S NOTE

Many thanks are owed to doctors W. Paul Murphy and Timothy Stanley for reviewing the nuances of malignant hyperthermia with me. I'd discovered the medical condition while reading a case study conducted using Lumbee subjects. I instantly became fascinated with the tribe's history and with the Battle of Hayes Pond. I took several liberties in regards to the events of that day in 1958, but if you'd like to read more about the Lumbee, visit them on the Internet at The Lumbee Tribe of North Carolina (www.lumbeetribe.com).

BIBLIOGRAPHY

(in order of appearance)

De Musset, Alfred. "Ballade à la lune." *Contes d'Espagne et d'Italie*, 1830.

Mansfield, Katherine. "Loneliness." *Poems*, edited by Murry (London: Constable, 1923).

Longfellow, Henry Wadsworth. "My Lost Youth." Arthur Quiller-Couch, ed. 1919. *The Oxford Book of English Verse: 1250–1900*.

Herrick, Robert. "To the Virgins, To Make Much of Time." Arthur Quiller-Couch, ed. 1919. *The Oxford Book of English Verse: 1250–1900*.

Van Dyke, Henry. "Inscription for Katrina's Sun-Dial." *Little Rivers*, 1895.

Turn the page for a preview of Ellery Adams's
next Books by the Bay Mystery . . .

Poisoned Prose

Coming soon from Berkley Prime Crime!

"Death by chocolate. That's what the coroner's report will read," Olivia Limoges said to the woman sitting next to her. She pushed away a plate still laden with a caramel brownie, a hazelnut petit four, and a square of peanut butter fudge. "I'll have to be rolled home in a wheelbarrow."

"That's why this place is called Decadence." Laurel Hobbs, local reporter and mother to twin boys, bit off the end of a strawberry dipped in white chocolate and moaned. "How can you resist the many, many temptations being offered to us? Here we are, two of the lucky few invited to this exclusive event, and you're showing restraint. Seriously, Olivia, try this one. Just take a bite."

Olivia glanced at the Amaretto cream puff and shook her head. "I think it was a mistake to drink multiple martinis during the cocktail hour. I could hardly refuse the chocolate martini I was given for the initial toast, and then Shelley pressed something called a Snickertini into my hand and stood there while I drank it. I didn't want to offend her on her big night and Michel would poison me at work tomorrow if I did anything to upset his beloved chocolatier, so down the hatch it went."

Laurel held up her hands. "No more talk of poisoning, strangling, or any other form of murder, please. I think we've had enough violence to last us several lifetimes. Besides, Michel would never turn on you. He's the head chef in the most celebrated restaurant on the North Carolina coast and you own the place."

Gesturing around the desserterie, which was filled with Oyster Bay's most influential townsfolk along with a dozen journalists and television personalities from out of state, Olivia shrugged. "The Boot Top can't compete with an establishment serving every guest a dark chocolate shopping bag filled with white chocolate mousse. And did you see what Shelley used as a garnish? Sugared raspberries and a Decadence business card made of fondant. Incredible."

"No, you probably can't compete with that. I guess you should be happy that Shelley doesn't serve seafood or the Bayside Crab House would be in trouble too."

"Speaking of the Crab House, I should pick up some treats for my niece. I saw some starfish lollipops on the counter. Each one is made of raspberry-filled chocolate and costs more than an entire Happy Meal, but she's worth it."

Laurel grinned. "It's a good thing you're an heiress. You could buy every last piece of candy in here if it took your fancy."

Olivia bristled. "Hey, I work as hard as the next person."

"You do. You spend all those hours between two restaurants and yet you stay so thin." Laurel shook her head in disbelief. "How can you be around such exquisite food all day long and not weigh a million pounds? If I weren't your friend, I'd really hate you. I still haven't worked off the rest of my baby weight and the twins are almost four! Oh well, now's not the time to count calories." She popped a truffle into her mouth. "Look at Shelley. She's sweet, beautiful, and clearly isn't shy about sampling her wares. A woman with Shirley Temple dimples and Marilyn Monroe curves. No wonder Michel fell for her. Ah, here he comes now."

Michel was glowing. Olivia barely recognized him out of his white chef's coat, but he cut a nice figure in his rented tux. "Can you get over my Shelley?" he asked, sitting next to Olivia and giving her a brotherly kiss on the cheek. "If I weren't madly in love with her, I'd be desperately jealous. She's got everyone under her spell. I told you she was an enchantress."

Olivia rolled her eyes. "Spare me, Michel. I've overindulged on tarts and cakes and bonbons and I can't stand another ounce of sugary sweetness."

"Then you should try the spicy chile chocolate," Michel suggested. "Or the bacon flavored." Olivia gave him a dark look, but he was too jovial to notice. He and Laurel began to compare notes on their favorite treats, going into endless detail about the perfect balance between sea salt and bittersweet chocolate.

"I'm going outside for some air." Olivia took her water glass and headed for the kitchen. Without asking permission, she breezed through the swing doors into the narrow space, surprised to find it empty of both wait and cooking staff. Shelley had hired servers from a local catering company for her grand opening and they were all busy in the main room, but where was the dishwasher? An assistant pastry chef or sous chef?

The kitchen was a mess. The sink was full of stainless steel bowls coated in dried caramel, jam, buttercream, and chocolate in every shade of brown. The remnants of crushed nuts, chopped fruit, and mint sprigs were strewn across the cutting board and every burner on the commercial stove was obscured by a dirty pot or sauté pan.

"Shelley's going to be up very late tonight," she said, unable to stop herself from picking up a bag of flour that had toppled from the counter onto the floor. "She's got to hire some full-time help."

Like many of the stores lining the streets of downtown Oyster Bay, Decadence had a small concrete patio out back where the merchants and their employees would take smoke or lunch breaks. Shelley had placed a pair of Adirondack chairs, a picnic table, and a potted fern on hers. The fern didn't look like it had long to live but Olivia decided to prolong its existence by dumping the contents of her water glass into its bone-dry soil.

She went into the kitchen, refilled the glass, and repeated the process three times before the soil was moist to the touch.

"I think it's a hopeless cause," a voice said from the alleyway behind the shop.

Olivia jumped.

"Damn it, Flynn." She scowled at the handsome, middle-aged owner of Oyster Bay's only bookstore. "Is this how you spend your evenings? Creeping among the town's garbage bins?"

"Only when beautiful women are nearby," he replied nonchalantly and sat down at the picnic table. "Is this how you spend yours? Dressing to the nines and watering half-dead plants?"

Olivia studied the man who'd once been her lover. He was as carefree and confident as usual. His mouth was always on the verge of curving into a smile and there was an ever-present gleam of mischief in his gull gray eyes. A textbook extrovert, Flynn loved to swap gossip with his customers and play with their children in the bookstore's puppet theater. He was lively and friendly and fun. Everyone liked him. He was everything Olivia was not and that's what had initially drawn her to him. However, their strong physical attraction hadn't been enough to hold them together and they'd both moved on to form more meaningful relationships with other partners.

"What are you thinking about right now?" Flynn asked. "You've got this look on your face. Like you've gone back in time and want to linger there a moment. Perhaps you are reminiscing about us?" He raised his brows and smiled a little. "We had some electric moments, didn't we?"

Trying not to let him see the accuracy of his guess, Olivia joined him at the picnic table. "Where's Diane? It's a Saturday night in June. The stars are shining, the ocean breeze is blowing, and the town is stuffed to the gills with tourists. So why aren't you out wining and dining your girlfriend?"

"Because we had a big fight," he said without the slightest trace of emotion. "And because I wanted the chance to talk to you."

"Oh?" Olivia's tone was guarded. "In the middle of Shelley's event? How did you know I'd be here?"

Flynn shrugged. "It was a sure bet that she'd invite you. Any small business owner with half a brain would. Do you know how many new customers I've gotten because you recommended me?"

"I love Through the Wardrobe." Olivia was careful to praise the store, not its proprietor. "I'd do anything to see it flourish. A town without a bookstore is an empty shell of a place."

Beaming, Flynn leaned toward her. "I'm so glad you said that. It makes it easier to ask you for a big favor."

Olivia gestured for him to continue.

"*The Gazette* and I are partnering to sponsor a storytellers' retreat next month. It's for people all over the region who make their living performing folktales. I'm going to schedule some children's programs at the shop and the paper will arrange for adult performances at the library. If there's enough interest, we'll use the high school's auditorium."

"That sounds wonderful, Flynn," she said sincerely. "But where do I come in?"

Olivia had to give her former lover credit. He didn't dance around the point or try to soften her up with compliments.

He simply opened his hands so that his palms formed a bowl and said, "I need help funding the event. The expenses were supposed be covered by the *Gazette*, a grant, and me. Well, the grant's fallen through. But we have to go on. Things have been set in motion. Hotel rooms have been booked. Ads placed. Invitations sent and accepted. But we don't have enough money to pay for it all. We need a philanthropist, Olivia. The storytellers need you."

"Don't lay it on too thick," she warned. "How much are we talking about?"

Eyes flashing in premature triumph, Flynn reached into his shirt pocket and withdrew a slip of paper. "I've itemized all the costs for you. This way, you'll have proof that I'm not heading out on a Caribbean cruise at your expense."

Olivia didn't unfold the paper. She tucked it into her Chanel evening bag and promised to look it over in the morning. "I never make decisions when my belly is stuffed with chocolate."

Flynn laughed. "An excellent motto. After all, chocolate stimulates the mind's opioid production, creating feelings of pleasure that will eventually wear off. But if you'd like to prolong the sensation of euphoria, I'd be glad to assist with that." He stood and held out his hand to her. She took it, allowing him to pull her to her feet. He studied her pale, silvery blond hair, which was swept off her brow in a modern wave, and then lowered his eyes to her necklace of moonstones and black pearls. His gaze drifted down the curves of her body, taking in the formfitting, vintage-style cocktail dress made of black lace with satin trim and Olivia's long, tan legs.

"I'd try to kiss you, but your police chief boyfriend would probably hit me with his baton."

Olivia pulled her hand away. "I don't need him to defend my honor. I can clout you all by myself, thank you very much." She smiled to take the sting from the words and wished Flynn a pleasant rest of the evening.

Once Flynn had gone, she hesitated for a moment at the

kitchen door and then decided not to return to the party. She walked down the alley and stepped onto the main sidewalk, heading for the public lot where her Range Rover was parked.

In order to reach her car, she had to pass by Fish Nets, the bar where her writer friend, Millay, worked. It was not an establishment Olivia regularly frequented as it reeked of tobacco, body odor, and stale beer. The music was too loud, the entertainment was limited to a stained pool table and decrepit dartboard, and the floor was covered in spilled liquor, discarded chewing gum, and chewing tobacco spittle. And yet, Olivia had grown up among its clientele. Her father had been a fisherman and most of the old timers within had known her since she was a skinny, towheaded girl with the shy, sea blue eyes.

Pausing at the door, she considered how ridiculous she'd look drinking whiskey with a group of work-worn men and women. She'd walk in wearing her cocktail dress and heels while Millay's patrons would be dressed in soiled and tattered jeans, frayed denim shorts or skirts, and T-shirts that had been washed so often that their logos and designs were no longer decipherable. Their skin would be bronzed by the sun and weathered by wind and worry. Their hands were scarred and dirty and their language coarse, but they knew her. They knew her story. They knew her mother had died in a tragic accident, that her drunkard of a father had abandoned her when she was only ten, and that she'd come back to Oyster Bay after a long absence in order to reconnect with the past and strive for a new and better future.

They've accepted me all along, she thought with a rush of gratitude and entered the bar. *These are my people.*

For a moment, her appearance stunned the crowd into silence, but it only lasted a heartbeat. Men and women warmly greeted her with catcalls and raucous shouts. Millay waved her over to the bar and polished a tumbler with a dish towel.

"Don't give me the stink eye. This one's clean," Millay said before pouring a finger's worth of her best whiskey into the glass. "It's the only thing in here that is, besides you. Aren't you supposed to be down the street with the rest of the snobs?"

"Why would I want to sip champagne and devour plates of sumptuous desserts with Oyster Bay's elite when I could be here, sitting on a wobbly stool and breathing in toxic air?" Olivia gestured at the taps. "Buy you a beer?"

Millay grinned. "Absolutely. But I prefer the King of Beers."

She reached into the refrigerator behind her and pulled out a bottle of Budweiser. Popping the cap off with a neat flourish, she clinked the neck against Olivia's tumbler. "In the immortal words of Minna Antrim, 'To be loved is to be fortunate, but to be hated is to achieve distinction.'"

Olivia laughed. "Despite your best efforts, I believe you are genuinely adored."

"In this place, yeah. Beyond these walls, I'm that girl the old biddies point and frown at in disapproval. I use too much makeup, my skirts are way too short, and I wear black boots all year long. I'm the scourge of the Junior Leaguers and I take pride in knowing they're afraid to look me in the eye." She pretended to claw at the air with her left hand, causing the feathers hanging from her black hair to swing back and forth. Millay's blend of several races had lent her an exotic beauty, but she preferred to celebrate her artistic nature by piercing her eyebrows, wearing rows of hoops in her ears, and dying the tips of her jet strands neon pink, orange, or green. Lately, she'd taken to adding accessories to her textured bob. Tonight, she wore crimson feathers, but at the last meeting of the Bayside Book Writers, the twentysomething barkeep celebrated the final round of edits on her young adult fantasy novel by decorating her hair with glittery Hello Kitty clips.

"That's why you're such a talented writer," Olivia said.

"You're fearless in life and on paper. You have the courage to be you, but you're also willing to be vulnerable. That's hard when you're used to wearing armor. Believe me, I know."

Millay shook her head in disgust. "What kind of crack was in that chocolate you ate? Don't go all fortune cookie philosopher on me, damn it. Hurry up and finish that whiskey. You need to wash that sugar out of your system."

Olivia complied. Millay immediately refilled her glass while a man sat down on the vacant stool to Olivia's right.

He lifted the faded John Deere cap from his head and said, "Evenin', ma'am."

"Good evening, Captain Fergusson." She gestured at her tumbler. "Would you join me?"

"Reckon I will. Thank you kindly."

When Millay had poured two fingers of whiskey, he turned to Olivia and she raised her glass. "'May the holes in your net be no bigger than the fish in it,'" she said, reciting one of the fishermen's traditional toasts.

He nodded and replied with one of his own. "May your troubles be as few as my granny's teeth."

Sipping their whiskey, they fell into easy conversation about the commercial fishing industry. Captain Fergusson supplied both of Olivia's restaurants with shrimp and had recently expanded his operation. He was now her primary source for blue crab and flounder as well and she often met his trawlers at the dock when they returned with full cargo holds. Olivia would chat with the captain and his crew as she made selections for the restaurants. She liked Fergusson and, more important, she trusted him.

Fergusson had cast off from the dock while it was still dark to fish the waters off the North Carolina coast for the past forty years. And it showed. He was grizzled, his pewter-colored beard was wiry, and his eyes were sharp from decades of gazing into the horizon. He was gruff, blunt, hardworking, and fair, and Olivia had grown quite fond of him.

As they spoke, other fishermen drifted over and inserted themselves into the conversation. Olivia bought clams, oysters, mussels, scallops, and a dozen different fish from many of them. Before long, she called for shots of whiskey for the entire motley crew. In between swallows, Olivia praised everyone she recognized for the quality of their seafood while the men and their wives shared predictions about the summer harvest. This naturally led to a discussion about the weather and Olivia realized that to a bar filled with fishermen, construction workers, farmers, and yardmen, each day's forecast had a direct effect on their livelihood.

"You'd best get ready for a hot, dry summer," one of the women told Olivia.

Another woman, clad in a lace-trimmed tank top that was several sizes too small for her generous chest, pointed a cherry-red acrylic nail at a man chalking the end of his pool cue. "Boyd said his pigs have been lying in the mud for weeks." She cocked her head at Olivia. "Do you know about pigs?"

"Only that I like bacon." Olivia smiled. "But I didn't think it was unusual for them to roll around in the mud. I thought that's how they kept cool."

"Sure is," a second woman agreed. "But it ain't normal for them to do it all the time. See, when they carry somethin' around in their mouths—a stick or a bone or somethin'—then you know it's gonna rain. When they just lie there in the dirt for days on end, a dry season's comin'."

A man wearing a black NASCAR shirt elbowed his way into the group. "The ants are all scattered too." He looked at Olivia. "When they walk in a nice, neat line like little soldiers, then we're gonna have a storm. I got a big nest right outside my front door and they haven't lined up in ages. It's no good."

"Woodpeckers aren't hammerin' neither," another man

added, and someone else mentioned how the robins had left his yard weeks ago and that he was certain they'd gone west into the mountains. "The animals know things we don't."

Everyone nodded in agreement and then one of the women turned to Captain Fergusson. "What's the sea been tellin' you?"

"She keeps her secrets close, but the moon says plenty." He put his whiskey down. Cupping his left hand, he raised it into the air, palm up. "We got a crescent moon right now and she's lyin' on her back like she's waitin' for her man to come to bed. We won't see a drop of rain until she gets up again. Mark my words."

The women tut-tutted and murmured about summers gone by. Summers of unrelenting heat. Long days of dry wind and parched ground. They talked of how the land had gone thirsty even though the ocean was close enough to touch. The salt had clung to people's skin, making them sticky, short-tempered, and lethargic.

Olivia spotted a local farmer, Lou Huckabee, on the fringes of the group. He'd been listening to the exchange closely. "I'll still get you all your produce, Miss Olivia," he said above the music. "Don't you fret."

"I know you will, Lou. And every piece of fruit will taste like it was plucked from the richest soil on earth, washed, and delivered straight to my kitchens. That's why I won't serve my customers anything else. You have a feel for growing things like no one I've ever met."

He dipped his head at the compliment, flushing from neck to forehead. "It's a callin', to be sure."

"To farmers," Olivia said, and held up her glass.

"To farmers!" the men and women around her echoed.

Next, they toasted fishermen, fishermen's wives, an array of different types of laborers, Millay, Olivia's mother, and on and on until Olivia was dangerously close to being drunk. Despite the close air and the way the whiskey made her feel overheated, she was too content to leave. And when Captain Fergusson began to tell a tale about a pod of dolphins changing into mermaids, she became as instantly enraptured as the rest of his inebriated audience.

While the old man spoke in a voice as weathered and worn as his face, Olivia thought about the note Flynn had given her. She glanced around at the people in the bar, reflecting on how each and every one of them had grown up listening to the stories of their parents and grandparents. Their elders passed down folklore on the weather, animal husbandry, treating ailments, courting, raising children, and more. And here they were now, sharing those same stories. Old, well-loved, and oft-repeated stories.

They are as much a part of us as our DNA, she thought. She knew that in the small, coastal town of Oyster Bay, the local legends focused mainly on the sea. She'd heard them over and over since she was little, but now she was suddenly curious to hear what tales Flynn's storytellers would bring to share with them.

A burst of laughter erupted as Captain Fergusson reached the end of his story. The woman in the tank top took a long pull from her beer and said, "Them mermaids might not be real, but my daddy saw the flaming ghost ship last September. Said it came out of the fog like somethin' sneakin' through the gates of hell. He was supposed to bring his catch into Okracoke that night so it'd be fresh for the mornin' market, but he sailed home with it instead."

No one laughed at her. Millay wiped off the bar and poured another round. "I've heard about that ship before. Would you tell me the whole story?"

The woman nodded solemnly, but there was a gleam of excitement in her eyes. Olivia saw it and smiled to herself. She'd seen the same spark in her mother's eyes every night at bedtime. Without fail, Olivia was sent to sleep with a spectrum of wonderful images and words floating through her mind. And though her childhood was long gone, a good story was no less magical to her now.

"A long time ago, a ship full of folks from England sailed to Okracoke," the woman began.

Olivia turned away from the storyteller so that she wouldn't see her take out her phone. She quickly sent a text to Flynn, telling him she'd be glad to help defray the costs of the retreat, and then turned the phone off and put it back in her purse.

When the woman was done with her tale of murder, robbery, and revenge, the talk returned to the weather, as it so often did at Fish Nets.

"It's hard to prepare for a dry season," Lou Huckabee told one of the fishermen. "I can irrigate, but nothin's the same as real rain."

"That's true enough," the other man agreed. "Much easier to get ready for a storm. You know they're comin' and you know that, by and by, they'll move on through."

Olivia sighed. "Still, we've had enough storms to last us a lifetime. I hope the big ones pass us over this year."

Captain Fergusson covered her hand with his and Olivia sensed that he knew she wasn't referring to hurricanes, but to the number of violent deaths that had occurred in Oyster Bay over the past few years.

She squeezed his hand. "I could use a season of peace and quiet."

"It's all right, my girl," he said as tenderly as possible. "Life ain't always easy and it ain't always fair, but there's beauty in every day. You just gotta know where to look."

Olivia considered this. She looked around the room and decided that he was right. Tonight, the beauty had been in this rough place filled with rough people. It had been in their lore and their legends and the way in which their stories bound them all together, weaving a spell of binding that could never be broken.

On impulse, Olivia told the captain about the storytellers' retreat. "They'll bring energy and tranquility and a little bit of magic to our town," she said, smiling widely.

For a long moment, the old fisherman didn't respond. Then he rubbed his bristly beard and slurred into his cup, "Outsiders tend to bring us things that we don't want. Sure, stories can be like a fire on a cold night. But they can burn too. There ain't nothin' can cut deeper or sting with more poison than words can. You'd best keep that in mind, Miss Olivia. Words have power and all things of power are dangerous."

And with that, he tossed back the last swallow of whiskey, slipped off his stool, and stumbled out into the night.

ABOUT THE AUTHOR

Ellery Adams grew up on a beach near the Long Island Sound. Having spent her adult life in a series of landlocked towns, she cherishes her memories of open water, violent storms, and the smell of the sea. Ms. Adams has held many jobs, including caterer, retail clerk, car salesperson, teacher, tutor, and tech writer, all the while penning poems, children's books, and novels. She now writes full time from her home in Virginia. For more information, please visit www.elleryadamsmysteries.com.

Truth can be deadlier than fiction . . .

ELLERY ADAMS

The Last Word

A BOOKS BY THE BAY MYSTERY

Olivia Limoges and the Bayside Book Writers are excited about Oyster Bay's newest resident: bestselling novelist Nick Plumley, who's come to work on his next book. But when Olivia stops by Plumley's rental she finds that he's been strangled to death. Her instincts tell her that something from the past came back to haunt him, but she never expects that the investigation could spell doom for one of her dearest friends . . .

**"Visit Oyster Bay and you'll long
to return again and again."**
—Lorna Barrett, *New York Times* bestselling author

facebook.com/TheCrimeSceneBooks
penguin.com